Second Half

Susanna Chelton Sheehy

Elden Publishing, LLC.

Elden Publishing, LLC
P. O. Box 421803
Atlanta, Georgia 30342

Book cover designed by Christy Bishop
Layout designed by J. L. Saloff

Fonts: Bookman Old Style, Myrid Standard

First Edition

Sheehy, Susanna Chelton
    Second Half

10-Digit ISBN: 0-9789271-1-7
13-Digit ISBN: 978-0-9789271-1-0
LCCN: 2007903434
Copyright information available upon request

Printed on Acid Free Paper in the United States of America

1.0

To family and friends.

What would we do without them?

Chapter One

"Tori, I told you I didn't want to do anything for my birthday." Jane Winslow stood in the doorway of her twelfth-story condominium looking at her best friend.

Victoria Vandor waited in the hallway holding a birthday cake. "Jane, it's noon and you're still in your bathrobe," Victoria exclaimed. "Are you sick?" She pushed past Jane and carried the cake to the kitchen. Putting it down on the counter, she turned around.

"No. I'm fine," Jane said, following her into the kitchen. "I just didn't feel like getting dressed. It's my birthday. I think if I want to spend it in my bathrobe, I can." Jane sat down at the table, put her elbows down, and propped her chin on her folded hands.

Victoria sat beside her. "You're scaring me, Jane. I'm the one that gets depressed. Not you. What's wrong? Is it your age?"

"I don't know. Maybe a little bit. I was washing my feet in the shower this morning and I got a good look at them. My toes are gross. They're old lady toes. I remember my mother's toes. They looked like that. You know, kind of creased up and down, and the nails are yellow around the edges, and there are calluses on them. I can remember thinking, *I sure am glad my toes don't look like that.* Now they do." Jane folded her arms flat on the table and rested her head on them."

Victoria stroked Jane's glossy white hair. "There's a remedy for that. It's called a pedicure. I have one twice a month."

"Really, Tori, your toes bother you, too?"

"Sure, old feet aren't pretty. That's what I'll get you for your birthday, a pedicure. Come on, get dressed. I'll take you to my salon."

"I don't think so, Tori. I just want to stay home today."

"Something really has got you down, Jane. If it's age, forget it. You're only sixty years old, and you've taken such good care of yourself, you'll probably live to be a hundred."

"Oh, great!" Jane stood up and started to pace. "So I've got forty years left of this misery."

"What misery? Jane, stop this. You're really scaring me."

"Everything scares you, Tori. But you just keep doing things anyway. I'm not afraid of anything, but look at me. I'm stagnating." Jane continued to pace.

"You've always been so happy. Don't you like your work anymore?" Victoria stood up and put her hand on Jane's arm. She looked up into her eyes. Jane at five foot ten inches was much taller than her petite friend, who stood only five foot two.

"No, I don't. I'm bored." Jane stopped and looked down at Victoria. "That's it, Tori. That's exactly it. I'm bored."

"Well, you'll retire in five years. Then you can travel. You've done so well. I'm sure you can afford it," Victoria said.

"Tori, I've traveled in my work. I've seen the world. I don't want to travel anymore." Jane started to pace again. "And besides that, I'm already semiretired." Jane had had a successful career in information technology. For the past couple of years she had limited herself to three days a week of consulting work. "Retirement isn't going to help. I don't have a family. I have nobody to share it with."

"You have me."

"I know, and I love you." Jane sat down at the table again. "But you have a family. There's only so much you can do with me." She sighed deeply. "No, I need a new interest, something that will consume me."

"I pulled myself out of a mid-life depression by gardening. That and art. Maybe you should look into something like that." Victoria sat down next to her and placed a hand on her arm.

"I hate gardening. That's why I live in a highrise condo. I don't even have plants on the balcony." She sighed. "I could try drawing. I might be okay at it. But honestly, it doesn't interest me much. Maybe photography?"

"There you go," Victoria said. "You always loved photography. Buy yourself a nice camera." She patted Jane's arm. "Come on, get dressed. Let me buy you a pedicure. Your toenails won't look creased and yellow if you paint them, and at my salon they buff off the calluses."

"Okay," Jane said. "Just give me a few minutes to get dressed."

"I can't find anything I want to look at here," Jane said, searching through the pile of magazines on the coffee table at the salon.

"No, there isn't much for people like you and me. It's all about child raising, and cooking large meals, fashions that would look ridiculous on people our age," Victoria said. "I don't even bother looking for magazines anymore. If I come alone, I usually just bring a book."

"See what I mean," Jane said, sitting beside Victoria. "Boring!"

"I'm not boring."

"That's not what I meant," Jane said.

"Anyway, you need to pick out a color for your toenails." Victoria handed her a color panel. "I was thinking red. I usually get a versatile shade of pink, but today I feel bold. I think I'll get red."

"Look at this, Tori. You can actually get black. I think I'll get that."

"Black?" Victoria said. "You really are in a bad mood, aren't you?"

"Yes. I'm getting black." She crossed her arms and looked straight ahead.

Walking down the mall after their pedicures, Victoria asked, "Would you mind if I went into this pet supply store? I need to get dog and cat food."

"No, that's fine," Jane said. "And, Tori..." She put a hand on her friend's arm to stop her. "I do feel a lot better. Thank you."

Victoria reached up and hugged her. "I'm glad. I can't stand the thought of you being unhappy." She opened the door to the store. "I still can't believe you had your toenails painted black."

Jane smiled. "I like my black toenails."

While Victoria filled up her cart with dog food, cat food, and various other pet supplies, Jane wandered over to the pets for sale. There were kittens of all different colors and breeds, and dogs of every sort. Some breeds she recognized and some she didn't. One of the cages had a small thin dog in it. It was white with gray markings on its face and head, and something looked familiar about it. She passed the cage and looked at the other dogs, but when she had seen them all, she returned to the cage to look at the little dog.

"It's an Italian greyhound," Victoria said, coming up behind her pushing the cart.

"That's why it looks familiar. It looks like Patricia's dog," Jane said. Victoria's youngest daughter Patricia had a retired racing greyhound. "Only much smaller."

"That's right. They're sort of a miniature of the greyhound. He's cute, isn't he?" Victoria started to push the cart toward the check out.

Jane followed her. "How much do you want for the Italian greyhound?" she asked the cashier.

Victoria turned quickly around to look at her. "Jane, you're not thinking of buying that dog, are you?"

"Yes, I am," Jane said.

"You're not an animal person. I don't think you've ever owned a dog," Victoria said.

"I need a change." Jane looked at the cashier. "Could I hold the dog?"

"Sure, I'll get someone to show him to you, but I'll warn you. That dog's been in that cage for three months. He's a little neurotic. His price has been reduced from $985 to $485." She paused and looked at Jane. "We were all surprised he didn't sell faster. He's really cute."

"Three months?" Jane said. "Poor thing." She followed the young man who had appeared from the back of the store over to the cage. He went through a door and she saw him on the other side of the cage. He took the puppy out and brought him to her. Jane just looked at the little creature.

Victoria had followed her over to the cage. She extended her arms to the little dog. He reached for her and she nestled him in her arms. "Oh, Jane, he is cute." She looked up. "Don't you want to hold him?"

"Yes," Jane whispered. She extended her arms. The little dog laid his face on her chest, nuzzling her chin with the top of his head. "I'll buy him."

"What?" Victoria asked. "Jane, you don't understand how much trouble puppies are."

"You've never complained."

"Yes, but I'm an animal person. I've had dozens of them. I know what I'm getting into when I get a new puppy."

"Well, I guess I'm about to find out how much trouble they are," Jane said.

"He'll end up living with me." Victoria smiled as if she really wouldn't mind too much.

"No, he won't. He's mine." Jane hugged the little dog to her chest.

They arrived at Jane's condo an hour later with dog food, a collar and leash, one bowl for food, another for water, and a large package of puppy pads. Add to that a crate, which Victoria had insisted on.

"He's going to be my companion," Jane had said. "You don't put a companion in a cage."

"It'll make him secure," Victoria said. "Believe me; you'll be glad you bought it."

Before they went up to the condominium, Victoria insisted on walking the dog. "You have to do this at least three times a day. That's the only way to house train him," she explained to Jane. When they had unloaded all of the supplies and assembled the crate, Victoria turned to Jane. "I probably need to go now. Are you all right?" She looked at her friend with concern.

Jane hugged her. "I feel a lot better. Thank you, Tori, for making me go out. I would've been miserable here alone all day."

"Will you be all right alone all evening?"

"I'm not alone. I have my puppy. Not only that, but Jeff is taking me to dinner for my birthday." Jeff was the owner of the plant shop where Victoria worked. He and Jane had had a brief affair that had progressed to a solid friendship. He was much younger than Jane. The romantic relationship couldn't have lasted. They'd both known it from the start.

"Okay, be sure that you put the puppy in his crate when you go out. You'll be sorry if you don't." Victoria kissed her best friend on the cheek and left.

Tori was right, Jane thought. *I should have brought a book.* She sat in the waiting room of her primary care physician. She was in for her yearly physical and had looked through all of the magazines. As usual she found nothing of interest to read. Her name was called, and she followed the medical assistant down the hall to the scale. She stepped up.

"Good, 135 pounds," the girl said. "You're always so slim. I don't think you've ever put on weight. How do you do it?"

"I think it's just metabolism. I've really never had to try. I guess it could have something to do with all the exercise I get," Jane said.

"You're lucky." They moved on to the exam room. Her blood pressure was good. Her pulse was steady. The EKG looked good. The MA left, and a few minutes later her doctor came in.

"Hello, Jane," she said as she stepped into the room. Jane had been her patient for nearly thirty years. They had developed a comfortable relationship.

"Hello, Gail."

She looked at the medical checklist that Jane had filled out, studied it for a few minutes, and looked up at Jane. "The only thing that's different on here is the number of drinks you have weekly."

"Yes, I have increased the amount of wine I drink."

"Do you think there's a problem?" she asked.

"Not with alcohol," Jane said, and looked her straight in the eye.

"But there is a problem. I can see it in your face." She reached over and patted Jane's wrist.

"I don't know exactly what it is. I'm just not happy. I'm not handling it very well," she said. "I'm not used to being unhappy."

"I'm not used to seeing you unhappy," Gail said. "It concerns me. Are there any physical symptoms?"

"Sometimes I think there are. I don't want to do anything, and it feels like I have no energy, but when I make myself ride my bike or run, I don't have any problem. I don't think it's physical." Jane took a deep breath and sighed.

"Sounds like depression."

"I've been trying not to say that."

"We have some good medications for depression these days. They don't have to make a zombie out of you any more. Do you want to try one?"

"Not really, but maybe I should." Jane sighed again.

"Well," Gail said. "I'll do a complete blood workup on you and an examination to be sure there isn't something going on inside. Would you like to take some samples of an antidepressant home, or do you want to call me with your decision on that."

"I'll call you," Jane said. "I want to think about it for a while."

On the way home, Jane passed The Camera Shop. She slowed down and pulled into the parking lot. She needed to do something to shake herself out of this rut she was in. She'd buy a camera. The first thing she noticed when she walked into the store was that the man behind the counter was beautiful. He was probably somewhere near her age. He had a full head of white hair, neatly cut. His features were carved like a statue, the age lines adding character. He was trim, with broad shoulders. Suddenly she realized that he was talking to her.

"I'm sorry," she said, feeling the blush rise up her face. "I was lost in thought. What did you say?"

"Can I help you with something?" he said, smiling at her.

"Oh, yes. I want to buy a camera."

"Did you have anything specific in mind?" he asked.

"No." She paused looking thoughtful. "Maybe this was a mistake," she said, and turned toward the door.

"Please, don't go. If you didn't want a camera, you wouldn't have come in." He came around the counter and approached her. "Tell me what you were thinking."

"Well." Jane swallowed. "I need a new hobby. I loved photography when I was young," she said. "But since that was, oh, maybe two-hundred years ago, I can't remember much about cameras, and even if I could I'm sure things have changed a lot. In other words, I have no idea what I had in mind."

"Well, I can help you there. Do you have any computer skills?"

"I'm just ending a forty year career in Information Technology," she said.

"You'll want a digital camera them. I'm sure you'll want to edit your pictures." Let me show you what is available," he said. "But first, let me introduce myself. I'm Gordon Fox. This is my shop."

"I'm Jane Winslow." She held out her hand. "It's nice to meet you." She let him show her through the cameras, and left with a new digital model, instructions on its features, and assurance that if she needed any help, he would be glad to oblige.

"Hello," Jane said, answering the phone.

"Hey, Jane, it's me, Tori. I just wanted to make sure everything went okay at the doctor today." She sounded anxious.

"I'm fine, Tori, but I appreciate you worrying about me. Nobody else does."

"I can't possibly live without you, so your health is important. How's the puppy?"

"I think he's doing okay. He poops and pees in his crate. So far, knock on wood, he only does it there. I think I might be able to live with that."

"I guess you're appreciating me making you buy it?"

"Very much, and the puppy pads, he doesn't sleep in his crate at night, though. He crawls under the covers with me and becomes a bed warmer." She laughed. "I'm not kidding. I've had to sleep naked just to keep from overheating."

"Well, you don't have to let him sleep with you. Ethel sleeps in her crate. By the way, what did you name him?"

"Fred, to go with Ethel, we need to introduce them. I want them to get along so we can all do things together." Victoria had a very small, short legged mutt named Ethel.

"I'm sure there won't be a problem. Ethel loves everyone." Victoria paused. "I know it's none of my business, but did you tell your doctor how you've been feeling lately?"

"I hope it is your business," Jane said. "You're all I have, Tori. My parents are dead. I don't have any siblings, except you." She took a breath. "She did a complete workup on me. If there's anything wrong, we'll know when the results come back. I already know there isn't, though. It's just like I told you. I'm bored."

"Do you want to have lunch on Thursday? I have the day off."

"Sure. Oh, I almost forgot. I bought a camera today. I'm going to start taking some pictures again. I've always loved photography. Did you know that you can edit your pictures on the computer these days?"

"Yeah, Ellen has one of those cameras. She takes pictures of the baby and e-mails them to Joe." Ellen, Victoria's oldest daughter had given them a grandson almost a year ago. "It's called a digital camera."

"I guess I haven't been paying attention. I mean, I'd heard of digital cameras, but I didn't know what they were." They made plans for lunch and hung up. Jane took her warm puppy, who was sleeping in her lap, out for a walk, and then went to bed.

Chapter Two

"My computer screen just went blank. I don't know what could be wrong," the shrill voice on the other end of the telephone said.

Jane was working on the helpline of the company she had worked for before semiretirement. She rarely worked the helpline, but they'd been desperate, so she agreed. "It just went black? Have you tried to turn it back on?"

"Oh, yes, I thought of that right away."

"Is it just the monitor, or is the computer off, too?"

"How could I tell?"

"Look at the computer and see if there's a green light on it."

"I already told you the screen is black."

"No, I mean the computer itself."

"Isn't the screen the computer?"

"No." Jane took a deep breath. Sometimes it was hard to think on the level of the average person, when you knew the stuff inside and out. "The part that makes the screen work is the box that's with it. It would probably be on the floor under the desk, or on the desk under the screen."

There was silence on the other end of the line. Jane imagined the woman looking around for the box. "Oh, that," she said. "No, there's no green light on it."

"Okay, look at the back of it for the cable that connects it to the wall," Jane said. "I want you to unplug that cable and plug it back in."

"I can't see back there," the woman said. "It's too dark."

"Can't you turn a light on, or turn the back of the computer around toward the light?" Jane asked.

"No, we're having a terrible storm. The lights are out."

Jane crossed her arms on the desk in front of her and dropped her head onto them. "I can't do this for another minute," she said.

"What?" the shrill voice on the line demanded.

"Nothing," she said. "Ma'am, computers work on electricity. It will come back on when the lights do."

"Oh. Okay. Thank you for your help." She hung up.

Jane immediately dialed the owner of the company. "Matthew, get someone to replace me. I have to leave."

"Is everything all right, Jane? Are you sick?"

She paused. She wanted to scream, *I quit. I'll never do any of this crap again.* But Matthew had been a good employer and a good friend. "Yes, I'm sick. I need to go now."

"Go ahead, Jane. I'll come down and take over," he said.

She felt very guilty on her way out the door. How could she do that to him? But she couldn't have stayed another minute longer.

When she got home, she took Fred out, then sat down at her computer and typed her letter of resignation. She would give notice for a month of part-time help so they could find someone else, but she knew she couldn't do this any more. Then she took her new camera out, put the leash on Fred, and went out for a walk.

They drove over to the Chattahoochee River nature trail. It was a wildlife preserve just outside of Atlanta. She would take pictures of Fred and of the preserve. She couldn't wait to start taking pictures again.

"You wouldn't believe what you can do with pictures these days, Tori." Jane felt excited for the first time in ages. She had called her friend to talk about it.

"That's what Ellen says," Victoria said. "Tell me about it."

"There are computer programs that let you edit the picture. If the eyes come out red, you can take the red out. It there's a shadow covering something important, you can take the shadow out. You can even remove an object you don't want. Like suppose you have a garbage can in the background or something."

"Do you have to use a digital camera?"

"No you can scan pictures from a 35mm with the right kind of scanner then you can edit them.

"Well, I can tell you're excited about it. I wish I was a little more computer savvy, so I knew what you were talking about," Victoria said. "Maybe on Thursday when we have lunch you can show me some of it."

"I will," Jane said. "I wanted to ask you, Tori, is there any such thing as a dog psychologist?"

"Why? Is something wrong with Fred?"

"Well, remember in the pet shop, the kid that showed him to me said he was neurotic?"

"That's right, he did."

"It's strange, but he hoards food," Jane said.

"What do you mean?" Victoria asked.

"When I feed him, he'll eat most of it, but then he'll start taking the little pieces out of the bowl into the living room. He acts like he's digging a hole, you know, with his little front feet scraping at the carpet. Then he puts the piece down and pretends to cover it up, pushing the carpet with his nose, as if it was dirt. Then he walks away looking really satisfied." Jane paused. "I think he might have a problem."

"No," Victoria said. "You have a problem. You just don't know how to think like a dog. That's instinct. They don't really even think about it. It's something that's just a part of them. If there's still food left when they're full, they hide it, so they'll have it when they get hungry again."

"It's not hidden," Jane said. "Anyone can see it. It's on the carpet."

"Have you picked it up?"

"No, I don't want to trigger some kind of panic attack. I mean if he comes back looking for it."

Victoria laughed. "It's just the act of doing it that they're after. You'll never let him get hungry again, so he'll never go looking for it."

"So, you don't think it's a problem."

"No."

The next morning, Jane got up early to jog. She always went to the park just after dawn in the summer. It was just too hot in Georgia to run in the afternoon. Fred looked so sad in his crate that she decided to take him with her.

"You're a greyhound, after all. A good run will be good for you." She put his leash on him, tucked a plastic bag in her fanny pack, and off they went. When they got to the park, she walked awhile to warm up, a good brisk walk. She smiled as she watched Fred. He picked his feet up so high it looked like he was prancing. He was almost smiling with joy.

After about a quarter of a mile, she started to jog, slowly at first, then she picked up the pace. Fred was keeping up just fine. She was watching for fatigue. He was just a puppy, after all, she didn't want him to overdo. She always ran three miles, but if he seemed to be tiring, she would just pick him up and carry him.

On about the second mile, a squirrel ran across the path. Fred took off after it. He pulled at the leash then crossed the path right in front of Jane. She side stepped to avoid crushing him, lost her balance and went down on her knees, skidding on the sidewalk about a foot before she put her hands down to stop herself. "Ouch," she screamed.

Fred stood at the end of the leash, looking guilty.

Jane rolled over to a sitting position and gazed at her knees. They looked like raw meat. They were scraped and bleeding. She stared at the palms of her hands. They weren't as bad as her knees, but they were bleeding too.

"Are you all right?" someone said to her from behind. "I saw you fall. Oh, look, you're bleeding." She looked at her knees as the voice moved closer.

"I don't think anything is broken, but I'm a mess," she said, turning around to the person who had spoken. "Oh, it's you." She felt herself blush as she recognized Gordon Fox.

"Jane Winslow, isn't it?" he asked as he knelt in front of her. He was dressed in running shorts and a T-shirt. Apparently, he liked the early morning as well. He was glancing at her knees. He took her hands in his and turned them palm up. "You're really scuffed up." He looked over at Fred. "He's just a puppy. He probably hasn't had enough training to run with you yet."

"I don't know how to train a dog. He's my first," Jane said. She tried to put her palms down on the ground to push herself up, but winced when they made contact with the pavement.

"Here, let me help." He stood and went around behind her. Putting his hands under her arms, he lifted her to her feet. "There." He circled around her. "Can you walk?"

"Of course, I can walk." She was feeling humiliated now. She took a couple of steps along the path, then stopped and gasped. "No, I can't walk. My ankle seems to have been damaged in the fall."

"Here," he said, putting his arm around her waist and helping her to the bench. Fred followed them over. "I think he knows he messed up. He looks apologetic." Gordon laughed.

"He should look apologetic." She stared at her puppy. He seemed so forlorn that her heart softened. "Don't look so sad, Fred." She extended her hand to him. "It's my fault for not training you first." The puppy trotted over to her offered hand and nudged it with the top of his head.

She stroked the little dog quietly for a minute then said, "I'm probably about a mile and a half from my car. I wonder how I'll get back."

"I'll go to the golf house and get a cart. It's just over that hill; won't take but a minute." Gordon started off at a jog.

"Sorry to interrupt your run," Jane called after him.

He looked back and waved. "I was almost finished anyway."

When they got to her car, she left the cart and limped over to the driver's side door. Fred followed quietly. Gordon watched from the cart. "It's your right ankle. Driving will be painful. Why don't you let me drive you home? I'll get a cab back."

Jane wanted to say no, but she was really in pain. She looked over at him. "...if you let me pay for the cab."

"Okay." He smiled. "I'll take the golf cart back. It won't take long."

When they arrived at the condominium, Jane stopped at the mailbox. She pulled the mail out of the box and tucked it under her arm. "Come on up," she said to Gordon. "You can call a cab from there. I really appreciate your help."

"I'm glad I was there. This early in the morning the park is a little deserted." He held the door for her, and put his arm around her waist to support her. "I hope you're not worried about bringing a strange man up to your apartment," he said, smiling.

She looked at him, noticing that they stood eye to eye. "You're not a strange man. I met you last week."

"I guess that's true," he said.

Jane unlocked the door and went in. Fred followed her in and after she took off his collar and leash, he went immediately to his crate and lay down on his bed. She sat down on a stool at the bar as soon as she could. It was the closest place to sit. She put down the mail and eased her aching ankle up onto the stool next to her. "The telephone is right there." She pointed, and then started looking through her mail. She picked up a magazine and threw it into the trash can beside her. She tossed a couple of flyers into the can, then another magazine.

"Why are you throwing away those magazines?" Gordon asked. "You haven't even looked at them."

"They don't interest me anymore," she said. "I'm not going to renew."

"Could I take them to my daughter? She loves those things."

"Oh, sure..." She looked up. "You have a daughter?"

"Yes, and two sons." He retrieved the magazines from the can.

"You don't think your wife will mind you taking a strange woman to her home?" she asked, feeling disappointed to find out he had a family. Was she attracted to him? She hadn't really thought about it, but his attention had been fun.

"My wife died six years ago; cancer."

"Oh, I'm sorry."

"So am I, but I've gotten used to it." He tucked the magazines under his arm and turned to the phone. "I think I'll call my daughter and see if she can pick me up. That would save us both the cost of a cab. The kids will be up and dressed by now."

"You have grandchildren?"

"I have seven grandchildren. They're a lot of fun, all the pleasure of kids, but none of the work. At least, only as much work as I want to put into it." He looked at her. "What am I telling you that for? You probably have grand-kids of your own."

"No, I never married, never had any kids," she said.

"Well, I guess you should make that call."

After he had talked to his daughter, he walked over to Jane and put the magazines down on the counter. "How's the ankle?" He looked down and lightly touched the swollen joint. "Where can I get some disinfectant and a wash cloth? We need to clean up those knees."

"Don't worry about that," Jane said. "I think I'll just

take a bath, wash everything." She held up her hands, palms out.

"That's a good idea, but just let me clean the grit out and disinfect. Okay?" He looked directly into her eyes. "You don't want infection."

"All right...Here, on the other side of the counter." She motioned around the wet bar. "There's water, cloths in the drawer, disinfectant in the medicine cabinet over the sink in the powder room." She pointed across the room.

"Great." He collected what he needed. "Jane, would you consider going to dinner with me tonight," he said, not looking up as he was bathing her knees.

"You don't think I'm too crippled?" She smiled.

He looked up at her face. "I'll carry you, if I need to. You need to eat something, don't you?"

"Yes, I guess so. I'd like to, but I'll limp and look pathetic. Are you sure you can live with that?"

Her phone rang. "I gave Kathy your number so she could call from her cellphone when she got here. That's probably her." He handed her the phone.

"Hello?" she said. "Yes, Gordon's here, hold on." She handed the phone to him.

"I'll be down in a minute, honey. Thanks." He hung up. "Well, 6:30 okay?"

"That's fine." She pulled a notepad over, picked up a pen. "When you get here, punch in this number," she said as she wrote it on the pad. "I'll open the door for you." She handed it to him and smiled. "Gordon, thanks for your help. It would have been tough to walk all that way back to my car."

"It would have, but I'm sure you'd have made it." He smiled and went out the door.

Jane felt a little flutter of something in her chest. Did she have a crush on this guy? She hadn't really felt this way about anyone in a long time. It might be fun to fall in love. "What am I thinking, Fred?" she said to the little dog. She stood up and shook her head. "At my age."

She limped to the bathroom and started to take off her clothes.

She had carefully bathed her wounds and disinfected them again. Then she put some rescue remedy cream on them, and pulled on a pair of jeans and a T-shirt. She looked fresher, but she was still limping. She put on an ankle support and that relieved some of the pain, but she still felt unsteady on her feet. She knew she should probably rest, but she just couldn't sit still.

"Fred..." Jane said as she closed the crate. "Don't worry, I won't be gone long. I just want to run to the bookstore. I need to buy a book on dog training." She blew him a kiss as she picked up her purse and limped toward the door. "I can't believe I'm talking to a dog, Fred," she said. "It's fun."

At the book store, she went directly to the animal section and scoured the shelves. How could you tell which book to choose? You probably had to know who these authors were, she thought. But she had never paid attention to animals before. She had no idea.

"Excuse me." She stopped a clerk who was hurrying by. "Could you advise me on these dog training books?" she asked.

"No, ma'am. I don't know anything about dogs. I'll see if I can find someone who can." The girl hurried off, but no one else came.

After a while, Jane settled on one of the books and started toward the check out. She glanced at a book display at the end of one of the aisles, and stopped short. The book on display was titled *Publishing Your Own Magazine*. She picked it up. Turned it over, flipped through the pages. That's it, she thought. *I'll publish a magazine that I'll like.* She smiled, and took both books to the checkout.

"Tori..." Victoria looked up from what she was doing at the plant nursery where she worked. Jane came hurrying toward her, limping badly, but smiling brightly. "Where's Jeff? I want to tell you both." She looked around.

"What happened to you?" Victoria asked.

Jane looked down at her hands. She was holding her books and her palms were facing up. The scratches were showing plainly. "Oh, don't worry about that."

"No, Jane," Jeff said, approaching her. He took one of her hands and turned it so he could examine the scratch. "Really, what happened?" He looked so concerned, she smiled.

"I tripped over my dog and fell on the pavement. You should see my legs. They look like raw meat from my knees to my shins," she said. "My ankle's sprained, too.

"Jane, I'm sorry," Victoria said. "I should have warned you to be careful until he was trained.

"It's not your fault," she said, soothing. "Anyway, you won't believe what happened. I went to the bookstore to buy a book on dog training and look what I found." She showed them the book."

"Publishing Your Own Magazine..." Victoria read the title out loud. "I don't get it." She looked at Jane.

"You're going to publish a magazine?" Jeff asked, taking the book and flipping through the pages. "Sounds like fun. It might be a lot of work, though."

"You know I've been complaining about being bored lately."

"That's true, and you were complaining about the magazines in the salon the other day. That's a great idea, Jane," Victoria said.

"I know. I'm so excited. I plan to spend the whole afternoon with my foot elevated, reading this book. I'll look at the dog training, too." She turned toward the door. "I just wanted to drop by and tell you two the good news."

"Want me to bring you some dinner tonight?" Jeff called after her. "So you can stay off that foot."

"No thanks, I've got a dinner date."

"...A date?" There was something in the way he said

it that made Jane stop and turn around. She looked up at him. His brows were drawn together.

"With who?" Victoria asked, oblivious to Jeff's scowl.

"Gordon Fox, the guy that owns The Camera Shop. I met him when I bought my camera." She was talking to both of them, but looking at Jeff. "He happened to be in the park when I fell. He pretty much scraped me up off the ground and took me home." She paused. "Jeff, do you want to talk about it?"

"No, I'm fine. Have a good time." He turned and went to his office and closed the door.

Jane looked over at Victoria. She lifted her shoulders slightly. "I thought the romantic stuff was over between you two," she said.

"It has been for a while, but I guess as long as we were both not seeing anyone, it was more comfortable." She started toward the office.

"Jeff." She knocked on the door and went in. "Mad at me?"

"Of course not..." He turned around. "I just feel strange about you seeing another man. I may be a little jealous, but mostly I'm worried that it'll interfere with our friendship. I'd hate that."

"You trust me more than that, don't you? I wouldn't let it interfere."

"You wouldn't want to let it, but if you got serious about this man, you might let it come between us anyway." Jeff was sitting at his desk facing the computer.

Jane put her hands on his shoulders. "You know me better than that."

He turned around and stood up. Pulling her into his arms, he rested his head on hers. "You're right, I do. You won't let it interfere. I guess I just have to get used to it."

"Well, there might not be anything to get used to. It's our first date. He's got kids—and grandkids. I really don't fit into his life."

"Are you interested?" Jeff asked.

She looked up into his eyes, held his stare for a minute. "Yes, I think I am."

"I think I'll have something to get used to then," he said, and kissed her lightly on the lips and pushed her gently away. "See you Sunday for our bike ride?" He sounded unsure.

"I hope so. It depends on this ankle."

"Oh, that's right. I'll call to check on you later in the week."

"You brought me a corsage? I haven't had a corsage since high school." Jane took the box from Gordon and opened it, extracting the small arrangement. She handed it to him to pin it on her blouse. She was dressed in a pale blue silk pantsuit. "An orchid, and it matches my outfit perfectly. Thank you."

"It does look nice," he said. "I'm glad you like it." They stood in the foyer of her apartment. Jane limped over to her purse. "Would you like to come in for a drink, or do you want to go ahead to dinner?"

"I made reservations for 7:00 p.m. at Four Seasons. We should probably go."

"Okay." She picked up her purse and limped to the door.

"Tell me about yourself, Jane," Gordon said, after they were seated in a corner booth in the quiet restaurant. "Do you have any family? How long have you lived in Atlanta?" He leaned back and waited.

"All I really have is my sister. I have an aunt and some cousins somewhere, but I haven't been in touch with them in years."

"Tell me about your sister, then, older or younger?"

"Younger." She smiled at the thought of Victoria. "She isn't really my sister. I was five years old when she was born. I lived next door. She became my live doll. Her parents were older when she was born. They loved her, but they really appreciated having me around to entertain her. Both of us being only children, we decided to adopt each other. She always introduces me as her older sister. I couldn't love her any more if we were blood."

"Does she live here?" Gordon asked.

"Yes, my parents and I moved away when I was a senior in high school. My parents were killed in a traffic accident while I was in college. I finished up and came back to Atlanta to be close to the only family I really had."

"I'm sorry. That must have been hard."

"I was sorry they died, but they were both very self-absorbed. We weren't close."

"It sounds so lonely."

"It wasn't. It would have been without Tori, but we always had each other."

"Tori, that's an interesting name."

"Victoria. Her mother called her Tori, so I did too. She prefers Victoria, though."

"What do you do for a living?"

"Nothing at the moment, I quit my job earlier this week. I burned out. I spent forty years in Information Technology...had a wonderful employer. I traveled. I loved it, but I just couldn't do it anymore."

"I've been lucky with The Camera Shop. I never tire of it. Of course, I love photography, so I don't just run the store, but do other things too," Gordon said.

Jane could see the passion for his work in his eyes. "That's nice. I've really enjoyed my camera. I'm learning to edit my pictures. I can't believe how the technology has changed since I was a kid."

"Have you taken pictures before?"

"It's always been sort of a hobby." She stopped talking as the waiter approached the table. They ordered wine and picked up their menus. They had been so engrossed in conversation she hadn't even looked at it. "What's good to eat here?" she asked.

"Everything... I particularly like the lobster. That's what I'll get."

"I'll have that too, then." She put down the menu

and smiled up at the waiter. Looking back over at Gordon, she said, "Tell me about your family. It sounded large and wonderful when you talked about it this morning."

"It is." He smiled proudly. "My daughter, Kathy, is thirty years old. Don't tell her I told you that," he said. "She thinks that's old." They both smiled. "She has two kids, both boys...let's see...Eric is three and Teddy is eighteen months. She's carrying a girl right now...due in a couple of months. My son Michael and his wife Jill have three girls, Joy, nine, Hope, seven, and Alexandra, three. Interesting names; aren't they? Michael is thirty-two. My son Grant and his wife Lauren have a son and a daughter, Gary, eight years old and Maggie, five years old. Grant, I think, is about thirty-five, yes, that's right," he said, somewhat relieved. "It's amazing that I can remember all of that."

"Wow," Jane said. "That's quite a family. Do they all live here?"

"No. Grant lives in Charlotte, and Michael lives in Savannah, but they're close enough that we get together at least a couple of times a year. It's quite a party."

Their wine arrived and they fell silent for a few minutes.

"What were you thinking just now?" Gordon asked. "You looked sad."

"I was thinking," she said, looking him in the eyes, "some of them are older than six. Your wife got to meet at least a few of her grandchildren."

Gordon didn't respond, but held her gaze.

"I'm sorry. Maybe I shouldn't have said that."

"No, I'm glad you did. I've often been grateful for that." He reached across the table and took her hand. "I appreciate you thinking of it." He squeezed her hand lightly and let it go when the waiter arrived with dinner.

They ate in silence. Lobsters are so hard to eat that they had to concentrate. Jane laughed a couple of times when she caught Gordon smiling at her while she splashed lobster mess all over her face. "I'm glad they gave us these bibs," she said, pointing to the plastic sheet tied around her neck. "I would hate to ruin my suit."

"I'd hate for you to ruin it, too. It looks lovely on you."

Jane felt herself blush and hoped the light was dim enough that he didn't see it.

They stood outside her door after dinner. She started to put her key into the lock, but Gordon stopped her. He turned her around to look at him.

"Would you like to come in?" she asked. "I could make some coffee."

"I'm not coming in this time," he said. "But I would like to kiss you."

She held his gaze, and said, "We're old people. Don't old people have bad breath?" She smiled.

"I haven't noticed old person breath on you. Have you noticed it on me?" He grinned back.

"Not so far," she said. He leaned forward and kissed her. It felt good. It was nice to kiss someone her own height. She had always gone out with men much taller. Jeff was 6'4". She wondered if she had done that on purpose.

"You cheated," she whispered. "You had a mint."

"Didn't want to take the chance..." He smiled and kissed her again. This time he lingered a moment on her mouth. It was perfect.

"I guess I didn't taste too bad, since you kissed me twice."

"You taste like heaven." He kissed her once more, this time nibbling a little at her bottom lip. Then he turned her toward the door. "Now let me see you safe inside, like a gentleman should."

Jane leaned against the closed door inside her condominium. That was fantastic, she thought. She looked around, and spotted Fred's big eyes looking at her from his crate. "Of course, now that the gentleman has seen me safely inside, I've got to walk you, right, Fred."

Chapter Three

"It's going to take a lot of work, Tori," Jane said to her friend the next day. "I've almost finished the book. First thing I have to do is work up a business plan. The person who wrote this book has a kit you can buy to do that. I think I'll get it." They were sitting at a table in a restaurant.

"How much will it cost to do this?" Victoria asked.

"Oh, it'll be a sizeable investment. That's the first thing they tell you in the book." Jane nibbled on a bread-stick. "But, I have the money. I've had a successful career, and I had a good financial advisor."

"Are you telling me you're rich?"

"Pretty much, yes, but you knew that."

"I never really thought of it that way. I guess because you aren't flashy about it." She paused. "Just don't run through your retirement money. I'd hate to have to support you."

"I won't. My retirement fund is safe until I'm sixty-five, and it's sizeable. What would I do with the rest of it anyway? I haven't got anyone to leave it to."

"That's true, and if this project could make you happy again, it's worth it. You were really scaring me for a while there." She stopped and looked at the waiter as he approached. "I'll have the soup and salad, please, honey mustard dressing, and tomato bisque."

"I'll have the same," Jane said. "And a brownie à la mode for dessert. Bring two spoons." She looked at Victoria. "We'll split it."

"You're such a bad influence, Jane. I'll get fat eating that stuff."

"You're cute when you're fat."

"Shut up." Victoria pouted for a minute then said, "How was your date with Gordon Fox?"

"Really nice. He brought me a corsage, an orchid. It went perfectly with the pantsuit I was wearing. And the lobster at Four Seasons? Delicious! We talked about my family, which consists of you, so that was short. Then we talked about his family, which is huge. He has three kids and seven grandkids and another on the way." She smiled remembering how proud he'd been.

"Where's his wife? Is he divorced?"

"No. She died six years ago. I think he said of cancer. We haven't talked about her much," Jane said, frowning. "I think he might still be in love with her."

"Did he kiss you?"

Jane laughed. "You can tell how close we are when you have no problem asking me about stuff like that. Yes. He kissed me." She blushed. "Three times."

"Was it good?" Victoria grinned.

Jane blushed. "See what I mean? Yes, the first one was wonderful, and they got better from there. You know what's funny? I noticed that he's about my height, maybe a little taller, but certainly not much. I've never dated anyone my height before."

"Well, that certainly narrows the field."

"You're right. I don't know if it was intentional, but it's nice to kiss someone without having to look up at them. I really liked it."

"Well, that's something I'll never experience. There just aren't many men who are my size."

"No, I guess not. But you'll never kiss anyone but Joe anyway." Victoria had a solid marriage.

"No. I'm okay with that, though," she said. "Do you have plans to see him again?"

"Well, no." Jane looked worried. "But when I asked him if he'd like to come in for coffee last night, he said, 'I won't come in this time.' So I'm hoping that means there will be a next time."

"If he doesn't call, you could always go over to his shop and buy something else."

"I've thought of that, and I will if I need to, but I'm hoping he'll call."

"Hello," Jane said, answering the phone. She stretched her back. She had been working on the computer all afternoon, getting started on her business plan.

"Jane, this is Gordon Fox. I wanted to check on your injuries. How are they today?"

"My ankle is still painful. I went to lunch with Tori today, and by the time I got back my ankle was throbbing. The thing that bothers me the most is that I can't jog, and I really enjoy jogging. I guess I won't be able to ride my bike on Sunday either." She prayed Jeff would understand. "I hope I don't completely lose my conditioning. At my age, *it goes fast*."

"You won't. You'll probably be able to at least take a good walk in another week." He paused. "I wondered if you'd have dinner with me again tonight. I know it's short notice."

"That would be nice." She felt a little flutter in her chest again.

"Good. This time, though, we'll go to my daughter's house. She has me over every Friday night. I'd hate to cancel with her," he said.

Jane felt suddenly nervous. She wasn't ready to meet the family yet. "Well, if you have a previous engagement, we can do it another time," she said.

"No, I'd really like for you to come. It's not a meet-the-family kind of thing. Neither one of us is ready for that. I'd just like to show off my grandkids a little. Please come."

"You tricked me. You already know I'm free," she said, and began to laugh.

He laughed too. "I didn't mean to be devious, but I was afraid if I told you first where we were going, you'd say you were busy."

"I probably would have, and with good reason. I haven't been around children since Tori's kids were small, and that's been awhile." She paused. "Okay, I'll come. I know you must be proud of them."

"Good. I'll pick you up at five thirty. It'll be an early evening. Maybe we could see a movie or something afterward."

"Sounds good, I'll see you then." She hung up the phone and looked down at the sleeping puppy on her lap. "I guess you need to go out pretty soon." She stood up, the puppy in her arms, and limped over to the coatrack. She took the leash and collar off the hook and put it on the dog. Then she put him on the floor. "Sit," she said in a commanding voice. He looked up at her, tail wagging, but did not sit. She was tempted to let him get away with it, but the book had said be consistent and don't say the command twice. Make him do it the first time, every time. She fixed him with a determined stare and he sat. "Good boy," she said, sweeping him up in her arms and kissing him. His skin was soft and warm under her lips and he smelled sweet and fleshy. "I really love you, Fred," she said. "Who'd a thought?"

After taking Fred out and practicing some of the commands she was teaching him, she put him back in his crate and picked up her purse. "I'm going to the bookstore, Fred. I won't be gone long," she said, laughing at herself for talking to her dog.

The first step in writing the business plan was to investigate her competition. She went to two different bookstores and a newsstand in the mall. Besides *AARP* and *Managing Menopause*, there was the *Arthritis Journal*. She also found two women's magazines of the type she was thinking of. She bought them all, took them home, and spent the afternoon reading them from cover to cover.

Around four o'clock she got up and took a shower.

She dried and styled her hair, and put on a lavender silk pantsuit. She wouldn't be wearing a skirt for a while, with her knees covered with ugly scabs. Gordon arrived promptly at five thirty, and she opened the door. As soon as she did, he reached out, took her face in his hands and kissed her. He wrapped his arms around her and deepened the kiss for just a moment. "I've been thinking about that for two days." He smiled at her. "I hope you don't mind."

She could feel the color rising in her cheeks. Why was she blushing? "No, that was nice." She stepped back. "Come in, I'll be ready in a minute."

He came in behind her. "Your corsage is in the car. I wanted to have my hands free." He walked over to the bar and sat on one of the stools.

"You didn't have to get me another one. The one you gave me on Wednesday still looks beautiful."

He smiled. "I wanted to." He started flipping through the magazines sitting on the bar while she gathered her purse and keys and put Fred in the crate. "I don't understand these magazines," he said.

"What do you mean?" She joined him at the bar.

He held them up, one at a time. "You're too young for *AARP*; you're too old for *Managing Menopause*. Do you have arthritis?" He held up the *Arthritis Journal*.

"No. How do you know I'm too old for *Managing Menopause*?" she said with a smile.

He looked up startled. "You are, aren't you?"

"Yes."

"Lucky guess." He flipped through the two women's magazines. "I thought you didn't like magazines."

"Those are supposed to be for older women, women over forty."

"Did you like them?" He stood and guided her to the door.

"They were okay, but mine will be better."

"Your what?"

"My magazine. Didn't I tell you I was going to publish a magazine?"

"No. Let's go. You can tell me about it on the way."

Jane limped beside him to the elevator. They went down to the lobby and out to the visitor's parking. Gordon took her to her door and opened it for her.

"You're such a gentleman. You'll spoil me."

"Can't have that," he said, with a mischievous grin. "Close your own door." He walked around and got into the driver's seat. "So tell me about this magazine."

"I've been noticing lately that I never can find a magazine I like when I go some place. You know, to the doctor's office or the beauty shop?"

He nodded.

"I used to like women's magazines. I enjoyed the articles and short stories. Reading about raising children was fun for me, even though I didn't have any kids of my own. I had lots of friends that had kids. Tori has two girls, and I did a lot with them when they were growing up. I enjoyed the recipes, even though they served six to eight, because I had friends over and their families. The fashion sections were always fun. I've always had the kind of figure that can wear anything. I even liked the hairstyles, although I've pretty much worn my hair the same way all my life."

"It's lovely, too." He reached over and brushed it over her shoulder with the back of his hand.

"Thank you," she said. "Anyway, those magazines don't work anymore for me, and they don't work for my friends who have families either. Empty nesters don't want to read articles about children's school problems or teenage temper. That's behind them. The fashions for young people would look ridiculous on people our age; and who wants to cook a meal for eight people, unless the family is visiting. So I've decided to publish a magazine for people over forty-five. I'm going to call it *Second Half*. I'm writing a five-year business plan now. The first step is to investigate the competition. Apparently, there isn't much."

"I know *AARP, Managing Menopause*, and the *Arthritis Journal* won't be competition, but how about those two women's magazines? They said for women over forty."

"They were okay, but didn't quite do it. The recipes were still for six to eight. The articles were pretty good, but you know what jumped out at me that was all wrong?"

"What?" Gordon glanced at her.

"The ads, they were still full of young beautiful models."

"Young and beautiful sells."

"Not to old people, old and beautiful sells to us."

"You're really excited about this," he said.

"Yes, I am. You know we may not be beautiful in the way we were when we were young. A young person might not even look past the lines, bulges, and gray hair. But we're still beautiful to each other."

"That's true. We are."

"It's just a thought at the moment, but I might design my own ads for my magazine, finding models who are older. We'll still use the most attractive people, and the picture editing that they use on the young models, but they'll clearly be older. I think that will appeal, don't you? I mean it's hard to build our self-esteem and self-worth on a young standard. We need to use our own standard."

"So you're going into the advertising business, not just the magazine business."

"That's right. Magazines support themselves on selling advertising space, that, and selling ancillary products. Well, I'm not just going to sell ad space. I'm also selling ads."

"Won't it drive the cost up? Do you think you'll be able to convince buyers?"

"I'll definitely need a powerful salesman but I'm not sure it will drive the cost up that much. I need to hire a commercial artist anyway for layout design, and I'll need a photographer. That's basically what an ad agency consists of."

"That's true, but won't that be a lot of work for two people?"

"At first we'll all work hard, but if the demand gets

too big, that's success. Then I'll be able to hire more people." She stopped, realizing they were sitting in the driveway of his daughter's house. "I'm sorry. I got so involved in what I was saying I didn't realize we were here. You should have stopped me."

"I didn't want to stop you. I was enthralled."

"Enthralled?" she asked.

"Enthralled." He got out of the car and before he could walk around, she got out. They walked up to the door together. Jane's stomach was fluttering.

"Don't be nervous. It's just a casual dinner. We won't stay long. We don't want to interfere with bath and bed time."

The door opened and a small pregnant redhead smiled up at them. "Hi, Dad." She reached up to kiss him on the cheek.

He put his arm around her shoulders. "Honey, this is Jane; Jane, my daughter Katherine." He smiled proudly.

"It's very nice to meet you, Jane. Come in." She stepped back to allow them in.

"It's nice to meet you, too. It's nice of you to include me in your dinner plans."

"We're happy to have you. I really enjoyed the magazines. Dad said you hadn't even looked at them. Would you like to have them back?"

"No thanks, you keep them."

"Rick," Katherine called up the steps. "Come on down. Dad's here with his friend. Would you like a glass of wine, Jane?" She went to the kitchen door. "You, Dad?"

"Sure, honey, that would be nice."

"I'd love one," Jane said. "She's about the cutest thing I've ever seen," Jane said to Gordon when Katherine had left the room.

"She is, isn't she?" he said, smiling proudly. There was the sound of small feet clumping down the stairs and seconds later, a small bundle of red hair and freckles launched itself at Gordon.

"Grampa!" he squealed as Gordon swung him in the air. This was obviously a common occurrence. A man came down the stairs behind the boy carrying a toddler on his hip. He was average height with brown hair and blue eyes. The toddler in his arms had red hair and freckles like his brother.

"Jane," Gordon said. "This is my son-in-law, Rick."

"It's nice to meet you."

"I'm glad you could come," Rick said, putting the toddler down on the floor and extending his hand. Katherine came back into the room carrying two glasses of wine.

"Would you like some wine, Rick?"

"Yes, but I'll get it. You stay here and talk to our guests."

"Grampa, who's she?" Eric looked at Jane, smiling from his position in his Grampa's arms.

"Oh, Eric, I'm sorry. Let me introduce you. This is my friend, Jane. Jane, my grandson Eric, and this little guy pulling on my pants leg is Teddy." Gordon reached down and scooped up Teddy so he had a child on each hip. They both gave him a sound kiss on the cheek.

"Janie," Teddy said.

"Janie," Eric repeated.

"That okay with you?" Gordon asked.

"I like it. It's nice to meet you both." Jane was feeling slightly out of place when Teddy reached his stubby little arms out to her. Jane reached and pulled him into her arms. He was a solid, little arm full, and it felt good to hold him.

"My children are not at all shy," Katherine said. "I hope you don't mind."

"Not at all. I haven't held a toddler for ages. I have a grand nephew, but he's only about six months old. I haven't seen him since he was three months old. My niece lives in Seattle."

"It must be hard to live all the way across the country from them."

"It is, but we make a point of seeing each other often."

Teddy reached up and took a lock of Jane's hair in

his little fist and yanked. "Janie," he called in a sing song voice.

"I'm sorry." Katherine reached to take the baby.

"That's all right," Jane said. "I guess we weren't paying enough attention to him." She pried the fat little fingers off her hair and said to Eric, "Can you take me to your playroom or where ever your toys are? I want you to show me what you like to do."

"The playroom is right through here," Katherine said. "I'll just finish up a few things in the kitchen then we'll eat."

Gordon sat on a couch and put Eric on the floor. Jane put Teddy down and sat beside Gordon. Rick came and sat in a chair across the room.

"Will you show me your toys and tell me what you do with them?" Jane asked. "I need to learn."

"Why do you need to learn?" Eric asked.

"Learn?" Teddy repeated.

"Because I have a grand nephew younger than you. So you can teach me how to play with him when he gets to be as big as you are."

Eric's chest puffed out and he started picking up toys and explaining them. Teddy mimicked his brother. Most of Teddy's explanations consisted of only one word, but the words were clear.

"They're bright kids, Rick. It's been a long time since I've been around children, but I don't remember them being so verbal this young."

"We're proud of them," Rick said.

"Where did the red hair come from?" She looked at Gordon. "Was your hair red?"

Rick tensed, but Gordon said, "Katherine's Mom had red hair. Two of my kids and five of my grandkids have red hair, too. Strong gene. My hair was very dark, but grayed early. Grant, my oldest son has dark hair, but it's graying, too."

"Dinner is ready," Katherine said from the door. The kids ran into the dining room. They all got up and followed.

"I wanna sit next to Janie," Eric howled.

"Ah...sit...Janie," Teddy echoed.

"No. You will both sit with me," Katherine said.

"Please, Katherine," Jane said. "I'm enjoying them."

Gordon smiled at her, and took her arm. "Sit here. I'll sit on the other side of Eric. Kathy, you can sit on the other side of Ted. It's a round table so we won't be sitting in a row."

"Well, if you're sure. They can be a mess." She sat and they started to pass around bowls of food. It was a nice meal of rotisserie chicken, rice, green beans, and gravy. After they were all served, Rick said, "Jane, are you from Atlanta?"

"Yes. I've lived here most of my life."

"Is your family here? Do you have children?"

"I never married. I don't have any children, but my sister is here. She has children." She stopped talking to take a bite of chicken. Her story sounded so lonely, but it wasn't. She had Tori and her family. She wasn't alone.

"What do you do?" Katherine asked.

They were trying to be friendly, but she was feeling a little uncomfortable. "I'm retired. I plan to..."

"Eric." Katherine spoke sharply. "Don't put your milk down next to your elbow...I'm sorry, Jane, go ahead."

"I plan to start..." She saw out of the corner of her eye Eric's elbow moving toward the glass of milk that was directly in front of her. She was poised to reach for it when something hit her on the face from the right side. Teddy was smiling holding an empty spoon right about the time she felt something that must have been strained carrots drip off her face and onto her blouse. Just then something cold and wet hit her chest and landed in her lap, spreading cold milk down her belly and thighs. She turned back to the table and encountered shocked faces.

"Eric! I told you..." The little boy looked at his mother with horror-filled eyes. The toddler started to cry.

Jane could feel the strained carrots still dripping off her chin. She giggled. Everyone looked at her. She giggled again, put her arm around Eric. "Do I look funny?" She asked.

"Really funny." Eric started to laugh.

Jane put her arm around both children. Eric was grinning, but Teddy looked concerned. "I wish you two wouldn't do that to me again." She squeezed each one. "But this time it was funny." She looked across the table at a smiling Gordon and said, "Could you show me the powder room? I need to clean up."

"We can still go to a movie if you want," Gordon said, following her into her apartment. I'm really sorry you got messed up."

"Don't worry about it, Gordon. I enjoyed your grand-kids. Milk washes out, and I don't think the carrots will stain my blouse," Jane said. "I don't really want to go to a movie. Truth is I don't like movies much...require too much sitting still."

"Do I have to go home?"

Jane turned around and looked at him. He looked worried. "No. I'd love for you to stay. I need to change these clothes and put them to soak, but then I have to walk Fred. I'd love some company."

He relaxed.

"Wearing milk makes me feel like I might go sour, though. Do you mind if I take a quick shower."

"No. Please, go ahead."

She went down the hall to her bedroom, took off the soiled suit and took a quick shower. Dressing in jeans and a T-shirt, she went back out to the living room to join Gordon. "So do you think Katherine liked me?" she asked.

"I know she did, and the kids loved you."

"I liked them too." She took Fred out of the crate and put his collar and leash on him. "Are you coming with us?"

"Of course." They were silent while they rode the elevator down.

"So," Jane said. "Tell me about your wife."

"I know," Gordon said, walking beside her. "We need to talk about her." He grew silent for a minute. "Her name was Margaret. I called her Maggie, but she wouldn't let anyone else get away with that." He smiled at this. "She was small, 5'3". I loved her very much. She was not an independent woman, never was employed. She stayed home, made the home, raised the kids, cooked the meals." He looked thoughtfully ahead. "She was my partner, my lover, and my best friend." He paused. They watched Fred relieve himself, and Jane picked it up in her fancy plastic bag that smelled like baby powder. They walked back to the building. It was starting to rain, so they ran the last few steps.

"When she found out she was terminal," Gordon continued, "she encouraged me to find someone else. She was such a loving person. She couldn't stand the thought of me spending the rest of my life alone. We were not old, you know, early fifties." He paused again. "I've never wanted to find anyone else. The kids have pushed, even gone so far as to introduce me to any single woman they knew around my age," he said. "And some not my age." They went into the building and got on the elevator. They were silent on the ride up.

"Would you like some more wine?" Jane asked, as they went through the door to her flat.

"No thanks," he said. "Until I met you, I thought I was like one of those birds that mate for life, no matter what, even if their mate dies. They live alone until they die." He put his hands on her arms. "But you make me feel like a kid again." He leaned close to her and kissed her. "I think about you during the day. I dream about you at night." He kissed her again. "Thank you, Jane." He put his arms around her waist and pulled her close.

She put her arms around his neck and gave into the feelings. He made love to her lips then moved his mouth to her jaw, then her neck. Standing the same height, lips were not all that was level. She could feel the hardening in his pants. It pressed against the same place that was quivering low in her belly.

"I want you real bad," he said in a husky voice.

"I want you, too. Take me right here on the floor or on the couch or down the hall in my bed." Her voice was a whisper.

He kissed her neck again then took her mouth and held it. Pulling back, sucking her lower lip as he went, he leaned his forehead against hers. His breathing was rapid. So was hers. "We need more time," he whispered.

"I don't."

He pulled back and looked into her eyes, held them for a minute. "Yes, you do. We both do." His arms tightened around her for a minute then he pulled away. "I'm going home. May I call you tomorrow?"

"Please?"

"Lock the door behind me," he said as he went out.

Chapter Four

"Then he just walked away, Tori," Jane said, standing in the greenhouse of the nursery where Victoria worked.

"You're kidding?" Victoria looked up from what she was doing. "Did he walk funny?"

"Stop it, Tori," Jane said. "I'm seriously upset about this. I feel like I was rejected. There I was asking him to take me right where we were, and he walks out. I just stood there with my mouth open for about ten minutes. I guess I thought he might come back."

"Has he called you since then?"

"Yes, he called the next day. It was Saturday. Said he had to go to Savannah to visit his son. He'd be gone a week. It's been over a week and I haven't heard anything from him." She looked down at the plant Victoria was potting. "I don't like being rejected."

"I guess you don't," Victoria said. "I'm sure that's the first time it's ever happened. Do you care?"

"About what?"

"Will it bother you, if he doesn't call you back?"

Jane was quiet for a minute. "Yes," she said. "That's what bothers me the most. I haven't ever felt this way about anyone before. I don't know what it is."

"Are you falling in love with him, Jane?" Victoria stopped what she was doing and turned to look into Jane's eyes.

"Maybe..." Jane looked down at the plant. "But, I'm going to stop it right here. If he can just walk away from me like that, I'm better off without him."

"Jane, don't pout."

"Thanks for the sympathy, Tori. You're supposed to be on my side."

"I am on your side. I'm furious with him for hurting you that way. I'd like to give him a good talking to, and I may if I get the chance. But, I would be just as mad at you if you hurt yourself by sacrificing your opportunities just because you got your feelings hurt." She'd put her hands on Jane's shoulders, forcing her to make eye contact.

Jane dropped her chin to her chest. "You're right, of course. But I may not have any opportunities. I may never hear from him again."

"Why don't you call him? You've never been shy about that kind of thing. I've got an idea. Ask him to go to Lillian's wedding with you this weekend."

"I'm afraid to do that. What if he says no?" She shook her head and closed her eyes. "I hate feeling like this."

"Jane, what's wrong?" Jeff came into the room. "Did that man hurt you? Do you want me to punch him?" He walked over to her and put his arm around her shoulders.

"No, I'll punch him myself. But thanks for the offer." Jane smiled up at Jeff.

"Well, I don't like to see you look so sad."

"It's nothing. I'm probably just being over sensitive. Anyway, I had another reason for coming here."

"What's that?" Jeff asked.

"I need a garden columnist. I'm going to put a gardening section in my magazine. I was wondering if either of you would consider writing a monthly article for me?" She looked hopefully back and forth between the two of them.

"Not me," Jeff said. "I hate to write, but Vic's good at that kind of thing. I wouldn't mind if it didn't take her away from her duties here."

"Gosh, I don't know how well I write, Jane. I've never done it before."

"Well, try. You'll have to be creative about it. Remember we're appealing to older gardeners. You may need to do some research. I was thinking about container gardening for apartment balconies, vegetables in potters, so you don't have to do a lot of bending, that kind of thing."

"That sounds like fun. I'll try it. You have to promise to tell me, though, if it's no good. I don't want you ruining your magazine because you're afraid to hurt my feelings."

"Of course, but I know it'll be good. You're good at anything you really want to do." She kissed Victoria's cheek. "I've got to go. I have an appointment to look at some office space."

"Office space?" Jeff asked. "You're really moving fast on this magazine."

"I finished my five year business plan last week. It's being reviewed by an advisor right now. I've got several freelance writers lined up to submit samples of their writing. I've talked to a couple of people about consulting on the fashion section, and hairstyles. I need to find a food section editor. Now, I've got you on gardening." She looked at Victoria. "I need a place for all of these people to work." Jane started for the door. "I need a secretary, too."

Jane looked at the office space and put down a deposit on it. It was perfect, not too much to start with. The location was great, right across the mall, only a mile from her house. She could walk. She made an appointment with the realtor to sign the lease and hurried on. She had an appointment with her financial advisor. He hadn't been happy about all the money she was using. Financiers just like to collect it. But when she made it clear to him that she was going to do this, he agreed to help.

After her morning appointments were finished, she went home and got Fred. They went for a walk and she was just about to fix herself some lunch when the phone rang. "Hello."

"Jane, this is Gordon Fox."

"Hello."

"I wondered if you'd have lunch with me. I know its short notice, but I'd like to see you."

"I don't think so. I was just about to fix some lunch for myself, and I have an appointment this afternoon."

"I know I shouldn't have run out like that, Jane, the last time I saw you. Please have lunch with me, so I can apologize."

The pleading tone he was using softened her. Why did she have no resolve when it came to this guy? "Gordon, I'm not used to being rejected like that. I don't like the way it feels. I'm not sure I want to set myself up for it to happen again."

"I know. I don't blame you for feeling that way, but just give me one chance."

She was silent. There was a tingling sensation in her chest. When did I become a marshmallow? she wondered.

"Please." He sounded so earnest.

"All right"

"Good. I'm downstairs. Shall I come up or will you come down?"

"I'll come down," she said, allowing herself at least that much control. She checked her hair and face in the mirror over the mantle, picked up her purse, and left. When she reached the lobby, she looked through the glass door to the parking lot. He was leaning up against his car with his arms crossed. Her heart gave a little jump. He was beautiful. It felt good just to look at him. Oh, God, she thought, *I am in love with him.* She'd never felt this way about a man before. I hope it doesn't show. She went through the doors and out into the summer heat.

He saw her coming, dropped his arms and smiled at her. "You look beautiful," he said.

"Funny," she said. "I was just thinking that about you." She felt awkward for a minute. "Where are we going?"

"Where would you like to go?"

"Some place simple, how about the mall?"

"Okay. Not the food court, though. I want to be able to talk to you."

"There are some nice quiet restaurants over there too." She went to the car and opened the passenger side door. Gordon closed it for her when she was settled and went around the car to the driver's side.

They rode in awkward silence for a few minutes.

"I panicked, Jane. I'm sorry."

"I figured."

"Please forgive me?"

Jane looked down at her hands folded in her lap. "You hurt my feelings." She laughed. "I sound like a child."

"You don't have to be a child to get your feelings hurt. You had a good reason to. I went to stay with my son, because I knew if I was here, I wouldn't be able to stay away from you, and I had some things that needed to be worked out." He reached over and took one of her clasped hands. "I should have explained that to you, but being near you makes me dizzy, and I can't think straight."

"You make me dizzy, too," she whispered.

"I'm glad." They pulled into a parking space at the mall and Gordon turned off the car. He tipped Jane's chin up to look at him. "I'm really sorry."

She smiled.

He kissed her. "I've missed doing that," he said. "I've done a lot of thinking in the past week, and a lot of it was about doing that." He kissed her again. "Let's go eat some lunch."

When they were seated across from each other in a booth, they ordered. Gordon looked across at Jane. "I put my house up for sale. It's way too big for me. The kids don't need for me to keep it anymore. It's going to be a bitch to move out of it. I've lived there for thirty-five years."

"Why are you selling it?"

"I need to let go. Michael helped me see that. He's the philosophical one of the group. That's why I went there.

He helped me realize that in a way I haven't let Maggie die, at least not for me. She's gone and I have to let go of her. I still have a life to live, one without her."

"You don't ever have to stop loving her," Jane said, "or stop remembering her."

He looked into her eyes. "I never will." He reached across the table and ran his finger down her cheek. "You're a lovely person. Do you know that?"

She smiled. "Of course I know that." They laughed. The food came and they fell silent while they ate. "Gordon, I was wondering..."

"What?"

"A very good friend of mine is getting married this weekend. Would you be my date to the wedding?"

"I'd love to. I love weddings. When is it?"

"Saturday at 3:00 p.m., reception to follow" She smiled. "You'll get to meet Tori, too. She'll be there."

"That's great. I've wanted to meet her. Tell me about your friend."

"Her name is Lillian. She started out as Victoria's friend. They work together at the nursery. She's young, mid- to late- twenties, going to school at Georgia State. She's studying Psychology. You know that's a long haul. You can't do anything with a bachelor's degree in it. You really have to go all the way to a doctorate. I was surprised what good friends we all three became, what with the age difference."

"That's nice. It's nice to have young friends. Tell me about the young man."

"I haven't met him. Tori has, she seems to like him. I think she said he's some kind of a commercial artist." Jane was quiet for a few minutes while she ate.

"What are you thinking about? You looked lost in thought."

"I was just thinking. I need a commercial artist for my magazine. I wonder if he'd be interested."

"That's a thought. I think I'd wait until after the honeymoon to ask, though."

Jane smiled. "I think you're probably right."

They finished lunch and Gordon took her home. He stood with her at the door to the building. "Jane, I have to go, I've got to stop by Kathy's house before I go to the store for the afternoon. Can I see you tonight?"

She looked at him.

"Please?"

"For some reason, when you say 'please' I melt."

"I'll have to remember that."

"Okay, but I'll cook. If I keep going to restaurants for my meals, I'll grow into a mountain. What time can you be here?"

"I'll be at the store until 6:00. I'd like to go home and shower before I come. So maybe 7:30."

"Okay, I'll see you then." She turned back to the door and started to put her key in the lock.

Gordon stopped her with his hand on her shoulder. He turned her around to face him and kissed her again. She couldn't believe how wonderful simply kissing him was. "See you then." He went to his car.

"I'm definitely in trouble," she said to Fred when she got to her flat. "I've never felt like this before."

The afternoon was fascinating. Jane interviewed two candidates for secretary. She'd interviewed secretaries before, but she'd never interviewed editors or publishers. She interviewed a couple of those that afternoon, too. She liked one of the secretary applicants. The other people wanted too much money. She'd investigated the field and knew what midrange salaries were. She'd have to look further. One of the sales people was of interest to her, too. She wished she had someone else to run them by. Oh, well. There were a number of sample articles from freelance writers in the mail. She read a couple of them. This was really a lot of fun.

At 6:00 she stopped her work and started to think about dinner. She looked in the refrigerator. There were three different kinds of lettuce, some blueberries. She looked into the freezer. There was a small bag of grilled chicken breasts. She took them out and put them on an oven tray, took out the lettuce and put it in a salad bowl, sprinkled some blueberries on top. Looking around the kitchen she spotted some almonds in a plastic container, sprinkled them on the lettuce. She put the salad in the refrigerator, and went back to work.

At seven o'clock she got up and picked up the warm puppy in her lap. "You need to go out, don't you?" She kissed him, again enjoying the warm sweet feel and scent of him. She put on the collar and leash and took him down in the elevator. They were just heading back toward the building when they saw Gordon pull up.

"Hello," she called. Fred was pulling at the leash when he recognized Gordon. He had developed a tender spot for him.

Gordon looked over at them and smiled. He reached into his car and pulled out a bouquet of daffodils. Jane stopped a few feet in front of him while Fred jumped on his legs and Gordon bent down to greet him. He'd changed his clothes. He always dressed casually, but tonight everything he wore looked brand new. His clothes adorned his body beautifully. She looked down at her own clothes. She had showered and changed, but had put on jeans and another T-shirt.

"These are for you." He handed the flowers to her then scooped Fred up into his arms. "Fred, my man," he said. "You okay?" He let the little dog lick his cheek and smiled over at Jane.

She smiled back. "He's doing great. I think I might be able to run with him soon," she said.

"Just be careful when you do." Gordon put the dog down and went to the door with her. He looked down at her feet. "You're not limping any more."

"No. It was just a twist...got better really fast." She opened the door. They went inside and got into the elevator.

"Have you started running again?"

"Yes, I've run once. I'll go again tomorrow."

"Good." They went into the flat.

"Would you like a glass of wine?" Jane asked.

"That would be nice."

"Red or white?"

"Red," he said. "Jane, is something wrong? You seem uncomfortable."

"Well," she poured the wine. "You're dressed so nicely and I'm in jeans."

He came up behind her and put his arms around her waist. "I like you in jeans."

"And it just dawned on me that you came here expecting a nice dinner, and all I have is chicken salad. I didn't even cook the chicken. It was frozen."

Gordon started to laugh.

"What?" Jane turned in his arms and looked into his eyes.

"Your point about a different standard just registered," he said. "What did you do all afternoon?"

"I had four interviews, two for secretaries, one for an editor, one for a publisher. Then I read some sample articles that were sent to me by writer applicants. Why?"

He smoothed her hair back from her face and looked at her. "I went to Kathy's house. She wasn't feeling very well, but insisted on feeding me. I wasn't hungry, but didn't want to hurt her feelings. I felt uncomfortably full all afternoon at the shop and was wondering how I was going to do justice to the meal you'd spent all afternoon cooking for me."

She smiled. "I didn't even think about dinner until 6:00."

"A chicken salad sounds great."

After dinner he followed her into the living room. Sitting down on the couch, he held his hand up to her. She took it and let him pull her down beside him. He turned her and pulled her across his lap so that her head rested on the arm of the couch. He leaned down and kissed her, then nibbled her jaw and her neck. His hand rested on her breast, and she sucked in her breath. He started to massage her gently.

"Gordon, before you get me begging again, promise you won't leave me this time," she whispered.

"I won't leave you." His voice was husky again. "I promise." He took a deep raspy breath. "I want you so much."

Jane laid her head back and absorbed the sensations. "Make love to me then. Please," she whispered.

"I will, but I'll take my time. I want to savor every inch of you." He kissed her mouth and started to move down her neck. His hand was under her T-shirt. "You have too much clothing on." He pulled her up and smoothly pulled the T-shirt over her head. Unfastening her bra he pulled it away from her breasts. They were full and firm. She had never had children. His eyes widened at the sight of them. "You're beautiful, Jane." He looked into her eyes then lowered his mouth to her nipple. She shivered. He massaged her right breast with his hand and devoured her left with his mouth. "I've dreamed of this," he whispered.

Jane's breath was coming in short gasps.

The phone rang. They both jumped.

"Ignore it," Gordon said.

"Look at the caller ID." Jane pointed over her head at the end table where the phone was.

Gordon leaned over and looked. "It's Kathy," he said. "She wasn't feeling well today." He handed her the phone.

"Hello. Yes, he's here, just a minute." She handed him the phone and took a deep breath.

"Hello." He sat up straight, bumping Jane as he did. She sat up and put her bra back on. "Okay honey, I'll be there as soon as I can get there. Just hold tight." He put down the phone.

Jane was pulling on her T-shirt.

"Jane, Kathy has gone into labor—six weeks early—and that's not good." He looked into Jane's eyes. "I'm sorry, but I have to go and stay with the boys while Rick takes her to the hospital."

"Of course, I understand," she said.

He stood up. "I swear I wouldn't go unless I had to." He looked down at her.

"I understand, I understand."

He grabbed her by the arms and pulled her around to face him. "Come with me?"

"No, Gordon, I'll be more comfortable here. I have a big day ahead of me tomorrow. Don't worry about it. I know you couldn't help this."

"I promised I wouldn't leave."

"You have to." She put her hand on his cheek. "I don't think you planned it or anything like that. Go on, hurry, they need to get to the hospital."

He kissed her and turned toward the door. He turned back. "Please come with me?"

"No. You need to be with your grandsons right now." She walked with him to the door. "Let me know what happens. I'll see you on Saturday."

The next morning Jane got up extra early and went to the park to run. She took Fred. He did very well. She stayed on her guard the whole time, but he never darted in front of her. He barked at a squirrel once, but didn't change his stride. The training was working. She slowed to a walk after running a complete circle around the park. That was three miles. "Good boy, Fred," she said as she ran water into a bowl that was left by the fountain for dogs. Fred sniffed at the bowl and stepped back.

"Some dogs won't drink after other dogs," a familiar voice said from behind her.

She turned around. "Gordon!"

He approached her from the path. He was dressed in running shorts and a T-shirt. She couldn't help but notice how well toned he was. His waist was trim, his stomach flat, legs muscled. There was that quiver in her lower belly again. "Are you finished running?" she asked.

"Yes, just finishing up," he said. His teeth were so

white and straight. She loved the way his eyes crinkled at the corners when he smiled.

"I guess everything is okay with Katherine. Otherwise you wouldn't be here."

"Oh, yes. It turns out that she let herself get dehydrated. Apparently when a pregnant woman gets dehydrated, she has contractions. She didn't dilate at all, and after they placed an IV catheter and ran some fluids into her, the contractions stopped. She stayed at the hospital overnight, but Rick came home about midnight."

"Good, I'm glad everything worked out."

"It's probably a good thing you didn't come with me. Eric had a nightmare, and Teddy threw up. I was busy pretty much the whole time."

"You're a good Grandpa," Jane said. "A good Dad."

"I love my family. I still feel bad about leaving you when I promised I wouldn't, though."

"Gordon, I didn't mean to give you the impression that I'm a woman who needs your undivided attention. I don't expect you to sacrifice your family for me."

"I don't think that about you. In fact, I'm amazed at your independence," he said. "But we were just getting through a rough spot, and I wish we just could have gotten through it."

"We did."

"Good." He smiled and picked up Fred who was pawing at his leg. "Have some breakfast with me?"

"I'd have to take Fred home first."

"Actually, my house is just over there." He pointed to a red brick two-story house across the street from the park.

"You're kidding? You live right on the park?" She looked back at him. "Are you sure you want to sell?"

"Yes, I'm ready. It is a nice place to live, but I can drive to the park. How about breakfast?"

"Well," she said, looking at Fred where he was panting in Gordon's arms. "I really don't eat anything but fruit for breakfast, but Fred could use some water."

"Good. Come on." He led the way, carrying Fred. "I

have blueberries, strawberries, bananas, and pineapple, and plenty of water. My cat probably won't like you very much, Fred," he said to the little dog. "But I'm sure you can hold your own."

"You have a cat?" Jane asked.

"Yes. Don't you like cats?"

"Sure. Tori has a cat. He's sweet."

"Well, mine's a nasty little creature that hates everything that lives. But, I'm kind of attached to her."

They walked across the street to the house and Gordon unlocked the front door. He walked in and put the little dog down. Going over to the sliding glass door, he opened it about six inches. "The back yard is fenced. I'll leave this open a little so he can go out if he wants." There was a hissing sound from the other side of the room. Jane turned around to look. A black, red and white cat stood in the corner. Her pose was classic. She was up on her toes, her hair stood up along her back. Her tail was puffed out and her mouth was open.

"She won't hurt him, will she?" Jane asked.

"She'll try, but she doesn't have any claws on her front paws. I don't think she can do much damage."

Jane extended her hand to the cat. "It's all right," she said. "We're friends." The cat hissed again and batted at Jane's hand. She jumped back. "She doesn't like me."

"She doesn't really like anyone but me," Gordon said.

At this point Fred decided to flee. He ran through the sliding glass door and out onto the patio. The cat took off after him. She cornered him against the fence. Jane and Gordon went out behind them. When Fred tried to skim past her to get to Jane, the cat swatted him soundly on the shoulder and sent the tiny dog somersaulting into the water bowl. Jane ran over to scoop him up. "She really doesn't like us," she said. "Maybe we should go."

Gordon came over to her and took Fred from her. "I'm sorry, old man. She's just got to establish herself." He started to put Fred down.

"Gordon," Jane said, putting her hand on his arm to stop him. "She really tried to hurt him."

"I won't let her hurt him, Jane, I promise." He put Fred down and the little dog leaned against his leg. The cat was sitting on the ground now, licking her paw. She looked over at Fred, stood up, and walked over. She rubbed against Gordon's other leg, then circled, eyeing Fred. Fred's eyes were the size of saucers. The cat slowly started to rub her head on Fred's side. Then she rubbed the length of her side against him. Fred was standing very tall, head back, eyes huge. The cat turned and rubbed the other side against him. Suddenly there was a rumbling sound coming from her. Gordon smiled. "She's purring." Fred sniffed her butt, which was now right under his nose. "They're forming an understanding."

"You understand animals very well," Jane said. "She scared me to death."

"She can be scary," he said. "Let's go inside and have some breakfast." They went into the house. Jane looked around. It was nicely furnished. The furniture looked old, but well kept. There were family pictures on the mantle. She made a note to look at them sometime. They went into the kitchen.

"What's her name?" Jane asked.

Gordon looked at her. "Baby."

"Baby!"

"I didn't name her. I got her for Maggie a couple of months before she died. She named her Baby. She loved cats."

"Tori's cat isn't like that. He's just sweet and cuddly. He loves everyone, unless you threaten Tori, or Ethel."

"Who's Ethel?"

"Tori's dog."

"Well, there's a big difference in male cats and female cats. The males are the nurturers. The females are the protectors. It's an instinct thing."

"Tori's always talking about instinct." Jane joined him at the counter where he was pulling fruit out of the refrigerator.

"You have to understand instinct to understand animals. Want one of my Harvest Muffins?" Gordon pulled a plastic bag out of the refrigerator with muffins in it. "They're full of healthy stuff," he said.

"Sure." Jane grinned back. Fred was still staying close to Gordon's leg. The cat had followed them into the kitchen, switching her tail. She sat next to them, now, licking her paw. Jane leaned down and touched her head. The cat pressed the top of her head into her hand and started to rub. After she had been stroked a few times, she hissed and walked away, switching her tail again.

Jane jumped back.

Gordon laughed. "She's a bitch. Just don't push her."

Chapter Five

"I'm telling you, Tori, that was such a mean cat. She tried to drown poor Fred in the water bowl."

"Cats are funny, especially female cats," Victoria said. "So this was Gordon's wife's cat?"

"Yeah, he got a kitten for her right before she died. He says she loved cats." Jane looked down at her toes. She and Victoria were having their pedicures. They had had their feet buffed and messaged and soaked in hot paraffin. Now they were wrapped in plastic and booties and propped on stools. "I guess I can't get black polish this time, since I'm wearing open-toed shoes to the wedding tomorrow."

"No, you can't," Victoria scolded.

"I think I'll get blue, to go with my dress."

"You can't get blue either. I think you should get something more conventional."

"Tori, don't be boring. The good thing about being old is that you can be unconventional. Besides, Gordon told me he likes me in blue." Jane smiled. "Imagine that, Tori, he notices what I wear."

"You're getting absolutely sappy about this guy, Jane. I can't wait to meet him."

"He's beautiful. His daughter, Katherine, called and invited me to dinner tonight. Apparently he always has dinner with her family on Friday night. Did I tell you I went there with him a couple of weeks ago?"

"Yes. That was the night he left you feeling rejected."

"Did I tell you he apologized for that?"

"Yes. Have you seen him again this week?"

"On Monday, and then Katherine got sick and he had to leave. Then I saw him again on Tuesday morning. He's called a couple of times, but we've both been busy. He's short-handed at one of his stores, so he's had to work late every evening. I've had so many sample articles to read and a couple more interviews. I'm not getting very far on this salesperson thing. I think I have narrowed it down to one secretary candidate."

"I'm having a lot of fun with this article," Victoria said. "I've decided to write one on container gardening and one on vegetable gardening in planters. We can decide later which one to use first. Coincidently, last spring I put tomatoes, cucumbers, and sugar snap peas in containers in my yard. I just didn't have a good spot for a vegetable garden. So I already have the research. And, of course, with the corporate business that I do at the nursery, I have research for container gardening of tropical plants, and some flowering ones. Lillian grows roses on her balcony."

"How do you feel about your writing?"

"I think it's pretty good. Joe likes it anyway."

"Joe likes everything you do," Jane teased. Victoria's husband obviously adored her.

"Lately, he does. A little jealousy does wonders for a relationship," Victoria said.

"You really did tease Joe with your close friendship to Jeff."

"You should remember that, Jane. It might come in handy."

"Poor Jeff, he's so used," Jane said. "Well, anyway, I hope Gordon's grandkids don't throw their dinner at me this time. It wasn't very comfortable sitting through dinner with souring milk on my blouse."

"I hope not, too. Tell me about them."

"Eric is three. He's really cute, bright red hair. Teddy is eighteen months. He has red hair, too. As far as I can tell, the whole family has red hair. Katherine, his daughter, is about the cutest thing I've ever seen, except for you, of course."

"I don't think cute fits me at this point," Victoria said.

"Yes it does. When you're only five foot two you'll always be cute, no matter how old you get." Jane went on. "Anyway, Margaret had red hair, and Gordon says most of the kids inherited it."

"Does Gordon have red hair?"

"No, his hair is white. He says it was dark before it turned white. But he went gray young, like I did."

"You have a good attitude about Margaret. You never talk like you're in competition with her."

"That would be dumb. Part of what I love about Gordon is how much he loved his wife."

"So you are in love with him?"

"No. I mean I think I could be, but it hasn't gone that far yet. I don't know where it's going, but I'm enjoying the feelings."

"I'm glad, Jane. You deserve that."

Jane unlocked her door and ran for the phone. "Hello?"

"Jane, this is Lillian. I wondered if we could come over for a minute this afternoon. I want you to meet Mark before the wedding. It just doesn't seem right that you haven't met him. I've just been so busy, the wedding and all."

"I'd love to see you, Lillian, but you don't have to worry about me right now. I don't feel left out."

"I know, but I'd feel more comfortable if we could just come by and visit for a few minutes."

"Sure, I'm getting ready to take Fred out. But I won't go far. Come on over."

"Who's Fred?" Lillian asked.

"We really haven't seen much of each other lately. Fred is my dog."

"I didn't think you were an animal person."

"I'm changing. I'll see you when you get here." Jane took Fred out of the crate and kissed his soft head. He rubbed the side of his head against her shoulder. "You really are a sweet little dog." She put his leash and collar on him and went down in the elevator. As soon as she put Fred down, he started to turn circles and lift his leg on plants and shrubs. He couldn't seem to walk straight for very long. He always had to turn a circle. At least he wasn't turning under her feet anymore.

She walked around the block with him and went back up to the condo. Just as she got into the door the intercom buzzed. "Yes?"

"It's us," Lillian said.

Jane buzzed them in and took Fred into the kitchen to give him some water. The doorbell rang and she opened it to her friend. Lillian looked wonderful, maybe a little thinner than usual, but radiant. Her ash blond hair was cut in a chin-length bob, her blue eyes were flashing. The young man was a little taller than Jane, quite handsome, a little stocky. His head was shaved. He wore a small beard in the middle of his chin, and a tidy mustache.

"You must be Mark." Jane shook his hand. "Please come in."

They all went in and sat down. "Can I get you something?" Jane asked.

"No, we're fine," Lillian said. "I just wanted to spend a few minutes so you two would know each other at the reception."

"Are you feeling nervous?"

"I'm just ready for it to be over with," Mark said.

"That's no way to start a marriage," Lillian scolded playfully. "I don't think Mark had any idea what he was getting into until my family actually arrived. You know I have three brothers and three sisters."

"Do you have any brothers or sisters, Mark?" Jane asked.

"I have one brother and one sister. My brother is my best man. My sister is a bridesmaid. The rest of the wedding party is made up of the O'Malley's." He nodded at Lillian.

Jane laughed. "I guess you have three bridesmaids, and maid of honor, and three groomsmen."

"That's right," Lillian said. "So who's this new man you're seeing, Jane? Vic says you're really serious about him."

"Tori talks too much."

"That's what she says about you."

They both laughed. "You'll meet him tomorrow. He'll be my date. Mark, Tori told me that you are a commercial artist. Tell me about your work."

"I work in advertising. I have for some time now. I've been pretty successful, but I've hit a kind of tough spot. I'm pretty much self-taught. I never did fit in very well in school, so I taught myself. But here's the thing, in order to get the really good positions, you need credentials."

"He'll overcome that, though, because he's the best at what he does," Lillian said, smiling up at him.

He smiled back at her. "She's crazy about me," he said.

"I see that," Jane said. "You know, I'm going to need a commercial artist on a magazine that I'm planning to publish. I'm just in the planning stages right now, but I was wondering if you'd be interested in anything like that?" She stopped. "Of course, this isn't the time to talk about it. You've got too much on your mind."

"That's all right, I would be interested. What kind of magazine is it?"

"We don't have time to get into a long discussion right now," Lillian said to Mark. "We have the rehearsal dinner tonight, and I have a million things to do." She turned to Jane. "I'm sorry it had to be such a short visit."

"I'm glad you came at all. We'll talk about it in more detail when you get back from your honeymoon."

"But what is the subject of the magazine?" Mark persisted.

"Now, don't get too excited, Mark," Jane said. "It's called *Second Half*, and it's for women over the age of forty-five. You might not be interested in that at all. Let's talk about it when all the excitement has settled down."

"It sounds great," Mark said. "Just the break I've been waiting for. It was nice meeting you. I'll look forward to seeing you at the wedding tomorrow."

Jane shook his hand and hugged Lillian. "I can't wait. See you tomorrow."

The phone was ringing again as Jane got out of the shower. She hurried into the bedroom and picked it up. "Hello."

"Jane, this is Gordon. Kathy told me she had invited you to dinner tonight. I wondered if I could pick you up."

"Sure, that would be nice."

"I'll be there around 5:30 again. Is that all right?"

"Perfect."

"I've missed you this week. I'm sorry I was so caught up in the store."

"That's okay, I was busy too. Have things smoothed out at the store?"

"Yes, for a while anyway, see you soon."

"I can't believe it, Fred," Jane said to the little dog as she towel dried her hair. "I'm kind of tingling at the thought of seeing him. You'd think I was a teen."

When Gordon arrived, she opened the door expecting him to kiss her. He walked past her and went straight to the bar. "Before we go, do you have any scotch?"

"Yes." She went over to the cabinet. "Is something wrong?" she asked as she pulled out a bottle of Chivas Regal.

"I just had to fire one of the clerks at the Marietta store." Gordon ran his hand through his hair. "I caught him stealing. I wonder how long that's been going on?"

"I'm sorry." She poured him two fingers of scotch, then another two for herself. "Ice? Water?"

"Neat is fine." He picked up the glass.

She expected him to swallow it in one gulp, instead, he sipped it. She laughed.

"What's funny?" he asked.

"Well, the way you came charging in here. I expected you to chug that and demand more. Then you just sipped it."

"I'm sorry. I shouldn't come charging in here ranting." He stood and crossed the space between them. "May I kiss you?"

"Of course you may."

He kissed her slowly. "Hmm, that's nice."

"Um-hm." She sipped her scotch.

"I think I'm tired of the store," Gordon said. "I think I might sell. I'll keep the studio. I still enjoy that, but the generation gap is getting wider between me and my employees in the store. The studio requires more professionalism. The people that work there have a better work ethic." He sipped again.

"What studio?" Jane asked.

"You didn't know that Fox had a studio, too? We do weddings, bar mitzvahs, portraits. Lately, since meeting Fred," he reached down and stroked the little dog, "I've been thinking about branching out into the pet portrait field."

"Have you ever done commercial photography?"

He looked up at her and smiled. "I can see the gears turning in that business brain of yours. No. I've never been interested in that. I'm more of a casual photographer."

"I'd like to see some of your work."

Gordon put down his glass and took her elbow. "Let's go, Kathy's expecting us."

"Okay, but I'm not letting you off the hook, here. I think I might have found myself an advertising artist this afternoon. Maybe I have a photographer, too."

They arrived at Katherine's house. Rick answered the door. "Come in, please." He stepped back and slapped Gordon on the back as he came in. He nodded at Jane.

"Janie...Grampa..." Eric wrapped his small arms around Gordon's legs. Gordon reached down and swung him in the air landing him firmly on his hip.

"Janie...Rampa..." Teddy toddled as fast as his stubby little legs would go. Jane leaned down and scooped him up. She brought him to her hip then held him slightly away from her.

"You've got a wet diaper," she said.

"Oh, Jane, I'm sorry." Katherine came into the room and took Teddy away from her. He started to cry. "He's soiled your blouse," she said, looking down at Jane's hip. Handing Teddy to Rick, she took Jane's arm. "Rick, would you please change him. I'll take Jane into the laundry room." She looked at Jane. "I have some wipes in there."

Jane followed her into the laundry room. "It's all right, Katherine. That's all a part of being around kids."

"No, it's not all right. Every time you're around my kids, they do something awful to you. I feel terrible." She pulled out a wipe and started to clean Jane's blouse.

Jane took her hand and pulled the wipe out of it. "I'll do it. Please, I'm fine." A timer went off in the kitchen.

"I have to go see to dinner. Are you sure you're all right?"

"Of course..." Katherine left and Gordon came into the laundry room.

"I'm sorry," Gordon said. "This is even worse than milk and strained carrots."

"It's all right." Jane was looking down at her blouse and dabbing with the wipe.

Gordon tipped her face up to look at him. "What's wrong? You don't look mad about getting peed on. You look humiliated."

"That's exactly the word."

"Why should you feel humiliated because Kathy's kid peed on you?"

"Because I should have known better than to put

him on my hip like that. It's just so obvious that I haven't been through this. I like kids, but when it comes to dealing with them, I'm stupid." She looked back down at her blouse. "I hate being stupid."

"There is no way you could ever be described as stupid. I would have done the same thing and I have three children and seven grandchildren."

"You're just being nice."

"No. I'm telling the truth." He put both hands on her cheeks and kissed her. "Now, let's go back out and start over."

She dried the wet spot with a wash cloth and straightened out her blouse. "Okay, I guess I'm ready."

When they got to the family room, Eric was playing with a toy next to his Dad. Teddy was sitting on the floor with his head bowed. He looked up as they came into the room. His face was streaked with tears. He looked at Jane, and said, "Ah..sowy..Janie."

"It's all right, Teddy." She reached down for him and he stretched his stubby arms up to her. She picked him up and put him on the dry hip. He put his small arms around her neck and laid his head on her shoulder.

"Janie, know what?" Eric called from below.

"What?" She looked down at him.

"Daddy is building us a tree house. Wanna see?"

"I would love to see," she said.

"You wanna come, Grampa?" Eric asked.

"You bet."

"Dad," Katherine called from the doorway. "Phone's for you. It's Sybil."

"Sybil?" Jane asked.

"My secretary."

"Oh. We'll go out without you. Join us when you can." Jane took Eric's hand and went out the back door, carrying Teddy."

Eric ran ahead. He pointed up a tree and started to dance in place. "See. It's almost done."

"That's one great tree house. How do you get to it?" Jane asked.

"Dad promised Mom he'd put the ladder up last. She thinks we're too young."

"I see," Jane said.

"Janie, why don't you like Grampa?"

Jane looked down at Eric. "I do like Grampa. Why would you think I didn't?" She sat down on a bench that was under the tree and put Teddy down on the ground.

"Mamma told Daddy, she wished you would marry Grampa. So I thought if you wouldn't marry him, you must not like him." He looked at her very seriously. "Mamma worries a lot about Grampa."

"I see." Jane took a deep breath. She wondered how to handle this without making things worse. "First of all, I like your Grampa very much. But we've only known each other for a little while. Marriage hasn't come up."

"Hasn't come up?"

"He hasn't asked me to marry him." Jane heard a door shut and looked up to see Gordon approaching them.

"So he doesn't like you."

"No," she said. "Eric, let's not talk about this right now. I'll come over one day, and we'll talk about it together. But don't mention it to anyone else...our secret, okay?"

"Okay." He looked puzzled.

"That's some tree house," Gordon said, smiling and looking up.

Jane nodded. "It sure is."

"Your mom says it's time for dinner." Gordon picked up Teddy. "Let's go eat. I'm hungry."

Jane smiled and took Eric's hand. They went inside.

Everyone sat down. Katherine told Jane that the boys had been told they had to sit next to her or go to bed without supper, so there was no argument. Gordon sat down next to Jane. The table was round so Gordon sat on her left, with Rick on her right, Eric next to him, then Katherine and Teddy.

They passed the food around. Again it was a lovely meal. Everyone dug in.

"Grampa," Eric broke the silence. "Why don't you like Janie?"

"What?" Gordon said. "I like Jane. Why did you ask me that, Eric?"

"Eric, remember," Jane said.

"Oh, yeah," Eric said. He looked down at his food.

Gordon looked at Jane. "Is everything all right, Jane?"

"Fine." She smiled and touched his arm. "Fine."

Katherine looked worried. She said, "Dad, Grant is planning to come down from Charlotte next week. Has he talked to you?"

"Yes. He and Lauren are coming on Thursday, and the kids of course. They plan to stay with me. He wants to go over the house, make sure he's gotten everything important to him out of it."

"I need to do that too." Katherine took another bite.

"Don't worry about it, sweetie," Gordon said. "You've got enough to think about now. I'll keep anything that isn't garbage, even if I have to store it."

"I'm just worried about your definition of garbage." Everyone laughed.

"So, will you tell me what went on between you and Eric in the back yard?" Gordon said to Jane when they got into his car to leave after dinner.

"Well, apparently he overheard his mother say that she wished I would marry you," she said. "He figured that I must not like you, otherwise why wouldn't I?"

"Jane, the kids have worried about me since Maggie died. Please don't be upset. No one is rushing you." Gordon sounded tense. His brows pulled together. "So why did he ask if I didn't like you?"

"I tried to explain that I liked you very much, but we hadn't known each other very long. I said that marriage hadn't come up. He asked me what I meant by that. I said that we hadn't known each other long enough for you to ask me. I guess that made him think you must not want to marry me," she explained. "Things are very simple with kids."

"You're right." He pulled into the visitor parking lot, got out of the car, and walked around to her door. She got out of the car and met him at the back of the car. "May I see you up?"

"Please."

They went into the building and up the elevator. Neither of them said a word.

"Would you like a drink?" Jane asked. "I need to take Fred out. Would you like to come with me?"

"Yes. I'd like a drink. Yes. I'd like to go with you to take Fred out."

"So," Jane said, on the way down in the elevator, "are we going to be polite all night and just answer questions?"

Gordon took Fred out of her arms. "No, we're going to have sex."

"Shut up," Jane said. She smiled to herself and got off the elevator. "Put Fred down," she said. "He needs to pee. He won't do it if you're holding him. He's a good dog."

Gordon put the little dog down. The three of them walked around the block.

"I'm ready for that drink now," Gordon said as they walked into Jane's apartment.

"You know where it is. Jane went into the kitchen to pour water into Fred's bowl. When she came back out, Gordon had a glass of scotch in his hand.

"Would you like something?" he asked.

"Yes, I would like something."

"What?" He looked into the liquor cabinet.

"Your body on mine."

Gordon turned around. "Jane, I was planning to make a move." He smiled at her.

"Well, I wasn't sure and I didn't want to chance it," she said.

He put his drink down and crossed the room to her. He took her in his arms and kissed her. "I want you so much," he said.

"I want you too."

Gordon kissed her again. He caressed her face and then ran his hand down her neck to her shoulder, then cupped her breast. "Let me see you," he whispered.

She started unbuttoning her blouse. "I'll do it," he said, gently removing her blouse. He slowly undressed her. When he had her naked he lowered her to the couch. "You're beautiful, Jane," he said. "I dream about you at night. The reality is even better than the dream," he whispered.

He moved down her body to the warm spot between her legs. "God, you're heaven." He nuzzled her with his lips. "You taste like honey," he said.

"Gordon...I...haven't done this," she whispered.

"What?" He looked up at her face.

"Oral sex, I haven't..."

`He looked at her for a minute then went back to what he was doing. "Jane," he murmured. "You taste so good." He moved back up to her face and kissed her.

She enjoyed the salty taste of herself. He kissed her jaw, her neck, her lips again. Kissing at the same height was nice, but sex at the same height was even better. She looked into his eyes as he entered her gently, slowly. They moved together as if they had practiced. She was sure he wouldn't last long enough for her to climax. No one ever had, but she could feel something building deep in her belly.

"Jane," Gordon whispered in her ear. "My Jane... beautiful Jane."

She could hear herself saying something, but couldn't make out the words. They came together in one long wave of pleasure. He fell against her as she wrapped herself around him, their hearts pounding, their breath ragged. They lay clasped to each other for minutes, maybe hours.

"Gordon," Jane whispered. "I had an orgasm."

"Um-hm, me too."

"You don't understand," she said. "I've never come with a man before."

Gordon pulled back a little, propped himself on his elbow and studied her eyes. "Have you come with a woman before?"

"Only myself."

"Seriously?" A smile pulled at the corners of his mouth.

"Seriously."

"No wonder you never married." He looked into her eyes again.

She smiled slowly.

Chapter Six

Some time during the night Gordon led her to her bedroom. There he made love to her again with the same sweet completion.

She woke to the feel of his lips on hers. "That's no fair," she said. "You got up and brushed your teeth."

"You taste delicious."

"Did you use my tooth brush?" She sat up to lean against the headboard. Gordon was sitting on the edge of the bed, fully dressed.

"No," He patted his shirt pocket. "I brought my own."

"You were planning."

"I was hoping."

"You're dressed. Are you leaving me now?"

"I have a lot to do this morning. If I can't find someone to work the Marietta store this afternoon, I'll have to close it to go to the wedding. I'd rather not do that."

"You don't have to go to the wedding."

"I want to."

"I appreciate that." Jane pulled the sheet over herself. It felt strange to be naked with him dressed.

"Don't cover yourself. You're beautiful." He leaned down and nipped her breast.

"Gordon, you made me feel real good last night. Thank you."

"Not bad for an old man."

"Not bad for any man." She touched his face beside his eye and traced the smile lines with her finger. "I love the way your eyes crinkle when you smile."

He kissed her again then got up. "I'll pick you up at about two o'clock."

"Okay. I'll be ready."

"Let's go to the dog park down at Piedmont," Victoria said, when Jane answered the phone a few minutes after Gordon left.

"What's a dog park?" Jane asked.

"It's a big fenced area where you can let your dogs run off leash."

"I don't know. Fred and Ethel are so small. They might get hurt."

"Don't be over protective, Jane. Besides, I hear they have a separate area for the smaller dogs. If the big dogs seem dangerous, we'll go in there. Come on, I want Ethel to meet Fred."

"Okay. It sounds like fun. You want to meet there or should I come and get you?"

"I'll come and get you. I'm ready to go and by the time I get there, you can be ready to go. We haven't got too much time with the wedding this afternoon."

"Sounds like a plan." Jane hung up and went into the bathroom to take a shower. The shower felt great. The warm water was delightful. She smiled at herself. Everything felt good this morning.

When Victoria arrived she called Jane from her car and Jane went down. She got into the passenger seat with Fred then slid him between the bucket seats into the back seat with Ethel.

"Some dogs fight. I hope they get along," Jane said.

"I don't think we'll have a problem. Fred's just a puppy and Ethel loves everyone."

They watched the exchange between them. Fred wagged his tail wildly and sniffed Ethel's face. Ethel was cooler, but wagged her tail and licked the puppy. They circled each other on the seat, sniffing butts and noses.

"They're fine," Victoria said.

"They are. I'm glad. You wouldn't believe how much I love that dog, Tori. I never realized how attached you get."

Victoria pulled the car out of the parking lot and onto the road. "So how did things go last night with Gordon?" she asked.

Jane smiled dreamily. "Great."

Victoria looked over at her. "He didn't walk away this time?"

"No, he stayed. Why didn't you tell me sex was so good, Tori?"

"I thought you knew. You're older than I am and you've had more relationships than I have. I assumed you had more experience."

"Apparently it wasn't the right experience," Jane said.

"And this was?"

"Oh, yeah."

"How did it go at dinner? Did the grandchildren throw their dinner at you?"

"No, but the little one peed on me." Jane laughed then sobered. "I feel so stupid when I'm around kids. I should have known better than to pick him up without finding out if he had a wet diaper first."

"Don't be silly, getting peed on is just going to happen when you're around babies. Did I tell you about the time Benjamin peed in Joe's face when he was changing his diaper?"

"Yes, you did," Jane said. "I guess you're right. I wish I could have seen Joe's face when that happened."

"It was pretty funny."

"You know, Tori, when I got cleaned up and went back out to the play room, Teddy felt bad about it. So I picked him up and he put his little arms around my neck and pressed his soft cheek against mine. It felt so good."

"That's nice. I remember that feeling. It was the nicest part about having the kids. I guess I'll get to experience it again with Benjamin. I hope I get to see him enough."

"Me too." They rode in silence for a while. Victoria pulled the car into the parking lot at the park and they got the dogs out.

"This is nice," Jane said. "Let's walk around the pond before we go to the dog park." They took a leisurely stroll around the pond then went to the fenced area designated for dogs. There weren't very many dogs in the park yet.

"I guess it's a little early on a Saturday morning for most people," Victoria said. "I understand the place is packed in the afternoon. Look over there, Jane, a greyhound like Patricia's."

Jane looked in the direction that she was pointing. The beautiful dog bounded up the hill toward a man standing at the top leaning on the fence. There was something familiar about him. "Is that Jeff?" she said.

"What would Jeff be doing here? He's not a dog person."

"I don't know, but I swear I think that's Jeff." She started walking in the direction of the greyhound.

"Jane, don't put Fred down until you know if that dog is okay with small animals." Victoria hurried along beside her. "Some greyhounds will kill them."

"I know." She hurried over to the tall man who was now stroking the dog and talking to it.

"Jeff," Jane said as she approached. He turned around and smiled when he saw her. She hurried up to him, put her spare arm around his neck and kissed him. "It is you," she said, stepping back and smiling. "What are you doing here with that dog?"

"It's one of Elizabeth's rescue dogs. I'm actually thinking of adopting him."

"I didn't think you liked dogs."

"I just didn't know anything about them until Ethel came along." He reached over, took Ethel out of Victoria's hands and turned her over on her back to tickle her belly. "There's my girl."

"I knew you'd come a long way with her," Victoria said. "But I never thought you'd want one of your own."

"I could use the company," he explained. He held Ethel down for the big dog to sniff.

"Be careful, Jeff." Victoria grabbed at Ethel.

"It's all right, Vic. Elizabeth tested him. He's small-animal safe."

"How could she test him?"

"I don't know, but she assured me he's small-animal safe. I wouldn't even consider adopting a dog that might hurt Ethel." He put Ethel down on the ground and the big dog sniffed her. She licked him on the nose and started walking around sniffing the ground.

"What do you think, Gabe?" Jeff said. The big dog followed her over to the fence. They sniffed the shrubs and each other and soon were dancing around playfully.

"Put Fred down, Jane. Let him join them," Victoria said.

"I don't know. He's really delicate."

"I can't believe how protective you are," Victoria said. "Gabe didn't hurt Ethel. He won't hurt Fred, and just look around, will you? There are only four, maybe five other dogs here and they're all way over there."

"Well, all right." Fred was squirming in her arms. She didn't know how much longer she could hold him anyway. She put him down and he ran over to Ethel and Gabe. All three of them postured and circled each other. They sniffed butts and licked faces then they started to play.

"You know it's almost like the big dog knows he has to be gentle," Jane said.

"Yeah, I think he's a pretty good dog," Jeff said. "And he listens to me. Elizabeth says that sight hounds are such free spirits that you can't let them off leash. She says that if something catches their attention they won't listen to you. Watch this: Gabe come," he called. The dog looked up from his game and reluctantly turned and loped toward Jeff. Jeff put his hand on the dog's head and rubbed his side. "Good boy. Go on back." Jeff waived and the dog trotted back to his companions.

"I think he loves you," Victoria said, and walked over to where the dogs were playing together.

"Well, it would be nice if someone did," Jeff said.

"Is something wrong, Jeff?" Jane asked. "You seem depressed today."

"No," he said, putting his arm around her. "I'm just feeling a little sorry for myself."

"Are you seeing a lot of Elizabeth?"

"We've been out a few times. She's coming to Lillian's wedding with me this afternoon...you going with the new guy?"

"Yes. I'm going with Gordon," Jane said. "Are we going cycling tomorrow? I've missed it for the last few weeks since I twisted my ankle."

"I'd like to."

"Good. Oh, Tori," Jane called. "Did I tell you I met Lillian's young man?" She turned back to Jeff. "Have you met Mark?"

"Yes, he's a nice kid."

"When did you meet him?" Victoria asked rejoining them.

"Yesterday. Lillian called and asked if they could come over. She said she just didn't feel right about me not meeting him before the wedding. They seem really happy."

"She's crazy about him," Jeff said.

"I noticed. He noticed too," Jane said. "I asked him if he'd be interested in hearing about my magazine and he seemed interested. I need a commercial artist. He doesn't have credentials, but I'd like to look at his work. I'm finding that the people with credentials either have jobs they're happy with, or want too much money."

"What are you looking for?" Jeff asked.

"First I need to hire an assistant publisher and editor."

"Who will they assist?" Victoria leaned down to pet Fred.

"Me, of course."

"You're not an editor or a publisher."

"I am now. I know what to do. I've studied it."

"What do you look for in people for those jobs?" Jeff asked.

"Well, for the editor, it would need to be someone with a marketing background. The education would be good, but experience works too. A combination is ideal, but I don't think I can afford that. They would need to have some knowledge of Finance. The publisher would probably need a business background of some kind, again, some knowledge of finance."

"And you can evaluate all this?" Jeff sounded surprised.

"She can do anything," Victoria said. "She's smarter than most people and she has lots of education."

"See why I love this sister of mine," Jane said. "Yes, I can evaluate it pretty well. Gordon is helping me. But all he can really do is back up my observations."

"This Gordon guy sounds like some guy," Jeff said.

"Are you jealous?" Victoria asked.

"Of course, I'm jealous. Everyone has a partner, but me."

"What about Elizabeth?" Jane asked.

"She's okay, but it's not going anywhere."

"Well, you've got us," Victoria said.

"When you have time for me."

"Do you need to talk, Jeff?" Jane asked. "You're starting to worry me."

"I'm just manipulating you," he said. "Make a woman feel sorry for you and they give you all sorts of attention."

"You're not going to talk, are you?"

"Nothing to talk about."

Jane picked up Fred. "Tori, we've got to go. I need to do some things before the wedding."

"You're right."

"See you in a while, Jeff. See ya, Gabe," Jane said, patting the big dog's head.

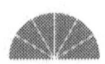

Jane pressed the buzzer on the wall to let Gordon up and went to the door to let him in. She laughed at her impatience. It would take a few minutes for him to get up to the 12th floor. She went back to the desk by the window where she had been working after lunch and started to straighten it up. The doorbell rang and she jumped. "I've got to get hold of myself, Fred," she said to the little dog and went to answer the door.

"Hello, pretty lady." Gordon pulled her into his arms and kissed her.

"Hello, pretty man," she said, kissing him back.

"I don't think I've ever been called pretty before."

"Maybe not to your face."

"Are you ready to go?"

She picked up her purse. "All set."

They rode the elevator down in silence. When they were in the car, Jane asked, "Did you find someone to mind the store?"

"Yes. One of the kids from the Buckhead store wanted some extra hours. He's doing it."

"Good. I'm glad you didn't have to close it. I'm sure Saturday is a big sales day."

"It is."

When they arrived at the church, Jane said, "Oh, look, Tori and Joe are already here."

"Where?"

"Over there, the little blond."

"You're kidding, that tiny little person standing next to the giant."

"That's right. The giant is her husband, Joe."

"I expected her to be tall like you."

"We adopted each other, remember?"

"You talk like she's a real sister. I guess I just forgot."

"Tori," Jane waved. There was a crowd standing outside the church. Victoria turned at the sound of her voice and smiled. She took Joe's hand and started pulling him in their direction.

"Jane," she said. "They haven't started going in yet.

I'm glad we saw each other so we can sit together. You must be Gordon," she said, extending her hand.

He took it and smiled at her. "And you must be Tori, I mean Victoria."

"You can call me Tori, if you want, I'm sure you've never heard Jane call me Victoria."

"That's quite an honor," Joe said. "She won't let me call her Vicki. I'm Joe."

"They're starting to go in now," Jane said, glad all the introductions were over. They walked toward the church door together.

"That's a beautiful corsage you have on, Victoria," Gordon said. "What kind of flower is that?"

"It's a hybrid. Different types of daffodil. It's my first. Jeff, my boss is teaching me hybridization at the nursery where I work."

"She's doing a great job of it, too," Jeff said from behind them.

Jane stopped and turned around. "Jeff," she leaned up and kissed him lightly on the lips. "I want you to meet Gordon Fox. Gordon, this is my very good friend and Tori's employer, Jeff Landrum, and his date, Elizabeth." She turned back to Gordon and drew in her breath. There was a look on his face. She wasn't sure what it was, maybe anger. It passed quickly and he held out his hand.

"It's nice to meet both of you."

He sounded fine. She must have imagined it.

"Hey, Jeff," Victoria said, and stood on tip toes while Jeff bent down so she could kiss his cheek.

Joe slapped him on the back. "Good to see you, Jeff," he said. "And it's good to see you too, Elizabeth." He kissed her on the cheek.

"You too," Elizabeth said.

"That's her first bloom," Jeff said, "but it's not her first hybrid. The others just haven't bloomed yet. I think we'll get some very interesting flowers."

"It is beautiful, Tori." Jane relaxed a little and looked at the flower. It looked like a daffodil, but it had six yellow petals around the base of it. In the center was the bloom.

It was white and was small at the base, getting larger at the top. Around the bottom of it were scalloped petals of yellow. When she looked up, Gordon was studying her face. Everyone else was looking ahead toward the door.

They were all seated in a pew together, Victoria and Joe, Jane and Gordon, Elizabeth and Jeff. The wedding was beautiful. Lillian's sisters and brothers all walked down the aisle, the women in gowns of blue; the men in navy tuxedoes. They all looked just like Lillian. Her parents walked together and proud. The maid of honor looked just like Lillian, too, but the best man looked just like Mark. Jane couldn't help but feel a little lonely. Nobody looked like her. She felt Gordon's eyes on her before he took her hand. He smiled at her. She smiled back.

"What a great reception," Jane said, as they sat down at a table with the other two couples. "Aren't you having any champagne, Tori?" she asked.

"Yes, I'll have some in a minute, but you know I'm not much of a drinker. I have to pace myself."

Joe laughed and kissed the top of her head. "She gets a little wild if she drinks too much."

"Oh, I'd love to see her get wild," Jeff said.

"I would too," Gordon agreed.

Everyone seemed to be having a good time. There was a band and dancing. Soon the newlyweds came into the room and walked around greeting and talking to people.

When they got to their table, Mark came straight over to Jane. "I haven't been able to think of anything else since we talked yesterday. I hope you will give me a chance to show you my work."

"I'm counting on it, but you need to be thinking of your bride right now," she said.

"Oh, well, I've thought of her, too."

"Where are you going for your honeymoon?"

"Hawaii, our parents split it between them. I think it'll be great."

"Don't think about the magazine again until you get back. It'll still be here when you do. I promise."

"Thanks."

Lillian joined him after talking to the other people at the table. She linked her arm through his and smiled up at him. She was beautiful in her white gown with her vale falling down her back.

"I'll give her enough attention." He smiled back down at her then looked back at Jane. "But I probably will think about the magazine a little." They moved on.

They left the reception at about 7:00 p.m. and headed for Jane's house. They had eaten, had some champagne, and danced a lot.

"What a great party," Jane said. "Aren't my friends great, Gordon?"

"Yes, they are. Victoria is as cute as she can be."

"See why I love her so much. You should have seen her when she was a baby. Although, I have to say, she just seems to keep getting cuter."

"And that gigantic husband of hers adores her."

"He really does, doesn't he?"

He parked the car and they went to the building. "May I come up?" Gordon asked.

"Please." Jane kissed him. It was a nice kiss, but maybe a little reserved. They got into the elevator.

"What is Jeff to you, Jane?" Gordon asked.

Jane took a deep breath. "So I didn't imagine that look I saw on your face when I introduced you?"

"You kissed him on the lips, Jane, even though you and he both had dates. That tells a story."

"What's the story?" Jane put her key into the door and went into the apartment.

"Have you slept with him?"

Jane took a deep breath and walked over to the bar. She pulled out a bottle of mineral water and took a glass off the shelf. "Would you like something?" she asked.

"Water is good."

Jane poured two glasses of mineral water, opened the small icemaker and put some ice in. She carried them over to Gordon and handed him one, then sat down on a bar stool.

"Gordon, I wasn't a virgin when you had sex with me last night. Did you know that?"

"Of course I did."

"I'm sixty-years-old. I've never been married, but I wanted a partner just as much as anyone else. I looked for one, and on the way I had some sexual encounters. No one ever made me want to be with them forever." She sipped her water. "You gave me my first orgasm last night." She stopped and took another sip. "Next to Tori, who is the only person who has ever truly loved me, Jeff is my best friend. That is never going to change." She looked straight into Gordon's eyes. "I'm not going to dignify your question with an answer. If you can't accept my friendship with him then we shouldn't see each other any more."

Gordon ran his hand through his hair. "I need to think about that," he said, and headed for the door.

"Make your decision now, Gordon. If you walk away from me again, I might not welcome you back."

He stopped with his hand on the doorknob. He stood there for a minute then left. The door didn't close all the way behind him.

Jane waited for a minute then walked over to close the door. It wouldn't close. She looked down at the floor where Gordon's foot held it open. Looking around the door she found him staring at the door frame.

"I'm acting like a jealous teen," he said.

"An accurate description."

"May I come back in?"

Jane opened the door and stepped back.

Gordon came in and closed the door behind him. He put his hands on her arms and looked into her face. "I can't stand the thought of another man touching you."

"After the way you made me feel last night," she

said, "and this morning, why would I ever want another man to touch me?"

"I want you to belong to me, to be mine."

She leaned forward and put her forehead on his chest. He picked her up and carried her to the couch. His movements were jerky.

"Gordon, I do belong to you," she whispered.

He pulled at her clothes. They heard something rip and she looked at the tear in her blouse.

"I'll get you another one." His lips were possessive as he pressed them against hers. Their tongues met with demanding pressure. He lowered himself on top of her.

"This won't work with your clothes on," she said, starting to tug at his shirt. In seconds he was naked. He entered her gently, but then he took her passionately. He embraced her so tightly that she couldn't breath, but she didn't care. She pulled him close and wrapped herself around him. He kissed her mouth, her face, her neck. They moved smoothly together for what seemed like always. She never wanted to stop. When they climaxed they came together, panting in each others arms.

"You know, Gordon," she said after she caught her breath. "If you had left, I would have let you come back. I just really didn't want you to leave."

"I didn't want to leave either."

Chapter Seven

The muscles in Jane's legs felt wonderful. She and Jeff had ridden about ten miles already. After about the third mile, her muscles ached so badly she didn't want to continue, but she pushed on. After about the seventh mile, the ache turned to that delicious burn of a conditioned muscle.

"Feeling better now?" Jeff asked from his bike beside her.

"Much," she said.

"I thought so. I can always tell with you. You smile when it starts to feel good."

"We'll go about five more miles then stop for lunch," she said.

"Okay, there's something I want to talk to you about."

"Really? What?"

"Wait till we get settled for lunch."

"All right."

They rode on mostly in silence, chatting occasionally. They talked about Jeff's work or about their mutual friends. After the fifteen mile marker on the Silver Comet Trail, Jane suggested they stop. There was a landscaped area just around the next bend with a picnic table. She pulled the lunch she had packed out of her saddlebags and started setting it out on the table.

"So, what did you want to talk to me about?" Jane asked, handing him a sandwich wrapped in wax paper.

"I've got this nephew—"

"You have a nephew? I didn't even know you had a sibling."

"I have a brother. He and I don't really get along well, mostly because of my nephew." He took a bite out of his sandwich then drank some water from the water bottle Jane handed him. "This kid is from his first marriage. He's remarried and has two kids with the second wife. That's fine. I know all marriages don't work, but he just abandoned David, the kid from his first marriage. His mother supported him and raised him alone, except, of course, for my help. I've participated as much as she would let me."

"Of course you would. You're such a wonderful man."

He smiled at her. "You just think that because you're my best friend."

"That's why I'm your best friend."

"Well, anyway, David grew up, did great in school all the way through and got into Harvard. Can you imagine? I talked Charlotte, my ex-sister-in-law, into letting me pay for it. She wanted him to turn down Harvard and go to Georgia State because she could afford it. She's very independent." He took another bite and chewed for a few minutes. "He finished his first year and did very well, but in his second year he got busted with a little less than an ounce of marijuana. Of course, Harvard expelled him." Jeff drank some water. "I got him a good lawyer and he got off with a slap on the wrist. We got him into Georgia State and he picked up where he'd left off."

"That's tough. I understand Harvard's position, but pot isn't dangerous. If he could make good grades even though he smoked...it's a shame he wasn't a little more careful."

Jeff smiled at her. "I was hoping you'd feel that way." He drank some more water. "Well, he wasn't careful again and he got caught, with a good bit more of the stuff. This time his mother didn't tell me. I guess Charlotte didn't want me to rescue him again. He went to prison for three years. While he was there, he finished college. He did it online…graduated summa-cum-laude, with a degree in marketing."

"Oh," she said. "I see where this is going."

"I'll understand if you don't want to even consider it, Jane, really." He paused and looked at the half eaten sandwich. "He can't get a job because of his background. Most employers do a background check these days. He's delivering pizza. I'm worried about him. He doesn't seem too depressed yet, but how many rejections can he take? He's really not a bad kid."

"I'll talk to him."

"He doesn't have any experience, but he's got a lot of drive and he's really smart." He took another bite and chewed slowly. "He says he doesn't smoke any more, but I can't swear to it. He's passed every drug test he's ever taken, but I think there are ways around drug tests."

"I don't care what he does on his own time, as long as he's careful and as long as it doesn't interfere with his work." Jane finished her sandwich and wiped her mouth with her napkin. "But Jeff, I won't let him ruin my magazine. I love you, but I'll fire his ass if he gets in trouble again."

Jeff smiled. "I know you will. That's the only reason why I brought it up. He doesn't have any knowledge of finance, or at least any official knowledge of it, but I'd be willing to educate him in it if it would help."

"That would be good. Have you talked to him about it?"

"No. I wanted to talk to you first."

They rode the fifteen miles back to where they started in relative silence. Jane felt good about this. She couldn't afford to pay what the people with perfect resumes wanted. Maybe her magazine would start with people who really needed a chance. That would be a double accomplishment.

"Jane, did everything go okay with Gordon last night?" Jeff asked when they had only about a mile to go.

She glanced over at him. "Why do you ask?"

"I saw that look on his face when you kissed me hello. It disappeared fast, but there was no mistaking it."

"He asked me what we were to each other. He asked me if we'd slept together." She rode in silence for a minute.

"What did you tell him?"

"I told him that next to Tori, you were my best friend and that I wouldn't dignify his other question with an answer."

"Was he satisfied with that?"

"I don't think so, but I told him that if he wasn't all right with you being my best friend, we wouldn't see each other any more. He did stay the night, so I think things are okay."

They rode in silence to the end of the trail where the car was parked. They loaded the bikes onto the rack and got into the car.

"Are you sorry you slept with me?" Jeff asked.

"No, but sometimes I'm sorry it didn't work."

"Me too, but other times I'm glad. It might have complicated our friendship. You're a great person, Jane."

"I think you're a great person, too."

"What do you think, Amanda, should the desk go here?" Jane asked the secretary she had hired. Amanda was the perfect candidate. Luckily she hadn't had to compromise on a secretary. They didn't get paid very much anywhere, even though they played such an important role. The two of them were directing the unloading of the furniture that Jane had bought for the office space she had leased.

"I think over here is better, facing this way," Amanda said. The delivery truck had just arrived and they were unloading the furniture.

"You're right. Put it there. It's your desk, your decision." She turned at the sound of the door opening.

Jeff came into the room smiling. "This place is great, Jane, perfect location." He looked around.

"Jeff, let me introduce you to my new secretary. Amanda Green, this is my very good friend, Jeff Landrum."

Amanda turned from where she was directing the placement of the desk. "It's nice to meet you." She extended her hand professionally and shook his. Then turned back to what she was doing.

Jeff shrugged. "Jane, where will your office be?" he asked.

"In here. Let me show you. They're unloading my furniture now. I need to be in there to supervise anyway." They went through an archway, turned right down a hall and into the first office on the right. The entire outside wall was a floor to ceiling window.

"This is nice."

"I thought so. There are two more offices on this hall for my assistant editor and publisher, then behind there is a large room where I plan to put cubicles for the rest of the staff. In the back there are two studio type rooms with big windows. I thought that would be good for my design group and my photographer." Jane smiled. "Did you just come by to see, or is there something I can do for you?"

"I wanted to see where you were going to be doing all this work, but I also wanted to get your telephone number. I talked to David and he's really excited." He looked around. "I guess they haven't installed the telephone system yet."

"They'll do that tomorrow, but I already know the number. I'll write it down for you, but David can call me at home.

"Great, I'll have him call."

They turned to look at the activity through the doorway. Two of the moving men were trying to maneuver a desk through the door. They had to turn it a couple of different ways to get it through. "Where do you want it, ma'am?"

"I think like this. I'd like to look out the window."

She motioned where she wanted it. They placed the desk and left the room again, returning in a minute with a credenza, then a couple of bookshelves and two chairs.

"Looks great," Jeff said. "I love the way you take charge." He leaned down and kissed her temple.

"Jane, oh, excuse me." Amanda stood in the doorway with Gordon looking over her shoulder. There was that look again. "There's someone here to see you." She made a fast retreat.

Gordon walked into the room. "Hello, Jane, I wanted to come by and see your new space." He looked at Jeff and frowned. "Hello, Landrum."

"Fox," Jeff said, stiffening his shoulders.

"Okay, you two cut it out." Jane stamped her foot and both men looked at her. "The way you're posturing and spitting at each other makes me feel like a female cat." She looked from one to the other. She had their attention. "Now, Gordon, Jeff is my very good friend, about the very best of my friends." She looked back to Jeff. "Jeff, Gordon is the man I'm seeing and very much enjoying. I insist that the two of you get along."

They looked at her and then Gordon looked back at Jeff. A smile started at the corners of his mouth.

Jeff started to smile too. "Well, I guess that's that." He extended his hand.

"I guess so. We've been told." Gordon shook Jeff's hand.

"Good," Jane said. "Now," she said, turning back to the room, "I'm happy with this room. I have to go and supervise the rest of the move." She hurried out.

After a minute both men joined her in the next room where she was directing the arrangement of the furniture into the same positions. "If they want to change it, they can," she said when they came in.

"Jane," Jeff approached her. "I'm going now. I really like your space and thanks for the other thing." He kissed her forehead again and looked pointedly at Gordon. When Gordon smiled, a little reluctantly, he left.

"What other thing?" Gordon asked approaching her.

"What?" She looked at him as he came toward her.

He pulled her into his arms and kissed her soundly. "Jeff said, 'thanks for the other thing.'"

"Oh, I'm going to interview his nephew for the editing job. He's having a hard time finding something and he has a degree in marketing."

"Oh, how're the interviews coming anyway?" Gordon didn't pursue the subject. Jane was glad. She didn't want to say anything about the marijuana problem until she had an idea of who the young man was.

"Not great. I can't afford the people with the best qualifications and I'm taking a chance on the others."

"Sometimes you just have to take a chance." Gordon brushed her lips again with his and released her. "Jane, I wanted to ask you something. All of my children and their families will be here this weekend. I had an offer on the house. I think I'll accept it. Michael decided to bring his family up while Grant was here so they could go through the house together. It's a big crowd." He brushed her hair with his hand. "I'd like for you to come to dinner on Saturday night, meet the whole group."

"I don't know, Gordon. Do I really belong there?" She looked away. "I mean that was your family home, a family that had nothing to do with me."

"The reason we're letting it go has something to do with you," he said. She looked away again and he put his finger under her chin and turned her to look at him. "This is a good thing for us, Jane, please, be part of it."

"Okay, Gordon, I'm nervous though. I think I might be in over my head."

"Me too," He kissed her again. "We'll drown together."

"Ms. Winslow, this is David Landrum. My uncle Jeff said you would be expecting a call from me."

"Yes, I'm glad you called. I'd like to meet with you to talk about my magazine."

"I'm really excited about it. When can we get together?" His voice was deep, but hesitant. Jane liked the sound of it right away.

"Is tomorrow morning too soon?" Jane asked.

"No. Where would you like to meet?"

"My office is at 1522 South Maple, across from the mall. Say about nine?" She thought early morning would be a good way to begin.

"That would be great. I'll look forward to seeing you."

Jane arrived at the office at 8:00 o'clock sharp the next morning. Amanda was already there. She looked at her through the glass door as she approached. She was actually quite pretty, although it was hard to tell with the mouse brown hair streaked with white and the horn rimmed glasses. The lenses were so thick that they magnified her eyes, but her features were nice, among them a sharp chiseled nose and full lips. Maybe she hadn't had anyone to tell her how to play up her looks instead of play them down. Or maybe she didn't want anyone to notice her. It would be interesting to find out. She was smart. There was no doubt about that. Why was she doing this kind of work? Surely she could do better. But she had no education on her resume. Jane made a mental note to find out why.

"Good morning, Amanda," she said, opening the front door.

"Good morning, Jane." Amanda's smile was warm. "Your appointment is already here I think. He's sitting in his car around the corner. He looked anxious when I passed him."

"I think we'll let him sit a minute then maybe I'll go out and introduce myself. I have some supplies to unpack in my office. Have you had any luck with the office machines I asked you to get?"

"Yes, it looks like leasing is really the way to go. You get a maintenance contract. That way, if anything goes wrong you don't have to pay for repair. You usually get some supplies along with the contract. I'm still comparing prices, but I'm almost ready to make a decision." She looked at Jane. "Of course, I'll present it all to you first."

Jane smiled. "I know you will. I'm sure I'll agree with you on it, but I do want to know everything." She went into her office and started unpacking her box of supplies. After a few minutes, she went back out to the reception area. "I think I'll go out and introduce myself now." Just then the door buzzed. She turned around to see a younger version of Jeff standing on the other side. She smiled and pressed the button to release the lock. "You have to be David. You look just like your uncle."

"My mom says I look like my dad, but he and Uncle Jeff are identical twins. I hope I'm not too early," he said.

"Identical twins!" Jane said. "How can I be such good friends with him and not know about an identical twin."

"They don't like each other too much."

"Well, anyway." Jane held out her hand. "I'm Jane Winslow, and this is my assistant, Amanda."

David shook her hand and then Amanda's. "It's nice to meet you. I really appreciate you giving me a chance to talk to you about this position."

"Let's go into my office."

David put his brief case down and pulled some papers out of it. "I have my resume here." He handed it across the table. "It doesn't look like much, but I've done some research about the magazine business since Uncle Jeff told me about this. I have a lot of learning to do, but I'm a good learner."

"Your uncle told me about your background, so why don't we get past that first."

"Yes, ma'am." He looked down for a second then returned his eyes to hers and made eye contact.

"I'm pretty open-minded about marijuana. I think it should be legalized. Putting a young man—a good student—behind bars for three years for it is counter productive if you ask me."

She leaned forward a little. "But it's not legal. That's the fact; and until it is, anyone who chooses to use it had better be very careful." She sat back again. "If you get into any trouble with that stuff again, this relationship is terminated. Understood?"

"Yes, ma'am."

"Now here's what I'm looking for in the position of assistant editor. Your initial work will center around finding our target audience and telling them about us. I have some ideas that we'll discuss later, but we need to know where they are and what they want to see in this magazine. It's a pretty big audience. We won't be able to confine our search to this area. This is not a niche production. So that means finding the most efficient and least costly way of reaching people, all of the people. Once we find them we'll need to develop long-term relationships. My editor will be responsible for the readers, finding out what they want, and getting it for them. The advertising will go to the assistant publisher. That can be a difficult relationship because sometimes the advertisers want something different than the readers. I expect whoever takes this job to be able to work out any differences that arise."

"It sounds exciting. I thought I'd start by studying our competitors," he said, waiting for her to go on.

She had an interview procedure that she had developed. She asked a number of questions that required problem-solving skills. She went through them with him, but she already liked this young man. "Do you have any questions for me?" she asked when she was finished.

"I wondered if you'd give me a more detailed description of the magazine. Uncle Jeff described it briefly, but he didn't know much."

"All right, it's called *Second Half* and it's literally targeted at people who are in the second half of their life. Do you think you'll have a hard time relating to that?"

"In some ways, I suppose, but I have relationships with people like that. I don't think my age will get in my way. In marketing you have to learn about your product whatever it is."

Jane smiled at him. "Good. The magazine will need to appeal to anyone forty-five years of age and older. I even plan to feature people of great longevity in every issue. I also plan to advertise using attractive older folks as models. I'm thinking of producing my own ads for everything. Clothes, cars, whatever we sell. I also have some ideas for ancillary products that can increase our income and grow our business. Marketing those would be up to you, too. You wouldn't be entirely alone. I plan to hire a staff of junior editors.

"Sounds great. I hope you'll consider me for the position." David picked up his brief case and stood.

Jane came around the desk and walked him to the door. "It was nice to meet you, David. I'll call.

David stopped at the door and looked down at her. "I really want this position. If you hire me, I'll make you glad you gave me the chance."

She smiled and walked out to the reception area with him. She watched him get into his car and drive away.

"I'm going to hire him," she said to Amanda.

"He sure does look like his dad," Amanda said.

"That man was his uncle you saw in here yesterday. But apparently he looks like his dad, too."

Chapter Eight

"Tori, did you know Jeff had an identical twin?" Jane asked. They were sitting on Victoria's back patio having lunch. It was early September and the weather was still warm, but not hot. There was a pleasant breeze keeping them comfortable.

"You're kidding. He never talks about him."

"Apparently they had a falling out. They don't see each other. I met his nephew yesterday. He looks just like Jeff, only younger." Jane popped a grape into her mouth.

"He has a nephew, too. Where did all this family come from?" She sipped her lemonade. "And to think, I've worried about him on holidays. How did you meet his nephew?"

"I interviewed him for a position yesterday. I'm going to offer him the job. When we went cycling on Sunday, Jeff asked me if I'd talk to him. Apparently he's had a hard time finding anything."

"But you think he'll do all right?"

"He's young, but he's very bright; did well in school. I'm going to have to take some chances here. Magazines always lose money at first. It's just part of the business, so you have to conserve your funds until you establish your customer base and get some big advertising contracts."

"You sound like you really know what you're doing."

"I don't suppose I'll really know until I've accomplished it, but I researched it pretty well." She pushed back from the table. "That was delicious, Tori. You're such a good cook."

"Thanks. So, do you know what the falling out was? I mean with Jeff and his twin."

"I think it had to do with the brother abandoning his son from his first marriage when he remarried. According to Jeff, David was raised by his mother. Jeff helped of course, but it doesn't sound like the boy's mother would let Jeff do much."

"That's terrible. How could you abandon your child?"

"I don't know."

"So how are things going with Gordon?"

"Good. He came by the office to see me on Tuesday. Jeff just happened to be there too. The way they stamped and snorted at each other was ridiculous. I don't agree with you about jealousy, Tori. I didn't find it fun."

"Really?" Victoria laughed. "And I enjoyed it so much. Well, I've always been a dumpy little housewife and you've always been a glamour queen. I guess we have different perspectives."

"You're not dumpy. Well, I told them to cut it out and they shook hands. I hope that's the end of it." Jane went on. "Gordon asked me to come to dinner on Saturday night. His whole family will be there. He sold his house and has about a month to move out. He's lived there for thirty-some years, so it's not going to be easy to do. Both sons and their families are coming to town to go through the house this weekend."

"That sounds like fun."

"I'm scared to death. Tori, I'm not used to that many people. I've lived a very solitary life. Not only that, but I just feel out of place. That was their family home. I'll be an intruder."

"No you won't, Jane. You're a friend of Gordon's."

"I'm a lover of Gordon's."

"Jane, his wife is dead."

"I know and he seems to have come to terms with it. I'm just not sure I have."

"Hello?" Jane picked up the phone.

"Hey, pretty lady." It was Gordon. "I hope I'm not calling too late." It was nine thirty, Thursday evening.

"No. You can call any time. Is everything all right?"

"Yes, I just miss you and I wanted to hear your voice. I've been so busy going through the house and packing things up I haven't had a chance to do anything else."

"I understand. Truth is I've been busy, too. I think I've finally decided on a printing company. I've checked out every printer in the area, and some not in the area. But I think I've finally found the best price."

"That's great," Gordon said. "Have you had any luck with employees?"

"Thanks for helping me decide on Amanda. She's already become my right hand. I've offered the assistant editor position to David Landrum. He accepted it promptly. I'll meet with him tomorrow morning to give him his first assignment."

"Good, I'm glad that worked out. I wish I could see you alone, but I'm afraid there won't be a chance until next week, with the family all here," he said.

"What about tonight, right now?"

"Grant and his family arrived this afternoon. I think I should introduce you to them before I go running off into the night after you." He laughed. "It's tempting, though."

Jane laughed too. "I guess I can see your point."

"I'll see you Saturday. Goodnight."

"Goodnight." She hung up the phone. "This is so much fun, Fred," she said as she burrowed under the covers to snuggle the warm puppy.

"The first thing I want from you is a plan of action," Jane said to David. She had seated him behind the desk in the office next to hers. She sat in the chair on the other side of the room. "I want you to write it out and present it to me. I want to know everything you plan to do before you do it."

"Yes, ma'am." The young man looked lost, frightened.

"David, please call me Jane. Ma'am just isn't going to work." She soothed. "I have guidelines for writing out a plan if you need them. I have some ideas I'd like to contribute too."

"I've read all of the magazines I could find in this category. Truth is there isn't a whole lot of competition. That also means there's no example to follow," David said. "I've got an appointment with the editor of another magazine, not a competitor. This guy is someone I knew at Harvard. He was in the masters program when I was a freshman. He's been very successful and has agreed to give me some tips. I think we can learn a lot from what's already been done."

"That's great." Jane smiled. "I want you to include in your report what you think you'll need in the way of staff. I want you to choose your own people, but all hiring of staff will be cleared through me." She rose and went to the door. "I'll leave you to your work. Any supplies that you need, tell Amanda about them. I'm always available if you want to talk." Jane left the room feeling excited. The kid was pretty smart and had obviously already put a lot of thought into this.

She went into the room behind the offices where the cubicles were being installed for the staff. Things were going well there. She had only put in one row of cubicles. She probably wouldn't fill them all at first, but later she may need to add more. Now she needed to concentrate on her search for an assistant publisher.

"Come on, Fred. Let's go for a run in the park." Jane picked up the little dog. "You're growing up, little guy. You seem heavier. Am I feeding you too much?" It was

Saturday morning. She had ended the day before feeling frustrated. She'd had two interviews in the afternoon and neither of the people was willing to negotiate in her salary range. She hadn't really liked them anyway, but there just had to be someone out there.

They got to the park and Jane put Fred through the little training routine she had developed for him. He was doing great. Then they started to run. Jane still watched Fred closely, but there was no problem. He trotted along beside her, watching the passing birds and squirrels with interest, but never breaking stride. When they had finished their run, she stopped at the fountain. Fred sat obediently beside her and she reached into the small fanny pack she was wearing and took out a bowl and a bottle of water. She poured some water into the bowl and put it on the ground for Fred, and then took a drink from the bottle.

"That's a great idea, bring his own, personal bowl," Gordon said from behind her.

She turned around startled to see Gordon and two other men standing there.

"Jane, these are my sons, Grant and Michael." They did resemble him now that she noticed. The red-haired one, Michael, was a little taller. Grant had dark hair heavily sprinkled with white.

"It's nice to meet you both," she said.

"And this is Fred," Gordon said. "He's sitting so well, Jane. You've done a remarkable job of training him."

"Release, Fred," she said to the little dog. He immediately ran over to Gordon who scooped him up.

"It's nice to meet you both," Grant said.

Michael nodded. "Is this the Jane that's going to dinner with us tonight?" he asked his father.

"This is the Jane," Gordon said.

"Great. We're going around again, Dad. It was nice to meet you, Jane. We'll see you tonight." They took off at a run down the trail.

"Nice looking sons," Jane said.

"I think so. Come and sit with me on the bench over here. Gordon pointed to a bench in the shade."

"All right," Jane said, following him over.

He carried Fred but put him down when they sat. He put an arm around her shoulders and pulled her close. He tipped her face in his direction and kissed her.

"Gordon, don't do that." Jane pulled away. "Your kids might see. And besides, I'm all sweaty."

"I'm sweaty too, and I don't care if my kids see." He squeezed her shoulder a little then withdrew his arm.

"I probably stink," Jane said.

"You smell great. Do I stink?"

"You smell great." She smiled.

"Tell me how everything went yesterday. I know David was starting, and you had a couple of interviews."

"Well, David is doing great. I gave him an assignment to draw up a plan of action. He'll need to define an audience, find a way to reach it, find a way to learn what they want from the production. He'll also need to create a mission statement. I also asked him to decide how much staff he'll need."

"Wow, that's a tall order. How did he react?"

"He jumped right in; spent the whole day in his office clicking away on his computer, and made a list of supplies for Amanda. I'm pleased. He's really enthusiastic. Now if I could only find a publisher."

"Still no luck? What do you need?"

"I need someone with an education in business, probably administration, some knowledge of finance would be good, and some sales experience. The publisher runs the business end of the enterprise...keeps the financials within the parameters. The publisher would handle the commercial end. That's where the sales experience comes in. He or she would have to sell our advertising capabilities."

"Sounds like a great job."

"The only problem is I don't have the money to pay someone with all those credentials. I can only meet midrange, but I'm offering some profit sharing potential. Nobody seems interested so far."

"Well, don't get discouraged, I'm sure someone will come along." Gordon patted her knee.

"Oh, one good thing happened yesterday afternoon. Tori brought her article for the gardening piece. It's really good. I swear. She just has so much talent. I'm really proud of her.

"That's great."

"Gordon, I was thinking while I was running this morning."

"Uh-oh..."

She elbowed him playfully. "Remember when we talked about your photography? You know I really do need a photographer. Please let me see your work."

"Jane, I'm enjoying watching you start this business up. You're so energetic and I know it will succeed, but I just really am not interested in anything like this."

She sighed. "Okay I'll back off, but I'd still like to see your work."

"I'll tell you what. If you let me take some shots of you, I'll show you my work."

"Shots of me? Why in the world. I'm not a model. I'm not even photogenic. I don't think there has ever been a good picture of me taken," Jane said.

"You just haven't come across the right photographer. You really should be a model. You're tall and thin and beautiful." He put his arm back on her shoulder. "Deal? You see my work. I take pictures of you."

"All right, but it won't work. You'll see."

"Good." He put his arm across her shoulders and pulled her close to kissed her.

"Dad," Grant said from behind them. Jane jumped back.

"That was fast," Gordon said, turning to look at his sons. "Have you been all the way around already?"

"I guess time flies when you're having fun," Michael said.

Jane could feel a blush rising.

"Want to come by for some breakfast, Jane?" Gordon asked.

"No thanks. I've got to take Fred home and I have some errands to run. I'll see you tonight."

Gordon rubbed his hands together. "I'll pick you up at five thirty. Okay?"

"You don't have to pick me up. I know the way."

"I want to. Please?"

"All right."

By the time Gordon arrived that evening, Jane was a nervous wreck. She pressed the button to let him in the lobby door and waited for him to ring her doorbell. When she opened the door to him, he pulled her into his arms and kissed her. He pulled back and looked into her eyes.

"What's the matter? You're shaking."

"I'm scared to death."

"Of what?"

"Your family."

"Jane, they're all nice people. I won't let any of the kids sit next to you. I promise you won't get food thrown at you or peed on." He pulled her into his arms and held her. He squeezed her tightly against him. "I can't believe you're this upset." He guided her to the couch and sat down pulling her into his lap.

"And that's another thing," she said, leaning into his shoulder and burying her head in his neck. "You're just too affectionate. They need to adjust to the fact that you're seeing another woman."

"Jane, there is no other woman. You're the only woman." Gordon kissed her until he felt her relax. "There, that's better. Jane, the kids know I'm seeing you romantically. I've told them so. They have no problem with it."

"Are you sure?" She sounded small and frightened.

"I'm glad it means so much to you, but there really isn't any reason to get yourself this worked up."

"Tori would say that I'm in a state."

"You are in a state," he said. "Now get up and let's go. I've reserved a room at an Italian restaurant over by the mall, but we have to go home to hook up with the family first. We'll drive over caravan style."

"A family caravan," she said, getting up from his lap. "I love family caravans. I'm always envious of Tori when I get to be in one of hers."

"Well, now you get to be in mine, as my partner."

They arrived at Gordon's house and went inside.

"Janie, Janie, Janie, Janie," Teddy said, toddling toward her, his stubby arms extended. She leaned down then looked up for Katherine.

"He's dry, Jane," Katherine said from beside her. "I just changed him."

Jane scooped him into her arms. He put his arms around her neck and pressed his soft cheek against hers

"Ah...wove...Janie."

"I love you too, Teddy." She felt tears pushing at the back of her eyes. I never cry, she thought.

"Janie!" She felt a tug on her skirt. Eric stood beside her, looking up. "All my cousins are here." He pointed at the sea of faces.

"I see that, Eric." She looked nervously at Gordon.

Gordon picked up Eric who was still tugging on her skirt. "I'm going to introduce you to my family, but don't worry. We don't expect you to remember all of the names the first time around."

She smiled faintly.

"This is my daughter in law Jill, and my granddaughter, Joy." Gordon waved at a pretty woman with wavy blond hair sitting on the couch with three girls. "This is Alexandra." He pointed to a younger child sitting on Jill's lap. "And this is Hope." He put his hand on the head of the girl sitting on the other side of Jill. He pointed across the room to his red-headed son. "You met Michael this morning. He and Jill and the girls make up his family. Then over here," he went toward the dining room table, "this is Lauren, Grant's wife, and Maggie. Over here is Gary. He pointed to an older child across the table. Grant should be down in a minute. Of course you know Katherine, and Rick is upstairs."

"We're all happy to meet you," Jill said, smiling. "I know it's a little overwhelming. I remember my first time meeting the family."

"Would you like a glass of wine?" Katherine appeared at her side holding two glasses. "The reservation isn't until 7:00 so we've got time. Here, let me take Teddy."

"No, Mommy." Teddy tried to hold on.

Katherine pulled him away. "Janie will be here all evening. Give her a chance to see the others," she said to him.

Jane sat down at the table with Lauren and Maggie. Gordon sat down next to her and put Eric on the floor. Jill came over and took another chair. Michael came over and stood behind Jill, his hands on her shoulders.

Jane's mouth went dry. She could remember Tori talking about her mouth going dry. Jane had never experienced it. She took a sip of wine.

"Tell us about this magazine," Michael said. "Dad says you're venturing into the publishing business."

She also remembered Tori saying that when she got nervous she couldn't swallow. Jane panicked. She couldn't swallow. She looked at Gordon.

Gordon looked back at her. His eyes crinkled.

She straightened and said, "I'm publishing a magazine for people in the second half of life." She put her hands under the table. They were trembling. "I started noticing that when I was waiting somewhere, like in a doctor's office or at the spa, the magazines didn't appeal to me anymore. They were filled with recipes that serve six to eight, and articles about raising children." She looked around the room. "Of course I guess you're all pretty interested in those things." Everyone laughed. She found herself laughing with them. "I used to like those articles. Even though I never had any children of my own, I had two nieces that I loved very much. Of course, I had friends who had kids too. But at this point, I'm not interested. Those magazines have nothing to offer someone of my years. So I decided to publish a magazine for people in the second half of their life."

"That sounds really interesting," Michael said. "Are you looking for a commercial photographer?"

"Yes." She looked up at him. "As a matter of fact, I am." She looked over at Gordon. He smiled.

"Really?" Michael sounded excited. "Why didn't you tell me, Dad?"

"I figured she'd tell you."

"Would you be willing to look at some of my work? I'm a commercial photographer."

"Yes, I'd love to see your work." She smiled.

Grant and Rick came down the stairs and joined the group.

"Grant," Michael said. "You should hear about Jane's magazine."

"First let me ask you." She smiled at Gordon then turned to Grant. "You wouldn't be interested in a publishing job, would you?"

"Yes I would," he said. "I've been trying to break into that field for a while now, but I don't have the credentials. I have the skills, but not the credentials. Try to get hired without the paperwork."

"We'd better go," Gordon said. "We don't want to lose our reservation and it'll take a little while to get this crowd into the restaurant."

"I wanna ride with Grampa and Janie," Eric squealed.

"Ah...ride...rampa...Janie," Teddy repeated.

"Let them ride with us, Kathy," Gordon said. She agreed and they went about the business of transferring car seats.

When they finally got on the way, Jane said, "Why didn't you tell me you had candidates for me?"

"I didn't want to get too involved with it. I figured that if they were interested, they'd speak up when you presented the opportunity. As a parent of adult children, I find that if I do too much instigating, I get into trouble."

"Well, I wouldn't know anything about that."

"Don't give them any special consideration," he said.

"Don't worry. I won't."

"I know." He smiled at her, picked up her hand and kissed the back of it.

"Grampa," Eric said from the back seat. "Do you like Janie now?"

"I always have, Eric."

They arrived at the restaurant and gathered in a group in the parking lot. Jane was holding Teddy and Gordon had Eric's hand. They all began to walk toward the building, moving together like a wave of people.

"I feel like a drop of water in the ocean," Jane said quietly to Gordon.

He smiled reassuringly.

When they got into the restaurant, Gordon gave them his name and the hostess showed them to a room off the hallway to the main dining room. The room was nice. There was art on the walls and a buffet table at the end of it. There were hors d'oeuvres and wine on the table. There were small bottles of soft drinks for the kids. Gordon poured two glasses of wine and handed one to Jane.

She took it and sipped. Rick reached for Teddy and carried him over to his mother. "He was asleep on my shoulder," Jane said. "I didn't even notice." She watched Rick carry the sleeping infant over to his mother.

Katherine sat down and adjusted him in her lap.

"There's not much room in her lap anymore," Gordon said, smiling at her pregnant belly. "Jane, you sit here on the end and I'll sit next to you. That way I can protect you from the kids. Joy, you sit on the other side of Jane." He pointed to the chair at the head of the table. "You'll have to protect her on that side." Joy smiled shyly and sat on the other side of Jane.

"You don't have to protect me, Gordon. I'm not worried," she said.

"No, I promised I wouldn't let the kids throw anything at you. Did I tell you what happened the first time Jane came to dinner at Kathy's?" He addressed the room as everyone sat down. There were fifteen of them so they took up two tables, but they were close enough to talk. Gordon told the story of the strained carrots and milk. Everyone laughed, even Eric. Jane laughed too. Soon the room was buzzing with conversation. It made Jane feel dizzy.

"Janie," Joy said from beside her. Jane looked down at the little girl. She had platinum blond hair and pale-blue eyes. Her skin looked like porcelain. She was beautiful. "Daddy said you have a dog. I love animals, but Grampa's cat won't let me pat her."

"You can pat my dog. He's pretty friendly."

"I thought maybe if you were going to the park tomorrow I could walk with you for a while."

Jane smiled. She could feel Gordon's eyes on her. "That would be nice. I'd enjoy the company."

"I wanna go too." The redheaded toddler from across the table called out. This must be Alexandra, Jane thought.

"You can't go. You're too small," Joy answered.

"I'm not too small." Hope, another redhead, called from the other side of Gordon.

"Mom!" Joy said.

"Girls, behave!" Jill commanded. "If you keep acting this way, no one will go. Jane won't go." The girls quieted. "We'll work it out," Jill said.

Jane heard Gordon laughing beside her. "What are you laughing at?" she asked.

"My family." He put his hand on her leg under the table. She jumped.

"Janie," Hope said, leaning around her Grampa. "Know what?"

"What."

"I have a dog."

"It's not your dog," Alexandra said. "It's our dog."

"It's a golden retriever," Joy said. "His name is Beau, because he's so beautiful."

"We have a cat, too," Hope said. "But he's not mean like Grampa's cat."

"Nobody is as mean as Grampa's cat," Gordon said.

"Did your Grampa tell you what his cat did to my dog?" Jane asked. "She knocked him into the water bowl."

"Into the water bowl?" Alexandra squealed. The table erupted with giggles. "Your dog must be small."

"He is small," Jane said.

"But that cat is so mean she could probably even beat up Beau," Joy said.

"Girls," Michael said. "It's not nice to talk about Grampa's cat like that."

Jane stiffened and looked at Michael. She'd forgotten that they were talking about his dead mother's cat. He was at the other end of the table talking to the dark haired boy sitting between him and Hope.

Gordon picked up Jane's hand under the table and squeezed it. She looked at him. He was smiling at her. "Gary likes to spend time with his uncle when he gets a chance. He's our next generation of photographer. They like to talk shop."

"That's right," Michael said. "Gary has computer smarts, too. He'll take photography to a whole different level."

The boy smiled shyly.

The waiter came around to take orders. Jane was feeling less dizzy now. She felt sorry for the waiter. It would be a miracle if all the orders came out right. The room buzzed with conversation.

"Well, no disasters. Your clothes are all still in tact," Gordon said on the way home.

"It was nice, Gordon. You have a beautiful family," Jane said a little sadly. They were alone in the car. They had transferred the car seats to Rick's car in the restaurant parking lot. Teddy had slept through dinner and was still asleep when they strapped him into the seat.

"Your eyes were the size of saucers when the girls started fighting." He looked at her closely. "You don't have to come to the park tomorrow if you don't want." He waited for a response. "Is everything all right, Jane?"

"I'm just a little bit overwhelmed, I think." She smiled and reached for his hand.

Chapter Nine

"What is that?" Jane woke to her own voice. Something was bothering her, a ringing noise. "Oh." She laughed at herself and reached for the phone. "Hello," she croaked into the receiver. She cleared her throat and tried again. "Hello."

"I woke you up. I'm sorry. This is Grant Fox."

"That's all right. What time is it?" She blinked her eyes and sat up in bed.

"It's 9:30. This house has been hopping for hours," he said.

"I usually don't sleep this late. I guess your family really wore me out," she said. "What can I do for you?"

"I was wondering if you were going to the park. I thought I'd walk over with Joy. Talk to you a little about my qualifications. I've got to go back to Charlotte tonight, but if you were interested, I could arrange to come back for a formal interview."

"I'd like that. Give me about forty-five minutes to get there."

"Okay. See ya there."

"Poor Fred, you must really have to pee." She put on her bathrobe and took him to the balcony. She had a dog litter box out there for emergencies. There was netting all around the balcony so he couldn't fall off. "You've really changed me, Fred," she said. "I'll do just about anything for you."

She took a quick shower, put on her clothes, gathered Fred and his water bowl, and left. When she arrived at the park, Grant and Joy were sitting on a bench waiting for her. She and Fred approached the bench. Fred sniffed the little girl then backed up, eyes wide. He pushed up against Jane's leg.

"He doesn't usually act shy," Jane explained. "I don't know what's wrong."

"I know." Grant laughed. "He smells that cat on you, Joy. Give him a treat."

Joy was holding a bag of treats. She reached into the bag and pulled one out. The little dog wagged his tail and took the treat. Joy reached down to pat his head. "Can I walk him a little?"

"Sure, but hold on tight to the leash. He's a greyhound. He'll run like the wind if you give him a chance," Jane said. She handed the leash to Joy and girl and dog started down the path.

Grant and Jane walked together down the path behind them. "I've been working for a magazine for about five years. I have some experience in the field. I just can't get past sales because I don't have the credentials. I was working on my MBA when Lauren became pregnant with Maggie. It was a difficult pregnancy. Lauren was sick all the time. She had to quit working and stay home. Of course we already had Gary, and he was a handful. I hired someone to stay with the two of them while I was at work during the day, but I needed to be home in the evenings. So I quit school. I should have gone back and finished, but I never did. Maggie was born with some health problems, nothing that we can't deal with, but with one thing and another." He stopped and smiled. "Truth is I could have gone back. I just didn't."

"You still can," Jane said.

"And I will if it'll make a difference to you."

"I don't really care about credentials. I'm finding all sorts of talent without paperwork." She laughed. "Tell me about your qualifications."

"I have the education even though I don't have the degree. I only lack a few courses, but my undergraduate degree was in finance and I do have the paperwork on that." He stooped and picked up a rock then tossed it into the stream running along the path. "It's my experience that's the best qualification, though. I've been in sales for five years. I like sales and I'm good at it, but I want to do more."

Jane laughed. "Did your dad describe the position to you?" she asked.

"No. He wouldn't talk about it. Why?"

"Because you just described what I'm looking for."

Grant smiled at her. "Will you give me an interview?"

"Yes. I'd like to see your resume. Talk in detail about what I'm looking for, what I expect, what I need."

"Uncle Grant, look," Joy called from the trail ahead of them. Fred sat in front of Joy. She had the leash looped over her hand. She held her hand out and said, "Shake." The little dog picked up his paw and put it in her hand.

"She taught him to shake hands." Jane laughed. "I didn't teach him that."

"Janie," Joy said. "What kind of dog is he again? I want one."

"You have a golden retriever."

"I know, but I want one of these. Can we take him back to the house and let the others see him."

"Well, I don't know." Jane looked at Grant.

"We won't let the cat hurt him." Grant smiled.

"Well, all right. We have to go slow with him though. He isn't used to a lot of people."

"You wouldn't believe it, Jeff. Gordon reserved a whole room. There were fifteen of us. Can you imagine having a family that big?" Jane and Jeff were riding the Silver Comet Trail again. They had started late that day because of her morning visit with Grant.

"That's what it's like when I go to my aunt's house. She's got a bunch of kids and they all have kids. It's quite a party," he said. "It's fun being a part of it."

"I had fun last night, but I felt out of place. I don't

know what the problem is; maybe it's just that I've lived such a solitary life. I've really never been part of a big crowd."

"You were part of Vic's family. But I guess that's not a really big family."

"No. All of Gordon's grandkids call me Janie. It's like they just accepted me as a part of the group. And there I was feeling like a sore thumb."

"A sore thumb..?"

"Yeah." They rode in silence for a while.

"How's David doing?" Jeff asked.

"He's only been in one day. What a time to start a new job—on Friday," Jane said. "I told him he could wait until Monday, but he wanted to start right away. I gave him a pretty big assignment, but he seems to be working hard on it. It'll be interesting to see what he comes up with."

"I hope he behaves himself."

"Don't worry about it, Jeff. If he doesn't, I'll take care of it. He sure does look like you. Why didn't you tell me your brother was an identical twin?"

"I'm not proud of it."

"You don't want to talk about it either, do you?"

"No." They turned around and headed back after their usual fifteen miles. "We should plan an overnight sometime, Jeff. Maybe bring Joe and Tori. She's riding pretty well now. Joe could take her on the tandem if it's too far for her alone."

"How's Gordon going to feel about you going on an overnight with me?" Jeff asked.

"I hadn't thought about that. Well, he doesn't own me. We're not even attached." She bit her lip. "Maybe he could come too."

"Maybe I'll skip it," Jeff said.

"What's wrong, Jeff?"

"Nothing, I'm sorry. I've just been a little down lately. I'll work it out." They were quiet for a while. "So do you think you'll hire Gordon's sons?"

"Grant is exactly what I'm looking for. We haven't

talked money, but I think he'd be willing to negotiate. He's looking for a chance to do something new. I haven't talked to Michael yet, but Gordon says he's good. Yes. I think I probably will hire them both."

"Here you are publishing a magazine for old people and staffing it with young people."

"Yeah, I thought about that. But that's okay. I'm just a little surprised they all seem so interested. I can't wait for Lillian and Mark to come back. The studio is looking really lonely back there. The magazine is really shaping up though. I'm having lots of fun with it. Did I tell you how good Tori's article is?"

"No, but I'm not surprised. She's an amazing little thing."

"She is."

"Jane," Amanda said, standing in the doorway to her office. "There's a Michael Fox here to see you. Were you expecting him?"

Jane looked up. "No, but he can come in."

"I guess I should have called first. I was hoping you'd have a minute to talk about the photography job." Michael was dressed in a suit with a tie and he carried a portfolio case.

Jane smiled at him as he came into the room. "Of course, sit down. I haven't really put together a job description on that one yet. I was hoping to talk your dad into taking the job, but he tells me he really isn't interested."

"No, Dad's more of a portrait man. And he likes wildlife and sports photography. He says he's going to get some shots of you though."

"I don't know why he wants to. I'm not photogenic. I just don't catch the light well," she said.

"You might be surprised. He's pretty good with light."

"Tell me what you've done, Michael."

"I worked freelance in Atlanta for a long time then went to Savannah. I heard there was more opportunity there. I have my portfolio with me. I keep it updated, just in case a chance like this comes along. I've wanted to get back to Atlanta. I'd like to live closer to Dad."

"I don't blame you. He's a good dad." Jane stood up and cleared the papers off her credenza. "Put it down over here so I can look at it." She flipped through his work. She stopped at a picture of a small woman with faded red hair. She stood by a window looking out. There was a reflection of her face looking back in the glass. The faces were looking past each other. Her expression was content.

"That's my mom. I thought about taking it out, but I think it's a pretty good shot. I hope it doesn't disturb you."

"No, of course it doesn't." She studied the picture for a minute. "She was pretty."

"She was." Michael flipped past the picture. He turned a few more and pulled one out of the protective sheet. "I think this one is particularly good." He handed it to Jane. He reached into a pocket of the bag and pulled out a couple of magazine pages. "This is the magazine I do a lot of work for in Savannah." He handed the pages to her. She looked through them.

"This is good work, Michael. I'm surprised you don't have your choice of jobs."

He smiled. "I think it's hard to break into any art industry, especially without a degree. There's just so much competition. It's hard to even get anyone to look at your stuff; and if they don't look, they don't know."

"You're probably right. I've never been much of an artist, so I don't have any experience with that."

"Hey, what are you doing with my girl?" Gordon said from the doorway.

Michael turned and smiled at him. "I'm hitting her up for a job, with no help from you, I might add."

"When did I become your girl, and how did you get past Amanda?"

"I brought her flowers and a vase, but no water, pretty tricky, huh." He kissed Jane on the cheek. "So what do you think of my kid's work?" He started flipping through the pictures. He stopped when he got to the one of Margaret. "This is a good one of your mom, Michael. Have I seen it before?" he asked.

"I'm sure you have. I took it shortly before she died."

"I can tell. She's so thin."

They talked so easily about her. Jane felt dizzy. She sat down suddenly feeling tingly and there was a black rim around her vision. Then everything was black. She could still hear them talking, though.

"Jane, are you all right?" She shook her head and blinked her eyes. Gordon was kneeling on the floor in front of her looking very concerned. "What happened? You turned pale and sat down. Luckily your chair was right behind you. Did you faint?"

"I never faint," she said.

"Jane," Michael came into the room with a glass of water. He handed it to her. "I didn't mean to upset you with that picture."

"It wasn't the picture for heaven sake," she snapped. "I don't think I've eaten anything today. That must be it."

"She's snapping at us," Gordon said. "She must be feeling better." He smiled at her. "I dropped by hoping to take you to lunch. Will you go with me?"

"Is it already noon? I guess I lost track of time." She looked up at Michael who still looked concerned. "Will you come with us, Michael? I'd like to tell you about the magazine, what I'm looking for in a photographer."

"Yes, but are you sure you feel up to it? I saw you turn white. I really thought you were going down."

"You make me sound like an airplane. I'm fine. I'll just have a glass of juice before we go."

Gordon stood up and extended his hand to her. She took it and he pulled her up. He held her by the shoulders and looked into her eyes. "You're sure you're all right?"

"You'll get on my nerves if you keep asking me that," she said, and went through the door. The two men followed her into a small break room across the hall. She opened the refrigerator and took a juice box out. "Would you like something?"

They both declined.

They went to lunch at the mall. Jane and Gordon sat on one side of the booth. Michael sat across from then. "Michael, when I researched my competition, I found one common denominator among them all. Some of them had pretty good articles. None of them cut the size of the recipes, though." She smiled. "But mostly I noticed that unless they were advertising for something that only older people use, they still used young models in the add. For example, if they were advertising for a fiber supplement, there would be some bloated looking senior in the ad.

"I see what you mean," Michael said.

"The other ads, like for underwear or cars or whatever, all had young-looking glamorous people in them. There was one ad for a minivan with a young woman and about five kids in the car. The reader base I'm looking at can't relate to that any more and doesn't want to."

"I'm guessing you want to design your own ads to appeal to the demographic you're targeting," Michael said.

"That's right. I'm also venturing into the advertising business. I've got someone in mind for layout design, but I plan to find my own models. We'll use the most beautiful seniors we can find and use all the air brush, and editing techniques that are used with the young people, only my models will be over 45 years of age. I plan for them to range all the way up in years to one hundred."

"Sounds great. I'd love to fill the photographer spot."

Jane smiled. "Are you sure you wouldn't have a problem photographing sixty-year-old women in their underwear?"

Michael flashed her a grin that reminded her of

Gordon. "These are going to be the most beautiful sixty-year-olds you can find, right? I think I can take it."

She laughed then went on. "I have limited funds. Magazine's always lose money at first. It's just part of the bargain. Until we develop some long term relationships with advertisers, we won't make anything. So to start with I figure I can only go about midrange of the pay scale, lower midrange. I've researched it pretty well. I can show you my figures back at the office if you want. I thought I'd offer some profit sharing capabilities. That way, if we work together to make a success of it, we're all better off."`

"That sounds good. I have a family to support so I can't take too much of a cut in pay. But I'd be willing to take a small cut in order to get started here."

"Jane. I hate to interrupt," Gordon said. "I need to go, but I wanted to ask you if you'll have dinner with me on Wednesday."

"That's right, Dad." Michael smiled. "I was wondering what you were doing for your birthday. Kathy's getting a little too close to delivering to do much. Grant and I will be gone."

"It's your birthday?" Jane said, smiling at him. "I guess I should treat then. Yes, I'd love to go to dinner with you on your birthday. How old will you be?"

"I'll be fifty-eight," Gordon said.

"Fifty-eight? You're younger than me. I turned sixty in July."

"You're kidding," Michael said. "I would have thought you were younger than him."

"Thanks." Gordon laughed and looked back at Jane.

She was looking down at her plate, frowning.

"Jane, two years is nothing at this point in life. Two years is nothing at any point of life." He put his arm across her shoulders.

"I know." She smiled at him. "It just took me by surprise. I thought you were my age."

"I am your age."

"I guess so."

"Tory, I can't show up empty handed, but what do you get for a man on his birthday."

"I usually play fun games in bed," Victoria said, and Joe smiled from his seat on the couch beside her.

Jane laughed. "I love you, Tori. I'll probably do that too, but I really have to have something else, but what?"

"What do you think, Joe?" Victoria asked her husband. The three of them were sitting in Joe and Victoria's living room after dinner that same night.

"What does he like? What does he do for fun?"

"You know what?" Jane said. "I don't even know. I feel like I've known this guy all my life, but I don't even know what he likes to do."

"Well, we know he's into cameras. Get him something for his camera."

"Tori, he owns a camera shop. What am I going to get him that he doesn't already have?" She fell silent and looked out the window. It was just dusk. The edge of the sky was still pink. There was a beautifully shaped tree set far back in Victoria's back yard. "What kind of a tree is that, Tori?"

Victoria looked out the window. "That's a sugar maple. They're really northern trees, but I've pampered that one so well that it's doing okay. In about six weeks it'll be the most beautiful color. They start turning a bright orange, then go to yellow, but different parts of the tree do it at different times, so you get different shades of orange, yellow, and the last of the summer green. It's beautiful."

"It's a beautiful shape too," Jane said. "Remind me to come and see it when it changes color."

"I will." Victoria smiled at her. "Jane, I've got just the gift for Gordon."

"What?"

"I saw it the other day and just couldn't pass it up. So I bought it. I don't need it, shouldn't have bought it."

"No," Joe said. "But that didn't stop you did it?"

"What is it, Tori?" Jane asked.

"It's a frame. What better thing to give a photographer than a frame."

"A frame?" Jane sounded disappointed.

"Think about it, Jane. They're always taking pictures. They must spend a fortune on frames."

"That's probably true. Well, show it to me. I'll buy it from you."

"Come on." Victoria jumped up and ran up the stairs. Jane followed her a little slower. Victoria went to her bedroom and took a box out of her closet. "It's a 5 by 7" She pulled it out of the box. It was a white and yellow polished pewter frame. There was a mat of white pewter surrounded by interwoven straps of white and gold pewter. "It's perfect."

"You really think so, Tori?" Jane asked. "How much is it?"

"Seventy-five dollars, it was on sale for half price," Victoria said.

"You're kidding. I wasn't thinking of spending that much."

"Oh, well, you don't have to pay me for it. I really think it's just the right gift, though." Victoria seemed a little disappointed.

"No, you're right. I don't have any other ideas. I want something nice. "I'll write you a check."

"You really don't have to, Jane."

"I insist." Jane put the frame back into the box and went downstairs to write a check.

"Hello," Jane said, answering her phone the next day in her office.

"Ms. Winslow, this is Mark Bradley, Lillian's husband."

"Hello, Mark. Are you back from the honeymoon already?"

"Yes ma'am. It was great, but I'm glad to be back. Lillian had to get back to school."

"I'm glad you had a good time. I suppose you'd like to come in and talk about the layout design job now."

"Yes ma'am. I had a hard time not thinking about it while we were away. In fact I did think about it, but I don't think it got in the way of Lillian's fun."

"I hope not. Have you got a portfolio?"

"Yes, ma'am."

"Mark, to start off, please don't call me ma'am. Call me Jane. We'll be working together if this arrangement works for both of us. We might as well be on a first name basis."

"Yes, ma'am, I'm sorry," he said. "Jane, when can I come in to see you?"

"Do you need time to prepare a resume or anything?"

"No. I'm all ready."

"Can you come in now?"

"I'd like to. Where are you located?"

She gave him the address and some directions. She told Amanda to expect him and then went back to designing a web site. In her research, she'd found that a successful web site was a *must* for a successful magazine. Who better to design it than her? Her computer skills were going to be a plus in this new venture of hers.

When Mark came in, she went over the job with him. It was pretty much the same info she had given Michael. "I've hired a photographer. You'll work closely with him. It's very important that we all work together as a team. I wish you could all have met each other before starting work, but that just doesn't happen. So, you're kind of at the mercy of my decisions. If I've made mistakes, I'll see them. If we don't function as a team, I'll find out why and take care of it."

"I've never had a hard time getting along with people. I'm sure I won't have a problem." He asked about Michael and Jane told him what she knew.

She looked at his portfolio. His work was excellent. "You're entirely self-taught?"

"Entirely, school just didn't work for me."

"Michael is too," she explained. "You should have a lot in common." She showed him the studio area. There were two big rooms, one for photography and one for design. He was obviously excited about the possibilities.

When he left, Jane said, "I'll be in touch with you soon."

"Thank you for the interview." He stopped at the door. "Ms. Winslow, Jane, I would love to have this job. I think I can do it well."

"That's great, Mark."

"I'm going to hire him, Amanda," she said when he left.

"I had a feeling you would."

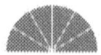

"I'm just so excited about the way things are coming together," Jane told Gordon on the way to the restaurant. He had picked her up promptly at 7:00 p.m., pinned a corsage on her, and kissed her until her knees were weak. They had taken Fred out for a short walk and left for the restaurant.

"I'm glad," Gordon said. "So you think both of my boys will work out?"

"Michael and I have already signed an employment contract. I was actually able to meet his present salary. I can't believe how much paperwork means in this world. It's ridiculous. His work is excellent."

"I've always thought so too. Of course, I'm his father." Gordon took her hand.

"I'm hoping Grant and I can come to an agreement. He said he could arrange to come down on Monday for a formal interview. It really isn't necessary. I already know I want to hire him. The only problem will be the money. He has a family to support and he told me that Maggie has some health problems. Of course, I have a decent health plan lined up, but they still need a good income."

"I'm sure you're planning to offer him a good income. He's really very motivated to make a change," Gordon said. "Honestly, I don't think he makes that much more than Michael."

"Really?"

"Of course, the company he works for tells him about his commission prospects, but I don't think he sees a lot of it. It's not that he isn't good. I just think the prospects aren't as great as they look." Gordon looked over at her. "I probably shouldn't be telling you all this."

"You know I'll do the best by him I can. I think the profit sharing option is good, though. I'm very determined, you know." She squeezed his hand.

"I know. Do you want me to drop you at the door?" Gordon said as they approached the hotel.

"No. I'll walk with you. Oh! The Four Season's again," she said. "This was the first place you took me. Will we eat lobster again?"

"If you want to."

They went inside and Gordon talked to the maître d'. He showed them to a small intimate table. It was a corner booth but the booth curved in a small semicircle. When they sat they were right next to each other, but with the curve of the table, they could also look at each other easily. They ordered wine and Jane put the packages she had been carrying up on the table.

"I have birthday presents for you," she said.

"You didn't have to do that, but I knew you would."

"This one is really from Tori. She thought it was the perfect gift, but since she picked it out, I don't really feel like I can take credit for it." She handed the larger of the packages to him.

He pulled the paper off and opened the box. "That's perfect," Gordon said. "Leave it to Victoria. You know that sister of yours is something else."

"I think so." Jane smiled. The waiter came and put

a candle down on the table and a small bouquet of roses. "That's nice," Jane looked around. "Does everyone get roses?"

"Not everyone," Gordon said. "Can I open my other gift?"

She smiled and handed the small box to him. "This one is from me. It isn't much. I realized when I started thinking about a gift how little I really know about you. I don't even know what you do for fun."

Gordon pulled the wrapping paper off the box and opened it. He took the tissue wrapped object out of the box and unwound the tissue. It contained a small white pewter figurine of a woman. Her hair fell over her shoulders to her waist in front and flowed to a point down the middle of her back. She wore a small pointed hat, cocked slightly to the left side. In her right hand she held a wand and in her left a crystal ball. The light from the candle caught the angles of the crystal and cast dancing specks of light on the back of the booth.

"It's beautiful, Jane."

"I found it in one of those awful glass cases at the Hallmark store. It just kind of grabbed me. I got so excited about it that I bought it and forgot to get you a card," she said.

"I don't need a card." He put the figurine down in front of him and slid a little closer to Jane. "I have something for you too, Jane." He slid his hand into his pocket and pulled out a small velvet sack.

"You didn't have to get me anything, Gordon. It's not my birthday."

He loosened the ties around the top of the sack and pulled out a ring. The band was interwoven strands of white and yellow gold. The setting looked like a tiny flower. There were six delicate petals that swirled to a point at the band. There was a diamond the shape of a tear set in a yellow gold scalloped base. Jane felt breathless.

"Jane," Gordon said softly. "Will you marry me?"

She looked at the ring closely. "It looks like Tori's hybrid," she said. "It's beautiful."

"It is her hybrid. I asked her to design a ring from it. She did. Then I took it to a jeweler for fine tuning and had it made. The diamond is only ½ karat, but I thought anything bigger wouldn't work."

"Tori knew about this? Gordon, I really hadn't even thought about marriage. I'm so old." She never took her eyes off the ring.

"I love you, Jane. I have since the first time I saw you. I didn't recognize it at first, but it didn't take long. I want to be a family with you. I want you to be my partner for the rest of our lives, however long that is."

She stared at the ring for another minute then looked up at Gordon. He sparkled when she looked at him. He was so beautiful. He had always sparkled when she looked at him. She could remember walking into The Camera Shop and thinking he was beautiful. She'd thought so every time she'd looked at him since. "I guess that's being in love," she whispered.

"I guess it is," Gordon said. "Jane you haven't answered me. Will you marry me?"

"Yes," she said, before she'd even thought it. "I want to be your partner too; for the rest of our lives."

Gordon released a breath and dropped his chin to his chest for a second. He took a deep breath and looking into her eyes, he kissed her. "Here," he said, taking her hand. "Let's put it on." He slid it onto her finger.

"It fits perfectly," she said.

"Victoria knew your ring size too." He kissed her again.

"Uh Uhmmm," the waiter said. "Congratulations, sir."

"Thank you, Drew," Gordon said, smiling at Jane. "We'll both have the lobster."

Chapter Ten

"Hello," Jane said, answering the phone in her office the next morning.

"Well?" Victoria's voice sounded anxious. "What happened? What was your answer?"

"What happened when?" Jane asked. "Answer about what?"

"Jane, you know what I'm talking about," Victoria insisted.

"No, I really don't, Tori. Explain." A broad smile on her face, Jane was clearly enjoying this.

"Never mind, I guess I need to go to work," Victoria said.

"You're off today, Tori. We're having lunch, remember?" Jane said. "You traitor."

"Why am I a traitor?"

"You knew Gordon was going to ask me to marry him and you didn't prepare me. Did Joe know?" Jane demanded.

"No, amazingly, I was even able to keep it from him. You have no idea how stressful the last two weeks have been for me," Victoria said.

"Two weeks, for a blabbermouth like you that must have taken years off your life." Jane was laughing now.

"It did. Now tell me, Jane. What was your answer?"

"What do you think?"

"I have no idea. You're completely unpredictable."

"Good," Jane said. "I wouldn't want to be predictable. Well, it looks like I'm getting married."

"Oh, Jane, I'm so excited."

Jane could almost see her petite friend jumping up and down.

"I think he's the most wonderful man, next to Joe, of course. He planned everything so well. Did the roses come to the table at a good time? Did he like the picture frame? It matched the ring perfectly, didn't it?"

"He said it was perfect and thanked you for it."

"You told him it was from me?"

"You picked it out. You didn't really think I'd take credit for it, did you? I got him something else."

"What did you get him?"

"A statue of a female wizard."

"Wouldn't that be a witch?"

"I guess so. Isn't that appropriate, since that's what he's marrying?" Jane asked.

"You're not a witch. You're a beautiful person."

"That's just what you think and you're prejudiced," Jane said. "You know, Tori, I'm worried. I love that man. I have no doubt of that, but I don't know if I'll ever be able to fit into that huge family of his. You know I've never really belonged to a family, except yours, of course, and I've always been slightly removed from that."

"You've only been removed when you chose to be, but I know what you're saying. I know you, and I know it'll be a big adjustment, but you'll do it, and you'll do it well. You do everything well."

"You're my best friend. That's why you say that. I'm not so sure."

"I know." Victoria paused. "Have you set a date?"

"Gordon wants to do it soon. He needs to wait until after Katherine has her baby so that he can be available to sit the other kids and help out when she gets home from the hospital. He's such a good dad," Jane said. "But he insists that we have a honeymoon. Isn't that nice? He also wants to have a wedding. I suggested that we just go to the justice of the peace, but he wouldn't have it, said he wants at least all of his family and mine involved."

"I'll tell the girls. I know they'll want to be there," Victoria said.

"That would be nice, but I'm not even going to look for my aunt and cousins. I never liked them much anyway. If you and Joe are there, and Jeff and Lillian, that'll be enough."

"We'll all be there. Will it be a church wedding?"

"I've never been very religious. Gordon says he's not either. You know what I've been thinking about?"

"What?"

"That tree in your back yard, the sugar maple. You said it would be beautiful in about six weeks. That's about right."

"That's a great idea."

"You wouldn't mind? It might create some work for you."

"I don't have a problem with work. You know that."

"I have an idea for a line of business clothes," Jane said to Anna Smart, the woman across the desk from her. "It would be an ancillary product for my magazine." The woman was a fashion designer. Jane had been interviewing them for the fashion section in her magazine.

"I've done a lot of suits and casual wear. Would you like to look at my portfolio?"

"Yes, very much." They put the bag down on the credenza and Jane flipped through it. "You've designed a number of bridal gowns, I see," she said.

"Yes. There's a big demand," Anna said. "It's not my favorite, but it's popular, and I'm good at it."

"I'm getting married in about a month." Jane looked at her. "Do you think you could design something for a sixty year old woman, something that doesn't make her look ridiculous?"

"A sixty-year-old woman with a figure like yours will be easy," she said. "I have a number of ideas."

"Do you think you can do it in a month?" Jane looked at her again.

"Once I get started, I can't stop," Anna said. "I'll

have the design finished by tonight. It'll take me a couple of days to figure out the materials. I'll make it myself." She looked up at Jane. "For a line of clothing I'd need a manufacturer, but for one item, I can do it myself. I could have it done in a week."

"I want to see designs before you do any sewing. Also, I'll have one bridesmaid at least. Do we need to get help to get them all done in time?"

"Maybe, I'll draw up the plans and bring them in tomorrow. I can leave them with your secretary," Anna said. She picked up her portfolio and left the room.

"I think she'll be able to do it," Jane said to herself. She reflected on the woman she had just interviewed. She was a young black woman, very bright, no credentials, but her work was beautiful.

"I think I may have found my clothing designer," Jane told Gordon over dinner that night. "She's going to bring some designs for a wedding dress for me. I made it clear that I wanted something that suited someone my age."

"That's great. Of course, you could put on a burlap sack and look gorgeous." He smiled. "Jane, let's take a ride over to the studio after dinner and let me get some of those shots of you that you promised me."

"You blackmailed me for, more like," Jane said.

"You can look at my work, if you're still interested after seeing Michael's."

"I'm still interested."

"Good. Will you let me photograph you tonight?"

"If you really want to, but Gordon, I'm telling you, I don't look good on film."

"Just give me a chance."

After dinner they took Fred over to the studio. Gordon said he wanted to take pictures of her with the little dog. When they got there, he took her to a room filled with lights. He turned some of them on, but not all.

There was a backdrop that could be changed. He flipped through a number of them and settled on one.

"I'm never going to be comfortable with all these lights shining in my face," Jane said.

"Look at Fred," Gordon said.

Fred was dancing around her feet, playing with the lights. She smiled. Snap. She looked up at Gordon. Snap. "You took a picture without warning me." Snap. "Stop it." Another snap. Fred pawed at her leg and she looked at him. Snap. She leaned down. Snap. She picked him up. Snap. "This isn't fair, Gordon." Snap. This went on for about half an hour. Gordon never said a word. He stopped from time to time to switch off lights and switch on others.

"I think we're finished," Gordon finally said.

"Well that's a damned good thing, because I'm just about to leave." Jane held the little dog and walked toward Gordon. "You never gave me a chance to smile or anything. Those pictures will be horrible."

"Bet they won't," he said as he walked around the room turning off lights. "Ready to go?" he said, stroking Fred and putting his arm around Jane.

"I guess so. That all made me feel a little confused."

"You, confused? I can't imagine." He laughed.

They drove back to her condo in relative silence. As they pulled into the parking lot, Gordon said, "This weekend, would you come with me to meet my parents?"

Jane drew in a sharp breath and looked at him. "You have parents?"

"Yes. Doesn't everyone?"

"Not at our age, no. You mean I'm going to have a mother-in-law?"

"She won't bother you, Jane. They live in assisted living at a retirement complex in Dunwoody."

She looked down at the dashboard in front of her.

"Jane, I love you with all may heart, but I'm not going to apologize for having a family." He reached over and took her hand.

"Of course you shouldn't, but I think we'd better

make a list of them all. I don't want any more surprises right now. Okay?"

When they reached her apartment, she got a note pad and pen and sat down on the couch. Gordon sat next to her and put his arm around her. "Of course you know my kids."

"Yes, but just to make the list complete, let's name them.""All right, there's Grant and Lauren, Gary and Maggie, that's one family. Then there's Michael, Jill, Joy, Hope, and Alexandra, another family. There's Kathy, Rick, Eric, Teddy, and, I don't think they've decided on a name for the little girl."

"All right, I'm pretty sure I can remember them. Your parents' names are?"

"Minerva, Dad calls her Minnie, and Gordon Sr."

"You're a junior?" She turned to look at him and he kissed her.

"Yes. I'm the oldest."

"You're the oldest? So you have brothers and sisters." She felt breathless.

"Brother and sister. My sister Brenda Adams and her husband Harry live in Macon. They have two grown children, Gwen, married to Leonard, with three kids," Gordon put his finger to his chin. "Will, Tommy, and Blair; Darlene is married to Todd, one child, let me see..." he tapped his temple, "an infant girl, Frances."

"Your brother?" Jane felt dizzy.

"Gerald, we call him Jerry. He's ten years younger than me. He has four children, but only one of them has a child. Let me see if I can remember their names." He kissed her temple. "See, you're not expected to if the rest of us can't," he said. "Jerry is married to Shannon. Their children are Breanne, she's the married one, the husband is Robert, baby is Robert, Jr. They call him Bobby, of course. Then there's Barbara, Arthur, and Scott." He squeezed her shoulder. "I can't believe I remembered them all."

"Is that it?" Her voice sounded weak.

"That's everyone who lives here." He got up and went into the kitchen.

"That's... everyone... who... lives... here," she said. Her mouth was moving, she thought she'd said the words out loud, but she didn't hear any sound.

"Joe, will you be my escort at the wedding?" Jane asked Joe at dinner on Friday night. She and Gordon were having dinner at Joe and Victoria's house. Katherine had called the day before and said she wasn't up to dinner. Then Victoria had called and invited them over to their house. "You and Tori are really the only family I have."

"I'd be honored to Jane," Joe said. "But I'm not giving you away. I'm keeping you."

"We're not doing the giving away part. It won't be a traditional wedding." She looked at Victoria. "You'll be my flower girl, of course. I'm having the same dress made for you as for me. It's just such a beautiful design, but mine will be pale blue, it's almost white but not quite, and yours will be royal blue."

"It's not flower girl, Jane. It's bridesmaid. Flower girls are children." Victoria was indignant.

"Well, you're so small you look like a child," Gordon said.

Victoria smiled. "Royal blue is one of my best colors."

"I know, and Gordon likes me in blue." Jane leaned in as he kissed her cheek. "I didn't want to wear a white dress. I'm too old for that. Pale blue will be perfect. We'll rent you a tux, Joe, to match Gordon's. They're charcoal," Jane said. "Have you talked to the girls?" she asked Victoria.

"Yes. Of course they're both coming. It's time to see Benjamin again anyway. We need an exact date, though. Have you and Gordon decided?"

"It looks like October 16th. Do you think the tree will be nice then?" Jane asked.

"It'll be perfect, and the weather will be nice too, as long as we plan it for the middle of the day when the sun is the strongest," Victoria said.

I'm going with Gordon to meet his parents tomorrow." Jane took a deep breath. "Can you believe I'll soon have a mother-in-law, a father-in-law, too?"

"That's nice. I love Joe's aunt and uncle, they raised him." Victoria said.

"I hope I do all right with mine." Jane looked at Gordon.

"You won't," he said. "She's a grouchy old woman and my dad is even worse. But they don't get around any more. We pay our visits and keep them as short as we need to."

"I have to say, I'm scared to death." She took a deep breath. "Gordon's whole family is coming the weekend before the wedding and they're having a big party at Katherine's house, so that I can meet them all. I don't know how I'll handle being with that many people."

"She makes my family sound like a pack of wolves," Gordon said.

"Jane, when we went to that convention in Savannah last year, there was a huge crowd at the dinner we went to," Victoria said. "You didn't have any problem with that."

"That was different. That was business. I never have a problem with business."

"You'll do fine, Jane." Joe reached across the table and squeezed her hand.

"Will you two come?" She turned to Gordon. "They can come, can't they Gordon?"

"Of course they can. This is your party too." He put his arm across the back of her chair. "Will you come?"

"We'd love to."

After dinner they went into the living room to relax for a minute.

"Will you have some brandy, Gordon?" Joe asked.

"Jane gave me some good brandy for my birthday this year. Would you like some, Jane?"

They both nodded and he poured three glasses.

"You don't drink brandy, Victoria?" Gordon asked. "Oh, that's right, you get wild when you drink."

"I do not." She blushed. "I just don't drink brandy."

The phone rang and Victoria picked it up. "Hello, yes he's here. It's for you, Gordon." She handed him the phone.

"I gave Kathy your number. She's due any minute," he explained.

"Hello." He listened for a minute. "I'll be right there, honey." He hung up. "This time it's the real thing," he said. "The contractions are five minutes apart."

"You go ahead," Jane said. "Joe and Tori won't mind taking me home."

"You come with me this time, please?"

"Let me take Fred home, she said, going to the door to call the little dog away from a romp with Ethel. "Then I'll come over there."

"Good idea. Thanks for dinner, Victoria." He kissed her on the cheek. "Joe." He shook his hand.

"Let us know when the baby gets here."

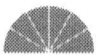

Gordon met Jane at the door about an hour later. "Come on in. I just got Teddy to sleep. Eric is still up. He promised he'd go to bed when I said I'd let him stay up to see you." She followed him into the playroom.

"Janie." He smiled up at her from his seat on the floor. He got up and crossed the room to kiss her on the cheek. His lips felt small and soft and sweet.

"What a nice greeting," she said.

"Grampa said I could stay up and tell you about my swimming lessons."

"You're taking swimming lessons?" Jane looked at Gordon. "Isn't three a little young for swimming lessons?"

Gordon laughed at the concern in her expression. "Kathy was on a swim team when she was growing up. She's had these kids in swimming lessons since they were infants. You'd be surprised how well this little guy can swim." He ruffled Eric's red curls. "She wants to put in a lap pool, but doesn't want to do it until all her children can swim."

"I guess that makes sense," Jane said. "I just hope she isn't rushing things a little."

"I think it'll work out fine," Gordon said.

"I really like to swim," Eric said. "We went to the big pool today. Me and my friend Kevin can swim all the way across the shallow end."

"That's great, Eric," Jane said. "Can you touch the bottom there?"

"Kevin can, but I only can with my big toe. Kevin's bigger than me."

"Well, you make sure the teacher is watching all the time," Jane said.

"She stands between us and the deep end."

"Good."

"Know what, Janie?"

"What, Eric?"

"Daddy finished the tree house. It's really neat. The ladder can role up and hook up high so that we can't reach it. That way Mamma doesn't have to worry about us going up there when she and Daddy aren't watching." He looked over at the stairs and whispered. "It's not for me. It's for Teddy. He's too little."

"Oh, I see. Next time I'm here in the daytime, I want to see it."

"Janie, Grampa says you and him are getting married, right Grampa?" He looked at Gordon for confirmation.

"That's right, Eric."

"Should I call you Gramma then?"

Jane felt a sudden chill. There were goose bumps rising on her upper arms. "No, you can still call me Janie," she said. There was that dizziness again.

"Jane, are you all right?" Gordon asked. "You look

a little pale. That's the second time you've gone pale like that. You aren't sick, are you?"

"No, I'm fine. I think I was just a little startled by Eric's question." She smiled at the little boy sitting between her and Gordon on the couch. Eric smiled back oblivious to it all.

"Well, it's time for Eric to run off to bed," Gordon said.

"Grampa, please let me stay up and watch *Nickelodeon* with Janie, just a half hour, please."

"Half an hour wouldn't hurt, would it Gordon?" Jane asked.

"No, I guess not, if you're sure you're all right."

"You're getting on my nerves again." She smiled at him.

"Well, I don't want to do that. You two settle in here." He turned on the TV and adjusted the channel. "I'll go check on Teddy."

After Eric had gone to bed, Gordon and Jane picked up the scattered toys and put them back into the toy box. "Come into the living room. It's more comfortable in there, unless you want to watch more *Nickelodeon.*"

"Well, it was fun," Jane said, following him into the living room.

Gordon sat down in a big easy chair with winged sides and put his feet on a foot stool. He held out his arms to her. Jane sat down in his lap. Her feet dangled over the stuffed arm of the chair and her head resting on the padded wing. Gordon wrapped his arms around her waist. They were quiet like that for a minute.

"Jane," Gordon said. "Michael thinks you're struggling with feelings about Maggie. I told him I didn't think so, but now I'm not so sure."

"Why do you say that?" She started to get up, but he pulled her back down. "I didn't even know her. Why would I have a problem?"

"You'd have to tell me that. I don't know, but you'd have to identify it before you could tell me." He relaxed his hold on her waist as she relaxed against him. "I just know that you fainted when you saw her picture."

"I don't faint."

He laughed and kissed her temple. "Well, you turned very pale and sat down. Then when Eric asked about you being called Gramma tonight, it happened again."

"Just coincidence."

"Well, I just wanted to tell you that nobody is expecting you to take her place. You have your own place. I hope you know that."

"Of course I do." She snuggled a little closer. He felt warm and sweet wrapped around her like this, but she was uncomfortable about something. What? She didn't know.

"What?" Jane woke up suddenly. They had both dozed off in the chair.

"Hello," Gordon said. She realized that he was holding the phone. He listened for a minute. "Kathy's all right?" She felt his breath release and noticed that his hand shook. "Seven pounds, seven ounces; she's beautiful. I'm so glad Rick." He listened for a minute. "Don't hurry, Rick. I'm fine with the kids." He paused again. "Jane is with me. We're fine." He said goodbye and hung up.

He pulled her close and put his head against her neck. He took a couple of deep breaths. "Thank God that's over," he said.

"I guess it's scary for a dad."

He pulled away and looked at her. "Terrifying," he said. "I hope she stops now. They have boys and girls. Why would they want any more?"

She kissed him. "I have no idea, but if it's that hard on you, I hope they stop too."

"Thank you for coming here with me. I love you, Jane."

"I love you too," she said. They settled against each other again. "Gordon, where are we going to live after we're married?"

"We haven't talked about that, have we? I was planning to move into the apartment I have over the Buckhead store when I close on my house next week. If you want we could look for a place of our own."

"We could do that. What kind of a place would you like to live in?" Jane asked.

"Truth is, Jane, I like your place. I'd like to move in there. I'd want to buy it from you. I don't want you to think I married you for your condo."

"I was hoping you'd say that. I don't really want to move. Of course, if you want something different, I will."

"My only problem is that I have to have a darkroom. I haven't seen your whole flat. Is there a space where I could put in a darkroom?"

Jane pursed her lips in thought. "The third bedroom has a walk-in closet. I've never even furnished that bedroom. I made the second bedroom into a guestroom. Not many people visit, but occasionally one of Tori's girls will stay with me. When I first moved in, I planned to make the third bedroom my office, but I work in the living room. I have a desk in there, and it's just more comfortable."

"Do you think I could run water in there?"

"I don't see any reason why not. I own the place."

"I could put Baby's tray in the laundry room. It's a self-cleaning tray, so there's never any odor or anything."

Jane jumped up. "Oh, shit! I hadn't thought about Baby."

"Jane," Gordon said, getting up. "Baby has been my companion for seven years. I can't just abandon her."

She looked at him. "Of course you can't, Gordon. I was just taken by surprise. Of course she's welcome. I just hope she doesn't hurt Fred."

"They'll learn to get along."

"Besides," Jane said, "she's Margaret's cat. You couldn't give up Margaret's cat."

"Jane, she's not Maggie's cat. She's mine."

"Which one's yours?" the woman standing next to Jane at the nursery window in the hospital asked.

Jane looked at her, confused. "This one, right in front." She pointed to the bassinet with the sign that read, Girl Thatcher.

"She's beautiful," the woman said. "Mine is the little boy on the end."

"Oh," Jane said. "He's beautiful, too."

"No, he isn't. He's the homeliest thing I've ever seen." The woman was smiling fondly as she spoke. "All of my grandchildren have been born ugly then grow up beautiful. Is this your first grandchild?" she asked.

Jane didn't know what to say. She could feel that dizziness starting and willed it away.

"It's her first," Gordon said. "My eighth." Gordon turned to look at the newborn infant. "She is beautiful, though, Jane, will you look at that hair?"

"It's black," Jane said, relieved that Gordon hadn't noticed her pallor. "And so thick."

"Like her Grampa. It'll gray early. Come on, let's go see Kathy." He took her hand and pulled her down the hall.

Jane smiled at the woman as they left. They reached Katherine's room and Gordon knocked. He cracked the door a little and called, "Kathy, it's Dad and Jane. Can we come in."

"Come on in, Dad," Katherine called from inside the room. They went into the room. Jane felt uncomfortable. She was feeling uncomfortable a lot these days.

"Hey, honey." Gordon hurried over to the bed where Katherine was sitting up looking surprisingly pretty. He put his arms around her and held her quietly for a minute. "I just can't wait to hold you every time you do this," he said.

"This was the easiest one, Dad. You know I'm good at having babies," she said.

"I know, but it still scares me to death every time." He released her reluctantly.

"Hello, Jane." Katherine held out her arms to Jane.

Jane leaned over to give her a brief hug. It actually did feel good to hug her, not uncomfortable.

"She sure is a beautiful baby," Jane said.

"She is, isn't she?" Katherine said. "Her name is Valerie Jane. The 'Jane' is for you."

"Katherine you shouldn't name your baby after me. I'm nobody to you." Jane was determined not to get dizzy, but her head really wanted to swim.

"Of course you're somebody to me. You're the woman who made my dad happy again." Katherine laughed. "But don't worry, if we hadn't liked the name, we wouldn't have done it. It sounds beautiful, don't you think? *Valerie Jane.*"

"It does sound beautiful," Gordon said.

"I guess Rick must be really tired. Did you leave when he got home last night? I think it was really late." Katherine said.

"I stayed," Gordon said. "Jane went home, but I wanted to be there in the morning to give the boys breakfast so Rick could sleep in. I think he got the sleep he needed."

"How did the boys react to the new arrival?"

"Eric is excited and Teddy agrees with everything Eric says," Gordon explained.

"I wonder how long that will last," Katherine said.

"Not long, so enjoy it while you can," Gordon said. "Jane and I are on our way to see your Gramma and Grampa."

"Oh, Dad," Katherine said, reached out and took Jane's hand. "Don't you think you should wait until after the wedding for that?"

"I thought about it, but I just couldn't trap her like that. She needs to know she still has a choice." They both looked at Jane.

"You two are scaring me. What am I in for?" she said.

They pulled into the parking lot at the retirement complex. Gordon took a deep breath and looked at Jane. "Brace yourself."

"Are they really that bad?"

"They're just very blunt. Whatever they think, they say."

They went into the lobby and to the elevator. Gordon said hello to a couple of the residents on the way through. They went to the second floor and down the hall to the last door. Gordon knocked. No one came to the door. After a few minutes he knocked again. Still no one came to the door.

"Maybe they aren't here," Jane said.

"No such luck." He smiled at her. "I never get a response to this. They can't hear very well and they don't like to wear their hearing aids. I'll have to unlock the door and go in, but I like to give them a chance to answer just the same." He pulled out his keys and unlocked the door.

"Gordon, I can't go in unannounced," Jane objected.

"You don't have to. You stay out here. I'll come and get you when we're ready." Gordon went through the door calling, "Mom, Dad..."

Jane could hear him talking loudly to them in another room. She tried not to listen. He came back to the door and motioned her in.

"Dad, Mom, this is Jane. We're getting married in about a month. Remember I told you about it."

"Well, look at that, Minnie," Gordon Senior bellowed. He was about Gordon's height and his features were very similar. But he had no hair at all. "This one is tall and skinny." He laughed walking over to Jane. "The other one was short and fat," he said to her. He turned to Gordon. "Never did understand your choice in women."

Gordon gave her a quick look and saw that she was smiling.

"Shut up, you big stupid blowfish," Minerva said. She came over to Jane. She was very small, maybe as small as Victoria. Her hair was pulled back in a tight bun at the back of her head. It was white and very thick.

Well, that's where that came from, Jane thought.

"Don't pay any attention to him," Minerva said. "He never did have any manners. I think tall and skinny is much better than short and fat."

Jane looked at Gordon and raised her eyebrows.

"Come into the kitchen with me and help me with the fruit tray I got for you." She took Jane by the arm and ushered her into the kitchen of the small apartment.

As she left the room she heard Gordon Senior say, "Why don't you go for a sexy woman for once? It would be a lot more fun for me."

"Sooo..." Jane said on the ride home. "I'm not sexy."

Gordon laughed. "I think I've expressed my feelings about you in that respect fairly well."

"Yes you have, but you have no taste in women," Jane said, and laughed softly.

Gordon reached for her hand. "You're taking this well. I knew you would."

"I liked them. Tori's mom got like that when she was their age."

"Really, so my parents aren't strange?"

"Well, they may be a little strange, but no more than Tori's mom," Jane said. "Your mom told me that if I didn't make you happy I'd have to answer to her."

"Uh-oh, you'd better make me happy."

"I will now," Jane said. "Before she said that, I was planning to make you miserable." They laughed together.

Chapter Eleven

"So how did Fox feel about you riding with me today?" Jeff asked. "Now that you're getting married, that is?"

"Jeff, is this going to tear us apart, because if it is, I'll call the whole thing off right now." Jane kept riding and never looked at him.

"Jane," Jeff said as he pulled his bike to a stop. "Stop...please."

She pulled to a stop, but didn't turn around. He approached her from behind, walking his bike.

"I'm sorry, Jane." He put his hand on her shoulder. "I'm having a hard time of my own right now. I'm happy for you. I really am." He squeezed her shoulder.

"Jeff," she said, and turned to look at him. "What's wrong? You've said that before. Why can't you talk to me?"

"It's just something I have to work out for myself, a mid-life crisis or something."

Jane put her hand on his arm. "Are you sure, Jeff? I'm worrying about you."

"Don't worry about me. Tell me about the way you're feeling. I can tell you're struggling."

Jane looked down at the ground. "I wasn't kidding when I said I'd call the whole thing off. I really need you because I think I might be having a nervous breakdown."

"That's silly, Jane. You're the most grounded person I know," Jeff said. He propped his bike against a tree and putting his hand on her other shoulder, turned her to look at him.

"When it comes to business, I'm grounded, but family scares me to death. Did I tell you Katherine named her baby Valerie Jane? She said *Jane* was for me. Jeff, I don't deserve that. Margaret did all the work. She went through the childbirth and motherhood. I've watched that with Tori. It's not easy. I don't deserve to have her babies named after me." She dropped her face into her hands.

Jeff pulled her into his arms and held her head against his shoulder. "Jane, you deserve it all. They wouldn't love you if you didn't. Margaret is gone. You have to let her go. They have. I'm sure they haven't stopped loving her, but they've let her go. They're allowed to love other people."

Jane cried into his shoulder until her sobs calmed and she started to breathe evenly.

"You know, Jane. I don't think I've ever seen you cry."

"I never cry," she said, pulling away and wiping her eyes and nose. "I never faint either, but I've done it twice in the past week and fought it twice." She sniffed. "I don't know what's happening to me."

"I think you've found your mate after all these years. And I think you love his family too...your family."

"I'm scared to death, Jeff."

"I would be too, but Gordon will help. I'll always be here for you. You know that, Jane. You're my hero," he said.

Jane reached up and put her arms around his neck. She kissed him then buried her head in his chest. After a minute they separated and got back on their bikes.

Jane met Michael and Grant at the door of the office the next morning. She was surprised, because she'd come in a little early. "You two sure are out early. Did you buzz to get in? I need to get keys made for you. Is Amanda here yet?"

"We just got here," Michael said. "Grant came to help

me unload my equipment until you have time to meet with him."

"Your equipment is coming already. That was fast."

"Since I've been working freelance I was able to pick up pretty fast. Jill wanted to go ahead and get the kids into school since the year has just begun. She's looking for an apartment today."

"How are the kids feeling about the move?" Jane asked.

"Joy's having a hard time with it. She's old enough to have made some pretty good friends. Hope's best friend moved up here last year, so she's excited about it. Alexandra is oblivious," Michael explained.

"I hope Joy doesn't have too much trouble adjusting," Jane said. She could remember how she felt when her parents told her she would have to leave Victoria.

"She'll be all right. Her mom and I will help her through it," Michael assured her.

"What about your family, Grant?" Jane asked. "How do they feel about moving?

"Gary has mixed feelings. He doesn't want to leave his friends, but he's excited about being close to his uncle Michael and his grampa. He's very interested in photography," he said. "Maggie's happy about it. She's excited about living in the same town with her grampa."

"Well, I hope the transition is smooth. Would you like to talk now, Grant?"

"That would be great." He looked at Michael.

"I don't think the moving van is even here yet. I'll go out back and look for it. I'll either be out back or in the studio."

"Okay, I'll be there in a while." Grant opened the door for Jane and Michael, and then followed Jane to her office. They went in and closed the door.

"Sit down." Jane motioned to the chair.

Grant sat and opened the briefcase he was holding. "I have my resume and references in here." He pulled out some papers and put them on the desk.

"That will be good to put in your file, but I already

know I want to offer you the job. I'm just not sure that we can agree on money."

"Well, let's talk about it," Grant said, "But first I'd like to say welcome to the family." He smiled at her. "I'm glad the old man found someone like you."

"Thank you, Grant, I hope I can fit in."

"You already have."

Jane and Grant joined Michael in the studio about half an hour later. "Is the truck here yet?" Grant asked.

"It just pulled up. Were you two able to come to an agreement?" Michael asked.

"Yes, we're finally going to be working together, brother." Grant put his hand on Michael's shoulder.

"That's great." Michael beamed.

Jane felt something warm and sweet spread through her. She smiled at them both.

"I won't be able to start until two weeks from today, but Jane already gave me an assignment to work on, a business plan and budget. I'll need input from you about what you'll need. Can we get together tonight before I leave? I plan to have an early dinner with Dad before I go," Grant said.

"I'll be at the house with Jill and the kids. I'm sure we can find some time. We can talk on the phone too. I've already spent some time on budget."

"I'd like for you two to come back to the office and meet David when you get a chance," Jane said. "He'll be here today. I plan to offer the job to Mark tomorrow, so you won't be able to meet him until you get back, Grant, but Michael, you will. The two of you will be working together very closely, so it's important that you develop good communication."

"I'll make sure I'm available when he gets here."

"Good, I'll leave you to your work." Jane turned to leave. "Come and get me when you're at a good stopping point."

"Jane?" Michael stopped her.

"Yes?" She turned around.

Michael closed the distance between them and put

his arms around her. "Welcome to the family." His hug was warm. He held her firmly but gently against him. Her eyes misted.

She swallowed and said, "Thank you, Michael." She turned and went back to her office and leaned against the closed door for a minute. There were tears running down her cheeks. She brushed them away with her hand. "I never cry." She reached for a tissue and blew her nose.

"Tori, I'm so excited!" Jane said at the nail salon. She'd left early that afternoon to meet Victoria for their appointment. "The magazine is really coming together. I have two of my department heads, my photographer, and I hope to hire my layout designer tomorrow."

"That's great, Jane. I didn't really think you would do this when you first mentioned it, but it didn't take long for me to realize you were serious."

"I have my fashion editor. I haven't seen her plans for my line of business clothes, but if the wedding dress is any indication of her ability, it'll be just what I want. You're my garden editor. All I need is a food and entertainment editor."

"Wait a minute. I thought I was just writing an article to get you started," Victoria said.

"You write really well, Tori. All it will involve for the garden section is to write an article for each issue. David will be responsible for finding out what the audience wants to know. You won't have to take much time away from Jeff. Please, help me out here." Jane put her hand on Victoria's arm.

"Well, all right. I guess I can do that."

"And get your picture taken with your project each month. That's all."

"My picture taken...Jane I don't want my picture in your magazine every month."

"Why not? You're perfect. You're beautiful, you're old, and you're the garden editor."

Victoria laughed. "I'll have to think about what you just said for a while. I don't know how to feel about it."

"Feel good."

"I'll try." She looked down at her toes drying on the stool with the little fan on them. "I like that pale pink color you got this time. Are you getting tired of the odd colors?"

"No. I just thought this would be nice for a change. I've chosen a beautiful color of pale blue for my wedding. It matches my dress perfectly," Jane said.

"You're not wearing open-toed shoes in October, are you?"

"If the weather holds out, I will. If not, well, at least I'll know my toenails match my dress. Thanks for showing me the glory of a pedicure, Tori." Jane kissed Victoria on the cheek.

"How are the plans for the wedding going? How many members of Gordon's family will be in it?"

"It'll just be his two sons. They're both going to walk with him. He couldn't choose a best man between them. His granddaughters, Joy and Hope wanted to be in it. I'm having dresses just like yours made for them. They'll look adorable in royal blue, a blond and a red-head. Everyone else opted to sit with his parents and help with the children."

"So he gave people a choice?"

"He wanted them all to participate if they wanted to, but *only* if they wanted to. I think it's really important to him that they all be there, though. Katherine suggested she leave the baby with a sitter, but Gordon wouldn't have it," Jane said. "Did I tell you Katherine named the baby Valerie Jane? I'm having a hard time with it."

"Jeff told me."

"I figured he would."

"I know this will be a big adjustment for you. I have faith in you, though. You'll make it," Victoria said.

"I hope so."

"Mark, this is what I want from you first. You have to decide what supplies you'll need and how you want to furnish the studio. Amanda has a list of the suppliers that are willing to give us a discount. Then you'll need to draw up a budget. Grant Fox, my assistant publisher, will be working the budget for the company. He'll be responsible for the final budget, but he'll require your input. At first we'll be lean, but things will be adjusted as we go along." Jane said, relaxing into her chair.

"I can't wait to get started," he said.

She had already explained her expectations and they had talked about salary. There was a knock at the door.

"Come in." Jane called.

Michael came in. "Amanda told me that Mark was here," he said.

"Come in, Michael. I want you to meet Mark, our new layout designer." She paused as they shook hands and exchanged greetings. "You two will work closely together, so it's important that you communicate well. I'm going to bring David in and introduce him, then I want the two of you to go and look at your space together. Spend a little time getting to know each other."

Jane called David into her office. He came and they exchanged greetings. "Michael, you and Mark are working with Grant on the commercial side of the business. David will be working on the other end of the business, the audience. He'll work more closely with my editors, but we're a team here so I think it's really important that we all take an interest in all of the positions."

"I couldn't agree more," Michael said.

David and Mark nodded agreement.

"Things are coming together really well at the magazine," Jane said to Gordon over dinner the next day.

"I'm glad. I know the boys have wanted to work together on a project like this for a while. They just had so many family obligations," Gordon said. "They wouldn't take my help. Not that I knew how to help."

"Well, I think they'll do well. I think we'll all do well. Tori is going to be my garden editor. Anna Smart will be my fashion designer. I told David that I wanted him to hire a short story and current interest editor. Now I just need a food and entertainment editor." She looked down at the soup she had served them for dinner. "I don't suppose you know anyone qualified for that position, do you?"

Gordon looked at her and smiled. "No, I'm sorry, I don't. You'll have to come up with that on your own."

"Darn," she said. "Gordon, is something wrong? You're quiet tonight."

"Jane, I'm just dealing with some feelings about the house. You know I'm closing on it tomorrow." He spooned some soup into his mouth.

"Oh, Gordon..." She sat back in her chair. "I was so caught up in myself I didn't even think about it. I know that's got to be hard."

"It is. Maybe I just need to go home. I won't be very good company until it's over," he said, putting his spoon down and getting up. He picked up his bowl and took it to the sink to rinse.

Jane got up and went over to stand beside him. "Is there anything I can do?"

"No, I don't think so." He turned and put his arms around her. "I love you, Jane. Please don't be mad at me for leaving tonight."

"Of course I won't," she said.

"I'll see you tomorrow." He released her and went to the door. "Bye, Fred." He rubbed the little dog's head and left.

Jane finished the dishes and went into the living room and sat down to read. She had just started a new book. It was hard at first, but she pushed herself and soon got involved in the story. She read for about an hour then the phone rang. She looked at the caller Id. It was Gordon. She picked it up.

"Hello."

"Jane, there is something you can do."

"What?"

"Come over here and stay with me tonight." He paused. She didn't say anything. "Please."

"I'll have to bring Fred."

"Bring Fred."

"I'll be right there." She felt very strange. It would feel horrible sleeping with Gordon in the bed he'd shared with Margaret, but she knew that he needed her. She gathered up the little dog, some of his food, her toothbrush, a change of clothes, and headed over to his house.

Gordon met her at the door. He stretched out his arms and she moved into them. He held her like that for a few minutes then picked up Fred. "We'll take him outside then go up to bed," he said. When they got to the bedroom they undressed and crawled in. He pulled her close to him, his chest to her back and held her that way through the night.

"Dad okay?" Jane looked up at Michael the next morning. He stood in the doorway of her office.

She nodded. "I stayed with him last night. I know this is hard for him."

"It is, but it's good for him, too." Michael came into the office and sat down in the chair across from her. "I know you're struggling too, Jane. I'm a pretty good listener if you need to talk."

"Your dad told me you were the sensitive one of the family."

"The artist. I can feel you struggling, though. I wondered why I was so compelled to include that picture of my mother in my portfolio. When you fainted, I realized there was something to be dealt with here."

"I guess I need to figure out what it is before I can talk about it," Jane said. "But thank you, Michael. I'll call if I need you."

"Jane, we all really are happy that you and Dad met

and not just because we've got someone to take care of the old man. You've given Grant and me a chance to do something we weren't accomplishing on our own. Thank you." He stood and walked to the door.

"Michael," Jane stopped him. "Where are you and Jill and the kids staying?"

"We've rented a suite for a week. Then we move into the apartment that Jill found for us. It's over in the Brookhaven area. Why?"

"This must be hard for you, too."

"A little," he said, and left her.

The weekend went by in a blur. Jane and Gordon went out to dinner on Friday night. Katherine wanted to cook for them, but Gordon wouldn't have it. Jane rode with Jeff again on Sunday. They increased their distance to twenty miles both ways. Jane needed to work out some nerves.

When Monday came, Jane went in early. She had a lot to do and wanted to leave early to take Fred to the dog park. She'd felt like she was neglecting him lately, with the activity at the magazine, and getting ready for the wedding. She had gone home at about three o'clock and changed into jeans and a T-shirt, had pulled on her socks and sneakers. She was gathering Fred's water bottle and bowl when the buzzer on the intercom sounded.

"Yes?" she said into the intercom.

"Janie, this is Joy. Can I come up?"

"Is anyone with you?"

"No." She sounded like she had been crying.

"When you hear the door click, open it. Take the elevator to the 12th floor. I'll meet you when you get off the elevator."

"Okay."

"Stay, Fred," Jane said, hurrying out the door and to the elevator. It seemed to take forever for it to arrive. Jane couldn't think of a reason Joy would be here alone.

Finally the doors opened. Joy ran straight to Jane and wrapped her arms around her waist. She was crying. Her small shoulders were shaking with her sobs.

"Joy." Jane put her arms around the child. "What happened? What's wrong?" Jane had started guiding her toward her flat.

"I ran away. I'm going back to Savannah." She hiccoughed.

"Oh," Jane said. "Why did you come here? How did you get here?"

"I rode the bus from school. I mean I rode the city bus. I didn't get on the school bus. I used my allowance." Jane took the girl into her flat and seated her on the couch. She sat beside her and put her arm around her. Fred watched them from his fluffy cushion. "I thought you might help me get to Savannah. I don't know how to get there."

"Oh. Why do you want to leave your family?" Jane didn't know what to do. If she made Joy go back home, the girl would hate her.

"I don't want to leave my family, but I can't go back to that school. I hate it there. I miss my friends. I don't have any friends here."

"You have me." Jane looked at Fred squirming to come to them. "Release, Fred," she said. The little dog scampered over to the couch, jumped up, and curled into Joy's lap. "And you have Fred. We don't want you to go back to Savannah."

"Janie, you don't know how awful it is to have to leave your friends and move to a place where you don't know anyone. Nobody eats lunch with me. Hope's best friend from Savannah moved here last year. She rides the same bus, so I can't even sit with Hope. I sit alone like some kind of outcast."

Jane smiled a little at the drama in Joy's speech. "You know what? I do know how it is. My parents uprooted me from my best friend, in fact we had adopted each other as sisters we were so close. I had to move to a place where I didn't know anyone too. You're right, it sucks," she said. "Don't you dare repeat what I just said."

Joy laughed and sniffed. Jane handed her a tissue. "What did you do?"

"I came back to Atlanta as soon as I was old enough, and I've been here ever since."

"I don't think I can wait that long." Joy's chin quivered as she looked up at Jane. "I can't even concentrate on my work at school. I feel so...I don't know."

"Out of place."

"Yeah."

"I know what you mean."

"How do you make it go away?"

"Grampa says you're a good student. You must like school a little."

"I liked my old school."

"Think about your schoolwork and think about me and Fred. Hey, you know what? Fred and I were just going to the dog park. It's this great big fenced area downtown at Piedmont Park. Why don't you come with us?"

"Okay," Joy said, looking away.

"Joy, please don't go back to Savannah. You're going to be my bridesmaid."

"I don't know how I'd get there anyway." She looked back at Jane. "Janie, you have to call my mother, don't you?"

"No, I don't have to, but I want to. She'll be worried sick. Atlanta is a big and dangerous city." She hugged the girl and said, "Please let me call her?'

"She won't let me go to the dog park. I'll have to go home and get punished."

"Well, I imagine you will have to pay for this one way or another, but maybe I can talk her into the dog park. Let me try?"

"Okay."

Jane picked up the phone on the table next to the couch. "Do you have the number?"

"Yeah," Joy picked up her backpack from the floor where Jane had put it and pulled a slip of paper out of one of the pockets. "I can't remember it yet, so I wrote it down."

"Smart girl." Jane dialed the number. "Hello, Jill, this is Jane."

"Jane, I'm sorry." Jill sounded panicked. "I can't talk. I've called all of my neighbors and Michael. Joy didn't get off the bus this afternoon. Hope said she didn't even get on it. I have to hang up; I might get a call—"

"Joy is with me." There was silence on the line. "Apparently she used her allowance to ride the city bus over here. She thought I might help her get back to Savannah." Jane looked down at the worried face of the girl beside her.

"Oh, thank God," Jill said. "I've been scared to death."

"I know you have. That's why I wanted to call right away. I know you can't wait to see her, but I was wondering if you would let me take her to the dog park for about an hour." She squeezed Joy's shoulder. "We're having a pretty good conversation and I'd like to finish it."

"I really need to see her right now, Jane."

"Of course you do. I'll bring her right home." Joy started to cry and Jane squeezed her shoulder again.

"No, you're right," Jill said. "If she came to you, you can have some influence on her. If I refuse to let her go, she won't listen to me about anything."

"Well, I hadn't thought of that, I just wanted her to spend some time with me and Fred." Jane felt suddenly nervous. She hadn't thought about the psychological implications at all. She just wanted to talk Joy out of running away.

"Go ahead, but we eat dinner at six thirty. Do you think you could be back by then?"

"Of course we will. Thanks, Jill. Would you like to talk to her?"

"Yes, please."

Jane handed the phone to Joy. She looked like she wanted to cry again. "Hello...I know...I'm sorry Mom...I love you too...Okay bye." She handed the phone back to

Jane. "Janie, if you don't mind, would you just take me home." She hugged Fred and kissed the top of his head. "I made my mom cry. I need to go home now."

"We'll go to the dog park another time."

"Promise?"

"Promise."

"Jane, thank you." Michael stood in the doorway to Jane's office the next morning. He came around the desk and kissed her on the cheek. "You really helped us out yesterday."

"I didn't do anything but be there. I'm just glad I left the office early," she said.

"You did a lot. We had a long talk with Joy last night. She hadn't told us how bad she was feeling. I guess we should have noticed. Sometimes parents get so caught up in what's going on in their own lives they forget to notice the children." He sat down in the chair across the desk from her. "Joy told us about how you had moved away from your best friend too, but had gone back when you were old enough. She assures us that she is going back to Savannah when she's old enough," Michael said. "We can live with that, as long as she waits until she's old enough."

"She probably won't go back, though. By that time she'll have friends here, I'm sure."

"That's what we're counting on." He got up. "But really, Jane, thanks."

She smiled and again felt something warm and sweet spread through her.

Chapter Twelve

"Jane?" David looked into her office. "Can I talk to you for a minute?" It was Wednesday morning and Jane had come in early again. She was planning to go to the dog park with Joy and Fred that afternoon.

"Of course, David, come in." Jane turned from her computer and watched him seat himself in the chair across her desk.

"I think I have a candidate for the article and short story editor's position," he said.

"Really? Tell me about it."

"He graduated with a degree in English, at the head of his class. His plan was to be an editor." David paused. "He graduated with me." He looked at her. "You know what that means, don't you?"

"It means he was in prison with you." Jane got up and walked to the window. She looked out for a minute. "Have you mentioned this position to him?"

"No. I wanted to check with you first." David watched her walk back from the window and sit down again. "I just talked to him last night. He's having a hard time finding anything."

"I've taken a number of chances on this magazine. I believe in all of you. Tell me why you believe in this person," Jane said.

"I knew him all the way through my three years in prison. He was as mad at himself as I was. He worked really hard at school. Eventually he wants to be a fiction writer. He might even write some short stories for us. I just think he deserves a chance. I know how hard it is to

get someone to give you one after you've been in prison."
David looked down. "I'll understand if you don't want to
do it."

"I'll talk to him. I want you to interview him first,
just like you would a total stranger. Give me your observations. Then I'll talk to him." She looked across the desk
at David and said, "Same thing goes for him as for you. If
he gets into any more trouble, no second chance here."

"I understand." David smiled. "I'll call him."

What a motley crew I have here, Jane thought. "I
think we're going to do very well. What do you think,
David?"

"I think so too." He smiled. She warmed inside at his
smile. He looked so much like his uncle Jeff.

As she drove through the visitors parking at her
condo, she noticed Gordon standing at the door to the
building. She pulled up and he came over to the car and
opened the passenger side door. "How long have you been
here?" she asked as he got into the car.

"About ten minutes." He kissed her and smiled. "I
heard you were taking Joy to the dog park and thought if
you didn't mind, I'd come along."

"Of course I don't mind. I'm delighted." She pulled
the car around to the parking under the building. "I can't
believe I haven't gotten you a key and a parking space.
We'll be married in less than two weeks." She shivered
lightly.

"Are you cold or are you getting cold feet," Gordon
asked, laughing.

"Neither, it's just that saying it out loud makes it so
real."

"It is real, Jane." Gordon squeezed her hand. "And
it's nice."

"I still don't understand why you didn't just move in
with me when you closed on the house." She had parked
the car and they were getting out.

"I don't want to live with you until we're married. I guess I'm just an old-fashioned guy."

They went to the elevator and pushed the button. The doors opened and they got in. "So," Jane said. "You just come over every night and have spectacular sex with me, sleep until midnight and then go home. Is that how old-fashioned people live in sin?"

Gordon pulled her into his arms and kissed her. He put his hands on her bottom and pulled her close to him. She could feel the bulge in his pants growing and she wrapped her arms around his neck. The elevator doors opened and they heard a gasp. They pulled away from each other and looked at the shocked face of the woman in the hall.

"Sorry, Mrs. Greenbaum," Jane said. "We got a little carried away." She took Gordon's hand and pulled him out of the elevator and down the hall. She was laughing when they got to the door.

"I think we shocked your neighbor," Gordon said, looking rather serious.

"Our neighbor. She's a terrible busybody. Who cares?"

"Easy for you to say," he said. "Your pants weren't bulging."

"Yes, they were," she said as she unlocked the door and ushered him inside. She pulled him over to the couch and started to unbutton his shirt. "Sit down," she said.

He sat. "What are you doing, Jane?" he said as she pulled his shirt over his shoulders.

"I'm having spectacular sex with you right here, right now." She smiled and kissed him. She moved from his mouth to his neck and then to his chest.

"Jane..." Gordon whispered reaching for her blouse. She pulled back. "I want you to take it off," he said.

"I will, when I'm ready." She put her hands back down on his chest. Turning him, she pushed him down on the couch. Running her fingers through the wiry hair, she circled his nipples with her thumbs.

"Jane." He reached for her again. "You're torturing me."

"No, I'm not. I'm loving you." She stood and stripped off her blouse, then her pants. When she was naked, she straddled his legs and unbuckled his pants. She stood and pulled them off of him then straddled him again. His penis stood erect. She took it in her hand savoring the feel of the soft skin. Leaning down she licked him and then took it into her mouth.

"Jane, you don't have to...you said you don't." He was gasping now.

"I've changed." She slipped her mouth around him again and ran her tongue the length of him. His hands were in her hair. He pulled her up to him and she straddled his waist. Gently sliding herself over him, she began to move. His eyes were closed and his breath came in short gasps. He put his hands on her hips and guided her until she forgot everything and they climaxed together. She felt weak and lowered her chest to his. His heart beat against hers and they quieted together.

"Oh, no," Jane jumped. "I forgot about Joy."

"It's all right, Jane." Gordon pulled her back down on top of him and wrapped his arms around her. "She won't notice that we're a little late. We even have time for a quick shower."

"I didn't know you were going with us, Grampa," Joy said when she opened the door to the apartment.

"You don't mind, do you?" Gordon leaned down to kiss her cheek.

"No," Joy said. "But I thought it would be just Jane and me."

"I'll stay behind if you want me to."

"It's up to you, Joy," Jane said.

Joy smiled. "I'm glad you're coming, Grampa. Where's Fred?"

"He's in the car," Jane said. "Let's make sure your mother knows we're leaving."

"Mom," Joy yelled. "Jane's here. I'm going now."

"Wait just a minute." Jill came into the room from the kitchen wiping her hands on an apron. "Oh, Gordon, I didn't know you were going too."

"I'm beginning to feel like I'm not needed around here any more now that you have Jane." He put an arm around Jill and kissed her cheek.

"We just didn't expect you," Jill said. "I just want to thank Jane for being there for Joy when she needed someone." She hugged Joy and kissed her head. "We were just so caught up in the move and all, we missed her distress."

"It's okay, Mom." Joy looked embarrassed.

"No, it's not," she said. "I won't do that again. Thanks again, Jane. We eat dinner at six thirty. It would be nice to have her back by then. She has homework to do."

"No problem," Gordon said.

They rode to the park in Gordon's car. Joy sat between them in the front seat holding Fred in her lap. The big area was too crowded with large dogs so they went to the area fenced off for small dogs. There were several in there and Fred immediately went to play with them. Joy ran along with him. Jane and Gordon sat down on a bench at the top of the hill. Gordon had picked up a small leather case off the back seat when they left the car. He opened it now.

"I developed these a while ago, but we haven't really had a chance to look at them." He pulled out a stack of pictures of Jane. The one on top was beautiful. She was picking Fred up and smiling at him.

"Gordon, you are good. That's the best picture of me I've ever seen." She took the picture and looked at it. "It's a good one of Fred, too."

"It's all in the lighting," he said, smiling at her praise. "Look at this one."

"Destroy it," Jane said. "I look like a giraffe. So does Fred."

Gordon laughed. He tore the picture in half. "I don't think you look like a giraffe, but it isn't flattering of either of you. I had planned to destroy it. I just wanted to demonstrate the difference. It's the way the light hits you and Fred that makes your necks look so long." He started flipping through the pictures. "Look at the rest of these."

Jane was amazed. They were good. "Are you sure you don't want to work on the magazine?"

"Only if I'm taking pictures of you," he said, "although I'd like to photograph Victoria too. She doesn't have the advantage of height that you do, but I think she'd look good on film anyway."

"Really?" Jane thought about it a minute. "I told her I wanted her to have her picture taken with her article for each issue. You could do that."

"That's not necessary. Michael knows his way around lighting. After all, I taught him. He can do it, but I'd like some shots of her. I wonder if she'd let me."

"I think she would," Jane said. "Gordon, what if you're taking pictures outside. What do you do about light then?"

"You adjust the position of the subject and the photographer and there are lens filters that help too."

"Who's taking our wedding pictures?"

"A protégé of mine from the studio, he's good. I'm coaching him on the proper positions and filters to capture you. Don't worry, they'll be good."

"Good, I'd like to have good wedding pictures." They looked over at Joy. She was talking to another girl about her age. Fred was playing with a small beagle and having a great time.

"She's growing up," Gordon said. "You know she's the oldest of the grandkids. We were so thrilled when she was born." He fell silent.

Jane watched his face. She felt like she was intruding. He had shared this grandchild with Margaret.

"Well, will you look at that?" he said. "She's got bumps in her T-shirt." He smiled and looked at Jane. "My little baby granddaughter is getting breasts."

Jane laughed and looked at Joy. "You're not supposed to notice things like that, Gordon."

"Of course I notice. I don't remember it starting that young, though." He drew his brows together in thought.

"How old is she? I've forgotten."

"She'll be ten in November, November 12th." He sounded so certain.

"Do you know all of their birthdays?"

"Yes, because I study my notes," he said, and kissed her. Then he quietly got up and went over to where Joy was talking to the other girl.

Jane watched him approach them and smile at the girl when Joy introduced him. He was so beautiful. He loved his kids so much. She couldn't believe how lucky she was.

"That was so much fun." Joy chattered on the way home. "Melissa's beagle and Fred got along so well. Melissa doesn't go to my school, but she doesn't live far away from us. I hope Mom will let her come over sometime."

"I'm sure she will," Gordon said. "They want you to make friends."

"It wouldn't be convenient. We couldn't ride the bus home together after school or anything." She paused thoughtfully. "I wish Fred was mine. He and Jellybean got along so well."

"Don't you think Jellybean will get along with Beau?" Jane asked.

"No. He's too big. But that's all right. We can meet her at the park with Fred again, can't we?"

"Sure," Jane said.

"Jane." David was standing at her door the next morning. "I've interviewed Lenny. I think he's qualified. He had some samples of his writing. I have them here for you. His credentials are good. I think he's learned his lesson about drugs. Will you still interview him?"

"Yes, I will." She looked at David. "If I get a bad feeling about him, I won't hire him, though, regardless of what you think."

"I know that and I respect it," David said.

"Any time this afternoon or tomorrow would be fine. Next week I'll be too busy. Gordon's family will be here and Grant will be getting started. If he can't come today or tomorrow, it will have to wait until I get back from Bermuda."

"I'm sure he'll come in today or tomorrow. He's very motivated."

At 2:00 that afternoon Amanda showed Lenwood Jones into Jane's office. David had told her that morning that he would be able to see her then. He was a small man, probably not more than about 5'8" and slim. He had short blond hair, worn in what looked like a spiked crew cut. He came into the room and shook her hand.

"I'm Lenwood Jones. I appreciate you giving me a chance to talk to you," he said. He smiled at her. It was a shy smile. Humble was the word that came to Jane's mind.

"Please, sit down." Jane motioned to the chair. She seated herself behind the desk. "I guess you know that David has informed me of your circumstances?"

"Yes ma'am." He bowed his head.

"I'm not going to judge you on that, Lenwood," she said, "but I want you to know from the beginning that if you get into any more trouble you won't get a second chance here."

"I know. David told me it's the same for him." He looked up at her earnestly. "I won't get in any more trouble. I don't ever want to go back to prison. I don't want anything to do with drugs any more."

There was something about this kid that Jane liked. He was cute for one thing. He seemed so genuine. "I've looked at your resume and your sample writing. It looks perfect for what we need." She thought for a minute. "Lenwood..."

"Call me Lenny." He smiled shyly again. "I hate Lenwood. How could my parents do that to me?"

"All right, Lenny, I was just about to ask you where you were from. Where is your family?"

"They're in Valdosta, Georgia."

"Do you see them often?"

"Yes. I try to go down every five or six months. My mom took the prison thing pretty hard. I'm trying to redeem myself." Again he looked embarrassed.

"All right, I'll take your application into consideration and let you know in a few days. Do you have any questions?"

"No, but I'd just like to say that I would really love to have this position. I think I can do it well. Thank you for the opportunity." He got up, shook her hand, and left.

Jane went out into the lobby. "Did you have a chance to form an opinion of him, Amanda?" she asked as she watched him walk to his car and get in.

"He's adorable. That's all I had the time to notice."

"He is. I'm taking a chance here, but I think I'll hire him. He's certainly qualified. We seem to be putting together a team of misfits." Jane turned to Amanda. "Except for you, of course."

"No," Amanda said. "I'm a misfit, too."

"You know, Amanda, I've become very dependent on you. You've done such a good job for me, but I really don't know much about you. Would you have lunch with me tomorrow? Let's get to know each other."

"There really isn't anything to know, Jane. I'm pretty dull." Amanda shuffled the papers on her desk. She didn't look up.

"Well, I'd still like to take you to lunch."

"All right, if that's what you want…"

The next morning Jane called Lenny and asked him to come in to talk to her that afternoon. Then she called Victoria. "Tori, I'll have most of my team assembled next week. I'd like to have a meeting with the group. What day do you have off? I'd like for you to be there."

"Jane, I don't know anything about meetings. Couldn't you just tell me what you want me to know?"

"Please, Tori, just this once. I won't ask you to come to all the meetings."

"All right, I'm off on Wednesday, but you know how shy I am. I won't say anything," Victoria said.

"That's okay. I plan to do most of the talking."

She went to lunch with Amanda, but didn't find out much about her. She has no family. She was the only child of a single mother who died a few years ago. She's never been married and she likes dogs. That was about it. Jane felt sad for her. She decided that after the wedding, she would try to draw her out a little more. Maybe talk her into putting some highlights in her hair or something. She looked so mousy with the gray streaks in the dull brown hair.

That afternoon when Lenny came in, Jane heard him in the lobby laughing with Amanda. He was teasing her about her organization. Amanda's work space was always in perfect order. Jane went out to where they were. They stopped when she came in.

"Sounds like you two are having fun out here. Don't stop on my account."

"That's okay," Lenny said. "I was starting to worry that she might put me in a drawer or something," he said.

His smile was contagious. Jane smiled back. "I think we're going to enjoy having you around here," she said.

"Does that mean I've got the job?" He was almost bouncing up and down.

"If you want it. Let's go into my office and talk about the terms."

He followed her into the office, giving Amanda a thumbs-up on the way.

After they had talked about salary and gone over Jane's expectations, she showed him to the area of cubicles. "Take your pick," she said. "The one on the end is Anna Smarts. She'll be our fashion editor, but besides that they're all available."

"I'll take the one on this end. I should be close to David since we'll be working together."

David came out of his office. "So you've got the job." He smiled. "I'm gonna love being your boss." He laughed and gave Lenny a playful shove.

"I'm gonna love being your flunky." Lenny laughed and swung at David's head. He ducked and they scuffled like children for a minute.

"Be careful you don't break anything," Jane said. But she was smiling. They really were just kids after all. The two of them looked so cute together. David was tall like his uncle, maybe even taller, six foot four, maybe five. Lenny was so small.

"I'm having a meeting on Wednesday at lunch time. I'll have food brought in," she said. "I'm going to assemble the whole group. Put it on your calendars. Lenny, let Amanda know about any supplies you need. Your computer is a laptop. You can take it home. But be very careful. Don't get it stolen. I can't afford to buy another one."

She left the two of them there and went back to her office. It was time to pack up and go home. She was having dinner with Victoria and Joe tonight. Gordon's family had all come into town. He was busy with them. Tomorrow night was the meet-the-family party and she was already feeling nervous.

"It's just not normal to have a family that big," she said to Joe and Victoria over dinner that night.

"Poor Jane," Victoria said. "I feel bad that you've been so lonely over the years."

"I wasn't lonely. I love my solitude. I guess that's a thing of the past." She took a bite of salad. "That's really good salad dressing, Tori. Did you make it?"

"Yes. I've finally learned how to make salad dressing. You cook it and cool it, then add the oil."

"Really, I never thought of that." Jane ate some more. "No, I really love that family. Those kids are so much fun, and they seem to be fond of me, too. I can't tell you how scared I was when Joy showed up at my house last week. Standing in the hall waiting for that elevator was the hardest thing I've ever done."

"That's parenthood," Joe said. "I guess it's the same for grandparenthood." He laughed.

"I can't be a grandparent. I've never even been a parent."

"Those kids will see you as their grandmother, Jane," Victoria said. "There's no way around that. You're filling that role."

"I know and I feel terrible about it. It's rightfully Margaret's." She put her fork down and leaned back in her chair. "I can't eat anymore. I'm too nervous. Everything was delicious, though." She got up and walked to the window. It was dusk, but she could still see the sugar maple. "The tree is beautiful, Tori. I hope it lasts another week."

"It will. There's still a lot of green on it." Victoria went to the window with Jane. "I just hope it doesn't rain. I'd hate to have to try and fit all of Gordon's family into the house."

Jane laughed. "I'll help you with the dishes."

Jane was waiting at the door when Gordon got there to pick her up on Saturday. He was about to kiss her when she whirled around and started to pace.

"You're scared to death again," he said. "Jane, I'm sorry my family scares you so much."

"You know, Gordon, before I met you, I never cried. I never fainted, and I never got nervous. Now I do all of those things."

"Wasn't there something else you never did before you met me, Jane?" Gordon stopped her pacing by putting his arms around her.

She smiled, remembering their love making. "That's true. You've given me lots of new experiences." She rested her head on his shoulder. "I'll be all right. Every time I see you, I know I'll be all right."

"Good." He buried his face in her hair. "You smell wonderful," he said. "Let's go. The caterers were setting up when I left Kathy's house a little while ago. Everyone should be arriving soon."

"I feel bad about doing this to Katherine when she just had a baby a few weeks ago." Jane gathered her purse and sweater. The evenings were cool now.

"She insisted." Gordon closed the door and locked it with the key Jane had given him. "I was planning to reserve a room at the restaurant again, but she wouldn't have it. I wouldn't let her do anything, though. I had the whole thing catered."

"You're good at that kind of thing, aren't you?"

"I've had to be for the past six years. Before that, Maggie took care of the social details." He put his hand on Jane's waist and guided her into the elevator.

"You're not expecting me to take over the social details now, are you?" She looked sideways at him.

"Of course not," he said. "I'm better at it than you."

"That's for sure."

They arrived at Katherine's house and parked the car. They had to park down the road. "Looks like everyone is here," Gordon said. "Jerry was going over to get Mom and Dad, but I guess he beat me back."

They went to the door. Jane's heart was pounding so hard she thought she could see movement in her chest. There was a humming noise coming from the other side of the door. Jane shivered when she realized it was the sound of voices.

"Cold?" Gordon asked.

"Cold feet." She smiled at him.

He opened the door and they went in. The room was so full of people that Jane felt dizzy again. Don't faint, you idiot. She took a deep breath and let it out slowly. Then she caught sight of Victoria and Joe across the room talking to Michael. The dizziness slowly subsided.

"Grampa!" Eric's familiar voice came from some-where below.

"Rampa!" Teddy was right behind.

Eric grabbed Gordon's hand and Teddy started to tug at his pants. "Hi, Janie," Eric said.

"Janie, up," Teddy said, reaching up to her. She leaned down and patted his bottom to check for wetness before she picked him up. It was comforting to hold him.

"Hello, Jane," Katherine said from beside her. "Come in and have a glass of wine."

"Thank you." Jane took the glass from her and Katherine took Teddy.

Gordon put Eric down and said, "Let me take you around the room and introduce you. The hum of conver-sation had stopped when they came in, but had subse-quently resumed.

"This is my brother, Jerry." She looked into eyes, the same color as Gordon's, showing the beginning of those beautiful smile lines. She smiled.

"It's nice to meet you, Jane. I can't believe my crazy brother managed to catch a woman as beautiful as you."

"Thank you." Jane felt a blush rise up her neck into her face.

"He's an incorrigible flirt." A pretty petite blonde stepped up to him. "I'm Shannon, Jerry's wife. We're so happy to meet you."

Gordon smiled at her and moved on. "This is Breanne and Robert," Gordon said, as they stopped in front of a young couple. The young woman was holding a baby. "This is Bobby." Gordon stroked the back of the infant's head.

"It's wonderful to meet you, Jane." They continued around the room until everyone had been introduced. Jane's head was spinning with names and faces.

"I'll never keep them all straight," Jane said to Gordon as he seated her in a chair next to his mother.

"Don't worry about it dear," Minerva said. "I don't even try."

"Get this girl some food, Gordon," Gordon Sr. said.

"She needs to flesh out a little. Of course that won't help with the height problem."

Jane smiled at Gordon.

"Jane doesn't have a height problem, Dad. I think she's beautiful."

The evening went well. Everyone had a good time. The meal was served buffet-style and people ate with plates on their laps. After the meal was finished, Grant stood and made a toast to the happy couple. Gordon kissed Jane, and she blushed.

"Before I met you, I never blushed either."

He kissed her again.

After a while Jane excused herself to go to the powder room. When she came out of the powder room, she noticed the back door was right next to it. She opened it and stepped out into the cool night. She took a deep breath of the autumn air and walked out into the yard. The tree house was finished and the ladder was folded and clipped to a hook on the tree. She unfolded it and tested it. It was very solid. She climbed up to the small porch on the front of the house. It was bigger than it looked from the ground. She opened the front door and went in. It was furnished with children's furniture. Sitting down on the floor she leaned up against the wall. Closing her eyes and taking a deep breath she relaxed for the first time all day.

She jumped at the sound of someone climbing the ladder. When the door opened and Gordon came through, she let out a breath. The moon was bright but she could barely see him in the shadows of the tree house. "Hey," he said, closing the door behind him. "Needed a moment of solitude?"

"Yeah."

He sat down on the floor beside her, put his arm around her, and pulled her close to kiss her. He deepened the kiss and put his hand on her breast.

She pulled her mouth away from his. "Cut that out, Gordon. This is not the time or the place."

He took a deep breath. "You're right."

They jumped apart when they heard someone coming up the ladder. The door opened and a light switched on. Gary stood in the doorway.

"Hey, Buddy. I didn't know there was electricity out here," Gordon said. "Join us."

"This is a cool tree house. I wonder if Uncle Rick would build one for me. I mean, when we find a house with a yard."

"Ask him," Gordon said.

They all looked in the direction of the door when they heard the sound of someone climbing the ladder again. This time it was Hope.

"Hope," Gary said. "Isn't this tree house great? It would be fun to spend the night in it."

"Yeah, it would. Wonder if Aunt Katherine would let us?"

"Janie, can we take the other kids to the dog park this week? I want to show it to them," Joy said as she came through the door.

"I think we can do that between dress fittings and such," she said.

Gordon smiled at her. "I love you, Jane."

"I love you, too, and my new family."

"You're not getting mushy, are you?" Gary asked, "because if you are, I'm leaving." Both girls giggled.

"You better leave then," Gordon said, "because we're getting mushy."

Chapter Thirteen

"Well, Jane, I'm here." Victoria stood in the doorway to her office. It was Wednesday, about eleven thirty. The meeting was at noon. "I feel completely out of place." She had a watering can in her hand.

"Did you bring the can as a security object?" Jane asked.

"No, I figured I'd kill two birds with one stone and water your plants while I was here." She went to the window and poured some water into a plant. "I hate that phrase. Why would you want to kill birds with a stone?"

Jane laughed. "I don't know, Tori."

"So you liked my articles. I have the crop of container vegetables that I'll have to harvest soon. Probably should get pictures now if you want to use them this year." Victoria dusted the plant and trimmed a broken leaf.

"I'll ask Michael if he can go to your house this afternoon. Would that be all right?

"Yes, but I'm not going to be in the pictures. I've decided I just can't do that."

"Well, that's disappointing," Jane said. "But I guess it has to be your decision."

"Uh-oh, every time someone says something is my decision, I end up doing what they want. I'm really not photogenic, Jane," Victoria said.

"I didn't think I was either, Tori, but these Fox guys are really good. It's all in the lighting. Give them a chance."

"I'll think about it. I've got some plants to attend to

so I'll see you at the meeting," she said, and left the room with her watering can.

At noon, Jane went into the conference room across the hall from her office. Everyone had gathered there. David and Lenny were playing catch with a wadded up piece of copy paper. Anna was keeping score about something. Jane didn't know the rules of the game they were playing. Michael and Grant were cheering for one side or another. Mark was laughing at the antics and Victoria was sitting quietly, but smiling.

"I see you're enjoying each others company," Jane said. "That's a good start."

The game stopped and everyone looked at her.

"Let's grab some lunch." She pointed to the sideboard where there were sandwiches and salads and fruit. "Then we can talk."

They all dug in and Jane was impressed by the buzz of conversation in the room. She gave them all a chance to eat and then said, "I think we can get started now, don't you?"

Everyone nodded.

"I hate going into a meeting where the leader of the group says, 'Let's go around the room and introduce ourselves and tell a little about ourselves,' Jane continued. "So I'm not going to do that. I'm going to introduce you to each other, even though most of you have already met. If you want to say something about yourselves, I'll give you the chance." Jane looked around the room. She had everyone's attention.

"I hope you realize that even though this is a business endeavor, we are all family in one way or another." She looked at Victoria who sat to her right. "This is Victoria Vandor. I've known her since the day she was born. We're adopted sisters. I call her Tori, but don't any of you dare." She looked around the room. "Tori is our garden editor."

She looked to Tori's right. "This is Mark Bradley. He married Tori's and my very good friend, Lillian, a few weeks ago. He's a self-taught commercial designer. He'll be our art director in charge of layout design, and he'll work closely with Michael on advertisement design."

She looked to the other side of the table and said, "This is Michael Fox. In a couple of days, he'll be my stepson. He's our photographer, and his older brother Grant," she nodded in his direction, "will also be my stepson in a couple of days. He is our production director."

Jane took a breath. "Over here is David Landrum. David is my best friend Jeff's nephew. Jeff is also Tori's boss at the nursery where she works. David is our managing editor."

Jane looked at all of the faces in the room. "At the end of the table on the right is Anna Smart. Anna is our fashion designer. She designed my wedding dress, and it is a work or art.

"On the other side is Lenwood Jones. Call him Lenny. He is our features editor. He'll be in charge of short stories and articles.

"At the end of the table taking notes is Amanda our support system. Treat her with respect. She is definitely an asset."

Jane looked around the room again. She picked up a couple of magazines and opened them to one of the first pages. "I plan to hire a food and entertainment editor. I have a hairdresser who will do a new style for each issue. Now I want to show you something. If you look at these credit pages on these established magazines, you'll get an idea of what a skeleton crew we are." She passed the magazines around. The credits took a whole page. "This means that we'll all be working very hard for the first year at least.

"I've set a date for the first publication. I want it ready by April 1st. The first year we will only produce quarterly. Once we have a strong customer base and a positive cash flow, we'll go bi-monthly.

Eventually I want to be a monthly publication. Of course we'll have to produce a sample publication. I want that done by December 1st. We'll need that for sales."

She looked around the room. "So, what do you think?"

Nobody said a word. They were all looking at her. "Grant," she said. "Will you give everyone a quick run-down of the business plan you outlined to me earlier this week? Then," she looked at David. "I'd like you to talk about your marketing plans."

"That was exhilarating, Jane," Victoria said, when the meeting was over and she and Jane had gone back into her office. "I never knew how professional you are."

"You're so funny, Tori." Jane gathered her purse and her sweater. "What time is our hair appointment?"

"At two this afternoon," Victoria said.

"Good, we've got plenty of time." They went out into the lobby. Amanda was sitting at her desk. "Amanda, why don't you come with Tori and me? We're going to get our hair done. I'm sure Harrison could fit you in. I'd love to see some highlights in your hair."

"No thank you, Jane," Amanda said.

"It's my treat," Jane said.

"No." Amanda smiled uneasily. "I prefer not to be too flashy. But thanks, I appreciate the offer."

Jane and Victoria left and drove to the salon in Jane's car.

"I think Amanda could be pretty if she tried," Jane said. "Her hair is so mousy looking, and the way she pulls it back in that tight bun at the base of her neck makes her look so severe. A few highlights and a good cut would make a world of difference."

"I had the same thought," Victoria said. "You know her teeth are crooked. I've wondered why her parents didn't have them straightened."

"She was the only child of a single mother. That's pretty much all I've learned about her so far. I guess a single mom doesn't have money for that kind of thing."

"I guess not, but you know, it's not unattractive. It's

not like her teeth stick out or anything, they just sort of fold over each other."

"Come in, ladies," Harrison, the man who had done their hair for all of their lives said.

"It's good to see you, Harrison," Jane said. "I want you to do the usual thing to my hair." He pulled her to a workstation then seated Victoria beside her. "You are thinking of a style for my magazine, aren't you?"

"Oh, I've designed a wonderful style for a sixty-year-old woman." He pulled her hair up and put a drape around her neck.

"I'd love to see a picture of it."

"You'll see it when I've finished with you."

"Don't you dare," Jane said. "I've always worn my hair the same way. It's what works for me."

"It's time for a change." Harrison smiled at her then at Victoria.

"He's right, Jane. You're due for a change. You trust Harrison. He won't make you look bad for your wedding."

"I know I'm going to regret this," Jane said. She closed her eyes and surrendered to Harrison's expertise.

"Janie, your hair looks great," Joy said on Thursday, when she picked her up for their last dress fitting.

"Thank you," Jane said. She hadn't quite gotten used to the feel of the hair around her face. Harrison had cut it in layers long enough to be swept behind her ear and out of her line of vision, but otherwise her hair fell around her face to her chin then tapered down to her shoulders where it hung in curls around her neck. Even Jane had to admit it was flattering. "I'm sure it'll bother me when I jog," she said. "Where's Hope?"

"I'm here." Hope ran out of the back room with Jill right behind her.

"Your hair looks wonderful," Jill said. "Are you sure

you don't need me to go with you to the dress fitting? They can be a handful."

"No, Tori's in the car. She can help me. I don't want to interrupt your routine," Jane said. "We'll be back by dinnertime."

"Are you still planning to take the kids to the dog park tomorrow? It's a teacher's work day and they're off. I can come along if you want," Jill said.

"I'd love you to if you want to, but I can handle it if you have other things to do," Jane said. "I know Gary is coming, but I'm not sure about Maggie."

"Oh, Maggie won't go. Lauren won't let her." Jill helped Jane get the girls into the car and buckled up, then said, "See you later. I think I'll let you take the kids without me tomorrow. It'll be fun to have a few minutes to myself."

The next morning Jane and Gordon set off to pick up the kids. Jane was driving Katherine's mini-van. She had Fred, Joy, Hope, Alexandra in a car seat in the seat behind her, and Erik beside Alexandra in another car seat. Gordon was behind her in his car with Teddy, also in a car seat, and Beau. Beau was a beautiful and good-natured golden retriever. Living in an apartment now, he was due for a good run. They stopped at Grant and Lauren's apartment to pick up Gary.

Jane waited in the car with the kids. Gordon carried Teddy in with him to get Gary. When he came out, he had Teddy and Gary. A minute later, Lauren followed him out of the house with Maggie. Jane smiled at them. She was glad Maggie was coming along. She hadn't had time to get know the little girl.

They arrived at the park and put both dogs on leashes and walked them to the fenced area. When they went through the gate, Joy carried Fred. It was early in the day, so there weren't very many dogs there.

"Let's sit on this bench over here." Gordon guided

Jane and Lauren over. He sat them down and went into the field with the children. The older children ran ahead. Gordon held Teddy and had Alexandra by the hand. Erik worked his little legs frantically trying to keep up with the big kids.

Lauren put her hand on Maggie's wrist and said, "You stay here with me. You're just here to watch."

"Okay, Mama," the child said, and sat between her mother and Jane.

The other kids went with Gordon into the middle of the field with the dogs. They started to play a game of catch. They were throwing a Frisbee back and forth. The dogs were both running after it. Beau caught it a couple of times and returned it to Gordon. Fred was determined to do the same, but never got near it. Jane laughed. She heard laughter beside her and looked down at Maggie.

"Tell me about yourself, Maggie. I haven't gotten to know you like the others," Jane said.

"Maggie has health problems and can't do a lot of the things the others can," Lauren said.

"Well," Jane said, feeling uncomfortable for the child. "Tell me what you can do then."

"I like to watch soccer on TV," Maggie said. Jane noticed that she looked up at her mother for approval. "I wish I could ride a bike."

"I'm sure in a few years you will," Jane said. "My sister, Victoria, didn't learn to ride a bike until she was a grown woman with children and grandchildren." She laughed, but fell silent when she saw the look on Lauren's face.

"Mom," Gary said. "Come and see what I taught Fred to do." Lauren looked at her son who was calling and gesturing to her. She looked back at Maggie.

"I'll stay with her, Lauren. Go with Gary," Jane said. She noticed Lauren's hesitation. "We won't move, we'll just sit right here."

"Come on, Mom," Gary persisted.

Lauren got up and went to her son.

"Janie," Maggie said, when her mother was out of

hearing range. "Do you think I'm healthy enough to play soccer?"

"Maggie, I don't know anything about your health," Jane said. "You look pretty strong to me, but your doctor would be the one to ask about that."

"Mama would be mad if I asked my doctor."

"Oh, I'm sure she wouldn't mind," Jane assured the child. "I'm sure she wants you to do whatever makes you happy."

The child looked at her mother playing with her brother. Her small eyes knit together. Jane felt uncomfortable for a reason she couldn't identify. Then Gordon approached them and sat down on the other side of Maggie. He settled Teddy on his lap and helped Alexandra on to the bench between him and Maggie.

"Are you two getting to know each other?" he asked.

"Yes, we are," Jane said.

Maggie smiled up at them.

"Aunt Jane, your hair looks wonderful!" Ellen said as she greeted Jane and Gordon that night at Victoria's door. Ellen was Victoria's oldest daughter. She lived in Seattle, Washington, with her husband, and infant son, Benjamin.

"Thank you, sweetie," Jane said, and put her arms around Ellen's neck and hugged her. She stepped back. "Gordon, this is Tori's oldest daughter, Ellen. Isn't she beautiful?"

"Yes, she is." Gordon said, and took Ellen's hand. "It's a pleasure to meet you. I've heard a lot about you."

"It's nice to meet you, too," Ellen said. "I guess you've heard more about Benjamin." She smiled proudly.

"I can't wait to meet him," Gordon said. They were having dinner with Victoria's family the night before the wedding. They had forgone the traditional rehearsal dinner due to the comparison in size of Jane's family and his.

"Come on in. Everyone is here." Ellen guided them into the living room. "Benjamin is at the age where he's a little shy with strangers, but he warms up pretty fast."

When they reached the living room, Jane put her arms around a petite, golden-blond girl with big dimples in her pretty cheeks. "Patricia, it's so good to see you. I don't see much more of you than I see of Ellen, and we live in the same city."

"You're right, Aunt Jane. We'll have to do better about that." She held her hand out to Gordon. "I'm Patricia, Victoria's youngest daughter, and this is my friend, Bob." Gordon shook the hand of the young man. "And this," Patricia put her hand on the shoulders of a tall, beautiful greyhound who stood at her side, "is my constant companion, Patch."

"It's nice to meet you, Patch." Gordon extended his hand, palm-up to the greyhound. The dog sniffed it cautiously then allowed Gordon to stroke his neck.

"Gordon," Ellen said from behind him. "I'd like to introduce you to my husband and son." She guided him over to a tall, studious looking young man standing at the window with an infant. "My husband, Alex, and my son, Benjamin."

"It's nice to meet you, Alex." Gordon shook his hand then held his arms out to Benjamin. The baby turned his head the other way and hid it in his fathers shoulder. "Benjamin," Gordon said to the child. "Come and meet your great uncle." He pulled the child gently from his father's arms. Benjamin immediately screwed up his face. Gordon bounced a little and started walking toward Jane. "And this is your great aunt, Jane," he said. "Isn't she beautiful?" Jane smiled. The infant smiled back.

"You're good with babies, Gordon," Ellen said.

"I have eight grandchildren. I learned early on not to panic if they start to cry."

"Gordon, would you like a drink?" Joe asked. He stood at a small bar in the corner of the room.

"I'd love one. What have you got?"

"I'm fully stocked. Name your pleasure."

Victoria came into the room carrying a tray of hors' d'oeuvres. "Jane, isn't it wonderful to see the whole group together?" she asked. "Hello Gordon." Victoria offered her hand and Gordon took it then leaned down and kissed her cheek.

"I get a kiss now, don't I? We're practically family." Victoria blushed. Benjamin, still in Gordon's arms, started to laugh.

The morning of the wedding was beautiful. They had planned the ceremony for three in the afternoon. The sun would be warm by then. People would be comfortable outside in the fall weather. The tree was perfect, mostly yellow and orange, with bits of green still sprinkled through it.

Jane got up and went for a bike ride with Jeff. They hit the trail at about 8:00 and rode for ten miles. Then stopped for a mid-morning snack.

"So, are we going to continue our Sunday rides now that you'll be married?" Jeff asked.

"Yes, if you want to. I told Gordon I intended to." Jane passed him the bunch of white grapes she had brought. "I don't think he'll mind as long as I can be flexible if something with the family comes up."

"Good, because I really look forward to our rides."

They fell silent for a while. Finally Jeff said, "You're pretty sure about this, aren't you?"

"Yes, I am." She looked at him. "I've questioned whether I'll be able to be what I should be for Gordon's grandchildren, and I've questioned whether it's the right thing to do as far as Margaret is concerned." She ate another grape. "But I've never questioned wanting to marry him. I guess I really love him."

"Good," Jeff said. "Maybe there's still hope for me."

"Are you all right, Jeff?" Jane said. "You seem sad lately."

"I don't know. Maybe I'm having some kind of midlife crisis." He looked thoughtful. "I'm thinking of asking Vic to become a partner in the nursery. Do you think she'd do it?"

"I don't know, but why would you do that, Jeff? That nursery has been your whole life."

"It's not enough any more," he said. "If I had a partner, I could take some time off and move around a little bit. It was just a thought." He looked at his watch. "We'd better get going. We've got a wedding to go to."

They rode back in silence. When Jeff dropped her at her building, he got out of the car and helped her unload her bike. "Jane, in a lot of ways I'm sorry I'm not marrying you today."

"Me too." She kissed him. "But that wouldn't have worked and we both knew it. I won't be able to ride with you tomorrow. Our flight leaves first thing in the morning," she said, "but next Sunday, for sure. We'll be home on Saturday."

"Next Sunday for sure," he said. "See you in a couple of hours."

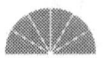

Jane was standing with Joe looking out the back window of the house. The families were seated on different sides of the tree. The few guests that were not family were seated behind them. Gordon, Grant, and Michael had walked the path between and were standing in front of the justice of the peace in front of the tree. Both girls had walked out, beautiful in their royal blue dresses. Victoria was on her way down the path now. "Joe, does Tori sparkle when you look at her?" Jane asked.

"Every time," Joe said. He put his arm around her shoulder and kissed her cheek. "Is Gordon's sparkling?"

"You don't see it?"

"No, he's not sparkling for me," Joe said. "Although, I do think he looks nice in his tux, as do his boys."

"You look nice in yours, too," Jane said, and patted his lapel.

"I think you've found the real thing, Jane. I'm happy for you."

The wedding march began and he held out his arm. "Ready?"

"Ready." Jane took his arm and they walked together down the path. Joe delivered her to Gordon's side and stepped behind them. Grant and Michael stepped to either side. The ceremony was short. Then it was time for Gordon to kiss her. He gently took her mouth with his. For a minute Jane forgot where she was and why. All she could feel was the comfort of his lips on hers. When he pulled away, she smiled shyly at him. He smiled just as shyly back. She was aware of the sound of a camera. Then they were walking back toward the house.

The reception was held in the back yard. The chairs were moved around the garden. Gordon had brought in a catering company. They had set up a table of food and a bar. The patio beside the house had been cleared for dancing, and there was a piano band. Gordon took Jane into her arms and guided her expertly around the patio.

"I didn't know you could dance. Why haven't we danced before?" Jane asked him.

"Just haven't had the time, I guess." He kissed her again on the dance floor.

"Gordon, we're in front of everyone." She could feel herself blush.

"We just got married. We're supposed to be in love." He kissed her again then turned to the crowd and said, "Please join us." He gestured to the dance floor. Victoria and Joe joined them. Then other couples began to fill up the space and Gordon and Jane retreated to a table under their wedding tree.

Chapter Fourteen

"So, Jane, wasn't the honeymoon good? I mean did you two argue or something?" Victoria asked.

"No. Why do you ask that, Tori? Don't I seem happy?"

"Well, you said you were so happy to be back."

"I wondered about that too, Jane," Jeff said. The three of them were riding the Silver Comet Trail on the Sunday after her return. Victoria was riding tandem with Jane in order to get her conditioning level up to speed with them.

"Oh, it was wonderful having Gordon all to myself for a whole week, but honestly, I think we should have postponed the honeymoon until a better time for both of us."

"Really, why?" Victoria asked.

"Well, I couldn't stop thinking about the magazine. You know I've just gotten my team assembled. I hated to leave before we really got started." They rode in silence for a few minutes. "Poor Gordon couldn't stop worrying about Katherine. He was afraid she'd need something and her brothers wouldn't take care of it for her."

"I took care of it," Victoria said.

"You took care of what?"

"I called her one day, just to check in. I thought with Gordon gone she might need some support." Victoria paused. "I do think there are going to be some rough spots with those grown siblings and their families all living in one city."

"Why, what happened?" Jane asked.

"Oh, nothing serious," Victoria assured her. "Katherine just had her one month follow-up with her OB/GYN and she couldn't get anyone to watch the kids. She said she was going to have to take them along. Of course, I volunteered to do it, so everything was fine. But she was mad at her brothers and their wives."

"I don't blame her. It seems like one of them could have spared her a couple of hours," Jeff said.

"Well, they all have a lot going on," Jane defended. "I do appreciate you doing that, though, Tori."

"Oh, I didn't mind. Those kids are adorable. That baby is so good. She didn't cry once. Katherine had left a bottle of breast milk. She said I should heat it up in the microwave, but I didn't feel comfortable with that, so I did it the old fashioned way, on the stove in a pan of water."

"How could she leave a bottle of breast milk? Don't tell me you can buy the stuff." Jeff said.

"Of course not," Victoria said.

"How did she do it, Tori?" Jane asked.

"She pumped it."

"You're kidding!" Jane and Jeff exclaimed together.

"Human beings can pump their breast milk?" Jane asked. She and Jeff stared at Victoria open mouthed.

"Of course they can," Victoria said. They stopped, parked their bikes, and walked over to a picnic area. "You two are so funny." Victoria put her saddle pack down on the table and started unpacking lunch. "I swear. The two of you know nothing about babies."

"I guess not." Jane sat down. "I hope I'm not in over my head."

"Of course you're not." Victoria spread out the cloth and put the sandwiches and salads and plates out. "If you ever need help, just call me." Victoria looked over at Jeff who was being very quiet. "Are you all right, Jeff? You look a little pale."

"I need some water." He sat down at the table.

Victoria pulled out a bottle of water and handed it to him. "You're not being squeamish about breast milk, are you?"

He took a gulp of water and shook his head.

"Anyway, Jane, those two little boys are cute, too," Victoria continued. "I just love the way Teddy repeats the last word of everything Eric says."

"Yeah, I do too. They're my babies. They were the first ones I got to know." Jane sat down and started to eat.

"They both called me Tori. I guess that's what your grandkids will call me."

"My grandkids," Jane repeated quietly, staring at the sandwich she was holding. "I guess so."

The next morning Jane arrived at the office early. There were a number of cars in the parking lot. Obviously a number of people had arrived early.

"Good morning, Amanda," she said as she walked into the office.

"Good morning, Jane. Did you have a nice trip?"

"It was wonderful. How did things go here?"

"I think everything went well. I've been ordering supplies for everyone and furnishing the studios. I assume that everyone is working hard on getting the place in running order. I have a couple of messages for you from manufacturing companies. Something about a clothing line and," Amanda flipped through some cards. "Something here about cookware."

"Oh, good, I was hoping I'd get some responses. Those are for my ancillary products. I'm planning a line of clothing and one for cookware." Jane picked up the stack of cards.

"This is really getting exciting. I'm glad I get to be a part of it," Amanda said.

"A very important part." Jane went into her office, made a couple of phone calls, and set up some appointments to meet with manufactures. Then she went down the hall to David's office. She knocked on the door.

"Come on in," David called from the other side.

"Good morning, David."

He looked up at her, startled. "I'd forgotten you were coming back today. It's good to see you. How was the trip?"

"It was wonderful, but I'm glad to be back. Is everything going well here? How's Lenny doing? Is he able to do some work along with all of that playing around?" she asked.

"Lenny is a real character, but he's a pretty smart guy, too. I've gotten a good response from the e-mail blast sent out last week. There has been some interesting responses about the types of articles people want to see." He showed her a stack of surveys that had been e-mailed back to them.

"I've had Lenny interviewing freelance writers. I thought it would be good to have some people that we use regularly."

"Sounds like a good idea." Jane sat down in the chair across from his desk and picked up the stack of papers. "Can I read through these?"

"Of course. I've logged them all on the computer," he said. "Lenny is assigning some of the article subjects to his writers. We'll see what we get."

"Any luck with subscriptions?"

"I've gotten us on the lists of all of the major subscription companies. You know, the one's that do the subscription service for doctor's offices and other professionals, you know, like accountants and lawyers," he said. "I'll have better luck with private subscribers when we get the sample issue completed."

"Looks like you're doing great." Jane got up, and taking the stack of papers, walked to the door. "Let me know if you need anything."

She went down the hall to the next office and looked inside. Grant had his head bent looking over some papers.

"Good morning, Grant," Jane said.

He looked up at her. There were circles under his

eyes and he looked drawn. "Hello, Jane." He yawned. "How was the trip?"

"It was great. Are you all right? You look tired."

"Maggie had an asthma attack last night. I never get much sleep when that happens," he said.

"I'm sorry. Is she okay?"

"Oh, yeah, she does fine with them. She just gets her inhaler and sprays it down her throat," he explained. "But Lauren and I get hysterical. We're having a hard time with that little girl. You know we almost lost her when she was born. For the first two years, it was touch and go. We fed her through a feeding tube until she was three."

"What does her doctor say? What's her prognosis?"

"Her pediatrician in Charlotte said that she was fine. She has asthma and probably always will, but it isn't very serious. He assured us that all the problems she was born with have been satisfactorily overcome." He rubbed his eyes. "I think the real problem now is with Lauren and me. I went to a support group up in Charlotte. Lauren never went, though. I don't really think it helped very much."

"I wish I could do something to help."

"I'm sure we'll work it out," he said. "Anyway, I've got some pretty good news."

"What's that?" Jane sat in the chair across from his desk.

"I think I'm close to our first ad sale. I've met with the prospect twice and they liked my ideas. I'm having Mark flesh out an ad. I'll meet with them again on Thursday."

"Already?" Jane almost bounced in her seat. "That's wonderful, Grant! Who is it?"

"A car dealership over on Roswell Rd. It's for their minivan. I thought about what you said about a young woman in the ad with five kids. I thought in our magazine we'd have a grandmother in the van with five kids and a young mother in the background. It happens."

Jane thought about the day she'd taken the kids to the dog park. "It sure does. I'm impressed, Grant."

"It's just the beginning. I've got a number of leads

in the pipeline. If this dealership likes what they see, we could go national." He looked back down at the desk. "I'm working on the budget right now. It's not as much fun, but just as important."

"Well, I'll let you get back to it then. Keep up the good work." Jane left him and went into the staff room. She checked Lenny's cube, but he wasn't there. She looked at her watch and frowned. She hadn't really given anyone hours to keep, but she expected them to put in a full day. It was nine thirty and he hadn't arrived yet.

"He never gets in before nine thirty," Anna said from behind her.

Jane turned and looked at her. "Is that right? Do you think it's a problem?"

"No. He's just not a morning person. He hardly ever takes a lunch break and it's not uncommon for him to stay late." Anna proceeded to her cube at the other end of the room.

Jane followed her. When she got to the cube she looked around admiringly. "Look what you've done here!"

One panel of the U-shaped counter had been tilted to make a drafting table. In fact, it was equipped with adjustable arms that could tilt it to the angle required.

"It was a built in feature," Anna said.

"Realy? I didn't know."

"Well, I did. I've worked in these things before."

"So how is everything going?" Jane sat down on a rolling stool that stood right outside the cube.

"Pretty well, I have some drafts of that suit you wanted for the first issue. Would you like to see?" Anna started to pull drafting papers out of her portfolio case.

"I'd love to." Jane took them and put them down on the tilted surface. "These are great, Anna. I knew I had talent with you. You don't know how many compliments I've gotten on my wedding dress."

"Have you decided on a manufacturer yet? I can make one to be modeled for the magazine, but if people start wanting to buy them, and I think they will, I won't be able to keep up with the demand."

"No, but I have a couple of appointments later this week. We'll have someone by the time we need someone," Jane assured her. "Is there anything I can do to help you, Anna?"

"Just the manufacturer, other than that, I'm enjoying my new job."

"Good. You know where I am if you need me." She stood up and noticed the light on in Lenny's cube. She went back down there and said, "Good morning, Lenny."

He looked startled for a minute, then smoothed his features into a smile and said, "Jane, I'd forgotten you were coming back today. It's great to see you. How was the trip?"

"It was wonderful, Lenny. I see that you're not a morning person."

"No. I thought since you didn't specify hours, that as long as I was productive, maybe it wouldn't matter. But if you want me to change, I will," he said.

"Let's see how it works for us. But if it doesn't, it will have to change."

"Yes ma'am. I mean all right."

"Show me what you've done for the past week." Jane sat down on a stool.

"All right." Lenny picked up a stack of papers. "These are all articles from freelance writers. I've made a list of the ones I liked." Lenny turned to his computer and started it up. "I put it in a spreadsheet, see?" He waited while the image came up on his screen. "Now over here on this worksheet," he said, clicking the next worksheet with his mouse, "are the ones I liked the most. Here are the writers I've interviewed and liked. I've given them all the assignments that David got from his e-mail blast. Their deadline is November 10th." He looked back at Jane. His eyes were bright with excitement. "It'll take me that long to read, select, and edit an article for our sample publication by December 1st."

"I'm impressed, Lenny. With this kind of work, it

won't matter if you're not a morning person." Jane smiled and got up. "Let me know if you need anything."

She moved on to Mark's studio at the back of the office suite. The door was closed. She knocked, but didn't get a response. Wondering if Mark wasn't a morning person either, she opened the door a crack. He was sitting at a drafting table working intently. She looked around the room. It looked like he'd been there for years. There were easels and drafting tables, racks of art supplies. Pictures were hung haphazardly all over the walls.

"Mark?" Jane said.

He jumped and turned around.

"I didn't mean to startle you. I knocked, but I guess you were lost in your work."

"Jane, it's good to see you. How was the trip?"

"It was great. How's Lillian? We haven't spent any time together in so long I've forgotten what she looks like. I need to change that." She sat on a stool beside him.

"She's still beautiful," he said. "And of course, she's still crazy about me." He dazzled her with his smile.

"Of course," Jane said, smiling back.

"She's busy with school, but I know she'd love to hear from you. Call her."

"I will." She looked at the drafting table. "Show me what you're doing."

"I'm working on the ad for the minivan." He turned back and showed her his work.

"It's beautiful." Jane looked it over for a minute. "You really are an artist. I envy you."

"Don't," he said. "I envy your business head and courage. We all have our strong points. That's why a good team is essential."

"You're pretty smart. Tell me, what you think about our team?" Jane asked.

"So far, so good," he said with a note of hesitation in his voice.

Jane folded her arms in front of her, and waited.

"I have a few reservations, but they're based on

instinct and I don't think that's sufficient to comment on. So I'll keep those reservations to myself."

"Hmm. You make me curious," Jane said.

"I'll speak up if I think I need to, but so far, I work pretty well with everyone. I love my studio." He looked around. "I could live here, but I don't think it would work for Lillian."

"No," Jane said. "And the truth is you're crazy about her too, right?"

"Absolutely."

"I'll see you later. I'm going next door to talk to Michael." She left Mark working on his design and turned to go to Michael's studio. "Oh!" she said as she almost bumped into him on her way out the door.

"Jane!" Michael put his hands on her shoulders to steady her and kissed her cheek. "It's so good to see you. How's the old man?"

There was a warm feeling in her chest. She realized she'd felt it before in Michael's presence. "He's fine. We had a wonderful trip. Was everything okay here?"

"Yes." Michael put his arm across her shoulders and guided her into his studio. "Except Kathy is mad at us because we couldn't help her out with her doctor's visit. I sent Victoria a thank you note for what she did."

"Apparently she really enjoyed it," Jane said.

"I would have been glad to help, if Kathy had given me a little notice. She's gotten a little spoiled living in Atlanta with Dad all to herself. He'll drop everything and run if she calls."

"I know."

"Truth is she's always been spoiled. She's the baby. I really can't criticize, though. I spoiled her as much as anyone."

"Well, she's adorable. How could you not?" Jane asked.

"You think she's cute now, you should have seen her at five." Michael started walking around the studio. "What do you think?"

"It looks like your dad's studio. Where did all these lights come from?"

"They're mine. I've been working for myself for a while now, you know."

"I really should compensate you for them. You've saved me a lot of money by having them," Jane said.

"I'm not willing to relinquish ownership. You're compensating me enough with the opportunity. Come here." He guided her over to a desk in the corner. He opened his portfolio case and pulled out a picture. "Look at this."

It was the wedding picture of her and Gordon. It was obviously right after their kiss in the ceremony. She vaguely remembered hearing a camera. They were looking at each other, smiling shyly. Both of them wore expressions of pure joy.

"We're both sparkling," she said. "We're both beautiful."

"That's what I thought. Matt did a very good job."

"Matt?"

"Dad's protégé from the studio. He's a student. Of course, Dad and I coached him. Anyway, I want to use it on the cover of the sample edition."

"Oh, I don't know about having my picture on the sample," Jane said.

"Why not, Jane? You're beautiful and it's your magazine. I think it's perfect."

"It is a good picture," she said. "And that's what *Second Half* is all about." She tapped her foot for a minute. "I'll think about it. Can I have this picture?"

"Yes. I already have copies."

"My life is just going by way too fast," Jane said to Gordon. They were lying side-by-side in bed, snuggling after making love for the second time that morning. "I can't believe it's already been two weeks since we got back."

"I know what you mean," he said. "I think it's because

I'm so happy. The store isn't even getting on my nerves any more. It was for a while."

"I remember you said you were thinking about selling it."

"I've changed my mind. In fact, my brother called me yesterday. He's interested in buying a partnership in it."

"Oh, really, how do you feel about that?"

"I think I like it."

Jane sat up and looked down at him. "You don't sound sure. You and your brother don't have trouble getting along, do you?"

"We never have, but we've never been real close either. He is ten years younger than me." Gordon sat up next to her. "I think it would be nice to have a partner. That way, I could take a little more time to work at the studio. That's what I really like to do."

"You should do it then. Couldn't you retain sole ownership in the studio?" Jane asked.

"I'd have to negotiate that with Jerry, but that's what I'd want to do." He got out of bed and went into the bathroom. "He's coming up from Macon next week," Gordon said from the other room. "You know, if he accepts, that would mean he'd be moving to Atlanta with his family."

"That's right, more family in town." Jane followed him into the bathroom and turned on the shower. "I'm getting desensitized to it."

"Good," Gordon said, his mouth full of toothpaste. "I was worried about you for a while there."

Jane sat on the edge of the tub. "I love Saturday mornings now that I have you," she said.

"I'm glad. I do too."

"I was thinking of calling Joy to see if she'd like to go for a hike with the dogs. Want to come?"

"I'd like to, but I have to go to the studio. I've got a couple of appointments this afternoon. Victoria's coming, too. I'm going to photograph her in her bridesmaid dress. I'd like to shoot you in your wedding dress, too."

"Michael does too. He wants to feature the dress in

the sample edition and he wants me to model it. I just don't know. Being a fashion model was not part of the plan." She got into the shower and ducked her head under the warm water.

Gordon got in behind her and kissed her shoulder. "Isn't the sample edition due for publication in three weeks?"

"Yes."

"Do you have another model?"

"No."

"Better change the plan."

Jane picked Joy up about an hour later. "Are you sure Hope doesn't want to go?" she asked as the child climbed into the car and hugged Fred.

"She's at Darlene's house, her friend from Savannah," Joy said.

"Have you made any friends at school?"

"Yeah, I'm not that lonely anymore. Melissa came over last weekend. I like her better than any of the kids I go to school with, but some of them are okay too," Joy said.

"Good. I felt a little bad about getting your dad up here to work on my magazine and making you unhappy."

"It's not your fault. He wanted to come up here anyway. He was always saying there was more opportunity up here."

They rode in silence for a while. "Janie?"

"Yes."

"Next Friday is my birthday. I asked Mom and Dad for an Italian greyhound."

"Oh, really, what did they say?"

"They said no. But I was thinking, if you and Grampa gave me one..."

"We can't do that if your parents said no."

Joy looked disappointed. "I didn't really think so,

but it was worth a try." She hugged Fred again and looked out the window.

"Someday you'll be able to make those decisions yourself," Jane said.

"You have to wait until your grown up to do everything," Joy answered.

"Not everything." Jane pulled the car into a parking space at the nature trail.

"What's this place? I've never been here before."

"It's a trail that runs beside the Chattahoochee River. I love coming here." Jane took Fred's leash and got out of the car. Joy got out and came around to the back of the car.

"Can I hold the leash?" she asked.

"Sure, but remember..."

"He's a greyhound," Joy said. "I won't give him the chance to run like the wind."

"So are we doing something special for your birthday?"

"Mom always lets us decide what we want for dinner and she bakes us a cake. If it's okay with Mom, would you and Grampa come?"

"If its okay with your mom, we'd love to."

They walked along the river for about a mile then turned around to come back. Joy asked about the ducks and geese on the river. Then she asked about the birds in the trees and flying overhead. There was a long legged-bird standing on one of the rocks. She pointed to it. "What kind of a bird is that?"

"I don't know and I can't believe I've never wondered," Jane said. She was surprised at herself for taking the birds for granted. "I've seen him out there before. You have a refreshing curiosity about things, Joy." Jane filed away the idea she had for a birthday present for Joy, a book about birds. She'd go to the bookstore this afternoon.

"Would you like to come to my house for lunch, Joy?" Jane asked when they got back into the car.

"Sure," Joy said, excitement lighting her face. "We'll have to ask my mom, though."

"Of course," Jane said, and pulled her cell phone out of her purse. "Here, call her."

Joy dialed the number and pressed send. She spoke to her mother then handed the phone to Jane. "She wants to talk to you."

Jane took the phone. "Hello."

"Yes, it was my idea." She paused, listening. "Yes, we'd love to. I'm sure Gordon doesn't have plans. He knows all of their birthdays, you know." She laughed. "I'll bring her home this afternoon."

"What did she want?" Joy asked.

"She invited us to your birthday dinner on Friday."

"Oh, good!" Joy said.

They arrived at Jane's building. She parked the car in the garage and they rode up in the elevator.

"When I grow up, I'm going to live on the twentieth floor," Joy said.

"You want to live in the sky." Jane laughed. She unlocked the door to her flat and they went inside. There was a hissing sound coming from the corner of the living room.

"Oh, no, Baby." Joy squealed. "How can you stand her, Janie? I'd forgotten she would be living with you now."

"She's not so bad," Jane said. "She loves Fred." They watched as Jane took the leash off of Fred and he scampered over to the cat. He sniffed her nose and she rubbed her head on him. Then he went into the kitchen for some water. "She even washes him. She likes to sleep in his bed, but she'll let him get in, too. It's really going better than I thought it would."

The cat looked at Joy again and hissed. "Well, she doesn't like me," Joy said.

"I'm not sure she likes anyone but Fred and Grampa. She doesn't seem to like me either." Jane had managed to get the cat to curl up on the couch next to her a couple of times, but when she tried to pet her she hissed. Gordon, however, could sit with her and stroke her and talk to her. She seemed to love him. He seemed to love her, too. Jane put her hand to her temple. She suddenly felt a little dizzy.

"Are you all right, Janie?" Joy looked up at her. Her face was swimming.

"I should sit down for a minute." Joy took her hand and guided her to a chair.

"You looked a little funny for a minute. Can I get you some water or something?"

"That would be nice, honey, over in the small fridge at the bar." Jane pointed to the wet bar.

Joy went over and pulled out a bottle of water. She took the top off and brought it to Jane. "What happened?"

"I'm not sure." Jane took a drink from the bottle. "But I feel better now, thank you. Let's have some lunch."

"Jane?" Michael stood in the door of her office on Monday morning.

"Come in, Michael." She turned from the computer and looked at him. "What can I do for you?"

He came into the room and sat down in the chair across form her. "Joy wants an Italian greyhound for her birthday."

"I know, she told me. She said you and Jill said no."

"Well, we didn't want to say yes without thinking it through first, but we've decided to do it. I was wondering if you could advise me about where to get one," he said.

"I got mine at a pet store," Jane said. "It was a spur of the moment decision. I could give you the name of the pet store. Maybe they have another one or they could tell you what breeder they get them from."

"That would be good."

"What changed your mind?"

"She's had the hardest time with this move. Hope

has her best friend here and Alexandra's too young to know the difference, but Joy has struggled," he said. "We were just afraid that if we gave her a dog on her birthday, Hope would want one too. But we talked to Hope and she wants an aquarium. Hope is kind of a nerd. We can deal with two dogs and an aquarium better than we can deal with three dogs."

"You have a cat, too, don't you?" Jane asked.

"Cat's are easy."

"Not Baby."

Michael laughed. "You're right about that, but Dad loves that cat." He stopped laughing and looked at Jane. "Joy told us what happened on Saturday, about your dizziness."

"I've made an appointment with my doctor. I just had a physical, but that's the third time I've had a dizzy spell. She at least needs to know about it."

"I agree," he said. "But I think you're having a problem with my mother. It seems to me it only happens when she's the topic of conversation."

"Joy and I weren't talking about your mother on Saturday."

"No, you were talking about Baby and you know that the reason Dad has Baby is because of my mother. Jane, I think it's an issue you need to deal with." He leaned forward, crossed his arms on the desk between them and looked her in the eye. "I think you need to grieve for her."

"I didn't even know her."

"No, and that's the problem. You feel like you're stepping into a place that is rightfully hers."

"It is rightfully hers."

"Jane, she isn't here to fill that place. You are," he said. "If you grieve for her, you'll be able to accept it, just like the rest of us have."

"I don't know how, Michael."

"Do you want to talk about it? I'm a good listener."

"I have to think about it for a while first, but thank

you. You're a wonderful man, Michael," Jane said. "Just like your dad."

Michael stood and went to the door. He stopped and turned around. "Oh, I forgot. When can we go to the pet store?"

"I don't know if I should go with you. The last time I went in there I bought a dog."

"I won't let you buy a dog—or a cat."

"I don't want a cat," she said. "Can you get away early this afternoon?"

"Sure." He started out the door again then stopped. "Jane, I've scheduled time on Wednesday afternoon to get some shots of you in your wedding dress. Remember we talked about it last week. You have it on your calendar, don't you?"

"Yes, but I'm still not happy about it."

"You will be."

Chapter Fifteen

"Well, I think we can wrap it up for today," Michael said.

"I think we can wrap it up for ever," Jane said. "You're as bad as your dad. You never even gave me a chance to smile at the camera."

"I didn't want pictures of you smiling at the camera." Michael was walking around switching off lights. They had been working in the studio on her wedding dress shots for about an hour.

"That is just the strangest feeling having a camera snapping at you every second or so." Jane went into the dressing room to change back into her suit. She was pulling on her shoes when she came back out. "Did you call the breeder the pet store told us about?"

"Yes, we've got a puppy coming tomorrow. Those little things are really expensive."

"I know. I got a deal on mine because he'd been in the pet store for so long. They told me he'd be neurotic, but he isn't."

"Well, they have champion quality, show quality, and pet quality. We definitely took pet quality. Still cost a pretty penny, though." He shrugged. "It's worth it if it helps Joy adjust to the move. I was wondering if you would keep it overnight."

"I'd like to, but I'm a little worried that Baby will hurt it," Jane said.

"Keep it in a crate. I have one in the trunk of my car. It'll be okay. It's a female, two months old. They've already spayed the thing. They don't want to take a chance on

breeding pet quality dogs. It makes them sound like damaged goods."

"I'm sure Joy will love that dog just as if it was a
champion." Jane went to the door. "I want to see those
pictures when they're developed. I'm going back to my
office. I have a few things to finish up before I go home."

She made a few stops on the way, checked in with
the other employees, then settled in behind her desk reading applications for food and entertainment director.

"Jane." She looked up. Michael stood in the doorway.
"I've got a couple of those pictures developed. I thought
you might like to see them."

"Only if they're good, I hate looking at bad pictures
of myself."

"They're good," Michael said. He put two pictures
down on the desk in front of her. "Don't touch them.
They're not completely dry yet."

"Michael, they're..."

She was interrupted by a commotion at the door.
"How dare you! You meddling bitch!" Lauren rushed up
to the desk and leaned across it. "You have no right to
interfere with my care of my child!"

"I'm sorry, Jane," Amanda said, rushing into the
room behind Lauren. "I tried to stop her, but she pushed
past me!"

"Lauren, what's going on?" Michael pulled her back
from the desk.

"Don't touch me, Michael!" Lauren wrenched her
arm away from him and pointed her finger at Jane. "Have
you ever watched your child gasping for breath? Have you
ever had to feed your baby through a tube? You should
know the facts before you start interfering!

Michael slipped out of the room.

"Lauren," Jane said. "I don't know what you're talking about. Sit down and explain it to me."

"Please, Mamma, let me go to the fizcalist." Jane
noticed for the first time that Maggie was clinging to her
mother's shirttail. She had tears in her eyes and was
pleading with her about something.

Michael came back into the room with Grant. "Lauren." Grant pulled her away from the desk and held her by the arms. "What's wrong? Tell me."

"When we went to Maggie's new pediatrician today, do you know what she asked him?"

"What?"

"She asked him if she was healthy enough to play soccer." Lauren was shrieking. "Can you believe it, without even talking to me about it first? And when I asked her why she did it, she said, 'Janie told me to.'"

"Daddy," Maggie said, pulling at his pants leg now. "Please let me go to the fizcalist. I want to play soccer. He said I could if I went to the fizcalist." Grant looked down at the tear stained face of his daughter. Then back at Lauren.

"What's a fizcalist?" he asked.

"A pediatric physical therapist, the new doctor said he wanted her to work with one until spring. He said they would decide then if she could play soccer." Lauren was sobbing now. She had her arms wrapped around her body defensively.

Grant looked again at the tear stained face of his daughter. He released one of Lauren's arms and put his hand on Maggie's cheek.

"You know we can't let her do it, Grant. You know we can't." Lauren begged him to agree. "She'll die, Grant. Don't you remember? You remember. You were there with me. All those tubes and she still couldn't breathe."

"Daddy, Mamma, please..?" Maggie wailed.

Michael scooped Maggie up into his arms and started talking quietly to her. Grant pulled Lauren into his arms and she buried her face in his chest. She was still murmuring something to him but the words turned to sobs and he closed his eyes and took a deep breath.

"Lauren," he said. "Where is Gary?"

She looked up at him, her expression confused. "Gary?"

"Oh, my God," Grant said. "Michael, would you take Maggie to your house?"

"Of course, Grant. I'll go by and pick up Gary. He'll be wondering why there's nobody home when he gets off the school bus."

"Yes, thank you." Grant looked back at Jane. "Are you all right?"

Both of her hands covered her mouth. She nodded. "I'm sorry, Grant. I didn't mean..."

"It's not your fault, Jane." Grant led Lauren out of the room speaking quietly to her.

"Jane, are you all right?" Michael asked.

"I'm sorry, Janie. I guess I was right. Mamma did get mad."

"I guess I gave you some bad advice, Maggie. I'll need to be more careful next time." Jane got up and went over to where Michael held Maggie in his arms.

"I know it doesn't seem like it right now, but I think it was exactly the right advice," Michael said. "Jane, this has been building for a long time. Kathy and I have both tried to talk to him about it, but he's as frightened as she is." He looked down at Maggie. "And I know that was scary, but I want you to know how proud I am of you. You really stood up for what you wanted."

"I really wanna play soccer," Maggie said. She looked at the door that her parents had just walked through. "Will Mamma be all right?"

"Everyone will be all right, Maggie." Michael kissed her forehead. He looked at her. "If the fizcalist says no, what will you do?"

"I'll do it anyway. I really wanna play soccer. I wanna ride a bike, too."

"I hope he doesn't say no," Michael said.

"Me too," Jane said.

"Me too," Maggie said.

Jane was afraid to face Gordon that evening. Michael had left the office with Maggie right after the incident. She hadn't seen any more of him that day. She'd worked as long as she could, but when she realized her lack of concentration, she went home. She and Fred went for a walk around the park and then came back to think about something to eat.

The walk had been good for her. Her nerves were steadier now. She pulled into the garage, and felt another surge of anxiety when she saw Gordon's car parked in the space next to hers. She went up in the elevator holding Fred and let herself into the flat.

Gordon was sitting at the bar. He had poured two drinks and was working on one. "Would you like one?" he asked.

"Yes. Thank you." Jane took off Fred's collar and hung it on the hook by the door. She went over to the bar and sat on the stool next to Gordon.

"Michael called me at the studio and told me what happened," he said. "Are you all right?"

She felt her face crumple and covered it with her hands. "I hate to cry," she said.

"I know." Gordon stood and put his arms around her.

"I'm sorry, Gordon. It really was just an innocent comment. I had no idea it would have such an impact."

"Tell me," he said.

"It was the day we were at the dog park, remember, before we were married. Lauren had gone to do something with Gary and while she was gone Maggie asked me if I thought she was healthy enough to play soccer." She sniffed and wiped her nose with a napkin. "I had seen the look on her mother's face when I told her I was sure she would learn to ride a bike, so I wasn't going to say 'of course you are.' I thought telling her to ask her doctor was the perfect answer." She blew her nose and walked around the bar. Turning on the cold water in the sink, she bathed her face.

"It was the perfect answer."

"No, it wasn't. I should have told her to talk to her mother about it."

"You're wrong. Lauren would have told her not to

ask." He rubbed his eyes. "Jane, they've both had a hard time seeing that little girl as a real person. I think when they look at her they see that fragile infant that almost didn't make it."

"You can't blame them for that."

"I don't, but she isn't that infant anymore. They've overcome those problems. She still has some health issues, but they aren't crippling." He took a deep breath. "She was going to rebel against their authority eventually. This was something that needed to happen."

"Maybe, but I feel terrible that I was the one that caused it."

"You weren't. Maggie was. She'd had enough. She asked your advice because she knew it would be good. And it was." Gordon rubbed his eyes again. "I just wonder if I should try to contact Grant. I hate what he's going through right now."

"Me too," Jane said. She remembered the look on Grant's face when he saw his tearful daughter begging for his support, then when he looked at his distraught wife. She didn't say anything about it. She could spare Gordon that.

"Would you like something to eat?" she asked. "I have some vegetable soup and some rolls?"

"That would be nice. I'll help you." He followed her into the kitchen. They worked together to prepare the light meal, ate in silence then cleaned the kitchen.

"Maybe I should call Michael," Gordon said. "He has Gary and Maggie. He'll have heard from Grant." The buzzer on the intercom sounded. Gordon went to it and pressed the button. "Yes?"

"Dad, it's Grant."

Gordon pressed the button and told him to come up. When the doorbell rang a few minutes later, Jane released a breath she wasn't aware she'd been holding. Gordon opened the door. Grant came in. He looked drawn.

"I guess you heard what happened today," he said to his father.

Gordon nodded.

"I'm really sorry, Jane." Grant looked at her. "I can't believe I let things get to that point."

"You're as scared as Lauren is, Grant." Gordon put his hand on Grant's shoulder. "It's completely understandable."

"Maybe, but Michael and Kathy have been warning me for a while." He rubbed his face with one hand. "I just didn't listen." He looked at his father. "Why didn't you say something, Dad?"

"You weren't ready to hear it," Gordon said. "Where is Lauren now?"

"She's in the hospital. I didn't know what to do, but she was so hysterical, I had to do something. I took her to the emergency room. They admitted her and gave her some medication to calm her. I stayed until she was asleep."

"Are the kids still with Michael?"

"Yes. Lauren's mother came in from Rome. She'll watch them until we work things out. I need to go and get them now, but I wanted to see you first." Grant sat on the couch and put his face in his hands. His shoulders started to shake. "I knew this was happening. Why didn't I do something, Dad?"

Gordon sat on the arm of the couch and gathered his weeping son into his arms. He pulled Grant's head against his chest and resting his cheek against it, he spoke quietly to him. Jane backed out of the room and went into the kitchen. She gulped a couple of times and poured herself a glass of water. She could hear Gordon's soothing voice as he spoke to his son.

A few minutes later Grant came into the kitchen. "I really am sorry you took the brunt of this, Jane. I hope you know you didn't do anything wrong."

"Don't worry about me Grant. I'll be fine."

"I want you to know that I'll continue to make the same effort I have for the magazine, but I may have to take some time during the day."

"I know. Lauren will need support."

"Yes, she will, and I need to take Maggie back to

the pediatrician and get a referral for the fizcalist." They smiled at each other. Grant crossed the kitchen, put his arms around Jane and hugged her. He kissed her on the cheek and left.

Jane went back into the living room after she heard the door close behind Grant. Gordon was sitting on the couch, staring straight ahead. She sat down next to him.

"That was brutal," he said.

Jane nodded. "It was. Is there anything I can do?"

"He's really a great kid, Jane. He didn't mean to let things get out of control. He really is frightened about that little girl."

"I know, he's told me."

"And Lauren's not crazy. I know she's let herself get worked into a state," he said.

They both smiled.

"That's Victoria's word, Gordon," Jane said.

"I know. It's a good word." He rubbed his eyes again.

Jane pulled his hands away from his eyes and said, "If you keep doing that you'll break blood vessels."

"I'll stop then." He smiled at her.

She held his hands in hers. "Do your eyes hurt?"

"No. It's just a nervous habit."

His eyes were watery. Tears, she wondered? "Gordon, how old is Maggie? I've forgotten."

"Let's see." He focused on something in midair. "She's five. She'll be six on January 14th." He paused in thought. "That's right, January 14th. Why?"

"I just thought she seemed older than that, even though she's so small."

They both sat quietly for a minute. Jane had let go of one of Gordon's hands and was holding the other in both of hers.

"You know what, Jane?" Gordon said. "Grant and Lauren have been way too stingy with Maggie. I think I'll work on developing a better relationship with that little girl." He smiled. His eyes dry now.

"So," Victoria said to Jane. They were in the propagation house of the nursery. Jane had dropped by before work to talk to her about her family disaster. "You've been married to the guy for one month and you've already put one of his family members into the psycho ward."

"Tori, this is not funny," Jane said. "I came here for support, not jokes."

"How many times have you told me to look for the humor in every situation?" Victoria asked. "I'm not laughing at you or at them, but you have to admit, that's got to be a record." She crossed the room to her friend and put her arms around her, being careful not to touch her with her dirt-covered gloved hands.

"What are you two doing?" Jeff said from behind them.

Victoria looked back at him. "I didn't hear you come in. Jane has put one of Gordon's children in the mental hospital, and I was just trying to comfort her."

"Tori, that's a horrible thing to say," Jane said, pulling away.

"I'm kidding." Victoria pulled her back close. "Jeff, Jane is having family problems and I'm trying to make her see that it's not the end of the world."

"What's going on? I never saw you upset so often before you met this guy." Jeff put his hand on her shoulder. "Do I need to do something?"

"No," Jane said. "But it's nice to know you would. I just need to stop sticking my nose where it doesn't belong."

"That's not true, Jane," Victoria said. "You didn't do anything but answer her question, and you answered it right."

"Okay, you're going to have to fill me in, you two," Jeff said.

"One of Gordon's grandchildren, the one that's named for his dead wife—"

"Tori, don't refer to her like that," Jane said.

"How else should I refer to her?"

Jane thought about it for a minute. "Well, I don't know, but not like that."

"Anyway," Victoria went on, "apparently the child had a hard time at birth. There was something wrong with her lungs. Is that right, Jane?"

"Yes, and they had to feed her through a tube so she wouldn't aspirate food."

"It was really tough going there for a while." Victoria was getting into the story. "The parents couldn't do anything but watch and hope."

"Don't be dramatic, Tori."

"Well it's true. Anyway," She looked back to Jeff and continued, "medical science was able to deal with the problems that the child had, but the problems that the parents developed during the process were never dealt with. They became very overprotective. The little girl had some minor health problems, but the parents blew them way out of proportion."

"Tori, you should write fiction. You're good," Jane said.

"This isn't fiction. It's the real thing." She smiled back at Jane. "Maggie lived to watch television. It was pretty much the only thing her parents would let her do."

"We don't know that was all they let her do," Jane said.

"She developed a keen interest in soccer," Victoria continued, ignoring Jane's interruption. "She learned everything she could about the game. She watched soccer teams from all over the world. More than anything in the world, she wanted to play soccer."

"Tori, you've even got me on the edge of my seat," Jane said. "What happens next?"

"When she was at the park one day with Jane, for just a few minutes her mother was out of hearing range and Maggie asked Jane if she thought she was healthy enough to play soccer."

"Don't tell me," Jeff said. "Jane said yes."

"No. Jane was smarter than that. She told her to ask her doctor. Isn't that a perfect answer?"

"Yes," Jeff said. "But I don't see where the problem is. It was up to the doctor. Isn't he the one who should make the decision?"

"Yes, but you've forgotten about the problems that the parents developed while they helplessly watched their infant daughter struggling for her life, back when she was born with all those problems." Victoria continued, "Maggie knew she couldn't tell her mother what she was planning to ask her doctor when she went. So she just sprung it on her."

"What do you mean?" Jeff demanded.

"She just asked the doctor, out of the blue, if she was healthy enough to play soccer."

"What did he say?"

"He said he wanted her to work with a pediatric physical therapist until spring soccer season, and they would decide then."

"I still don't see the problem," Jeff said.

"With all the built-up anxiety, it drove the mother over the edge of her carefully guarded sanity, and she lost control. She charged into Jane's office accusing her of being a...what was it, Jane?"

"A meddling bitch."

"A meddling bitch. Grant had to take her to the emergency room and they admitted her to the psycho ward."

"I don't know if that's where they put her, Tori," Jane said.

"Of course it is." Victoria looked at Jane and took a deep breath. "I'm sorry, Jane. I guess I shouldn't have had any fun with it. The thing is they can deal with stuff like this very well these days. There are drugs that can help. There are all kinds of therapy. I've even heard that massage therapy can help with this kind of thing. It's true what Gordon and Michael said. This needed to happen. Lauren will get the help she needs now and Maggie will be able to really live the life she fought so hard for."

Jane's face crumpled and she covered it with her hands. "I wish I could believe that. I just feel so bad about the whole thing."

"Jane, you never cry." Jeff put his arms around her and her sobs increased in tempo.

"Jane," Victoria said. "Whenever I feel like this, what helps me the most is getting my hands in the dirt. Here, give me your hands."

Jane looked at Victoria as she pulled her hands, one by one, away from her face and placed gardening gloves on them. She put a clay pot in front of her and started spooning soil ingredients into it.

"What are you doing, Tori?"

"I want you to mix this soil. It needs to be mixed thoroughly. See all of these seedlings over here? They each need to be transplanted into a pot this size." Victoria stood back. "You instruct her, Jeff." She turned and went to the far end of the greenhouse to gather more pots.

"Tori, I'm dressed for work. I can't dig in the dirt."

"You'll be fine. Just take off your blazer."

Jeff took Jane's blazer by the collar and helped her pull it off over her gloved hands. Then he started to tell her how to crush the pieces of moss and mix the soil.

"Is this good enough?" Jane asked.

"It's fine," Jeff said.

Victoria looked over at the pot Jane was working on. "You would never have let me get away with that, Jeff. There are still clumps in there. Mix some more, Jane."

Jane went to work on the pot. It actually felt good to crush the lumps of moss between her fingers and thumb. She wiped her face with the back of her hand. The greenhouse was moist, not hot really, but moist. "You know, this is kind of fun."

Victoria looked over at her pot. "What do you think, Jeff?"

"Looks pretty good to me."

Jane wiped the other cheek with the back of her wrist.

"Here," Victoria said. "Jeff, show her how to put this seedling in."

Jeff started to instruct Jane on potting the seedlings.

Something snapped. Jane looked up, recognizing the sound. "What are you doing here?"

Michael stood in the door with a camera draped around his neck. He was looking down at it. "I was worried about you after yesterday, so..." Snap.

"Stop that," Jane said. She noticed the smiles on Victoria and Jeff's faces. "You two stop smiling."

"When you didn't show up at work this morning, I called Dad at the store." Snap. Snap. Snap. "He told me you were planning to stop here." Snap. Snap. "So I came by to make sure you were all right." Snap. Snap. Snap.

"Why did you bring a camera?" Jane asked.

"Jane, keep planting. I've prepared all these pots. Put the seedlings in before they dry out," Victoria said.

Snap. Snap.

Jeff started to move the pots and seedlings in front of her. "Hurry Jane, their roots will dry out."

Snap.

"I take a camera everywhere I go. Photography is my life, remember." Snap.

"Are you two in on this with him?" Jane looked at Victoria and Jeff.

Snap. Snap.

"They're in these pictures, too, Jane." Snap. "This wasn't planned." Snap. "But it's gonna be great."

"Stop it." Jane picked up a clump of dirt and flung it at Michael. He dodged out of the way just as Victoria was bringing another pot from the other side of the room. The soil hit her on the cheek.

"Hey," she said, and putting the pot down, she picked a clump of dirt, leaned across the work table and smeared it on Jane's blouse.

"Tori, I was aiming at him. Hitting you was an accident." She picked up another clump and flung it at

Victoria. Jeff jumped behind Jane and wrapped his arms around her locking her arms to her side.

The camera snapped five times in succession then Michael grabbed Victoria around the waist with one hand and caught her hand just before it flung another clump of dirt.

"That's enough, ladies," Jeff said.

They were all laughing by this time.

"You were right, Tori. Getting my hands in the dirt did help. I feel much better now." She looked down at the seedlings she had planted. "I hope these will do okay."

"They will," Victoria said. "Why don't you take one with you?"

"I don't know. I'm not good with plants."

"You're changing, Jane. Give it a try. I'll help."

"Okay." Jane picked up one of the pots. "Michael, I have to go home and change before I can come to work. I'll see you in a while."

"Great. I'll walk out with you," he said, and they left the nursery together.

Chapter Sixteen

"Happy Birthday," Gordon and Jane said together, when Joy answered the door on Friday night. Jane carried a large black bag on her shoulder. She handed Joy the package she was carrying in her hand, and handed the bag to Jill who took it into the other room.

Gordon handed Joy a package he was carrying and she smiled and offered her cheek to both of them for a kiss.

"How does it feel to be in the double digits?" Gordon asked.

"I don't feel much different than before," Joy said. "But I'm having a nice day."

"Joy was our first grandbaby," Gordon said to Jane. "We loved the name they chose. A joy is exactly what she's been from day one." He picked her up and held her in his arms.

"Grampa," Joy said, and began to laugh. "I'm too big for this."

"You'll never be too big for this," Gordon said. He kissed her neck which made her squeal.

"Dad, would you like something to drink?" Michael asked. He was standing in front of the liquor cabinet. "There's wine in the kitchen. How about you, Jane?"

"A glass of white wine would be nice."

"Same for me," Gordon said.

They all went into the kitchen while Joy took her gifts and put them on the dining room table.

Jill was busy preparing dinner. "I'm so glad you could come. Joy was really excited about having you. She chose vegetable lasagna, mixed salad, and garlic bread for dinner. I hope that's all right with you. Joy has decided to be a vegetarian."

"Really?" Gordon said. "Imagine that. Dinner sounds great to me."

"Me too," Jane said. "I do eat meat, but not very much."

"Joy says she won't eat anything that had a face or had a mother." Jill smiled proudly. "She's growing up way too fast."

"Grampa!" Hope flew into the room and wrapped her arms around Gordon.

"There's my carrot top." Gordon swung her into his arms and kissed her cheek soundly. "How do you feel about your sister getting so old?" he asked as he set her back down.

"I'm happy because I'm right behind her," she said. "Hi, Janie."

"It's good to see you, Hope," Jane said. "You and I haven't really spent much time together. We need to get together sometime and talk. I'd like to get to know you better."

"Okay," Hope said. "I have a present for Joy, too." She held up a small package. "I bought it with my allowance."

"That's nice, Hope," Gordon said.

"I'll put it with the others." Joy held out her hand. "Thanks, Hope."

Suddenly there was a wailing sound coming from the other end of the apartment. Jill stopped what she was doing. "Michael, Alexandra is awake. Would you get her?" she asked.

"Sure." He left the kitchen.

"I figured she would be up late tonight, so I let her nap a little longer than usual. Gordon, would you check on the puppy in our bedroom," she said while Joy was out of the room. "She's still in the bag you brought her in. There's a crate in there. Maybe she should be transferred to it."

"Sure." Gordon left.

"Thank you for keeping her, Jane."

"I thoroughly enjoyed it. I'd have a hard time giving her back if I didn't know I'll get to see her often. She's really sweet," Jane said.

"She didn't keep you up all night crying?"

"Sorry to tell you this, but she slept in the bed with us, along with Fred and Baby."

"You're kidding." Jill turned the oven off and steered Jane into the living room where Michael and Gordon were talking.

"Everything's just fine," Gordon said.

Alexandra was comfortable in her father's arms until she saw her mother. Then she stretched her chubby arms out. Jill took her and snuggled her to her neck. "We'll give Alexandra a few minutes to wake up. Then we'll have dinner," Jill said.

"Maybe I should open my presents now." Joy smiled at the adults as they sat on various chairs in the living room.

"We usually do it after dinner," Jill said.

"I think Joy has a good idea," Gordon said. "We might even want to go out for a short walk before dinner." He smiled at Michael.

"Let's do the present opening now," Michael said to Jill.

"All right."

Joy went to the table where she had put her gifts. She brought the three packages into the living room, put them on the floor, and sat down behind them.

Hope reached over and grabbed the one she had given her. "I'll tell you when you can open mine."

Joy looked at her. "Why?"

"You'll see."

Picking up Gordon's package, Joy pulled the pretty paper off of it. It was a framed picture. She looked at it. "Grampa, thank you, it's beautiful." She turned the picture around to the room so that they could all see it. It was a picture of Joy, Jane, and Fred at the dog park.

Joy had her hand in front of Fred, palm up. His paw was touching her palm. Jane was smiling beside them.

"That's beautiful, Gordon," Jane said. "You do such good work. I wish..."

"Not interested, sweetheart." He kissed her cheek. Michael, Jane, and Gordon exchanged a smile.

Joy picked up Jane's package. She pulled the paper off. "Jane, thank you. This is great." She held three books in her hands. One about birds, one about flowers, and the last, a book about reptiles.

"I wasn't sure about the reptiles," Jane said. "But I figured if we ever see one on our hikes, you'll probably want to know what it is."

"Thank you, Jane, Grampa." Joy got up and gave each of them a hug and a kiss. Then she reached for Hope's gift.

"No. You'll have to open Mom and Dad's gift first." Joy looked around.

"Mine too," Alexandra wined.

"Mom, Dad, and Alexandra's gift," Hope corrected.

"I'll get it." Michael got up and went down the hall of the apartment. When he came back into the room, he walked right up to Joy and handed her the puppy.

"Uuuhh!" Joy said. "A puppy, you really got me a puppy." She sniffed and tears filled her eyes. The little dog squirmed in her arms and turned to lick her face. It was a beautiful fawn color with no markings.

"I think she might need to go outside. Put her leash and collar on," Jill said.

Hope handed Joy her package. Holding the little dog under her arm, Joy tore the paper of the gift. The little dog licked her face and wagged its tail. Inside there was a small pink collar with rhinestones around it and a matching leash.

"It's beautiful, Hope, thank you!" Joy put the collar on the little dog and all of them went outside to watch her pee. At dinner the dog sat in the crate Michael had placed in the dining room. Beau sat beside it, sniffing the little dog protectively. The meal was wonderful. Everyone was happy, especially Joy.

"Tori, I don't have a food and entertainment director for the sample edition," Jane said. She was sitting in Victoria's kitchen on Sunday morning before they met Jeff for their bike ride.

"What do you want me to do about it?"

"We'll have to do it together."

"Jane, this magazine is your project." Victoria gave her a level glare. "I think I've already helped a lot."

"I'll do the writing. I just need recipes," Jane said.

"Use your recipes."

"I don't cook." She looked thoughtful, remembering feeding Gordon every night for the past month. "I mean nothing but easy stuff."

"Isn't easy stuff what we're looking for here?"

"Yes it is." Jane looked at her hands. "I guess what I'm really asking for is your salad dressing recipe."

"Why didn't you just ask?"

After she had typed the ingredients and instructions on the notebook computer she had brought with her, Jane said, "What kind of lettuce did you use with your salad?"

"That was my own Mesclun."

"Isn't that some kind of hallucinogenic drug?" Jane asked, and then laughed.

"I think it's spelled differently. Anyway, you didn't hallucinate, did you?" Victoria asked.

"No. Is Mesclun a type of lettuce? Did you grow it?"

"It's actually a mix of greens. I used spinach, arugula, and endive—the endive is really important. You could really put any lettuce you wanted in the salad, but you've got to have the endive."

"What was the curly stuff, I really liked that."

"It was curly endive. There was Belgian endive in it, too. They're two of my favorites."

"What was the green stuff you asked if I wanted sprinkled on top?"

"I told you, don't you remember? It was parsley and cilantro. Joe doesn't like it in his salad, but I do, so I do it separately."

"I'll note that it's optional," Jane said. "Then let's see, you had nuts in it. What kind?"

"I don't remember what I put in that night, but I always use either almonds or walnuts. They're heart healthy, but they have to be raw. You can't toast them or sugar them or anything like that."

Jane typed away at the notebook computer she had brought with her. She tapped her chin with her finger. "There was cheese, too. What kind was it?"

"Jane, that was months ago. I don't remember. I usually use blue, gorgonzola, or goat cheese. Take your pick." Victoria huffed. "You better give me credit on this article. If I'm going to do the work, I want the credit."

"We're doing it together," Jane said. "You're getting grumpy in your old age, Tori."

"I am not old."

"Now, how about chicken? I could make a vegetarian version stopping with the nuts and cheese, but if you wanted to you could add chicken." Jane typed some more.

"Why would you want a vegetarian version?"

"A lot of people are vegetarian. Did I tell you Joy is a vegetarian?" Jane asked.

"Joy is a child. She isn't going to read *Second Half*." Victoria looked out the window. "Jeff's here. Shut down your computer. Let's ride. I'm riding my own bike today."

Jane closed the notebook and put it back in its case. She carried it out to the car and the threesome headed for the Silver Comet Trail.

"Jeff, are you coming to Gordon and Jane's for Thanksgiving?" Victoria asked as they rode down the trail. It was crisp and cool outside. The sun was shining and the air was clear.

"For a while...my aunt would be disappointed if I

didn't go to her house at least for a few minutes." He groaned. "I guess I'll eat too much this year. I always do, but I usually only go to one place."

"You don't have to come to our place if you don't want, Jeff."

"David wants me too. He loves that magazine and he's pretty crazy about you, Jane. He's bringing his mother, too."

"I'm very impressed with him, and if he's still smoking pot, I can't tell."

"Oh, he's a pot head? You hadn't told me that, Jane," Victoria said.

"Oops."

"You two aren't keeping secrets from me, are you?"

"No," Jeff said. "Jane was just being discreet. He spent three years in prison, finished school there and had a hard time getting a job when he got out. Jane agreed to give him a chance."

"That's nice of you, Jane."

"I wouldn't have done it if I didn't think he could do the job. And Lenny, his friend is good too. He's just the cutest thing, all full of fun and games, but a great worker. He wrote the short story that we'll put in the sample edition. It's about a sixty-five-year-old woman who becomes a private investigator. It's been done before, but his slant on it is entirely new and quite amusing."

"Was Lenny in prison, too?" Victoria asked.

"Yes, they graduated together."

"Why was he there?"

"I don't know. I assume it was marijuana, like David," Jane said. "I didn't think to ask."

"Well, I can't wait to read his short story," Jeff said.

"Lenny's mother is coming up from Valdosta. I don't know about any of the rest of his family. It'll be nice to meet her."

"Is Anna coming?" Victoria asked.

"Yes, but she'll be by herself. She says she doesn't have any family."

"Everyone has family," Victoria said.

"I don't," Jane said.

"You have us and we're coming. Did I tell you that Patricia and Bob will stop by before they go to Bob's house?"

"Yes, I'll be so happy to see them."

Thanksgiving Day was cool and windy. There were low clouds in the sky and brightly colored leaves were falling in the wind. Jane looked out the window of the living room.

"You're up early," Gordon said, coming into the room from the hallway.

"I couldn't sleep." She smiled and kissed his cheek. "Did you know you snore?"

"I think someone might have told me that before."

"That's right. You had a wife before me." She turned and looked back out the window.

"Are you dizzy, Jane?"

"No." She laughed. "I'm fine."

"I'm looking forward to the party this afternoon." They had rented the banquet room in the building and catered a traditional Thanksgiving dinner, insisting that all the vegetable dishes be prepared without meat products. All of Gordon's family was invited. Victoria and Joe and their family were coming, all of the members of the magazine, and Gordon's staff at the store and studio. It would be a big group."

"I'm a little worried about how Lauren will feel. I haven't talked to her since the problem we had," Jane said.

"Grant says she's all right. He says she's mostly embarrassed." Gordon brushed her hair behind her shoulder.

"That's what he says, but the few times I've seen her, it looks more like anger on her face than embarrassment."

"Well, I guess you rocked her boat a little. She'll

come around. She's a lovely woman, really, Jane. She's just had a tough time."

"I'm sure you're right." Jane just couldn't forget the frightful scene that had taken place in her office.

The two of them showered and went down to the banquet room to decorate. They spent a nice morning making the place festive and went upstairs to change for the party. It was planned for two in the afternoon. They wanted to make a day of it. There was an indoor pool the kids could use, and dinner would be served around four, so it wouldn't be too late night for the youngsters. Gordon had hired a dance band for any adults that wanted to stay after dinner for a while. It was going to be a great day.

When the guests started arriving, Jane and Gordon greeted them. First to arrive were Victoria and Joe, but the rest of the group wasn't far behind. Before they knew it there was a full room. The kids changed their clothes next door in the pool locker rooms and the parents took turns watching the pool.

Joy, Hope, Alexandra, and Michael were the first in the water. Jill sat on the side of the pool dangling her feet. Grant and Gary were in next. Katherine held Teddy, but Eric dove right into the pool.

"He really can swim," Jane commented to Gordon.

"He's done really well. He doesn't have a lot of stamina. You can't let him get to far out because he gets tired and goes under, but he's building his conditioning. I think by next spring, he'll be completely water-safe." They watched as Rick reached out and put a hand under Eric when he started to struggle.

"That's great. Teddy does well, too. Is he in lessons?"

"Yes, but it'll be a little while before he can take off that floating swim suit they have him in," Gordon said.

"This is wonderful, Dad." Katherine said as she approached them holding Valerie. The kids are having a blast. "Where's Maggie?"

"She's inside with Lauren," Jane said. "I saw them

sitting over by the window talking. I guess I should say something to Lauren, try to smooth things over."

"Let me try to get Maggie away from her first," Katherine said. "Here, Dad, you hold Valerie Jane." She handed the baby to Gordon and hurried off to the banquet room.

"You all right, Jane?" Gordon asked, looking at her with concern.

"I'm fine. You need to stop asking me that or I'll get irritated." She sighed, "I am worried about my relationship with Lauren. I don't want to be a source of friction in your family."

"I don't want you to either, but there is always some friction in a family. We'll deal with it." Gordon bounced Valerie when she started to fuss, and sat in a rocker beside the pool. He started to rock, holding the infant in his lap facing the pool.

"You look adorable," Jane said. "Where's a photographer when you need to take a picture of a photographer?" She remembered her camera in her purse and hurried off to get it. When she went into the dining room, she noticed Katherine and Lauren talking animatedly. Maggie cast a pleading look in her direction. Jane smiled, grabbed her camera, and hurried back to Gordon.

She hurried up to him and pressed the button.

"Hey, warn me first," Gordon said. He'd been making a face at the baby.

She pressed the button again.

"See how it feels?" Click, click. "I hope mine turn out at least half as good as yours."

A few minutes later Katherine came back into the pool room with Maggie dressed in her swimming suit. "I guess she was successful in talking Lauren into letting Maggie swim," Gordon said.

"I guess that's my cue to have a word with Lauren," Jane said.

"If you're all right with it, Jane, just don't stress about it."

She leaned down and kissed him and went back

into the banquet room. She put her camera away and went over to where Lauren was sitting by herself looking out the window.

"Lauren," Jane said. "I just wanted to try to get back on track with you. I want you to know that I didn't mean to overstep my bounds with Maggie. I'll be more careful from now on."

"Grant thinks it needed to happen. He says we were smothering her." Lauren said, looking out the window.

"But you don't agree?"

She looked at Jane for a minute then turned back to the window. "I don't know."

"Lauren, what can I do to help us get past this?"

Lauren was quiet for a minute. Then she whispered, "Leave us alone."

"All right." Jane stood. She wasn't sure what she felt about Lauren's words. Was it anger, hurt? Whatever it was, she didn't like it.

"I'm afraid for her to exercise," Lauren said, as Jane turned to walk away.

Jane turned back to her. "I understand that."

"No, I don't think you do."

Jane waited for Lauren to say more, but she didn't.

"I guess it didn't go very well," Gordon said, when he came back into the room with Valerie asleep on his shoulder. Jane had been talking to David, Jeff, and David's mother at the bar when he came in. She excused herself and went over to the little play pen he was putting Valerie into.

"Why do you say that?"

"The look on your face."

"She hates me. I think she blames me for everything. I don't think she believes things ever needed to change," Jane said, rubbing her eyes.

"Don't rub your eyes. You'll break blood vessels." Gordon took her hands.

They smiled at each other. For a minute it felt like there was nobody else in the room. "I'll stop then."

"It'll work out, Jane. Go in by the pool and watch

Maggie play in the water. I promise," Gordon said, looking into her eyes. "It'll work out."

Jane hurried out of the room. She could hear Maggie's happy squeals before she got to the pool.

"Watch, Daddy," she squealed as she jumped from the side of the pool into her brother's waiting arms.

"I hope so," Jane whispered.

Dinner was served buffet style. When the caterers came to set it up, the parents and children were coming in from the pool. They had all changed back into their clothes. Their hair was wet, except for Maggie.

When the child saw Jane directing the caterers, she ran over to her. "Janie, did you see me swimming?"

"Yes, I did." Jane stooped to look at the child. "I didn't know you were so comfortable in the water."

"I swim at the fiscal therpist. It's great fun. I get to walk on a treadmill and I'll start to run some next week."

"That's great, Maggie," Jane said, looking around for Lauren. "Where's your Mamma?"

"She's still in the locker room. She had to pack up the hairdryer. She had to make sure my hair was dry before we go outside."

"That's a good idea." Jane stood up when she saw Lauren come back into the room with a duffle bag. "Maybe you'd better go back and sit with her. We'll be serving dinner soon and Grampa's going to make a little speech."

"Okay." Maggie grabbed Jane's hand and kissed it. "I love you, Janie." She scampered off to her mother.

"Now I'm going to cry," Jane said.

Gordon put his arms around her from behind. "I saw that. I think I might cry too." He turned her in his arms and held her for a minute.

"It's passed, Gordon. I'm all right now. I managed not to make a spectacle of myself." She pulled back a little and kissed him.

"Good, me too," he said. He stepped back and spoke

loudly to the crowd. "Everyone find a seat. We'll have dinner soon and I'd like to say a few words to you first."

The room was bustling with activity for a while, but soon everyone was comfortable at one of the tables. Gordon stood and began by introducing the two newest members of his family.

"First I'd like to welcome my eighth grandchild to the family, Valerie Jane, slumbering peacefully over in the corner. I hope her mother gets a chance to eat some dinner." The laughter was subdued. "Now, I want to welcome my beautiful, new wife." He held out his hand to her. "Stand up, Jane." She did. He kissed her. She blushed and sat back down.

"You never look shy, Jane," Victoria whispered.

"Shut up."

Gordon went on to talk about the magazine and how it had come together. How nice it was that his sons would finally be able to work together. He talked about Victoria and Joe and their family, how much they mean to Jane. He finished by talking about the shop and the studio. He ended by inviting everyone to enjoy the food.

"Before we all eat," a voice called out from the group. Everyone looked over to where Lenny was standing. "I'd like to say something." He had everyone's attention. "One of the reason's I wanted to be here tonight and one of the reasons I wanted my Mom to be here," he looked adoringly at the old woman sitting next to him, "is because it being Thanksgiving, I couldn't think of a better time to say Thank you, Jane." He held up a wine glass. "You've given me a chance I may never have gotten anywhere else. I think that's true pretty much for all for us at *Second Half*. From the bottom of my heart, I want to say, 'Thank you.'

Glasses clinked, people cheered, and Jane blushed.

Chapter Seventeen

Jane sat in her office looking out the big window onto the street. It was a cold December day. The sun was shining, but there was an icy wind. She watched the people on the street snuggling into their jackets and hurrying to get inside.

"Jane, are we interrupting you?" David stood at the door of her office. Lenny and Anna stood behind him.

"You're interrupting me staring out the window," she said. "What can I do for you?"

The three of them filed into the office. Anna and David sat while Lenny remained standing. He walked around the office looking at pictures, books, whatever he could find.

"You have a hard time sitting still, don't you, Lenny? You're as bad as a kid," Jane said.

"I am a kid. I just can't seem to grow up."

Jane looked at her team. "So, what's up?"

"Anna and Lenny have come up with an idea for an ad campaign," David said. "We'd like to run it by you."

"Great, go ahead."

Anna began, "I've about finished the designs for the first set of 'business comfortable' clothing. I was thinking a fashion show would be a good idea."

"A fashion show?" Jane didn't look enthusiastic. "I hadn't intended to get into the modeling business when I started this."

"I know, but I think it would be great for the line of clothing," Anna said. "I was thinking we could make the show for charity. Maybe use one of the prominent country clubs for it. Invite the whole city. Donate some tickets to the leading industries in town. That way we could appeal to the uniform segment of the market."

"You think your designs could translate to uniforms?" Jane asked.

"Easily."

"This sounds expensive." She wasn't at all sure this was a good idea.

"It would be, but I think it would pay off. With the sample edition already in all the newsstands and magazine racks, people will have seen the wedding clothes," David explained. "Since I've distributed samples to all of the waiting rooms in Georgia, I've had a tremendous subscription response. I've even gotten a pretty good response from the subscription companies."

"You've done a spectacular job, David," Jane said. "All of you have." She looked at Lenny. "What does this have to do with you?" she asked.

"I'm pretty much here for moral support. Anna told me about her idea first. I encouraged her to take it to David." Lenny stood behind Anna. He put his hand on her shoulder. "She's a pretty smart cookie," he said, smiling fondly at her.

"Get me an estimate. I need to know what it will cost before I can make a decision," Jane said. "Have you thought about the cost of models?"

"We thought we'd start with you and Victoria," Lenny said.

"That's out of the question!" Jane said. "I am not a fashion model and neither is Tori."

"Okay, okay!" Lenny said. "Michael has hired some very beautiful women. I don't think it'll be too bad."

"Anna, if you want to get into the uniform market, you'll have to have a line for men. Have you thought of that?"

"Yes, I'm already working on it."

"How's the manufacturer working out?"

"Good. They do good work."

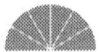

The phone was ringing when Jane opened her front door. She rushed to pick it up. "Hello."

"Could I speak to Gordon Fox?" a female voice asked.

"He isn't here right now. Could I take a message?"

"Who am I speaking too?"

"I'm his wife."

"Mrs. Fox, I didn't realize Eric had a grandmother. I thought she was dead."

"I'm Gordon's second wife. Is there something I can do for you?" Jane was starting to get irritated.

"Do you know how I could reach Mr. Fox? I'm calling from the children's hospital. Eric and my son Kevin had a swimming lesson this afternoon. Katherine had to go to the airport to pick up Rick, so I volunteered to take Eric. There was an accident at the pool. Eric is all right, but they're going to keep him overnight for observation. I can't get hold of Katherine. Her cell phone is off..."

Jane couldn't hear anymore of what the woman was saying. Her ears were ringing and she couldn't breath. She sat down and took a deep breath.

"Mrs. Fox, are you there? My concern is that Eric is so agitated that I'm afraid he'll pull his IV out. I have to physically restrain him. I was hoping his grandfather could come here and calm him down until I can reach Katherine."

"I'll be right there," Jane said.

"Good, I'll tell him his Grandma is coming."

"No, that will confuse him. Tell him Janie is coming."

Jane wrote a quick note for Gordon on the dry erase board in the kitchen and hurried out the door. She didn't even remember the drive to the hospital. Luckily it was only one exit north on highway 400. She hurried to the information desk, found out the room number, and ran to the stairs. She couldn't wait for the elevator.

When she rushed into the room she found a stout dark haired woman sitting on the bed restraining a sobbing Eric.

"Janie!" Eric shrieked when he saw her. She ran to him and pulled him into her arms being careful to protect the IV. Eric buried his wet face in her neck. "I drowned, Janie. I thought I could make it to the other side, but I started to go under. I kicked as hard as I could and tried to yell, but the water came in my mouth. It went in my nose and my tummy." The horror of the experience spilled from the sobbing child.

Jane turned around, sat on the bed, and rocked him back and forth. "I'm so sorry, Eric, so sorry." Jane spoke softly to Eric. His sobs were still coming hard, but he had stopped struggling. His grip on her neck was so tight it hurt, but Jane didn't care. Her blouse was wet from his tears. "I'm sorry, baby," she repeated.

"I thought I could make it in the deep end, so I swam out there when the teacher was with Kevin." Eric's small voice was steadying some now. "But I just couldn't do it." He hiccoughed again. The sobs were slowing now, and he was loosening his hold on Jane's neck. She eased him down onto her lap and cradled him against her chest.

"You're all right now, Eric," Jane said. "Everything will be okay," she said.

"When I threw up the water, it went up my nose again. It hurt real bad," Eric said.

"I'm sure it did."

"Then they put a tube in my throat. That hurt, too." His breath was coming in short gasps. "And look what they did to my arm." He held up the arm with the IV in it.

"Oh, Eric, you've been through so much. I wish I'd been with you," Jane said.

"Me too." He buried his head in her chest and wept gently. She rocked him back and forth.

Jane looked across the room at the woman standing by the window. "You must be Kevin's mother."

"Yes, I'm Susan. I'm so sorry. I had just gone to the

locker room for a minute. The instructor was with them, but when I got back I saw him under the water. He ventured out on his own, but we should have been watching him more closely."

"Accidents happen," Jane said. "Why did they intubate him?"

"His lungs were full of water. He couldn't breathe. I'm not sure what they did, but it worked. They have him on antibiotics to avoid any infection and they want to watch him overnight."

"If you need to go now, that's fine," Jane said. "I'll stay here until Katherine can be located."

"All right, if I can't reach her beforehand, she'll come to my house to get him." Susan left the room quietly.

Jane settled onto the bed more securely and resettled Eric. After a minute the door opened and Gordon came in looking anxious. "Hey, buddy," he came to the bed and stroked Eric's head.

"Grampa, I drowned." Eric turned to look at Gordon but did not relinquish his hold on Jane.

"You drowned, Eric. That must have been terrible."

"It was." He buried his face in Jane's chest again. Gordon sat down on the bed beside them and continued to stroke Eric's head. Speaking quietly to him, he leaned down and kissed his brow.

"Thank you, Jane." Gordon put his arm around her and kissed her cheek.

"I don't even remember the drive over. I hope I didn't run over anyone."

"I didn't see anything on the road on my way."

The three of them sat quietly together. Jane didn't know how long, just that it felt good to hold Eric. He had stopped crying now and his eyelids were looking heavy. He still clung to her, but not as tightly.

The door opened and Katherine rushed in. For the first time since Jane had arrived, Eric released her and stretched his small arms toward his mother. She scooped him up and he clung to her neck, much the same as he had with Jane.

Guiding the IV line safely to Katherine, Jane and Gordon slipped off the bed and walked to the window together. Katherine was crying. There were tears on her cheeks and her eyes were red. Gordon gave her a minute then went over to them and put his arms around the small group.

"Everything's all right now, Kathy, poor Eric's had a very bad time, though."

"I just can't believe this happened. I guess I pushed him too hard. Rick always told me I was pushing too hard."

"This isn't your fault, Kathy. Accidents happen."

"It's my fault." Eric started to cry again.

"No, baby, it isn't." Katherine rocked him. "Oh, Eric, I'm sorry."

"It's okay, Mamma," Eric said.

Jane smiled at the scene before her. "Where's Rick?" she asked.

Katherine looked over at Jane as if it was the first time she'd noticed her. "Jane, Susan said that you came as soon as she called. Thank you so much."

"Of course, I love this little boy."

"Rick is in the car with the babies. I have to take them back home. Rick will stay the night with Eric. I just had to see him." She buried her face in the child's hair again, still crying. "I want to stay, but I'm still nursing Valerie."

"I'll go get Rick," Gordon said. "You can stay at least until Eric goes to sleep. I'll take the babies home. I can handle them that long."

"Oh, Dad, would you?"

"Of course. Do you have a bottle prepared for Valerie Jane?"

"Yes."

"Then we'll be fine. I'll go on now. I'm sure Rick needs to see Eric, too."

"I'll go too," Jane said. She leaned down to kiss Eric on the head and he put his arms around her again.

"I love you, Janie." He pressed his cheek against hers.

"I love you, too, Eric." Jane sniffed. "I can't believe how easily I cry these days." She smiled at Katherine and dashed a tear from her cheek.

Katherine squeezed her hand and smiled.

When Jane got to the car, Rick was hurrying away. He stopped and put his arms around her. "Thank you," he said, hurrying toward the hospital.

"I'll take Kathy's van home with the babies," Gordon said. Jane looked in the window. Both kids were slumbering peacefully in their car seats. "She can bring my car when she comes. I gave Rick the keys."

"I'll go home and walk Fred, and then I'll join you."

"You don't have to, Jane." Gordon pulled her into his arms.

"I want to."

He leaned back and looked at her face. "You've really adjusted to this family. It's scary, isn't it?"

"Terrifying, what if...no I won't even think it."

"I know." Gordon put his hand on her blouse. "You're drenched. You should probably get out of these wet clothes. Where is your jacket? You must be freezing."

"It's Eric's tears," she said, rubbing the wet spots on her blouse. "I guess I forgot my jacket in my rush." She shivered, noticing the cold for the first time.

"Eric's tears and snot and drool," Gordon said. He took off his jacket and wrapped it around Jane. "You take this. Kathy's car is still warm. I'll see you in a while." He kissed her quickly, then kissed her again more deeply.

An hour later, Jane rang the doorbell at Katherine's house. Gordon opened it with a smile. "I'm glad you're here. I was just giving Teddy his dinner." He went back to the kitchen.

"Where's Valerie?"

"She's still sleeping. I figured I'd let her sleep until she's hungry. I think that's what you do at her age."

Teddy was sitting in the highchair eating some kind

of noodles. "Hi, Janie," he sang, when she came into the room.

"What are you eating, Teddy?" she said as she sat beside him.

"Mac and gronie," he said. She looked at Gordon.

"Macaroni," he said. "Easy Mac." He picked up the box and showed it to her. "He loves it."

Teddy picked up his fork and stabbed a few more pieces. "Ah wove it," he said, stuffing it into his mouth.

The crying started in the other room and Gordon said, "I'll get her. Teddy's pretty self-sufficient, but would you stay with him in case he needs some help?"

"Sure." Jane looked back at Teddy. He was smiling at her. "Is there anything I can get you, Teddy?"

"No." He stuffed more macaroni into his mouth.

Gordon came back into the kitchen. "If you two are all right, I'll go up and change her before I give her the bottle."

"We're fine," Jane said. She got up and went to the refrigerator. The bottle of breast milk was in the door. She pulled it out and put a pot of hot water on the stove. She adjusted the heat and put the bottle in then turned back to Teddy. His bowl was empty and he was smiling at her.

"Cookie, please," he said.

"Can he have a cookie?" Jane asked Gordon, as he walked back into the room.

"Sure, they're in that cabinet." He pointed. "You started the bottle heating," he asked as he put Valerie on his shoulder and started to bounce. She was crying and squirming in his arms. "Kathy says you can heat it in the microwave, but I'm just not comfortable with that," he said, as he bounced around the room.

Jane laughed.

"What are you laughing at?"

"You bouncing around the room. It's the cutest thing I've ever seen."

"Bouncing makes them happy. Haven't you ever heard the phrase 'bounce a baby'?" Gordon continued to bounce.

"Yes, but I always visualized it on one's knee."

"At this age, it has to be the shoulder." He stopped at the stove and picked up the bottle. He rotated it a few times then holding the baby in the crook of his arm, he tested the milk on his wrist. "Perfect." He sat in the rocker in the corner of the room and offered the nipple to Valerie. She took it into her mouth and started sucking the milk out noisily.

"She's a good baby, isn't she?"

"Yeah, she is. They can be tyrants, but she's not," Gordon said. "I think it's the red hair. All the redheaded kids have been tough, but the others are easy."

"Well, her hair is certainly not red. I don't think I've ever seen a baby that young with that much black hair," Jane said.

"A lot of them are born with black hair and it falls out and comes in another color, but hers hasn't fallen out. I think it's going to stay. It'll probably gray early, though, like mine."

"Mine too." Jane watched Gordon rock the baby as he fed her. "I love you, Gordon."

He looked up and smiled.

"Rampa," Teddy said. "Down."

"Just a minute, Buddy," Gordon said.

"I'll get him," Jane said. She looked at the food smeared all over his face and picked up a clean dish towel. She dampened it with the faucet and cleaned his face and hands. Then she took the tray off the high chair and lifted him out of it.

"Ah go playroom." Teddy toddled out of the room. Jane started to follow.

"He's all right, Jane. Stay here with me," Gordon said. "He'll let us know if he needs anything."

She sat back down at the table. "You've done a lot of this," she said.

"A lot." He smiled at the feeding infant in his arms.

"I haven't done much at all. I sat for Tori's girls when they were little, but not a lot. I mostly did stuff with them with Tori along," she said. "In fact, you should have seen the look on my face when Tori told me that women actually pump their breast milk." She laughed remembering how pale Jeff had gotten and how surprised they both had been.

"I try not to think about that."

"Jeff got squeamish about it too."

"It's not so much that I'm squeamish, but I have a problem envisioning my little girl pumping her breast milk. Oh, God." He closed his eyes and shook his head.

Jane laughed. "I guess that is hard."

After Gordon had fed Valerie the whole bottle, he burped her and said, "Let's go check on Teddy." They went into the playroom. Teddy had spread pretty much all of the toys around the room and seemed to be having a wonderful time.

"Hi, Rampa," he said. "Ah show games." He started picking up different toys and showing them to Gordon. Some of his explanations were easy to understand and others were not.

Jane wandered over to the window and looked out. It was dark out, but she could see the tree house. She remembered the nice little party she, Gordon, and the older kids had had out there. She was remembering Gary's fear of them getting mushy, when Teddy pulled on her skirt. Coming back to the present, she looked for Gordon. He was sitting in a chair. Valerie was lying across his lap on her stomach and Gordon was bouncing his knee. She smiled and looked down at Teddy.

"Janie." He held a picture frame up to her. "Look." She took the frame and looked at it. It was a picture of Margaret holding a baby. It must have been Joy or Gary. She was smiling down at the infant. Her face was radiant.

"Ramma," Teddy said.

Jane was trying to go somewhere, but she couldn't move her legs. She struggled as hard as she could, but they must have been stuck in cement or something. There were sounds all around her, but she didn't know what they were. Maybe she was paralyzed, but what had happened. She tried to remember.

There was crying. Oh, that's right, the babies. They were taking care of the babies.

"Jane, wake up, sweetheart." She heard Gordon's voice from a distance. "It's all right, Teddy," he said.

"Dad, what happened?" Whose voice was that? It seemed far away too. She tried to open her eyes, but she couldn't move her eyelids either.

"Jane fainted, Kathy, would you take the kids up to bed. I'll bring her around." It was Gordon's voice again. "Wake up, Jane. Please, baby." He kissed her cheeks.

She opened her eyes and blinked at him. He was very close. "Oh, thank God," he said, kissing her mouth and pulling her into his arms. He sat cross-legged on the floor and rocked her back and forth.

She laughed. It was what she'd done with Eric earlier that evening. "What happened?" she asked, struggling to sit up in his arms.

He held her to his chest. "I don't know. One minute you were looking out the window and Teddy was talking to you and the next you were on the floor." He stopped. "What's this?" He picked up the picture frame and looked at it.

She looked at it, too. "He called her Ramma," she said. Tears started in the lower lids of her eyes and then fell over her cheeks.

Gordon stiffened. "Jane, you've got to deal with this. You scared me to death." He released her from his hold and got up from where he sat on the floor. He held his hands down to her. When she took them, he pulled her to her feet then scooped her into his arms and carried her to a chair. "Do you need to elevate your feet? Are you still dizzy?" He seemed concerned, but he was clearly mad at her.

"Gordon, I didn't do it on purpose."

"You're purposely not dealing with it." He was pacing. "Jane, for God's sake," he paused, worry returning to his face. "Did you see the doctor? There's nothing wrong, is there?"

"I saw the doctor, I'm in perfect health," she said. "I don't know how to deal with it, Gordon. When I figure that out, I will." She stood and walked to the door. "In the meantime, you can storm and rant all you want. I'm going home."

"I am so glad you talked me into this, Tori," Jane said, as she pulled her horse to a stop beside Victoria's. "How did you find this place?"

"On the Internet" They went horseback riding. It was something they had done as children, but it had surely been thirty years or more since she'd been on a horse.

"You're actually using the Internet now, Tory. I'm proud of you."

"Yeah, I've finally gotten fairly comfortable with a computer."

"Well, anyway, like I was saying, thanks. I feel much better," Jane said, as they continued down the trail. "They had just cantered across a clearing in the trail and the exhilaration and the wind in her face had refreshed her.

"So, anyway," Victoria said. "Tell me the rest of what happened last night. Did you and Gordon ever make up?"

"No. I was walking Fred when he came home. I saw him pull in. I'm pretty sure he saw me too, but he went straight up to the apartment and closed himself in his studio. He must have slept in there, because he never came to bed. I missed him, although I have to say it's the first good night's sleep I've had since we married. He snores."

"Jane, I never told you about ear plugs?" Victoria asked. "Did you see him at breakfast?"

"Yes, but we didn't speak. He leaves earlier than me. That's why I was still there when you called." Jane looked at Victoria. "Tell me about ear plugs."

"I can't believe I'm so remiss. All men snore. I'll get you some," Victoria said. "I'm glad you decided to take the morning off and come with me. You've been working too hard lately. Remember you're supposed to be semi-retired." Victoria wound her horse through the trees of a large pine forest.

"I know, but working on the magazine is more like fun than work."

"You still need some recreation." She paused. "So, Jane, is this the first time you've encountered Gordon's *asshole potential?*"

"What's that?" Jane asked.

"Surely I've explained my theory of asshole potential versus bitch potential?

Jane laughed. "No, I'm pretty sure I would have remembered that."

"Well, all men have asshole potential, some more than others. The only reason why we put up with it is because we women have our bitch potential.

"Tori, you don't have bitch potential. You're the sweetest person in the world," Jane said.

"I don't think Joe and the girls would agree with you on that," Victoria said. They were quiet for a minute while they guided the horses across a stream.

"Tori, they all would agree that you're the sweetest person in the world."

"Well, they might think I'm sweet, but they would tell you that I do have bitch potential. Truth is that I think if wives and mothers don't bitch enough, then they're not doing their jobs properly." The horses scrambled up the bank of the creek.

"That was fun, but I have to say, I'm not as confident on a horse as I was when I was young," Jane said. "Remember how we used to just jump on the horse without a saddle and take off."

"It has nothing to do with confidence. You're not as stupid," Victoria said, laughter filling the air.

"You're right. So all men have asshole potential and all women have bitch potential, go on."

"I have a scale to measure these potentials. You can't measure it with a scale from one to ten because say you said a man was a nine on the asshole potential scale. That would have to mean that he is a serious asshole most of the time, but suppose he is hardly ever an asshole, but when he is, he's really terrible."

"I see what you mean."

"So it has to be a double reading, like your blood pressure. Top number represents how often he displays his potential, bottom number represents how bad it is. Same goes for bitch potential."

"So what's Joe?"

"He's a two over eight. A nine or a ten would mean physical violence. Joe wouldn't ruffle my hair, but he can be a real butt verbally."

"Really, Tori? I can't imagine. He seems to just fawn over you most of the time."

"Yeah, he's good, that's why he's a two. It doesn't happen often, but when it does…"

"So what are you on the scale?" Jane asked. They were quiet again while they maneuvered past a fallen tree in the path.

"I'm a four over nine. I do it more often, though I have to say since menopause and the end of PMS we may have to revise that, but when I do I'm truly bitchy."

"I thought a nine meant violence."

"Nine is minor violence. I've actually shoved him before."

Jane laughed heartily.

"It's not funny, Jane. I'm really ashamed of that. I wouldn't tell just anyone," Victoria said.

"I'm sure that's true, Tori, but how far could you push him, you're five foot two and he's six foot four. I don't think you're much of a threat."

"It's still not okay."

"No, but Joe forgave you, right?"

"Yeah."

"Maybe Gordon will forgive me for fainting then." She

looked at the clearing in front of her. "Does this path lead us back to where we came from?" she asked Victoria.

"Yes. You want to run across the clearing?"

"Yes, I do." Jane urged her mount forward and they ran beside each other. The rhythm of the horse and the wind in her face were delightful. Life is really so good, she thought.

"So how would you rate Gordon?" Victoria asked when they stopped.

"Well, I've really only seen it this one time..."

"Now, be honest. You said he got upset when you kissed Jeff at Lillian's wedding and you told me that his lovemaking was possessive that night."

"Yeah, but if I have to get him mad to do that to me, I'll do it more often," Jane said.

"What about when he walked away from you that first time you made out?" Victoria looked at her seriously.

Jane laughed. "You're right. That sucked, but it was fear not meanness."

The horses were gently wandering down a wide road now and they were side by side. Victoria looked at Jane steadily.

"Okay, maybe that was a hint of the asshole potential to come. But still this has been the only really unreasonable incident we've had."

"So at this point, and I must remind you that you've known him only half a year, what do you think?" Victoria was so serious that Jane couldn't stop laughing.

"One over six," Jane said.

"Well, you're still in the honeymoon stage. I have a feeling that will change. What would you say about your bitch potential?" Victoria asked.

"Five over eight."

"Jane, you're not that bad."

"Well, I'm not violent, that's true, but I'm bitchy often and I'm good at whatever I do."

"That's true." They rode in silence for a few minutes. The barn came into sight and Victoria said, "So why do you think you faint when you encounter Margaret." She looked at Jane with concern. "Maybe we shouldn't talk about this now. If you faint, you'll fall off the horse."

"I'm not going to faint, Tori. It seems to only happen when I'm with one of the family and one of them is talking about her."

"What does it make you feel?"

"They seem to talk about her so easily. They smile. No one cries. It's like she's just in the other room. I just can't help remembering what stage of life she was in when she died." Jane leaned down and patted the horse's neck. "Remember a few years ago, Tori, when you were so depressed? The girls were gone, Joe wasn't paying attention anymore?"

"I'll never forget it."

"Remember how you and Joe fell in love all over again, and then the kids started being a part of your life again?" Victoria nodded. "Well, that's when Margaret died. It's so sad."

"It is sad, Jane, but now Gordon has you. So do the rest of them. They still love her. They've just let her go and moved on."

"But Margaret is dead. She has nothing. I feel guilty."

"For what?"

"For enjoying the family that she created, for having one of her grandchildren named after me, and for having wild passionate sex with her husband."

"He's *your* husband, Jane. Obviously those grand-kids will remember her. Wasn't it Teddy, the toddler that showed you the picture?"

"You're right. I just can't seem to come to terms with it."

"You will."

"Will I still have Gordon when I do?"

"If he's worth having."

Chapter Eighteen

"Janie." Jane looked up at Maggie as she ran in the door of her office. "I just came from fizcal therpy." Her hair was wet and her cheeks were rosy. Grant came into the office behind her.

"How'd it go?" Jane asked as she embraced the child and pulled her into her lap. She was sitting at her desk. She had gone home after riding with Victoria, showered and changed, and gone into the office to tie up some loose ends.

"I love it. I've started running on the treadmill now. Coach says I'm pretty good. I hardly ever have to stop to use my inhaler."

"That's great. What does he say about soccer?"

"He says, in the spring, we'll start with half a game and practice at ten minutes on, ten minutes off." Maggie was bubbling.

"That sounds great to me." Jane looked up at Grant. He was smiling. "Sounds like she's doing well," Jane said. "How's Lauren doing?"

"Still adjusting, but not fighting it any more," Grant said.

"Dad, can I go tell Uncle Michael?" Maggie asked.

"You know where he is," he said, "but don't run too fast. You're supposed to be cooling down."

"Okay." Maggie walked slowly out of the room. Then the sound of running feet faded down the hallway.

Jane and Grant smiled at each other. "Thanks, Jane, for helping out with Eric. I shudder every time I think about how close we came to losing him."

"Me too. Susan said he was unconscious when they pulled him out of the water." She rubbed her eyes.

"I should have been on the call list. I've been in town long enough to establish that. I think we'll all revise our call lists now." Grant sat down in the chair across from Jane. He leaned forward and looked at her. "Kathy told me what happened at her house. Jane, I don't know how to help, but I want you to know that you have your own place with us. None of us are expecting you to take Mom's place."

"I know, Grant. I don't know how I'm going to work that out, but I have to do it some way." She rubbed her eyes again.

Grant reached over and took her hands. "You'll break blood vessels if you keep doing that."

"I just wish your Dad would speak to me again. He hasn't spoken to me since...I miss him." She looked down at Grant's hands holding hers. They looked like his father's hands.

"He will. I talked to him this morning. You scared him. That makes him feel vulnerable. That makes him mad." He released her hands and she felt a fleeting loss. "He'll come around, but you still have to deal with whatever is bothering you about my mother. Michael thinks we should each talk to you about our separate relationships with her. He thinks if you can get to know her a little, you'll be able to grieve for her loss and move on."

"I'm not sure I have the energy for that, Grant."

"Jane, you have more energy than anyone I know. Look at what you've done here, just because you were bored."

"Daddy," Maggie said running back into the room. "Uncle Michael wants to take me for a bike ride." Michael came into the room behind her.

"I was looking into tandems," Michael said to Grant. "I think we could get one fitted for me on the front and her on the back. That would start her out slowly."

"I have a tandem," Jane said. "I used to ride it with Tori. She didn't learn to ride a bike until she was in her fifties. She knows how to ride now and I don't use it. Maybe you could have the back seat fitted for Maggie."

"That would be great, but I'll have to talk to the fizcal therapist," Grant said. "If it works, we'll fit it for me on the front." He elbowed his brother. "You can get one for your kids."

They all started to leave the room. Grant stopped by Jane and leaning down he kissed her temple. "We'll talk more about this another time. Don't worry about Dad, he won't hold out long."

"So, are you ever going to speak to me again?" Jane said over dinner that night. Gordon had brought takeout chicken home with him. He'd gotten home before her, which was unusual. When she got there the table was prepared and they sat down and ate silently until Jane spoke.

"I'm sorry." He looked up at her. "You scared me to death and I've had a hard time getting over it."

"Are you over it now?"

"I'd like to be."

"How can I help you get over it?" Jane stood and walked around the table. She knelt beside him.

"Jane, what are you doing?" He looked embarrassed.

"I've missed you. You didn't sleep with me last night. When you don't sleep with me, we don't touch. I want you to touch me."

"Don't you think we should talk about our argument?" he asked.

"After you touch me." Jane stood and dropped her pants on the floor beside him and took his hand. "Touch me here." She guided his hand to her bottom.

"Jane," Gordon said, smiling at her. "Most women don't think this is the proper solution to a conflict."

"I'm not most women." She knelt next to him and started to unbutton his pants.

"This isn't fair, Jane." He tried to take her hands. She dodged his grasp and opened his fly. Releasing his swelling penis, she took him into her mouth. "God," he said. "Jane..." He put his hands on her waist and moved up under her blouse. "You're not wearing a bra." He gasped as she slid her mouth over his cock. "Jane..."

She stood, straddled him and guided herself smoothly over him. "You've starved me, Gordon." She was looking down at him. She moved her mouth over his as she rose and fell on his lap.

"One night, Jane," he gasped.

"That's too much."

"We can't solve our problems with sex," Gordon said the next morning. It was Saturday. They had spent a glorious morning in bed and were eating fruit and harvest muffins in the kitchen.

"What problems?" Jane asked.

"I won't say that you didn't distract me," Gordon said. "But we have to deal with this. It can't be healthy for you to keep passing out. What if you hit your head when you fall?"

"I hate the fact that I fainted, Gordon. I'm not exactly the type of woman who swoons."

"I know. That's why I'm not going to stop pushing you until you deal with it."

"How? I don't know how?"

"I want you to go to a therapist with me. We'll work on it together." He leaned across the table and took her hands.

"Oh, I don't know, Gordon. It seems so personal. I don't want to share it with anyone else." Jane pulled out of his grasp and put yogurt spread on her muffin.

"Jane, you don't have a problem with therapy, do you?" He looked at her.

"Of course not."

"You know it's a powerful tool. It doesn't mean you're crazy. It's more of a self-exploration exercise."

"I've heard."

Gordon put his hand under her chin and forced her to look at him. "Promise me you'll think about it." He paused, waiting. "Please?"

"All right, I'll think about it." She leaned forward and kissed him. "Right now I need to take a shower and get dressed. I'm taking Joy, Hope, and Gary Christmas shopping at the mall today."

"Maybe you are crazy," Gordon said. "Want me to come along?"

"No way, we're shopping for you."

The mall was crowded. It was only a week before Christmas and everyone was busy doing the last minute stuff. Jane felt a moment of panic when she saw all the people and realized she was responsible for three children under the age of ten. They weren't quite ready to strike out on their own, but they were too old to hold your hand. What if they got lost in the crowd?

"Okay, guys, stay with me. If anyone gets lost, I'll die."

All three kids dissolved into laughter. "You won't die," Hope said. "We'll go to lost and found and they'll broadcast for you over the loudspeaker."

"Really?" Jane looked from one face to another.

"Yeah," Gary said. "I've been lost lots of times. That's always what happens."

"How do you find lost and found?" Jane asked.

"You just go into one of the shops and tell the lady behind the counter that you're lost. She calls lost and found and they come and get you," Joy said.

"The lady behind the counter won't let them take you until security shows them an ID," Hope said. "Then they take you to this nice play room with all kinds of great toys and send out the page."

"They even have computers," Gary added.

"Sounds like you like the place a little too much," Jane said. "Do you just want to go there and wait for me?"

Gary laughed. "I thought about it. I hate being the only man in the group." He puffed out his chest. "But I do need to find a gift for Grampa and Dad and Uncle Michael. I guess I should do something for Uncle Rick, too. Now that we live here, I have a lot more people to buy for."

"Have you got any money?" Joy elbowed him.

"Yeah, I mowed the lawn all summer, I got twenty-one bucks."

"Wow," Hope said. "I only have fifteen. I already spent some of my savings." She glanced at Joy.

"I plan to help out, guys," Jane said. "I'm loaded and looking for a place to spend."

"Does it count as our gift if you pay for it?" Gary asked.

Jane hadn't thought about that. They might not want her help.

"I think so, if you put some of your own money on each gift and choose the gift yourself," she said, feeling proud of her adlib.

"Okay, let's get started. I want to go to the Nature Store," Joy said. All three kids agreed that was the place to start. Jane followed them through the mall. They seemed to know exactly where they were going, she noted. The mall took on a whole different dimension when experienced with kids.

After a couple of hours they stopped for lunch. It was a late lunch and the crowds had died down. They decided to go to one of the restaurants in the mall instead of the food court.

"This is nice," Jane said, as they sat at a square table. It was better than a booth. They were all looking at each other. "It's quiet in here. My treat, guys, anything you want."

They studied the menu. The waiter came. He looked first at Jane and said, "May I get you a drink?"

Jane laughed at his implication. "Just water for me, thanks."

"I want a hamburger with fries," Gary said to the waiter. "And a chocolate shake." He glanced at Jane.

"That's fine," she said.

"I want a cheeseburger with fries," Hope said. "And I'll have a milk shake too, but vanilla.

"You guys are gross." Joy wrinkled her nose. "I'll have a veggieburger," she said. "Are the fries cooked with animal products?"

"I don't know, ma'am, I could ask," the waiter said.

"That's all right. I'll have a garden salad as a side. No bacon, vinegar and oil for dressing."

"Is egg all right, ma'am?"

"Yes, egg is all right. And I'll have bottled water, please." She looked at Jane. "Mom says I need complete protein. I haven't decided if I'll eliminate eggs, too. I need to research it."

"I see. Well, I think I'll have a veggieburger too, but I want coleslaw as a side."

They all dug into their meals. Shopping worked up a powerful appetite.

"Can we go to the dog park now, Janie?" Joy asked.

"Are we finished shopping?" She looked around the table at the other kids.

"I am," Gary said. "I could take Beau."

"Beau's my dog," Hope said.

"If you're going to fight about it..." Jane said.

"We'll share him. Let's go. Please, Janie," Hope said.

"All right, we'll go home and pick up Fred then we'll go to Joy and Hope's house and get Beau and Isis. You need to call your Mom, Gary, and make sure it's all right with her. Maybe she and Maggie would like to come."

"I doubt it." Gary looked uncomfortable.

"I'll tell you what, I'll call her."

They made the various stops and gathered the dogs together. Then Jane pulled out her cell phone and called Gary's house. "Lauren, this is Jane."

"Is everything all right?" Lauren asked.

"Yes, we had a very successful shopping trip. Listen, the kids want to go to the dog park. I wanted to ask your permission to take Gary. We'll only be a couple of hours."

"That's fine."

"Good. I wondered if you and Maggie would like to come along."

"No, it's too cold for Maggie. She'll get sick."

"That's all right, you don't have to go. It is cold outside. I just thought that since the sun is shining, if Maggie bundled up she'd be okay, but if you don't think so, we'll do it another time." She paused. She could hear Maggie's little voice saying something to Lauren. "Lauren, are you there?"

"If you wouldn't mind coming by, Maggie wants to go with you." Lauren's voice was cool.

"We'll come by. I hope you'll come along, too."

"I don't think so." Lauren hung up the phone.

Jane looked at the dead phone in her hand. Well things were certainly not healed between them, but at least she was going to let Maggie join them. They stopped to pick her up.

"You kids stay here with the dogs. I'll go in and get Maggie," Jane said. They were in her SUV. The dogs were in the back behind a separator she had recently had installed.

"No, Janie," Gary said. "Let me." He hopped out of the car and ran up the walk to the door of the apartment. A few minutes later he emerged from the house with Maggie by the hand and Lauren behind them.

"The kids want me to come. Are you sure it's all right with you?" Lauren said, leaning in the passenger side door.

"I'm delighted. Get in."

Gary got into the back seat with Hope and Joy,

Maggie scrambled onto the bench seat next to Jane. Lauren got into the passenger seat. "I've got seat belts for everyone. Buckle up." They set off for the dog park.

There weren't very many people there for a Saturday afternoon. The group settled in a corner of the large run and the dogs started to play. Jane smiled at the difference in size. Isis, Joy's puppy, was even smaller than Fred. Of course she was only a puppy, and Fred was fully-grown at eight months old. Then there was Beau. He dwarfed them.

"Isn't it interesting how Beau seems to know he has to be gentle with the smaller dogs?" Jane said to Lauren. They were standing on the edge of a game the kids were playing with the dogs. They tossed a ball, the first dog to get it would return it to a child, seemingly at random and that child would toss it again.

"It's almost like Beau takes turns letting the little ones get the ball," Lauren said. They watched in silence for a while.

Maggie played with the group. Jane could feel Lauren's tension beside her.

"Janie." She looked at Joy who was calling her. "Look what I taught Isis." She had the little dog sit, and then Joy backed away from her and stopped. "Come," she said. The little dog stood and romped to her owner. When she reached her, Joy said, "Sit." Isis, wagging her tail, looked at her. Joy stared at her a little harder and the dog sat.

"That's wonderful, Joy," Jane and Lauren both said.

"I remember what you told me. Make them do it the first time every time. Never repeat the command."

"Why did you name her Isis, Joy?" Lauren asked.

"Isis is the Egyptian Goddess of protection." Joy looked fondly at the little dog.

Jane and Lauren smiled. The little dog couldn't weigh more than five pounds. The ball was tossed back and forth a couple of times then Gary got it and heaved it in Jane's direction. Beau hung back letting the smaller dogs go for the ball, but the pitch was too high. Neither of them could get it. Jane started to back up to try and stop it from going over the fence and into the forest beyond.

"Watch out, Janie!" All three kids yelled at one time, but it was too late. Her heel collided with a fallen tree branch and she sat down hard on the ground. When she landed she felt something soft, damp, and a little bit warm spread across her bottom and squeeze out between her buttocks and the hard ground.

"Oh, no, what was that," she said, looking up. All four kids and Lauren were standing around her looking concerned.

"Are you all right, Jane?" Lauren asked.

"I'm not hurt, but something is definitely not all right." She stood up and looked around at her bottom. There was brown gooey stuff all over it.

"It's dog do," Maggie said. All four kids giggled. Jane looked at Lauren.

She straightened her face quickly. "Oh, Jane," she said, stiffly controlling the corners of her mouth. "Kids, this is not funny," she said, and then lost control. All five of them laughed uncontrollably while Jane crossed her arms and looked on.

Jane wasn't unhappy. It was good to see Lauren laughing and to see her joining in the fun. She smiled at them and chuckled. "Well, now what?" she asked. "I can't get into my car like this," she said.

"We're not ready to go home anyway," Hope said.

"But we will be eventually."

"There's a hose over there," Gary said. "I could hose off your butt."

"Gary, don't say butt," Lauren admonished.

"I could hose off your pants," Gary corrected.

"It's forty degrees out here. I'd freeze," Jane said. Remembering her cell phone she pulled it out of her pocket. "I'll call Grampa. Hopefully he can bring me a change of pants."

The kids ran back to their game and Lauren sat down on the bench again, this time by herself. Her face was more relaxed than Jane had seen it since before that horrible day in her office, maybe ever.

"Gordon," Jane said, when he picked up the phone at the apartment. "I need your help."

"Are you all right, Jane? What's wrong?" His concern anchored her.

"Don't worry so much, Gordon. Everyone is fine. I was just wondering if you could bring me a change of pants. I'm at the dog park with the kids and Lauren."

"Lauren's there?"

"Yes, and she's having a grand time," Jane said, not caring about her sarcastic tone.

"Tell me what's going on, Jane."

"I was playing ball with the kids and somehow I managed to sit in dog shit."

Gordon laughed. "I'll be right there." He hung up and she closed her cell phone and put it back in her pack. She walked over to the bench Lauren was sitting on. Lauren moved over.

"I'm not going to sit next to you like this," Jane said. "I'm not going to sit at all. I'll just stand over here until Gordon comes."

Looking down at her hands, Lauren smiled. She and Jane were silent watching the kids for some time.

"Grant told me you fainted at Katherine's the other night. Are you all right?"

"Yes." Jane took a deep breath. "I seem to be having a hard time coming to terms with Margaret."

"I can understand that. He loved her very much." Lauren looked up at Jane. "Do you feel competitive with her?"

"No, it isn't that. I think I feel guilty."

"For being in love with Gordon?"

"Yes." She grabbed the ball as it bounced toward her and threw it back to the circle of kids and dogs. "And for loving her family so much. She created this wonderful family. It's just so unfair that she had to go, and I'm basking in the glory of it." Jane felt the dizziness trying to take her and put her hand on the back of the bench.

"Are you all right?" Lauren stood and started toward her.

"I'm fine, Lauren." She waved her aside. "Gordon wants me to go to a therapist with him. He says we'll work this out together. I'm just not comfortable with it."

"I know what you mean. Grant insisted on me going to one with him after...I'm sorry I called you a bitch, Jane." Lauren sat back down and looked at the ground in front of her.

"I've been called worse," Jane said. "Anyway, how is it? I mean therapy. I know it's none of my business, but do you think it's helping?"

"Yes, I do." Lauren said. "I hate to admit it, but I do."

"I guess I should try it. It's just that I've always been able to work things out for myself."

"You've always lived by yourself, right? You've never been married before?"

"No."

"Janie, watch," Joy called. Jane looked over at the circle of kids. Joy threw the ball and Fred caught it in midair.

"That's great!" she called back

"You're not by yourself anymore, Jane."

"No, I'm certainly not." She and Lauren exchanged a smile. "Oh, good, there's Gordon." Jane hurried over to him. He was carrying a bundle in his arms.

"Phew!" He laughed. "I can't wait to hear about this."

"Just give me the clothes." She snatched the bundle away from him and looked around for a place to change.

"Those thick shrubs over there will shield you. I'll stand watch," he said. "Hey Lauren." He bent and kissed her cheek. "I'll be back in a minute."

Jane ran over to the shrubs and ducked behind. Gordon stood at the side watching her as she took off her pants.

"Gordon, you can't stand watch if you're looking at me."

"Sure I can." He smiled wickedly.

She pulled on the clean pants and then slipped back into her shoes. Turning her back to him, she said, "Is there poop on my sweatshirt?"

Gordon put his hand on her bottom and started brushing at something on the seat of her pants.

"These are the clean pants. What's on them?"

"Nothing," he said.

Jane laughed and turned around. "Then stop patting my butt."

"It's fun." He circled her waist with his arms and kissed her.

She leaned into the kiss. He tasted sweet and warm. Gordon put his arm across her shoulder and they walked back to Lauren.

"I brought you a plastic bag to put the soiled pants into." Gordon pulled a kitchen trash bag out of his back pocket. Jane stuffed the pants into it.

"Thank you, sweetie," Jane said. They sat down on either side of Lauren. Maggie came over to them and crawled into her mother's lap.

"It's rest time," she said. "Coach says I can do anything any other kid can do, I just have to pay special attention to myself."

"Special attention?" Gordon asked.

"Listen to my body, if it says rest, rest."

"And your body says rest?" Lauren asked.

"Yep, and it says water." She looked at Jane.

"Oh, of course" Jane pulled the bottle she had packed out of her bag and a plastic cup. She poured some water and handed it to Maggie. Soon all the kids were asking for water. Jane gave it to them then poured a bowl of water for the dogs.

"You set a good example, Maggie," Jane said.

Lauren buried her cheek in Maggie's red curls and smiled.

Chapter Nineteen

"Jane?" David stood in the doorway of her office. "I've got an estimate on the fashion show."

"All right, let's see it." She felt good every time she looked at David. He looked so much like Jeff. He handed her the papers he had in his hand.

"It's a pretty good sum, but I think it'll pay off. Until we have renewal subscriptions and a bigger advertising client base, we'll need to rely on earnings from our ancillary products."

"I know. I'm just not sure that this is the way." Jane looked at the numbers on the paper. "It's a lot of money."

"It is." David tapped his fingers on the desk. "It's your call, of course."

"I'm not walking down a runway."

"That's what you said."

"I meant it." She looked into David's eyes.

"I believe you."

"Do you have a time frame on this?"

"Late February or early March. We want to get people while they're still bored with the winter, but close enough to spring that they're thinking about wardrobe change." David was intense.

"I didn't know you had an interest in the fashion industry, David," Jane said.

He looked bashful. "Anna's convinced me. She's something else. She has Lenny wrapped around her finger. I think he's in love with her. You should spend some time with her. She's great."

"You're right. I haven't spent enough time with her. I've been really impressed with her work." Jane looked out the window.

Jane went to Anna's cubicle and knocked on the desk. Anna turned around and blinked her eyes. "Oh, Jane, sit down." She motioned to the rolling stool under the desk. "Is there something I can do for you?"

"Yes, I haven't spent nearly enough time with you. I'd like to take you to lunch today. I want you to tell me why I should shell out the bucks for this fashion show." Jane sat on the stool.

"I'd love to have lunch with you, but first I'd need to show you my sketches." Anna turned to her portfolio and pulled it out.

"Were you expecting this or something?" Jane asked.

"I'm pretty much always prepared to sell my work," Anna said. "If you're not, no one looks at you."

"Show me," Jane said.

The work was incredible. Jane had described to her what she wanted, but Anna had gone far beyond Jane's expectations. Her business line was perfect: all comfortable, and all wash and wear. And she couldn't have made better choices for the materials. She also showed Jane a more formal line of clothing. Everything was designed to look perfect on someone over the age of forty-five, though it was versatile enough for younger businessmen and women.

"Anna, I'm really impressed. You're right! We need to show this to the working community, to the whole community," Jane said. "Are you ready for lunch?"

"Well, I think I've already sold my work. You don't have to take me to lunch."

"I want to."

A singsong voice started at the end of the room and advanced toward them. "Oh, my sweet Anna, won't you have lunch with me." Lenny appeared around the corner of the cube. He jumped back when he saw Jane. "I'm sorry, Jane. I didn't know you were here."

"I guess not," Jane said. "Anna's having lunch with me today. I'd invite you to come along, but I'd like to spend some time with her alone. How about you and I have lunch tomorrow?"

"I'm off tomorrow. I'm taking a long weekend to go to Valdosta to spend Christmas with the family. I guess I could change my plans."

"That's not necessary, Lenny. We'll do it after Christmas. I hope you have a wonderful time." Jane looked at Anna. "Are you ready?"

"I'll meet you in your office in five minutes," she said. "I just want to run to the ladies room."

Jane left the cube with Anna and Lenny still in it. She could hear them speaking quietly to each other. She wondered if there was a romance beginning there. Anna was black and Lenny was white, but these days that didn't mean anything. She wondered how his mother would feel about it. Well, it was none of her concern.

They went to lunch. Jane enjoyed it, but really didn't get to know Anna any better. Just like Amanda, she didn't talk about herself very much. She said she didn't have any family.

"What will you do for Christmas?" Jane asked.

"I'll enjoy a day off to myself," she said. "It's what I do every year."

"Gordon and I are having dinner with Tori. Would you like to join us?"

"Thanks, Jane, but I'm happy enjoying a day of self-indulgence." Anna smiled and looked straight into Jane's eyes. It was disconcerting. "I'm fine, Jane, I'm not lonely."

"I wasn't feeling sorry for you. I just thought it would be fun. I'd like to get to know you," Jane said.

"You know me," Anna said, and ate her dessert.

Jane ate her dessert. She was disappointed. Apparently it was hard to get past arms length with Anna. Well, they weren't family. They were co-workers. Her work was certainly excellent.

When she returned to the office, Mark was waiting

for her holding a box. "I've got the samples of the cookware I had made," he said. "Have you got a minute to look at them?"

"I can't wait. I loved your designs. Let's go into my office." She led the way. Mark put the box down on the credenza and reached into it. He put the samples on the table in a line. There was a half pie pan, a quarter pie pan, a half loaf pan, single muffin pans, and half and quarter cake pans.

"Those are great. I love the *Second Half* logo on them," Jane said.

"These are the metal ones. I have the same designs being made in Pyrex," Mark said. "I'm working on a two portion slow cooker."

"Great idea, we could make small portion appliances of all kinds really. It's all been done before, but not with the *Second Half* flair." She smiled up at Mark. He was grinning proudly. "You've done a wonderful job with this, Mark. I know it wasn't what you're used to doing."

"It was fun. I'm an artist. I love to try new things."

"How's Lillian? I don't see enough of her. She's so busy with school. I stop by the nursery sometimes to see her, and Tori. They're lucky they get to work together."

"She's fine, focused on school as usual."

"What will you do for Christmas?"

"We'll go to my parents for dinner on Christmas Eve, and then spend Christmas day together. We decided we'd like to start some of our own traditions on Christmas day."

"That's a great idea. Have you got any ideas about marketing this stuff?"

"I've designed a few ad layouts, but other than that, marketing isn't my strong point."

"We'll put David to work on it. Anna may have some ideas, too. She came up with a fashion show for the line of clothing."

"Good idea. I'd better get back to work."

"Hey, get your coat. Let's go for a ride." Michael stood in the doorway of Jane's office. It was about an hour before quitting time.

"Where are we going?"

"You'll see when we get there." He took her coat off the rack and brought it over to her.

"All right." Jane put it on, got her purse, and followed him out the door.

"I had a call from one of the modeling agencies I use," Michael said, when they were tucked into the car and on the road.

"What did they want?"

"They wanted to know who the model on the front of *Second Half* was, said they'd like to lure her away from her current agency with a better contract."

"You didn't tell them how to reach me, did you?" Jane frowned.

"I told them the model was the owner of *Second Half* and that she wouldn't have consented to doing those pictures if she hadn't been getting married that day anyway." They laughed together.

"That's the truth."

"Why are we at a cemetery?" Jane asked, as they pulled into the parking lot.

"I wanted you to come with me to visit my mother's grave."

"Oh, Michael, I don't know. You know about the problem I've been having." Her hand shook as she put it on his arm.

"I won't let you fall, Jane. I think this might help." He took a poinsettia out of the back seat and got out of the car. He came around to her side. She had already gotten out, but stood leaning against the car door. "It's worth a try." He looked earnestly into her eyes.

"All right." She followed him around the building and down a path. He waited for her when the path widened and took her arm.

"Are you feeling all right?" he asked.

"So far." Jane loved his smile. It was like his father's, but a little wider. His lips were a little fuller, too.

They walked arm in arm across the lawn to a plot on top of a slope. There was a stone bench beside the grave. There was a stoneware vase at the foot of the grave. Michael placed the plant in the vase and motioned for her to sit down. He sat beside her. The headstone read:

Margaret Fletcher Fox
Beloved wife of Gordon Ryan Fox
Beloved mother of Grant Ryan, Michael Gordon
and Katherine Sarah

Michael put his arm across Jane's shoulders and squeezed. "Take a couple of deep breaths."

She let a breath go first then took two slow deep breaths, being careful to exhale completely each time.

"I could see you holding your breath, Jane," Michael said. "You okay? Your color is coming back."

"I'm all right. I don't know why it has this effect on me."

"I think I do." They sat quietly for a minute then Michael started to talk. "After Mom died, Dad used to come out here and sit for hours. It worried us to death. He didn't bring a book, or a magazine, or anything. He just sat and stared. Katherine would come looking for him, and then she'd call me or Grant and ask us to come and get him. I told her she just had to let him get through it his way."

Jane could feel the tears fighting for release. She swallowed.

"I was her least favorite child," Michael whispered.

"Oh, Michael, I'm sure that's not true." Jane turned to him, startled by his statement.

"Oh, yes, it's true, at least until the end. We got close at the end. I don't mean she didn't love me. She did. I always knew that, but she didn't like me." He paused and looked at the grave. "She was crazy about Grant. He was so handsome. He looked like Dad with his dark hair and sparkling blue eyes. He always made good grades. They were both crazy about Kathy. She was just so cute.

We were all crazy about her." He laughed then fell silent for a minute. "I had red hair and freckles, and I was a fat kid. She used to say I was a hefty. I didn't do very well in school, either. It didn't bother Dad. He could see my artistic ability. He taught me to take pictures as soon as I was old enough to hold a camera. Mom couldn't believe that someone who didn't do well in school could succeed. But I just didn't fit in at school."

"It sounds sad. I've never thought of you as sad," Jane said. She looked at Michael. Smile lines were beginning to form beside his eyes, just like his fathers. "You weren't sad, though, were you?"

"Sometimes when I was very young, I was. But when I got old enough to understand it, I wasn't anymore. The kids in the neighborhood would tease me about being fat or about the red hair. One day she came running out of the house swinging a wooden spoon and screaming for them to get out of her yard if they couldn't act civil." He smiled at the memory. "Her red hair was flying and she was swinging that spoon. I realized then that she loved me. She just didn't understand me." He was quiet for a minute. "I was lucky I had Dad. He always understood me."

"You were lucky. I'm lucky too," Jane said, looking again at the headstone.

"Then when Jill and I sprung our little surprise just before Lauren and Grant's wedding, Mom was furious. She never did forgive Jill."

"What surprise? I always assumed that you and Jill were married first, since Joy's the oldest grandchild."

"We were married first because Joy is the oldest grandchild."

"Oh."

"That's right." He frowned. "Lauren and Grant got engaged the way they were supposed to. They spent a year planning their wedding. Mom got really involved. She was having a grand time. About a month before the wedding, Jill told me she was pregnant. We didn't know what to do." He turned quickly to Jane. "Not abortion. That was never considered. We were happy about the baby, but we didn't want to throw a wrench into the wedding plans. So we eloped."

"What was the problem then?"

"When we told Mom and Dad about it, Mom insisted on making an announcement. She didn't want it to be too obvious that the baby was early." He shrugged. "I tried to make her see that it really didn't matter these days if a baby is early, but..."

"She forgave you, though, I'm sure."

"Oh, yeah, everyone was happy when Joy was born. She was eight pounds of adorable, with a full head of blond hair." He smiled. "She forgave me and learned to tolerate Jill, but she never liked her."

"That's too bad. Jill's such a lovely person."

"Yes, she is." They sat quietly for a while.

"Thank you for telling me all this, Michael. I'm not sure why it helps, but it does."

He put his arms around her and kissed her temple. "I thought it would. Are you dizzy? You're shaking."

"No, I'm cold."

"Let's go"

Jane fumbled with her keys at the door to the apartment. Before she could get the key into the lock, though, the door opened. Gordon pulled her into his arms and dragged her into the living room. "Where were you? I was worried."

"I'm sorry. Is it late? I didn't realize." She looked at the clock. It was 7:00 p.m. "It is late. That was inconsiderate of me. I should have called."

"Well, you don't have to report to me." Gordon laughed as he kissed her firmly. "But I did worry. You're usually home before me."

"Michael took me to the cemetery to visit Margaret's grave," she said as she turned to the foyer table and put down her keys and purse. She took off her coat and hung it in the closet.

"Really," Gordon said. "Why did he do that? It's not her birthday or anything."

"He took her a poinsettia."

"That was nice. Were you all right? Did you get dizzy?"

"Once, but Michael pointed out that I was holding my breath."

"Really, I wonder if that's always been the problem."

"Gordon, did you know that Michael thinks he was her least favorite child."

"He was, in a way. The truth is that she worried about him the most. He frustrated her." Gordon went to the bar. "Would you like something to drink?"

"That would be nice. Do we have any more of that single malt scotch?" Jane sat down on one of the stools. "I can't imagine her feeling that way. He's so tuned in to the world around him, the people around him too. I love all your kids, but there's something special about Michael."

"That's what I've always thought." Gordon poured her drink and handed it to her. "They're all special in their own way, but he's so warm, so genuine."

"That's it exactly." She sipped her drink.

"She always had him on some kind of a diet. He was a hefty," Gordon said.

"That's what he told me."

"I tried to tell her that it was just baby fat. It would come off by itself as he grew up, but she didn't believe it because the other two kids weren't fat. Poor kid, he was always eating carrots and celery when the others had cookies. I had to take him out for a hamburger once in a while." Gordon laughed at the memory.

"He's beautiful now, fit and athletic looking."

"I knew he would be. Truth is he was just like Maggie when she was a kid. I've seen pictures. She was a fat little girl. She was a trim adult until she started having the kids. Then she got plump. I liked her that way, though."

Gordon smiled and looked at Jane. "Are you hungry? Have you eaten?"

"No, I haven't eaten, but I'm not hungry. Would you like me to fix you something?" Jane asked around a yawn. She felt drained, but not dizzy.

"I can fix something for myself. I've fed myself for a long time now, Jane." Gordon went into the kitchen.

Jane followed him in and sat down at the table. "Michael said that he and Margaret got close right before she died. He didn't elaborate. What happened?"

"When she found out she was terminal and told the family, I guess I pretty much fell apart. I just couldn't face it. I looked for cures and, well, I didn't spend a lot of time with her, just being with her." He continued to pull things out of the refrigerator, but he looked sad.

"I'm sorry, Gordon. You don't have to tell me."

"I want to. Anyway, Grant and Kathy, sort of, went into denial, I think. They kept coming to the house. They were all living in Atlanta at that time. They'd be all cheerful and try to joke with her. She appreciated it, but it wasn't what she needed." He started constructing a sandwich. "But Michael, true to form, knew exactly what she needed. He would come by after work and just sit with her. Sometimes they'd talk. I'd hear them in the other room just chattering away. I don't know what they talked about. I didn't want to know." He carried the plate to the table and sat down next to Jane. "Sometimes they'd just sit together, quietly. He'd hold her hand or she'd put her head on his shoulder." He took a big bite of the sandwich.

Jane laughed and wiped her eyes.

"What's funny?" Gordon said with his mouth full.

"I don't know. I'm close to tears and you're eating a sandwich." She dabbed at her eyes.

"I know the story, Jane. I've shed a lot of tears over it. It can still make me cry, but I've learned to live with it, in fact it makes me happy as much as sad. I was married for thirty-five years to a wonderful woman who loved me. Now I'm married to another wonderful woman who loves me. How can I not be happy?" He took another bite and chewed slowly. "Eating is part of living and I'm alive and I'm hungry."

"Are you ready for a bike ride?" Jeff asked when he called on the Sunday after Christmas.

"I don't know, Jeff. It's only thirty degrees outside. I'm sure Tori won't want to go."

"We've already loaded her bike on the truck. We're on our way to your house. If you don't want to come, though, we'll understand."

"I won't," she heard Victoria say in the background. "No way, if you fools are going, so am I."

"We've decided not to have a picnic. It's too cold for that, so we're going to ride to a spot Vic found on the trail, and stop for lunch at a restaurant. I called ahead to make sure they were open. It's kind of a local spot."

"Sounds like fun." Jane hung up the phone and hurried to get ready.

"You bundle up and wear gloves. I don't want you getting sick," Gordon said as she pulled on her long johns and winter tights.

"I'll be careful." She kissed him as she left the room.

He followed her out to the living room and watched as she packed her bag with water and light snacks.

"Do you have plans for the day, Gordon?" she asked.

"I'm going over to Kathy's. All the kids are meeting over there for lunch. We're planning one big birthday celebration for all three January birthdays."

Jane stopped what she was doing and looked up. "Three January birthdays?"

"Yeah, Hope will be eight on January 12th, Maggie will be six on January 14th, and Michael will be thirty-three on January 20th."

"Maybe I should be there, Gordon. Why didn't you tell me?"

"I think it was understood right from the start that these Sunday bike trips were important to you. Nobody expects you to be there when they plan things on Sunday." Gordon patted her shoulder. "Don't worry about it, Jane. I'll tell you what we decide."

"Okay, but if you decide to have the party on a Sunday, I'll cancel my bike trip for that day. I'm not inflexible, you know."

"I never thought you were. I just want you to do what makes you happy."

"It makes me happy to be a part of your family."

"Good," Gordon said. "That makes me happy, too, but you're not going to miss anything today. You go ahead and have fun with your friends. I think the friendship between you and Tori and Jeff is very valuable. Since you married me, I'm not jealous of Jeff any more. I hope you know how lucky you are to have them." Gordon went back down the hall to his studio and closed the door.

She watched him go. He was right, of course. She was lucky to have such good friends. Baby brushed up against her leg. She looked down at her. "Does your dad have any friends?" she asked the cat. Baby sat and looked up at her then she rubbed the side of her face on Jane's leg. The buzzer sounded and Jane went down to the lobby.

"So tell us about Christmas with the clan," Jeff said as they sat down to lunch. The restaurant was cozy. There was a lit fireplace. It had been a cold fifteen mile ride to get there and the warmth felt good.

Jane laughed. "It is a clan, isn't it, the Fox clan. It was nice, but the kids were...I don't know how to describe it."

"Over stimulated?" Victoria asked.

"I think that's it," Jane said. "I mean, they got all sorts of great gifts. I expected them to be really happy, but they bickered and fought with each other. Even Teddy had a temper tantrum, and he's always happy."

"He should turn two pretty soon, shouldn't he?" Victoria asked. "He'll be getting started on his terrible two's. I imagine you'll be seeing a few more tantrums."

"That's true." Jane looked thoughtful. "I need to get Gordon's birthday list. I guess I need to know when these things are. He told me this morning that there are three family birthdays in January."

"That reminds me, Jane. Joe and I are going out to Seattle for Benjamin's first birthday. We were hoping that you and Gordon could come."

"I'd love to do that. I wonder if Gordon can get away," Jane said. "If not, I'll go without him. Give me the dates when we get back today. Okay Tori?"

"Okay."

"Jane," Jeff said. "I thought you were only spending Christmas Eve with Gordon's family."

"That's right, apparently it's a tradition in their family for all of them to get together on Christmas Eve and exchange gifts between the families, then on Christmas they have celebrations of their own. We had Christmas dinner with Tori and Joe," she said. "How was your Christmas, Jeff?"

"It was great. I put a big fire in my wood stove, read a book all day, drank a couple of cocktails made with that Glenfiddich you gave me, and went to bed."

"I thought you went to your aunt's on Christmas," Victoria said. "You could have had dinner with us. I've always wanted you to join us. We have a great time."

"We do, Jeff. Don't spend Christmas alone again. Come to Tori's with us." Jane was worried. Jeff seemed downhearted. She looked at Victoria and saw concern on her face, too.

"I didn't feel like company, otherwise I would have gone to my aunt's house." He'd been looking at the menu, but looked up at the silence from his companions. "Don't look at me like that. I can spend a day alone if I want."

"Of course you can," Jane said. "We just care about you, Jeff. Gordon was pointing out this morning how lucky we three are that we have this friendship. I hope you both know how much I love you." She looked from Victoria to Jeff.

"Of course we do, Jane," Victoria said. Jeff nodded.

"Talk to us, Jeff. What's bothering you?" Jane prodded.

"Now don't get all mushy on me, Jane. I'm just restless or something. I don't know. I need to make a change, but I don't know exactly what change. I'll figure it out." He looked at the menu again. "Now what are we going to eat?"

Jane and Victoria exchanged a look. "I'm going to have the grilled salmon and warm peppered slaw," Jane said.

"I think I'll have that, too," Jeff said.

"We'll make it three." Victoria put down her menu. "Jeff," she said. He looked at her defensively. "I've been thinking about what you suggested. I mean about buying part of the nursery."

"What do you think?" He relaxed.

"Maybe if you taught me about the business end of it, I could handle it. I think it may be a good idea. Joe liked the idea, too."

"Good," he said. "That reminds me, Jane. Joe and I ran into Gordon at the sporting club when we went to play racquetball the other day."

"Really, I didn't know he played racquetball," Jane said.

"He was with his brother. He told us that his brother was going to buy in to the camera shop." Jeff looked at Jane. "He's not in financial trouble or anything, is he?"

She shook her head. "No, but thanks for the concern I see in your eyes. He wants to have a little more freedom. He's getting a little tired of the shop and would like to spend more time in the studio. This way, he could do that without really giving up the business." Jane thought about her conversation with Gordon this morning. "You know, I realized this morning that I've never met any of Gordon's friends. I wonder if he has any." She paused as the waiter came to take their order. "And if he hasn't got friends, I wonder why." She continued after the waiter was gone. "He's a great person and lots of fun."

"All of his friends were probably couples that he and Margaret knew together," Victoria said. "When she died, he probably just didn't fit in with them anymore. I've seen that happen after divorce, too."

"Jane, are you all right?" Jeff stood and moved to her side. "You're white as a sheet."

She blinked at him and dropped her head. He caught her as she slid from her chair.

"Wake up, Jane," she heard Victoria's voice from what seemed like a great distance. "Our food will be here soon and I'm hungry. If you don't wake up, I'll leave you here and eat my lunch."

"Vic!" Jeff said. "Some friend."

Jane blinked her eyes and looked at Victoria.

"There you are. Don't get up too fast." Victoria was bathing her face with a dampened napkin that she had dipped into a glass of ice water.

Jane sat up slowly and looked around. She was lying on a bench seat against the wall of the restaurant with her feet propped on a seat cushion. "I did it again?"

"You sure did." Victoria said, and stood up. "I think you scared Jeff to death."

Jeff sat down on the seat beside her and put his arm around her shoulders as she swung her feet over the side of the seat.

"I'm so embarrassed," Jane said.

"Do I need to call Gordon to come up here and get you? I'm not sure you should ride your bike home," Jeff said.

"I'm fine, Jeff. This happens sometimes when I talk about Margaret." She stood shakily and Jeff helped her back to her seat just as the food arrived. "Good, I'm starving," she said, and started to eat. Victoria followed suit. After a couple of bites, they both looked up at Jeff.

"Aren't you going to eat?" Jane asked.

"I've lost my appetite."

"I didn't puke, Jeff, I fainted." She pointed to his plate. "Eat," she said.

He picked up his fork and took a reluctant bite.

When Jeff and Victoria dropped her at her condo, she said, "I'd appreciate it if you wouldn't tell Gordon that I fainted. I'm working this thing out, but it upsets him. I'd rather he didn't know."

Chapter Twenty

"I'll call you in a day or two," Jane said to the woman sitting across the desk from her. "I just need to review your application with my assistants and see if either of them wants to interview you." She looked to be about Jane's age. She was a little bit plump, but not really fat. Her experience was perfect for the food and entertainment editor position. She had worked as a school dietitian and then had opened her own catering business. She had a degree in Nutrition and Dietetics, and had been to culinary school. She was also very personable.

"I'll wait to hear from you then." She stood up. "Mrs. Fox," she said, stopping at the door. "I loved your sample edition of *Second Half.* I took a subscription card from it and I've already subscribed. You looked beautiful on the cover. Was that Mr. Fox with you?"

"Yes it was," Jane said.

"So you really did get married that day?"

"Yes, we did."

"I thought I recognized that look," she said. "I'll wait to hear from you."

"Thank you, Christine," Jane said.

Jane got up and went down the hall to Grant's office. She knocked on the door.

"Come in," Grant called. "Hello, Jane," he said as she sat in the chair across from him "What can I do for you?"

"I think I've found a food and entertainment editor. I wondered if you'd like to interview her. Actually," she corrected, "I'd like for you to interview her. I always feel better if I can get another opinion."

"I'd like to, yes," he said.

Jane put the application on the desk. "I thought you'd like to read this over before you do. You can arrange to meet with her when it's convenient, but I'd like to get this position filled as soon as possible."

"I won't drag my feet," he said. "How's the old man?"

"He's fine. We'll see you on Saturday. I'm looking forward to it." She got up to leave the room.

"That's right, the birthdays. Maggie's so excited to be having her birthday celebrated with her big cousin and her uncle."

"Grant, when you're finished with that application, give it back to me. I want David to interview her, too. I value his opinion and he needs the experience."

"He's doing great, by the way. I really enjoy working with him. He's a bright kid."

"He is."

Jane returned to her office and took her coat off the peg. She grabbed her purse and went to the reception area. "I'm going out for a while, Amanda. I'll be back in about an hour." She got into her car and headed for the cemetery. She'd been thinking about it ever since she'd fainted when she was with Victoria and Jeff. She'd felt better after visiting the cemetery with Michael. She'd actually been able to talk about Margaret with Gordon afterward, without feeling dizzy.

It was ten days into the New Year. It was nice to have the holidays behind her. They'd been fun, but hectic. She looked forward to them next year, but was glad she could put a year between them. She pulled into the parking lot and went to the grave. Sitting down on the bench, she looked at the stone vase at the foot and wondered where the fresh flowers in it had come from.

"I don't know what to do now," she said to the headstone. "Maybe I should just sit and stare, like Gordon did." She couldn't believe she was talking out loud. Was she talking to Margaret, or was she talking to herself? "Do you hate me for loving your family so much?" she asked. "If she answers me," Jane said out loud, "I won't faint, I'll die."

"Who are you talking to?" The voice was close to her ear and she jumped up and screamed. Gordon caught her as she quickly whirled around and lost her balance.

"Gordon, you scared me to death. Why did you sneak up on me?" she demanded, but she allowed him to steady her.

"I didn't sneak, Jane. I walked right up behind you. I thought you heard me." He held her close when she tried to pull away.

"Let me go." Jane struggled and looked around.

"Are you afraid Maggie will see me holding you?" Gordon relaxed his hold on her, but just a little. "Jane, I told you. Maggie wanted me to find love again."

She pushed away from him and he let her go. "I guess you brought the flowers?"

"I did." He sat down on the bench and pulled her down beside him. "Today is our wedding anniversary," he said. "Maggie's and mine."

"Really?" She looked at him. "You came here to be with her. I'm sorry. If I'd known, I wouldn't have come."

"I came here to honor her memory. I can't be with her, Jane. She isn't here. I was leaving when I saw you park and get out of your car. I followed you. Maybe I shouldn't have interfered."

Jane didn't say anything. She stared at the headstone.

"I used to think I would find her here, right after she died. I'd come here and wait, hoping that somehow she'd touch me, be with me. But she's not here. She's not anywhere." Gordon put his arm around his wife. "Except for in the faces of her children and grandchildren, and here of course." He tapped his chest.

Jane was still silent. Gordon put his hand on her chin and turned her face to him. "We're not cheating on her, Jane. I love you, completely separately from her."

"Gordon, do you believe in an afterlife?"

"Never have put much faith in it, but I guess no one really knows."

"Suppose there is one. How will the three of us deal with each other?"

"God I love you, Jane," Gordon said. "I think that if there is an afterlife, it translates completely differently than this one. I think we'll do fine."

She looked back at the headstone. "One of the things that made me fall in love with you, Gordon, is how much you love her."

"One of the things that made me fall in love with you is that you value that."

They sat quietly together, staring. It was all right, Jane realized. "I need to go back to the office," she said after a while.

"Me too." Gordon got up and offered her his hand. She took it and he pulled her to her feet. "I'm showing Jerry around. I wanted to see how well he catches on before I make my decision." He pulled her into his arms and kissed her. She stiffened, but he touched her cheek. "Relax, Jane, we're alone."

She relaxed and they turned to walk down the hill. "How is he doing?" she asked.

"He's not as stupid as I thought he was." They laughed together. "I think we're going to make a deal and I'll be able to fulfill my dream."

"That's great, Gordon."

Amanda greeted her at the door when she returned to the office. "David and his father are in your office. I think something is wrong."

"You mean his uncle, don't you?" Jane looked in the direction of her office.

"That's right. I keep forgetting. They look so much alike."

Jane took off her coat and hung it on the rack by the

door. When she went into her office David was standing with his back to her. His head was bowed and Jeff had a hand on the back of his neck. The other hand was on his shoulder.

"When am I going to stop screwing up, Uncle Jeff?" David said.

"This wasn't your fault, David."

Jane went straight to him. Putting a hand on David's arm she turned him to face her. His eyes were red and swollen. "What's wrong, David? You're not in trouble?"

"It's not me, Jane, it's Lenny." David sat down and put his face in his hands. "He called me around 2:00 a.m. He's in jail. He wanted me to post bail."

"You didn't do it, did you?" Jane sat in the chair across from him and leaned forward.

"No." David looked up at her.

Jeff put his hand on David's back. "He came to me wondering what to do," he said to Jane. "I brought him here to tell you about it."

"What did Lenny do?" Jane asked.

"It's bad, Jane. I thought he was clean, but apparently he's been doing cocaine. He got really messed up last night and stole a car."

"He stole a car!" Jane sat back. "I can't believe it."

"It's worse than that, Jane." He rubbed his eyes. Jane pulled his hands away from his face and held them.

"Tell me, David."

"He's been dating Anna for a while. I don't know if you were aware of that."

"I suspected."

"Well, he went to her apartment and they had an argument. I guess they must have been making a lot of noise, because a neighbor called the police. Lenny forced Anna into the car, but by the time he got her there the police had arrived." David took a deep breath and stood up. He started to pace. "I guess he must have tried to run away from them or something. Anyway, he wrecked the car. Anna was hurt pretty bad. She's in the hospital."

"Oh, my God!" Jane got up and went to her desk. "What hospital is she in?"

"Northside. Her condition is serious, but stable. I already checked. I don't know the details. I thought I'd go over there after I told you." David stopped pacing and picked up an envelope that was sitting on the desk. "This is my resignation, Jane."

She took the envelope and tore it in half. "Not accepted"

"Jane, this is my fault. I thought he was clean. I've brought shame to the magazine."

"You haven't done anything, but a very good job, David. You may have introduced Lenny, but I hired him. I knew I was taking a chance."

"I told you she'd feel that way." Jeff put an arm across David's shoulders and squeezed.

"The question is what to do now." Jane was flipping through her rolodex.

"He had a large amount of cocaine on him when he was arrested. His cube needs to be searched." David took a deep breath. "But I'm afraid to go near it."

"You are not to go near it. In fact I want you to leave here for a while." She looked at Jeff. "Will you take him home and get him cleaned up."

"I'll take him home," Jeff said. "He can clean himself up."

"One of my former co-workers is married to a City of Atlanta policeman. I'll call him. Find out what we need to do." Jane came around the desk to David. "Don't take on the whole world, David. This was not your fault. It's your responsibility to keep yourself out of trouble, not Lenny." She stood on her toes and kissed his cheek.

"Thanks, Jane. I just hope Anna will be all right."

"Me too."

Jane knocked on the door to the hospital room. There was no answer so she pushed it open a little. "Anna, it's me, Jane. May I come in?"

"Yes, come in, Jane." Anna sat up in her bed. Her head was bandaged. Her nose was swollen and one arm lay across her lap in a cast."

"Well, you really got banged up," Jane said. She put the vase of flowers she was carrying on a table and went over to the bed.

"This is the story of my life. Did you know that, Jane?

"I don't know anything about your life, Anna."

"My mother was a junky. I was born addicted to heroin."

"I'm sorry. That's a really tough way to start," Jane said. "But you've done very well. You didn't let your bad start hurt you."

"I didn't let it ruin me, but it did hurt me."

Jane was silent. She didn't know what to say.

"I didn't want to date Lenny. I've pretty much stayed away from men...pretty much stayed away from everyone. He just wouldn't take no for an answer." She looked down at her casted arm. "I broke it off as soon as I found out about the drugs. I have to stay far away from that stuff. I've already been an addict once."

"Through no fault of your own."

"Doesn't matter, once an addict, always an addict. The only defense is to stay away from it, but it just seems to follow me around." She sniffed. "You know what's stupid?" She looked up at Jane. Her brown eyes were swimming with tears. They spilled over and ran down her cheeks. "I really love him."

Jane pulled a tissue from the box on the table beside the bed and wiped Anna's tears. "We all love him, Anna. The hard thing is that you can't just stop loving him because you discovered he's no good."

Anna took the tissue from Jane and scrubbed her eyes. "And he is no good, Jane. He'll go to prison again for this and when he gets out, he'll do it again. He can't do anything else."

"I'm afraid you're right. He won't try to come back to the magazine, though. He knows I won't take him back. I know it doesn't feel like it right now, Anna, but you'll get through this."

"Oh, I know. I manage to get through everything. I'm a rock."

Jane wondered what other horrors lurked in this innocent child's background. Maybe some day she'd be close enough to find out. Anyway, Anna had talked to her more just now than she ever had before. "Anna, I'm going to call the whole group together tomorrow to talk about what happened. I know you can't be there, but I just wanted you to know. It's going to be hard on everyone. Lenny was a big part of the magazine."

The next morning Jane arrived early at the office. Everyone was already there. Victoria was waiting for her in her office. "Where's the seedling I gave you?" she asked.

"It's at home. Gordon's helping me with it. He's pretty good with plants."

"How's it doing?"

"I think it's doing well. What is it?"

"It's a banyan tree."

"A banyan tree, you mean like those trees that grow in Florida with all the roots that hang from the branches."

"That's right."

"What do I want with one of those? They can't live up here and they get too big to stay in the house."

"I'm trying my hand at the art of Bonsai."

"Tori," Jane said. "You just never quit, do you?"

"Of course not, so what's this meeting about?"

"I'll tell everyone together. Let's go into the conference room."

They went into the other room. The whole group was there, except Anna and Lenny, of course. They all looked around expectantly when Jane shut the door behind her.

"Anna and Lenny won't be joining us." Jane told the story in as few words as possible. All faces registered concern for Anna and hurt and anger for Lenny's betrayal.

"This is hard on us as a group. When you start something like this magazine, you become very close to the people involved," Jane said. "I'm available to talk to anyone any time, of course, but I think it will probably help if we voice our feelings as a group."

"I feel guilty," Mark said.

"Why?" Jane asked.

"I had reservations about him in the beginning. I decided to get to know him before I said anything. He convinced me. I liked him. Maybe this could have been prevented if I'd said something."

"I don't know, Mark," Grant said. "I think you were right not to go on your first impression. First impressions can be deceiving. I liked him, too, right from the start."

David sat in the back of the room quietly. Jane hoped he would say something. He needed to express his feelings, but she didn't want to force him.

"I didn't know he'd been in prison before," Michael said. "I'd never have guessed. He just seemed so... wholesome."

"I knew he'd been in prison before," David said from the back.

"David," Jane said. "You don't have to—"

"I need to, Jane." He held up his hand. Facing his coworkers, he said, "He was in prison with me."

The room was silent. All eyes were on David.

"I got my degree there. When I got out I had a hard time finding a job. I was delivering pizza and getting very discouraged. When Jane gave me this chance, I brought Lenny with me." He rubbed his eyes. "So don't feel bad about being taken in by him. I've known him for five years and I believed he was clean," he looked up. "Like me."

"That must have been tough, David," Mark said. "Being in prison..."

"It was, but it was my fault I was there. I got caught selling marijuana." He looked around the room "I learned something from it, though. I'm never going back there." He looked around the room again. "I also want you to know that I gave Jane my written resignation yesterday. She tore it up, but if any of you want me to go, I'll go."

"Who's going to do your job, David, me?" Grant said. "I've got enough to do."

"I believe in you, David," Michael said.

"This has been almost as hard on you as it has on Anna," Victoria said. "No one wants you to leave, David."

"I'm glad that's settled," Jane said. "Anybody else need to say something?"

"Do you think this will affect the magazine in any way?" Grant asked.

"I don't know. We're so new, not that well known yet, but it may come up. I had a friend of mine who is part of the Atlanta police force search Lenny's cube last night. Luckily there was nothing illegal in it. So we won't have any complications there." She paused. "The press will be at the fashion show next month of course, and if they get wind of this there will be questions. We'll just have to deal with it. We haven't done anything wrong and I just think we should not comment on it."

"I agree, Jane," Grant said. "I guess we'll be looking for another features editor."

"That's right, if any of you know anyone, let me know. I'll start looking." They filed out of the room leaving Jane, Victoria, and David.

Victoria got up and gave David a kiss on the cheek. "I'm proud of you, honey. You're a good man, just like your uncle."

"Thanks, Vic." David blushed.

Jane smiled. "See ya later, Tori." She waved as Victoria left the room.

"Ready to get back to work?" Jane asked.

"Almost," David said, looking up at her. "I'd like to go to the hospital to see Anna first, if that's okay."

"That's fine. Tell her I'll be by later."

"What color are you going to choose today?" Victoria asked Jane, as she studied the color panel at the nail salon.

"Well, I was thinking black when I came over here, but I'm starting to feel a little better. It was a stressful morning. It's been a stressful couple of days." Jane chose a nice red color and sat down.

"Red, that's the first time you've chosen anything normal. You must be relaxing." Victoria said.

"I got pink once." She looked out the window. "Oh, here come Lauren and Katherine and Jill. I told you I called them, didn't I?"

"Yes, and you told me to tell Lillian. She just drove up."

The door to the salon opened and a gust of cold air swept through the shop while the three ladies filed in. Another gust hit when Lillian came in a second later. Jane got up and went over to the group.

"I'm so glad you could all manage to come. This is the most wonderful therapy. Victoria introduced it to me last summer." She embraced them all one by one. "Of course, everyone knows each other, except Lillian." She moved over to Lillian and took her arm. "Lillian," Jane turned to the others. "These are my..."

They all three chuckled. "What are we, Jane?" Katherine asked, still smiling at the confused look on Jane's face.

"...friends," Jane said, and fell unusually silent.

"Well, that's definitely true." Katherine stepped forward. "Actually, Jane, we all met at your Thanksgiving feast, but just to refresh, Lillian," she said, "I'm Gordon's daughter, Katherine, and these are my sister's in law, Jill and Lauren."

They nodded at each other. "Jane says that this is wonderful therapy. Have you ever had a pedicure before?" Jill asked.

"No, I haven't." Lillian said as they all found seats around the U shape of the chairs that were set up for the service.

Lauren had hung back a little, looking shy, but she stepped forward now. "I haven't either. I've heard that they soak your feet in hot paraffin. Sit here, Lillian." She pointed to the seat next to her. "I wonder what that feels like."

"It's great," Jane said as she and Victoria sat down. The way the tables were arranged they could all see each other. "I thought this was a great idea. In fact, I was thinking that maybe we should form a group and do something nice together every couple of months."

"You know, Jane, Lauren and Katherine and I have been talking about starting a *Mom's night out*. It would be even better if the two of you joined us," Jill said.

"Are you sure you wouldn't mind that we're not moms?" Jane said.

"I'm a mom," Victoria said. "And you're a step mom and a grand mom."

"That's right, Jane," Katherine said.

"Besides," Jill put in. "It's not to enjoy being a mom that we want to get out, but to take a break from it. It's probably a good thing to have members of the group who aren't preoccupied with it."

Jane glanced at Lauren. She was studying the color panel and staying conspicuously silent. "How do you feel about us joining your Mom's night out group, Lauren?" Jane said.

"I'd like it, Jane. I'm not sure I'd be able to make all of the nights, though," she said.

"Lauren's been our holdout," Katherine said. "I'm not sure she trusts Grant with the kids," she said.

"Of course I do." Lauren smiled stiffly. "It's just that he works really hard. I'm home all day. It's not fair to ask him to work at night, too."

"My thought was this," Jane said. "And don't feel at all bad about telling me it won't work. I was thinking about Saturday afternoon. I don't know about all the rest, but Gordon always watches some kind of sports event on Saturday afternoon."

"Michael, too," Jill said.

"Joe, too," Victoria said. "He always asks me to watch with him, but I just don't really want to."

"I like sports," Lauren said. Everyone looked at her with interest. "Not as much as Grant does, of course." She looked around at everyone again. She smiled slowly. "I suppose I could give up one Saturday a month." She laughed then sobered. "But with the men all involved in sports, can they really be watching the kids?"

"I think they can," Victoria said. "I remember feeling that way, but after what we've been through lately, I've realized how much Joe loves our kids." Everyone looked at her. "I know they do some stupid things, but I think they care enough to pay attention to the important stuff."

"What's happened lately?" Lauren asked, and then flushed. "Oh, I'm sorry, Victoria. That's none of my business."

"If I wasn't open to talking about it, I wouldn't have mentioned it," Victoria said. "A little over a year ago, our youngest daughter was beaten and left for dead by her boyfriend."

"Oh, no!" Lauren said.

"What did you do?" Katherine asked.

"What could we do?" Victoria said. "She was out in California and we went out there and got her. She was covered with bruises and broken bones. We gathered her things and brought her home. It was strange, though. Joe blamed himself completely."

"Why?" Lauren asked.

"He felt that he had always been so close to Ellen, our older daughter, that he had neglected Patricia, the one that got hurt." She stopped and looked down at her feet while the attendant put them in plastic bags after dipping them in paraffin then put them in booties. Everyone had stopped for the same reason.

"So tell us," Katherine said.

"Well, we brought her home and tried to nurture her back to health. Let me tell you, that was hard. No matter what we did, we just couldn't reach her. I got frustrated. Then I got angry. She wouldn't even try to help herself."

Jane touched her arm. "You don't have to bare your heart here, Tori."

"I know, but we're all learning to be friends here. I want them to know me," she said.

"We won't push if you don't want to say any more," Lauren said.

"Oh, she wants to say more," Lillian said, and then chuckled.

"Shut up, Lillian," Victoria said, smiling at her. "Anyway, after I realized that no matter what I did, I couldn't make a difference to her, I just kind of took care of myself and watched. Not Joe, though. First thing he did was talk her into going to a greyhound rescue shelter. She's always loved animals." She paused again as the manicurist dried her feet and started to buff. "We found a dog there that had been so abused that he cowered on the floor and watched you as if he thought you might hit him. Patricia bonded with him immediately."

"Those dogs are huge," Jill said. "I saw one the other day at the pet store. It looked just like Fred and Isis, but huge."

"I know. I was scared. What if the thing was viscous because of its bad beginning?" Victoria said. "But Patricia reached him and he reached her. She kissed her father on the cheek that night and thanked him." She wiped a tear. "It was beautiful."

All of them sniffed.

"Don't you think she should write novels?" Jane said. "Isn't she great?"

The room rocked with laughter.

"Anyway, Lauren," Victoria said. "My point is that the dads really do care. They'll take care of the kids when you aren't there."

"I suppose you're right. I know Grant loves them. I just really get scared every time I can't see her." She looked up quickly. "I mean *them*." She looked down again. "Truth is I don't worry as much about Gary as I do about Maggie." Her face flushed.

"Of course you don't," Katherine said. "Maggie

almost didn't make it when she was a baby. I don't know if I could have come through like you did."

"Me neither," Jill said. "In fact, I was much more afraid when I was carrying Alexandra than with any of the others, because of what I'd seen you and Grant go through. Michael was, too."

"Really?" Lauren looked around the room.

"She almost didn't make it?" Lillian asked. "What happened?"

Lauren reached next to her and grabbed Lillian's hand. "It was awful. I hardly even remember giving birth to her. I just remember asking the nurses to let me see her." She paused and let go of Lillian's hand. "Grant had been with me, just like when Gary was born, but the doctor pulled him away as soon as the baby was out. The nurses just cleaned me up and put me on a gurney and took me to a room. I kept saying, 'Where's my baby?' I want to hold her."

"Oh, Lauren," Jane said. "That must have been awful."

"It was. Then the doctor and Grant came into the room. Grant was the color of ashes. The doctor told me there was a problem. He said he wasn't sure she'd pull through." Lauren looked at her hands for a minute. Everyone was quiet. "Grant held me and we both cried. I'm not sure how long." Her shoulders relaxed. Jane had never seen her look so relaxed. The room was quiet while the attendants set up small fans on everyone's toes.

"I'll tell you what, though." Katherine broke the silence. "Maggie is something else. She's beautiful, she's smart, and she's determined. She'll do fine."

"That's the truth," Jill said.

"I think you're right," Lauren said. "In one way I wish she'd be more pliable." She looked around the room. "So I could take care of her. In other ways, I'm so proud."

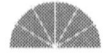

Chapter Twenty-One

"Have I ever told you how much I love my little sister?" Jane asked Gordon on the way to Grant and Lauren's house for the birthday party that Saturday.

"Maybe once or twice..." He laughed. "What did she do?"

"When I got us all together for pedicures the other day, she told a story about a problem they had with Patricia last year. It had the affect of making Lauren open up. She talked about the whole experience with Maggie. I don't even think she'd ever told Jill and Katherine about it."

"That's great," Gordon said. They rode in silence for a while. "It'll be nice to see Grant and Lauren's new house furnished. I haven't seen it since I helped them move in. You know, Gary's planning to talk Rick into building him a tree house like the one in their back yard."

"Do you think Rick will do it?"

"I think so, if he can find time. His business is doing great, Kathy says."

"If he can't, I think I'll hire someone to do it. Everyone should have a tree house when they're growing up." Jane looked out the window.

Gordon picked up her hand and kissed the back of it. "Did you have a tree house when you were growing up?"

"No. And I didn't miss it until I saw Eric and Teddy's."

"And Valerie Jane's."

"You always call her by both names."

"I like the way it sounds." Gordon pulled into the driveway beside Michael and Jill's station wagon. "It looks like everyone's here. Did I tell you Mom and Dad would be here?"

"No, how about Jerry and Shannon?"

"Them too."

"Were you afraid I wouldn't come if I knew?"

"A little." Gordon smiled at her. She reached over to touch the smile lines beside his eyes and he pulled her close and kissed her. He cupped her chin with his hand and deepened the kiss. For a minute Jane forgot where she was.

There was a tap on the window and loud giggling from outside. "Grampa, stop kissing Janie and come in. The party's started without you," Maggie's voice piped. She stood outside Jane's window with Hope and Michael.

"Busted by the birthday babies," Gordon said, a smile spreading across his face.

Jane could feel a blush rise up her neck to her face. "You know, Gordon, before I met you, I never blushed—"

"Or cried or fainted." Gordon leaned close to her for a second. "Anything else?" He grinned wickedly.

They laughed together as they got out of the car.

Maggie grabbed both of their hands and started to pull; Hope had Jane by the other hand. Michael fell in next to Gordon. Jane heard him say, "If I'd realized you were about to kiss her, I'd have held them back a minute." He smiled at his dad.

"Thanks, but I didn't realize it myself until it happened. Happy birthday," he said, putting his hand on Michael's shoulder.

"Grampa, Janie," Teddy said, charging toward them when they came in. "There's a playroom," he said clearly. He grabbed Gordon's hand and said, "Mon...au...shoya." He was dressed in jeans with an elastic waist and a tiny polo shirt. He was wearing running shoes on his little feet.

"Teddy, you look so handsome!" Jane said as she

followed him and Gordon down the hall. "Gordon," she whispered. "He's not a baby any more. He's a little boy."

"You have to pay close attention, they grow up fast."

They climbed the steps to a room over the garage. It was big and had large windows on each end. There was a wet bar in one corner with a refrigerator. The rest of the room was a playroom. There were toy boxes and a computer. One entire wall was an entertainment center. All the kids, except for the baby, were in the room engaged in various entertainments.

"Grampa!" Joy pulled herself away from the show she was watching on TV. She ran to Gordon and hugged him as he swung her up in his arms.

Gordon put Joy down and they walked around the room visiting with each child.

"Hey, Dad." Grant came into the room. "Isn't this a great playroom?"

"It sure is," Gordon said. They were standing behind Gary as he worked on the computer. "Gary was showing us his photo-editing program. It's great. I think I'll get one and have Gary train me."

"I can do that, Grampa." Gary looked over his shoulder for a second.

"I know you can." Gordon smiled at Grant.

"Come down to the living room with the grown ups, Dad. Jane would probably like a glass of wine." He put his arm around Jane's shoulders. "I know you're just dying to see Gramma and Grampa again."

"I didn't tell her they were coming until we got here," Gordon said.

"That was smart." They started down the stairs.

"Janie, wait," Hope called. "You too, Grampa. I want to tell you about the aquarium I got for my birthday."

"Tell us," Gordon said. They walked down the stairs to the kitchen.

"It's thirty gallons. I've got twenty-five fish in it. I can't wait to show it to you."

"Hope, that's huge," Jane said. "It must be beautiful. Tell me about the fish."

"Hope has always loved fish," Gordon said.

"Actually, Grampa," Hope said. "It's the whole underwater world I love. I like the plants, too, and the rocks. I love working with the stones and gravel. In fact, I've found really nice gravel. It doesn't change the pH of the water."

"You're so smart, Hope," Gordon said.

"She is. Have you been to the aquarium in Chattanooga yet?" Jane asked.

"No, I keep asking, but everyone's too busy. I think they're just not interested."

"I'll take you," Jane said. "I've wanted to go, but nobody wants to go with me either."

"That would be so much fun, Janie! When can we go?" Hope was jumping up and down.

"Well, next weekend, Grampa and I are going to Seattle to see my grand nephew. When we get back the next week, I'll need to spend some time at the magazine. So let's say three weeks from today. Can you stand it?"

"I think so."

"Can I come, or is this *girls* only?" Gordon asked.

"It's okay with me if he comes, Janie, how about you?" Hope replied.

"I'd love to have some time with just you, Hope, but I'm always happy when he's around."

"You can come, Grampa," Hope said. "We'd better go into the living room. Dad's got a toast planned."

Gordon and Jane followed Hope into the room. The whole group was gathered. All of the children had come down from the playroom. Katherine was holding Valerie and talking to Teddy. Lauren was involved in an animated conversation with Gary. Jill sat on the couch holding Alexandra. Gordon guided Jane over to his parents and kissed his mother then embraced his father.

"Gordon, I figured you'd have put some weight on her by now," Gordon Senior said while eyeing Jane. "The other one was fat within months of your marriage."

"The other one was pregnant within months of our marriage," Gordon said, then looked at Jane and shrugged.

"I don't think he could fatten me up if he tried," she said. "I think it's metabolism."

"Well, even with the tall and skinny look, you're cute," Jerry said, joining them.

"Shut up, Jerry," Minerva said to her youngest son. "It's good to see you again, Joan."

"Jane," Gordon said. "Her name is *Jane*." He widened his eyes at her.

She smiled easily at him.

"Could I have everyone's attention?" Michael called from the end of the room. "I'd like to make a toast." He was standing behind the couch. Hope and Maggie were standing beside him. He picked Maggie up and stood her on the back of the couch. Then he helped Hope climb up to the back of the couch on the other side of him. He held them both around the waist. "Dad," he said. "Step a little closer to Jane and hold her tight."

Gordon stepped in beside Jane and put his arm around her waist. "My pleasure," he said. "I've got her."

Jane looked at him questioningly.

"I want you all to look at the three of us," Michael said. "Do we have anything in common?" he asked the group.

There was a rumble of laughter.

"I want to thank my mother for the dramatic, if challenging, coloring." He held his glass of wine up and said, "To Mom. Thanks for our birthdays."

Hope held her glass of juice up and said, "To Gramma." Maggie followed suit.

Jane felt the lightness come to her head. Gordon tightened his hold on her. She exhaled then took a deep breath, smiling all the time.

"Are you all right?" Gordon whispered in her ear.

She nudged her elbow into his ribs, separating them slightly. "I'm fine." She smiled at Michael as he glanced at her with concern.

"I'd also like to toast my dad," Michael said. "Without both of them, the three of us, and a good number of the rest of you, wouldn't exist. Happy Birthday, Hope, Maggie," he said.

"Happy Birthday, Uncle Michael," Maggie said

"Happy Birthday, Dad." Said Hope.

Jane smiled and chatted all the way through dinner. Only Gordon noticed that she didn't eat much. She was silent on the way home.

"Jane, you can't expect him not to honor his mother on his birthday," Gordon said as they opened the door to their apartment.

"Of course I don't, Gordon. What do you think of me? What must everyone think of me?" She hung her coat in the closet and started down the hall.

"Everyone loves you, Jane." Gordon put his hand on her arm and turned her to him. "Jane, have you thought any more about going to therapy with me? I felt you tense when Michael made that toast. Let's get to the bottom of this."

"I tensed, but I didn't faint. Now leave me alone. I need to lie down."

"Jane, you can't just learn how to avoid fainting. We need to work this out."

"Why can't you just let this go? It's my problem, not yours," she snapped.

"Jane!" Gordon turned her to face him and held her by the shoulders. "Don't forget, I've buried a wife. I've watched helplessly while someone I loved died. This scares me to death."

"I went to the doctor about it. I'm fine. This is a psychological problem."

"That's why I want us to go to a psychologist to deal with it," Gordon said.

"I'm nauseated. If you don't let me go, I'll throw up on you."

Gordon released her and she ran down the hall to the bathroom. After she'd emptied the meager contents of her stomach into the toilet, she washed her face, rinsed her mouth, and went to the bed to lie down.

Gordon came into the room and sat down on the bed beside her. "Are you all right?"

"I am now. I just need to go to sleep."

"Jane, it's getting worse. Now you don't faint, but you vomit."

"I'm sure something I ate didn't agree with me. That's all."

"You didn't eat anything, Jane." They were both silent for a minute. "We're not finished talking about this, Jane."

"Not now, please?" She closed her eyes. After a minute Gordon got up. A second later she heard the door to his studio shut.

Jane stripped off her clothes and dropped them to the floor. She crawled between the sheets naked. Fred burrowed under the covers and stretched out beside her.

"Oh, Fred," she said. "Why is this so hard for me?" She snuggled the warm little dog and drifted off to sleep.

On Monday morning, Jane got to work a little late. Amanda greeted her as she came in. She went to her office and hung up her coat. Sitting down at her desk, she put her head down on her crossed arms. Gordon had insisted that she not go cycling on Sunday. She had agreed, whether it was because she really didn't feel well, or she just didn't have the energy to argue, she wasn't sure.

The phone rang and she picked it up. "*Second Half,* Jane Fox."

"Jane, this is Lenny," a familiar voice said.

"Hello, Lenny, where are you?"

"I'm still in jail. No one would post bail. Not even my mother."

"I hope you're not calling to ask me to," Jane said.

"No. I know better than that. I'm calling to apologize."

"Have you called Anna to apologize?"

"Yes, but she won't take my calls. She has caller ID. She won't pick up," he said. "I don't blame her."

"I don't either."

"Jane, I didn't intend to let this happen again. When I took the job with you I meant to stay clean. I just couldn't."

"I believe that, but it doesn't make a difference. You'll never come back here, Lenny."

"I know, and the truth is I think prison is the best place for me. I do my best work here," he said. "Jane, I plan to keep writing. I was hoping you'd let me send you my articles. If not, I'll send them to other magazines, but I'd like to give you first chance at them. I'm a drug addict, and a thief, and not really fit for society, but I'm also a brilliant writer."

Jane took a deep breath. "Send them to me. I'd like to see them. If they're good, I'll print them."

"Thanks, Jane."

"Lenny, I hope you'll be all right," she said. "And if you ever get out..."

"Yeah..?"

"Don't come near us again."

"I won't."

She got up and went down the hall to Anna's cube. She wasn't surprised to find Anna working at her drafting table. "I guess it's a good thing it was your left arm that got broken in the accident," Jane said.

"Very lucky," Anna said, managing a smile that didn't quite reach her eyes.

"I'm glad to see you back, Anna. We've missed you around here."

"I was only gone a few days."

"We still missed you," Jane said. "I just talked to Lenny."

"You're not letting him come back here, are you?"

"Trust me more than that, Anna." Jane put her hand

on Anna's shoulder. "I did tell him he could send me his articles and short stories from prison. I said if they were good, we'd publish them. That's only if it's all right with you."

Anna looked into Jane's eyes. "I think they'll be good. He's very talented." She looked back down at her work. "We should publish them."

"Do you want to read them first?" Jane asked.

Anna stopped her work and stared straight ahead for a minute. "Yes, please."

"All right, Anna, if you want to talk, I'm always willing to listen."

Anna looked at her. Her eyes were warmer than usual. "Thanks Jane. I'll let you know if I need you."

Jane left the cube and walked back toward her office. Michael joined her about half way down the hall. When they got to the office Grant came in behind them.

"Are you all right, Jane?" Grant asked. "You looked so pale when you left the house on Saturday."

"I'm fine. I had a little virus or something. It's gone now." She sat down. Michael didn't say anything, but she noticed him looking at her.

"You still look pale," Grant persisted.

"I just talked to Lenny," she said. "It's hard for me. I was very fond of him."

"And yet you still have to reject him," Grant said. "I know that's hard."

Jane looked at Michael. He hadn't stopped watching her since he came into the room. "Michael, what are you thinking?"

"I think this problem you have with my mother is bigger than we thought. I think Dad's right. You need to get help with it."

"Jesus!" Jane stood and started to pace. "Six months ago nobody knew my business. Nobody tried to tell me how to deal with my problems."

"Six month ago you were alone. You're part of this family now," he said.

Grant had watched the exchange quietly, but now

he said, "That's true, Jane. I know you only married Dad, but you got all of us in the bargain, and that includes Mom's memory."

She sat back down behind her desk and put her face in her hands. "I shouldn't have done it. It was a mistake. I'm just not cut out for a family."

"Too late. You might be able to leave us," Michael said. "But you love Dad too much. I can see it in the way you look at him."

"I can feel it when you're together," Grant said.

Jane looked up at the two men in front of her. They both looked like their father, but different too. They were separate people and she loved them both. She thought of their children and their wives. They'd become so close to her heart. Katherine and her family meant so much to her. She could still feel the way Eric had clung to her in the hospital. She sniffed and pulled a tissue from the box on her desk.

"I couldn't leave you either. I couldn't leave any one of you. I love you all."

"I hoped you felt that way," Michael said. "So let Dad make an appointment. Let's work through this."

"I'll talk to him about it after we get back from Seattle," Jane said. She looked up at Michael and Grant. "I promise." Michael leaned across the desk and kissed her cheek. Grant did the same and they both left.

"I'm so excited that the four of us are doing this together," Victoria said, as they drove from the airport in Seattle to Ellen and Alex's house.

"Are you sure we shouldn't have rented two cars?" Jane asked. "We might not always want to do the same thing."

"You and Gordon will only be here four days. If you want to go off and do something, you can take the car. Joe and I want to spend as much time as we can with Benjamin," Victoria said.

"That's true," Jane said. "We'll want to be with Benjamin as much as possible, too. I can't believe how fast they change, Tori. Did I tell you how much Teddy has grown?"

"You did," Victoria said. "I know what you mean, though, they go from babies to children over night."

"And Valerie is sitting up and playing with hand toys, you know, rattles and plastic keys, that kind of thing."

"Jane, you're such a grandmamma," Joe said.

"I'm not their grandmother."

"Yes you are, Jane," Joe said, oblivious to the fear in her voice.

Gordon squeezed her hand.

"Here we are," Victoria said as they pulled up to a large house in a neighborhood of equally large houses.

"They've done well," Jane said. "I can't believe that wild, crazy Ellen owns a house like this."

"Me neither," Victoria said. "But she does, with Alex, of course." They all got out of the car and walked to the front door. Joe rang the door bell.

After a minute it swung open. Alex stood in the entrance, his hair standing up at all angles.

"You've been messing with your hair," Victoria said. "What's wrong?" She charged into the house with Joe right behind her.

"I just can't get Ellen to calm down. I can't make her stop crying," Alex said.

Gordon and Jane stepped back on the walk way. Alex hadn't seemed to notice them.

"Is she in the bedroom?" Victoria asked as she hurried down the hall. "Where's Benjamin?"

Joe put an arm across Alex's shoulders and steered him toward the inside of the house. "What's going on, Alex?" Jane heard him say as she stepped forward and shut the door.

"I don't think we belong in there right now," she said to Gordon.

"I think you're right. Maybe we should find a hotel.

I know Ellen said they had room for us, but under the circumstances…”

“You’re probably right.” They had walked back out toward the car. “Oh, look, Gordon, they’re so close to the water.” Jane pointed around the side of the house. They could see the opening of the harbor.

“There’s a foot path. Let’s take a walk while we wait for things to calm down inside.” Gordon put his arm around her and guided her to the path. There was a cold breeze blowing, but they were bundled up well. “The first year with the first child is always really hard on a marriage,” he said.

“Tori has been worried about that. She said the first year of marriage is hard enough, but Alex and Ellen were expecting Benjamin when they got married,” Jane explained as they walked. The cold air was delightful. She raised her face to the breeze. “I guess I probably shouldn’t have told you that.”

“It doesn’t matter. That’s what happened to Michael and Jill, too.”

“I know. He told me.” She looked at Gordon and smiled.

“They had a hard time, too. There wasn’t anything we could do, though, but be there for support,” Gordon said. “The hard thing is that you get attached really fast to the in-law, the one your child has married, and you know if the marriage doesn’t work, you’ll have to give them up.”

“I hadn’t thought about that,” Jane said. “I’m crazy about Alex. I hope they work through it.”

“I do too.”

They walked in silence for a while. The breeze coming off the water was wonderful. Soon they turned back toward the house.

“Is that Joe coming this way?” Gordon asked.

“Looks like it.”

When they reached each other, Joe said, “I think things are under control inside now. Victoria can really pull things together when she has to.”

"Maybe we should find a hotel, Joe," Jane said. "This much company is just too stressful."

"Maybe," Joe said, "but let's go in and talk about it first, okay?"

They went in the back door and stopped in a small mudroom to brush off their shoes. Joe led them through a spacious kitchen and into the living room.

Ellen hurried over to Jane and hugged her then hugged Gordon. "I'm really sorry about the greeting, but I'm so glad you're here. Alex has already put your bags in your room."

"Ellen, are you sure you don't want us to find a hotel? It's hard to have this much company in your home," Jane said.

"I insist you stay."

"Please stay," Alex said. "Don't get her started again." He walked to a wet bar in the corner of the room.

Ellen frowned in his direction.

"Would anyone like something to drink?" Alex asked. "I've got beer, wine, soft drinks."

A wailing sound came from down the hall and Ellen said, "Benjamin's up," and started down the hall. Victoria and Jane followed her, leaving the men in the living room. Ellen went to the crib and picked up the baby. He was standing up holding on to the rail. She pulled him into her arms. He looked at Victoria and Jane then buried his face in his mother's shoulder.

"He's shy when he first wakes up. He'll warm up in a minute," Ellen said.

"Of course he is," Victoria said. "Who wants to wake up and look at a bunch of strange people first thing? I'm sure he's wet. I'll get a diaper ready." She went to the change table.

"Benjamin, you remember Granny," Ellen said. He picked up his head and turned to look at Victoria. He grinned and buried his head again. "And this is..." She looked at Jane.

"Janie. Gordon's grandkids call me *Janie*."

"This is Janie." Benjamin turned his head, laid it flat on his mother's chest and smiled at Jane.

"What a cheerful boy," Jane said.

"Let's get a clean diaper and go see Daddy," Ellen said. Benjamin giggled.

Jane and Victoria watched and played peek-a-boo games with him while Ellen changed his diaper and put a warm sleeper on him. She set him down and he toddled out the door and down the hall.

"There's my boy," Alex said, scooping him up in his arms. He bounced a little.

Jane looked at Gordon and smiled, remembering him bouncing around the room with Valerie. He smiled back.

"Gordon was just telling us about the first-year marital problems Jane and he are having," Joe said.

Gordon stiffened and Alex stopped bouncing. They both looked at Joe.

"Did I say something wrong?" Joe asked.

"I'm sure Gordon didn't expect you to share that with Jane," Victoria said.

"I didn't expect it, but if I'd been trying to hide it, I should have kept my mouth shut."

Jane went to his side and kissed his cheek. "Keep talking," she said. "I can't wait to hear this."

"Well, I was just telling them about how you faint every time the family talks about..." He stopped and looked at her.

"Better get ready to catch me," she said, and leaned in and kissed his lips. "I know what you're doing," she whispered in his ear.

"Anyway, since I've already buried one wife, I don't want to bury another," he said, after he squeezed her waist. "I want to work this problem out. Your wife is your *soul mate*."

A beeping sound started in the kitchen. Ellen said, "My casserole needs stirring," and started for the kitchen.

Jane and Victoria followed her in.

"I just can't do anything right for him any more," Ellen said. She opened the oven and pulled out the dish.

"It's a really tough time," Victoria said. "Starting a marriage is hard and having a baby is hard on a marriage. Put the two together and it's twice as hard."

"I'm sure that's true," Jane said.

"Are you and Gordon really struggling?" Ellen looked at Jane as she stirred.

"Well, yes," Jane said, realizing it was true. "I just love him so much, his family, too. But I'm really struggling with—"

"The first wife," Victoria said. "She faints every time someone mentions her."

"I do not, Tori," Jane said.

"I've seen it happen," Victoria said. "Remember when Jeff had to carry you—"

"Shut up, Tori."

Ellen laughed. "*I* haven't fainted. In fact, I can't imagine you fainting, Aunt Jane. You're always such a rock."

Jane looked at Ellen. She was smiling easily for the first time since they'd arrived.

"Not only do I faint," Jane said as she sat down at the kitchen table and propped her chin on her hands, "but I blush and I cry and I vomit."

"You vomit?" Victoria asked.

"That's right. When Michael made a toast to his mother on his birthday, which I know was completely acceptable, I controlled the urge to faint, but when I got home, I threw up."

"Aunt Jane, you're kidding." Ellen sat down next to her and took her hand.

"No. Gordon wants to go to therapy together, but I just want to deal with it myself," she said, squeezing Ellen's hand back. "I'm starting to think maybe he's right, though."

"What bothers you about therapy?" Ellen asked.

"I don't know for sure. I've just always been so independent. I've always coveted my privacy, too."

"I've been trying to talk Alex into couple's therapy," Ellen said. "He doesn't want it either." She looked at her hand joined with Jane's. "I just love him so much, but we can't go on like this. I want to try everything before we just give up." She pulled her hand away and brushed away a tear. "He's finally agreed, but I don't think his heart is really in it."

Victoria put her arms around Ellen's shoulders and kissed the top of her head.

Jane looked into Ellen's eyes, and said, "Thank you, Ellen. You're right." She brushed a tear away from Ellen's cheek. "I'm sorry you're having a hard time." The three of them embraced.

"What's going on in here?" Gordon asked, walking into the kitchen.

"We're cooking," Victoria said as they moved apart.

Chapter Twenty-Two

"Tell us what the plans are," Victoria said to Ellen when they sat down to dinner. They had all gone to their rooms and freshened up then met back in the living room for a cocktail.

"Well, Benjamin's birthday is on Saturday, so we're having some friends in for lunch. Since they're babies, we don't want to do it over dinner. That's suicide hour."

"I remember that," Victoria said. "You were the worst. You were so horrible between about 4:30 p.m. and 6:30 p.m. that Dad started calling it cocktail hour," she said, squeezing Joe's hand.

"Hasn't changed much," Alex said.

Ellen glared at him.

"You know, Alex," Victoria said. "Your hostility is inappropriate. If you have something to say, just say it. It would be more honest."

"Sweetheart," Joe said. "Don't—"

"No, she's right, Dad," Ellen said. "Don't just snipe at me, Alex. Why don't you just say what's bothering you?" She looked at him. "It's not like nobody's noticed."

Alex took a deep breath and looked around the table. "I apologize. I shouldn't have acted like that." He pushed his chair back and got up. "I think I'll take a walk."

"Alex, please don't leave," Jane said. "Stay and talk to us. Maybe that would help."

"I don't think so," he said, and grabbing his jacket from a peg on the wall, headed for the door.

"I'm sorry," Ellen said when the door slammed shut. "He just seems to hate me these days."

"What's going on, Ellen?" Victoria asked.

"I can leave if you're not comfortable talking in front of me," Gordon said.

"No, Gordon, you're family now," Ellen said. "He wants me to go back to work and I just really don't want to leave the baby."

"Is there a problem with the money?" Joe asked. "We might be able to help a little."

"It isn't money," Ellen said. "His parents are rich and he makes a good living. He says I'm too preoccupied with Benjamin. He can't believe I would leave a career I've worked so hard for. He says I'd be happier, and easier to live with." She looked down at her plate.

"Do you think there might be some truth in that?" Victoria asked.

"Yes, I do, but there's a problem." She looked up at the faces around the table. "I'm pregnant again. Even the company I worked for before I had Benjamin won't hire me back now."

"You're pregnant again and Alex expects you to find a job?" Jane asked.

"He doesn't know. I'm afraid to tell him."

"He hasn't threatened you in any way?" Joe leaned closer to his daughter, reached across the table, and put a hand on her wrist.

"No, Dad." She squeezed his hand. "He isn't like that." She leaned back in her chair. "I'm afraid if I tell him, he'll leave me. How will I raise two kids by myself?"

They all sat silently for a few minutes. Benjamin smeared strained green beans on the table of his high chair.

"Can't you trust him more than that?" Gordon asked. "Even if he left the marriage, don't you think he'd help you raise the kids?"

"You're right. I do trust him that much. I'm just not sure he loves me enough to stick it out." She sniffed. "And I do love him that much."

"Something in the relationship must be going all right if you're pregnant again," Jane said.

Ellen blushed. She spooned another bite into Benjamin's mouth. "I guess that's true."

"Honey," Victoria said. "You can't keep a secret like that for long."

The back door opened and Alex came in. "Do you think the four of you could manage Benjamin for a while? I'd like to take a walk with my soul mate."

"I haven't finished feeding him yet," Ellen said.

"The two of you go. I think between the four of us we can do it," Victoria said. She stood and lifted Ellen by the elbow. "Go with your husband, Ellen. Give him a little of your time. Benjamin will be fine with us."

They all watched as Alex held Ellen's jacket for her and the two of them walked out the door. They watched through the French doors that opened onto the back patio as they walked down the footpath side by side. Both had their hands buried in their pockets and their heads bowed.

"What do you suppose it was about that birth control lesson I gave her that she didn't understand?" Victoria asked.

"I don't know," Joe said. "We went over it together. It was clear to me."

Benjamin grabbed a handful of green slime off his plate and hurled it at his Grampa.

"Monster!" Joe said. "You couldn't be the reason for their problems, could you?" He wiped his face with his napkin and tickled the baby's belly.

Benjamin squealed with laughter and they all pointed their attention to him.

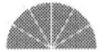

"By the time they got back that night, the four of us had managed to feed and bathe Benjamin, and then get him to sleep," Jane said to Jeff two Sunday's later. They were sitting in another restaurant on the bike trail.

"How did the rest of the weekend go?" he asked.

"It went beautifully. We had a great time at the little birthday party they had planned," Victoria said.

"How did you do with the mother-in-law?" Jeff asked. "Didn't you have problems with her last year?"

"Yes, but luckily she really hit it off with Jane."

"She writes short stories," Jane said. "You're not going to believe the story she wrote about meeting Tori for the first time. I'm going to publish it in the summer issue of *Second Half*."

"I think I remember something about that," Jeff said. "Did she make fun of you, Vic?"

"Yes, but she made fun of herself too. It really is good."

"I just can't believe that Ellen didn't say anything to you about what went on between her and Alex on that walk." Jane looked back to Jeff. "They were fine together when they got back. He told us about the baby. I mean about the pregnancy. He even acted happy about it, but they weren't really affectionate."

"No, and they still sniped at each other," Victoria said.

"But she didn't tell you anything?" Jane demanded.

"Nothing," Victoria said. "But they're still together. So I guess there's hope."

"I don't think I can stand that. I need to know what's going on."

"What are you going to do, Jane, demand details?"

"No, but, this sucks."

"It does," Victoria said. She reached over and patted Jane's arm. "But we'll just have to wait and see."

Jane arrived at the office early that Monday. Christine Pharrs was starting today as Food and Entertainment director. She also needed to talk to David about a new article and short story editor. They were running out of time.

"Good morning, Jane," Amanda said as she came

through the door. "Christine is waiting in the break room. I gave her a cup of coffee."

"Thanks, Amanda." Jane went into her office and put her coat up then she went across the hall to the break room. "Christine, come into my office. Let's get started." She guided her across the hall and to the chair in front of the desk. "I have an idea for your section. I want to have a yearly cookbook," she said. "I love the recipes you have for single and double portion muffins for this issue. I think we should publish a cookbook for all of our recipes."

"I've thought of that too," Christine said. "In fact I've written short poems about each recipe. They're sort of a mnemonic to help people memorize the recipes."

"That's a wonderful idea. It suits the audience perfectly," Jane said. "I'd love to see a sample of your work."

"I'll print what I've done so far and bring it in."

"That's great." Jane stood. "Let me show you where you'll be working." She guided her out the door and along the row of cubicles. "Take your choice," she said. "All but one of them are empty."

Christine chose the cube next to Anna's. She liked to be close to artistic people, she said.

"I want you to tell me what you need. I can put in a small kitchen for experiments over here in the corner." She pointed out the space, "But I can't be elaborate at this point."

"I'll use my own kitchen. The office will be for writing and organizing."

"I can't afford much staff for you right now, but you can have an assistant if you want one."

"I'll think about it."

Jane went back toward her office. She stopped at David's office on the way. The door was shut so she knocked.

"Come on in," David called. He had his head bent over some papers, but he looked up at her as she sat down across from him. "We're doing great on subscriptions. Our magazine is in every type of waiting room you can imagine."

"That's great. Have you had any luck looking for a features editor?"

"Yes, I've got two candidates in mind. I've interviewed them, but their qualifications are pretty much equal to each other. I like them both," he said. Flipping through his papers, he pulled out two resumes and handed them to her.

"Good, I'll call them," she said. "I'm also planning a book review segment. Do you think either of these people would work on that?"

"Yes, I think either one of them would." David looked down at his desk. "Of course, it's up to you."

"David, you're not still feeling responsible for what happened with Lenny, are you?"

"I guess I always will."

"No, you won't." Jane got up and walked to the door. "I'll interview them and give you my impressions, but you're going to decide who to hire for what. I want you to gain your self-confidence back." She went out the door and down the hall to Grant's office. The door was open. "Got a minute?" she asked Grant. He was standing at the window looking out onto the street.

"Sure, come in." He turned back to the room.

"Is everything all right?"

"Yes, I'm just waiting for Lauren to drop Maggie off. She goes to the physical therapist this morning." He sat down at his desk. "Lauren still won't take her."

"That's all right. We can spare you for an hour a couple of times a week."

"I usually try to do it in the afternoon. Maggie is in kindergarten in the morning, but this week there was a conflict."

"How's she doing?"

"Great. I've got her on a soccer team for spring season. She starts practice next week. Her first game is March 20th. I hope you and Dad can be there."

"We wouldn't miss it," she said. "Tell me what's new on the advertising front."

"I've got some really exciting stuff to show you,"

Grant said. "By the way, David and Anna have done a spectacular job on that fashion show. We're sold out. People are talking about it all over town."

Jane spent about an hour in Grant's office going over the sales and the budget. Things were going better than she'd hoped for. It looked like they were about half way to breaking even when the first issue came out in April. Depending on how well it was received, she may be able to go to every other month instead of quarterly issues. That would be great. By their one-year anniversary, they might be able to make back their initial investment. That would mean profit in the following year.

She wanted to interview David's candidates before the weekly meeting on Wednesday morning. It would be great to have three new people on board by then, she thought as she made her way back to her office.

The phone was ringing when she got to her office. "*Second Half*, Jane Fox."

"I love the sound of your name, Jane Fox," Gordon said.

"I do too," she said. "Did you just call to tell me that?" She sat down.

"No, I called to remind you that we're going to Teddy's birthday celebration tonight, and to remind you that this weekend we promised to take Hope to Chattanooga."

"I remembered the birthday celebration, but Chattanooga had slipped my mind. Do you still want to go along?"

"Hope said I could come so don't try to shake me."

"I wouldn't. Should we go overnight or just make a day trip?"

"I think I'll ask Jill about it. Hope's at the age where kids get nervous when they leave home overnight. When Michael was that age, he couldn't even spend the night next door without me having to get up at midnight to go and get him."

"Really, why?"

"Who knows? I can't remember being that age."

"I'll ask Michael," Jane said. "We'll get both opinions."

"Good idea." Gordon paused. "Wanna have lunch with me?"

"Yes, but I can't. I've got a lunch appointment."

"Darn!"

"Yeah, darn!"

"Will anyone else be here?" Jane asked, as they stood at Katherine's door.

"No, since he's only two, Kathy didn't want to over stimulate him. Birthdays are special, but the little guys don't handle too much spotlight very well."

"I noticed that at Christmas," Jane said. "I'm glad it's just us. I've missed those dinners we used to have with Katherine's family."

"You know, I have too." Gordon pulled her closer and kissed her just as the door opened.

"Are you two at it again?" Rick asked. "Come in." He stood back.

"We're newlyweds, remember? Surely you remember what it's like being a newlywed," Gordon said as they went inside.

Rick took their coats and hung them in the closet. There was some kind of racket coming from the playroom. "With that going on all the time," Rick said, "I have to admit it's hard to remember the newlywed stage."

Katherine came out of the kitchen and headed for the playroom. "Hey, Dad, Jane," she said as she went by. "I'll be right back." She hurried into the playroom and they could hear her peacemaking maneuvers.

She reappeared a few minutes later with Teddy in her arms. "Grampa, Janie," Teddy squealed as he squirmed to the floor. He ran to Gordon to be scooped up. Flinging his arms around Jane's neck, he pulled the three of them close together. "Aum...two."

Jane noticed Eric move slowly into the room looking sulky.

"You're growing up fast, big guy," Gordon said. "Happy birthday."

"Happy birthday, Teddy," Jane said, and then kissed his soft cheek. "Hello, Eric. How do you feel about your little brother getting so old?"

"You're not supposed to talk to me," Eric cried, then dissolved into tears.

"I'm sorry." Jane looked at Katherine.

Katherine rolled her eyes and said, "It's not your fault, Jane." She scooped Eric up and carried him up the stairs. They could hear his wails fading down the hallway.

"Aren't you glad you skipped this part, Jane?" Rick asked. "Would you like a glass of wine or some lemonade? The kids are having lemonade."

"I'll have lemonade, too," Jane said. "I've never seen Eric act like that. Isn't he feeling well?"

"He's fine. He's just not used to being in Teddy's shadow. He doesn't remember this time last year." Rick went to the kitchen.

"Where should I put your presents, Teddy?" Jane asked, indicating the packages she carried.

"Au shoya." He squirmed out of Gordon's arms and led them to the dining room. "We eat here on spishal cashons." He beamed. "Au got a cake, too."

"That's exciting!" Gordon said. "Let's go back to the playroom."

Rick came in with lemonade for everyone. In a few minutes Katherine came in carrying Valerie and holding a subdued Eric by the hand.

"I'm sorry, Grampa and Janie. I'm good now." He looked down at the floor.

"I love you even when you're bad, Eric," Gordon said. "Come and give me a hug." Eric ran to his Grampa and hugged him then turned to Jane.

She held out her arms and he moved into them. He

kissed her cheek with his small soft lips and she felt that familiar warmth inside.

"Who else do you need to apologize to?" Katherine asked.

Eric looked sulky again.

"Do you want to go back to time out?" Rick asked.

"I'm sorry, Teddy," he said.

"'s okay, Eric. Wanna play...airplane game?" Teddy asked.

"Okay." The two of them knew the parts of the game so well that in a matter of seconds they were playing happily with toy airplanes.

"Teddy loves his older brother so much," Katherine said. "I think we spoiled Eric a little when he was the only one." She sat down on the arm of the chair Rick was sitting on.

"That's natural, everyone does it," Gordon said as he took Valerie out of her arms and went back to sit on the couch beside Jane. "It wasn't too much fireworks for a birthday," he said.

"That's been going on all day. Don't be surprised if it happens again," Katherine said.

The next day Jane interviewed both of the candidates for editor. Early in the afternoon she went into David's office. "I liked them both. I told them you'd set up a time to talk to them this week. You decide which one should be offered which position. I'm hoping to have them on board by the end of the week."

"Are you sure, Jane?" David looked trapped.

"David, don't look so worried. I trust you, now trust yourself. I agree with your assessment of them. Don't you trust me?"

"Of course I do. It's just—"

"Stop thinking that way." She reached across the desk and squeezed his hand. "Now get to it."

When she left David's office she went to Michael's

studio. The door was closed. She knocked. The door opened and Daniel, the man Michael had hired as his assistant stood back. "Come on in," he said.

She went into the studio. "Is Michael around?" she asked. Daniel was probably in his late forties. He was a tall thin man with a bald head. He wore a fringe of graying brown hair around the lower part of his head and over his ears. He had side burns and a trim beard, very artistic looking.

"He stepped out for just a minute. Is there something I can do for you?" he asked. He had an easy smile.

Jane smiled back. "I hope you'll be at the meeting tomorrow. I haven't seen you at them before."

"I wasn't sure I was invited," he said. "I'd like to come."

"You're part of the team. Of course you're invited." She looked around the room. "Are you and Michael set up for the fashion show next week? David tells me that we're sold out."

"We're ready."

"Does Michael need to hire extra help? I want film as well as photos."

"Film is my area of expertise," he said. "We could handle it by ourselves, but Michael has lined up one of Gordon's students to help. I think it's the one that took your wedding pictures."

"Oh, that's good. He did a great job."

"He was going to clear it with you at the meeting tomorrow."

"You worked with Gordon before you worked with Michael, didn't you?" Jane asked. She hadn't paid very close attention to what Michael told her about Daniel.

"That's right. I've been with the family for years. Michael's like a son to me. I went with Michael when he got old enough to go commercial. Gordon wasn't interested in that kind of thing and I was."

"I know. I tried to hire him," Jane said.

"Gave you a firm *No*, I'll bet."

"Yes, but, he asked me to marry him instead. I'm happy with that."

"I'm happy for both of you. I worried about Gordon being all alone like that."

"He wasn't really alone. He's got a tremendous family. I find myself overwhelmed sometimes," she said.

"I know. Hard to give all of them the time they need, isn't it?"

"Do you have family, Daniel?"

"Wife, daughter in college."

"I hope to meet them some time."

"I'm sure you will."

Jane let herself into the apartment and put down her packages. She'd taken the last part of the day to do a little shopping. She needed underwear. Her life had been so full for the past six months she hadn't had time to buy any. Gordon had asked her why she did laundry all week long instead of just saving it for the week end. That's when she realized she needed to buy underwear.

She went into the kitchen and poured herself some water, squeezed a lemon wedge into it, and sat down at the table. The phone rang.

"Joan, this is Gordon Senior. Is Minnie over there?"

"No, isn't she over there?"

"She went to the doctor on the bus a couple of hours ago. I just looked out at the parking lot. The bus is back, but she isn't."

"Could she have gone to a friend's apartment?" Jane felt panicky. She hadn't dealt with anything like this before.

"I checked with all her friends. None of them are home."

"Gordon should be home soon," Jane said. "I'll leave him a note and come over to help you look for her."

"I'd appreciate it. I'm worried. It's not like her to disappear."

Jane wrote a quick note on the dry erase board and headed out the door. She watched the sidewalks and street corners all the way to the retirement complex. When she arrived she hurried up the stairs and rang the bell. After a couple of minutes of waiting she rang the bell again. What if he didn't hear the bell? He wore a hearing aid. Maybe he didn't have it on.

The door opened quickly and Minerva stood in the doorway. She looked upset. "You're here," Jane said. "What's wrong, Minerva?"

"I can't find Gordon. I've looked everywhere. I'm worried sick." She leaned heavily on her cane and swayed. Jane jumped to her side and wrapped an arm around her shoulders. "Come over here and sit down." She guided her to a chair.

Now Jane was feeling hysterical. She had to resist the urge to giggle. "Let me try to straighten this out," she said. "Gordon Senior called me about twenty minutes ago and said that you had never come home from the doctor. He said the bus had come home, but you weren't on it."

"I was on it. I came in and he was asleep on the living room couch. He must not have had his hearing aid on because he didn't hear me. So I went over to play bridge with the girls like I do every Tuesday afternoon." Minerva wiped a tear off her cheek. "He must have forgotten and gone looking for me. Where could he be? He forgets his way around sometimes, you know."

The front door opened and Gordon Junior came in followed by Gordon Senior. "Mom, don't cry," he said. "Dad's right here." He went over to Jane and put his hand on her shoulder. "Are you all right? I should have prepared you for this."

"You scared me to death, you old fool. Not to mention what you did to poor Joan." Minerva got up and let her husband pull her into his arms. They hugged and Gordon Senior dried her tears with a wrinkled handkerchief he pulled from his pocket.

"I don't really understand what happened," Jane said.

"Once I remembered that today was bridge day, I went to the pool room to play with the guys. Whenever she plays bridge, I play pool."

"That's right, I forgot," Minerva said. "Why didn't you leave me a note?" She blew her nose in the handkerchief and tucked it into her pocket.

Jane winced.

"And why didn't you call Jane to tell her it was a false alarm," Gordon Junior asked.

"I didn't leave a note for the same reason you didn't leave a note. We're supposed to know. And I did call Joan back but she'd already left."

"Jane, her name is *Jane*." Gordon was getting agitated. "And you should have waited for her to arrive."

"I meant to, but I forgot."

"You forgot?" Gordon's voice was rising.

"It's all right, Gordon." Jane put a hand on his arm hoping to avoid a scene.

He smiled down at her hand and put his over it. He took a deep breath. "You're right, everything is all right now, but we need to talk, Dad. I think it's time that you and Mom had a little more help."

"We don't need any help. We do just fine," Minerva said.

"That's right, son," Gordon Senior said. "Every time some little thing goes wrong, you want to get us a keeper. We don't need a keeper. We have each other and we do fine."

"I'm not talking about a keeper, Dad. I'm just talking about someone to help you organize things and keep things straight so this doesn't happen any more." Gordon started to sound angry again.

Jane squeezed his hand. "Let's go, Gordon. They need to have their dinner and so do we. We can get together and talk about this later."

"All right," he sighed. "But we will talk about it," he said. Then he kissed his mother and hugged her warmly, tapped his Dad on the shoulder and they left.

"I'll see you at home," Jane said as they walked out.

Gordon stopped her as she started for her car. He turned her around and kissed her. "I'm sorry, Jane. I shouldn't let them get to me like that, but they're so stubborn."

"I can see how hard it is. I'm completely out of my element here. I didn't even have *young* parents."

"You seem to be handling the elements pretty well," he said, "better than me. I'll see you at home." They went to their separate cars.

Chapter Twenty-Three

"I can't believe I let the two of you talk me into this," Jeff said as they picked their way along the wooded trail on horseback.

"Are you really not having fun?" Jane asked, stopping her horse and looking back at Jeff bringing up the rear.

"No, I'm not. What's wrong with bikes anyway?" he said.

"I just thought this would be fun for a change," Jane said, looking concerned.

"Why are you leaning back like that, Jeff?" Victoria asked.

"I'm afraid of that thing," he said, pointing to the saddle horn. "I have organs to protect, you know."

"Jeff," Victoria said, pulling her horse along side his. "Push your heels down in the stirrups a little." She bent and positioned his foot. "Then grip with your knees." She slipped her hand between his knee and the saddle. "That way you can absorb the impact in your knees and thighs so it won't hurt your genitals."

Jeff turned crimson and Jane roared with laughter. "Tori, you are so funny!" she said. "You're just so straight forward."

"We all know that's what he's concerned about," Victoria said. "Now squeeze my hand with your knee," she said turning back to Jeff. "Ouch!" She pulled her hand free. "That's good. Try riding like that."

They moved forward in silence for a while. "This does feel better," Jeff said.

"Are you ready for a good run?" Jane asked, as they came to a clearing. She urged her horse forward and they all cantered across the field.

"Look at him," Victoria said, as they pulled to a stop. "Just like an old cow hand."

"You look great on that horse, Jeff," Jane said.

"Shut up, you two," Jeff said with a smile. "I've never ridden a horse before."

"Not even in camp when you were a kid?" Jane asked.

"No," he said. "Now finish the story about taking Hope to the aquarium yesterday."

"It was great. We asked her parents if they thought we should stay overnight. Gordon says kids at that age tend to be afraid to be away from home at night."

"I remember that. It didn't happen too often with Ellen, but Patricia would call in the middle of the night crying and one of us would go out and get her," Victoria said.

"That's what Gordon said about Michael. Anyway, her parents didn't recommend it, so we did a day trip. It's only about an hour and a half drive. We started early, had breakfast on the road, then we got to the aquarium and went through. Have you ever been there?"

"I haven't," Jeff said.

"I went with the girl scouts years ago," Victoria said. "I remember being very impressed. You start at the top and work your way down, right?"

"That's right. It was great going through with Hope. She could name all the fish and plants. She even knew the names of the rocks. She's such a smart girl," Jane said. "In fact all of Gordon's grandchildren are remarkable. His children are too."

"Sounds like you're talking about your own children and grandchildren," Jeff said.

"Be careful, Jeff," Victoria said. "It wouldn't be a good thing for her to faint or vomit while riding a horse."

"Shut up, Tori."

"You vomit now, too?" Jeff asked.

"Yes, if I can control the fainting, I vomit."

"I think I'd rather faint," he said.

"Obviously you've never fainted," Jane said. They crossed a stream and rode silently for a while. "You know, I was noticing the other day when we had that problem with Gordon's parents. The only time he gets rattled is with me and his parents."

"What problem with his parents?" Jeff asked.

"Yeah, what problem with his parents?" Victoria repeated.

"I didn't tell you about that?"

"No, you didn't. Tell us."

"They kind of lost each other." She told the story. "Gordon got so frustrated trying to talk them into getting more help. It was like when he tries to talk me into therapy."

"You're a stubborn old fool, too," Jeff said.

"I am not." Jane turned to look at her two best friends. "You're laughing at me."

"No, we're laughing with you," Victoria said.

"I'm not laughing."

Wednesday morning Jane arrived at the office to find Victoria watering plants. "I'm glad you came for the meeting," Jane said. "You should see my banyon tree. It's doing beautifully. Gordon has even wired one of the branches to make it curve dramatically. Have you done that with any of yours?"

"Not yet. I've done some aralias that way, though. It's fun. Jeff's going to sell them in the shop in the spring."

"Have you thought anymore about buying into the business with Jeff?"

"Yes, Joe and I have scraped the money together. We close the deal next month." Victoria continued around the room with her watering can.

"That's great, Tori."

"I hope I don't ruin Jeff's business. He's going on a

bike trip in the fall, around the world or something like that. I'll be completely in charge. I sure hope I'm not in over my head."

"I didn't know he was planning a bike trip around the world. How can you ride your bike around the world?" Jane asked. "I guess he and I haven't talked much lately."

"I think he'll fly across the oceans." Victoria stopped and looked at Jane. "I'm a little worried about Jeff. He seems restless."

"I need to get together with him and have a chat." Jane made a mental note to call Jeff. "Ready?" She got up and guided Victoria across the hall.

David was already there with his two new employees. Michael and Daniel were also there. Amanda sat at the end of the table with her note pad. Grant and Anna came in together.

"Has anybody seen Christine this morning?" Jane asked.

"Here I am." Christine hurried in with a large basket of warm muffins wrapped in a linen cloth to keep warm. She put tubs of yogurt spread and butter on the table. "I brought breakfast."

"I knew I liked you," Grant said as he took a muffin and passed the basket.

"I brought olive oil spread for people who don't use dairy products." Christine pulled a tub out of her bag. "And napkins." She put a stack down on the table.

"Thank you, Christine," Jane said. "I think we can get started now. David, I'll let you introduce our new team members."

David looked to his right at a woman who appeared to be in her mid fifties. Her hair was salt and pepper. She was slightly heavy with graceful features. "This is Cassandra Butts. She will be our book review editor. She comes to us with excellent qualifications and a sparkling sense of humor. I think you will all enjoy working with her."

"Thank you, David. I'm very happy to be here."

David turned to the man on his left. He wore a suit and tie, and looked very professional. "This is Tom Johnson. Tom will be our features editor. He is also a very talented writer. I know you will all enjoy his stories."

"I'm glad to become a part of your group," Tom said.

"We're all happy to welcome you. Now, we've got five weeks until the first issue comes out on April 1st. That's a lot of work. This Saturday is our fashion show. Anna and David have done a wonderful job of putting it together. David tells me we've sold out. We have a full house. I'm hoping to sell a good deal of the clothing line." She smiled at David and Anna.

"Michael, are you all set up for pictures?"

"We're ready to go. I've got Matt lined up to help out and Daniel will take care of the Video end of it."

"That's great."

"I've got more good news." Jane looked at Grant. "I'll let you talk about this."

"It looks like we'll be about halfway to making back our..." Grant paused and smiled at Jane. "... to making back *Jane's* investment. I guess I feel a little possessive about this place."

"That's great!" Jane said. "I want everyone to feel that way."

"Anyway," Grant went on, "I think we can afford to publish bi-monthly instead of quarterly. If my predictions are correct and things keep going as well as they are, we'll break even at our one-year anniversary."

Everyone cheered and congratulated each other. Even Anna smiled.

Jane stood and the group quieted down. "Look around the room, Tori." Everyone looked around the room. "We've become more diverse."

"You're right. It's not just a bunch of young people and us any more."

"That's right," Jane said, looking over her team. They chatted together, got to know the newcomers, ate muffins, and then dispersed to their own areas.

The country club was bustling on the night of the fashion show. The runway was set up in the huge banquet room. There were rows of chairs as far as Jane could see. She stood at the end of the runway and looked at the people starting to file in.

"Exciting, isn't it?" Anna said from behind her.

"Yes it is," Jane said. "I'm just glad I'll be in the audience and not on the stage. Are you nervous?"

"A little, but I have to get used to this in my line of work. Hopefully, I'll be narrating a lot of fashion shows."

"You could be modeling clothes, too, if you wanted to."

"I don't want to." Anna turned when someone called her name. "I'm needed in the back. You'd better come back, too. People are beginning to arrive."

There was an open bar in the back of the room along with hors d'oeuvres tables. People were milling around them talking. Jane turned and went back stage. There were small dressing areas set up for the models.

One of the models rushed over to Anna. "Stephanie is sick. She can't be here." The girl looked panicked.

"It'll be all right, Janet." Anna calmed the girl and looked around the room. She turned to Jane. "You'll have to do it."

"Oh, no! I told you I'm not walking down a runway. That was clear from the start." Jane backed away.

"I planned it without you, but things go wrong and sometimes you have to stretch yourself." Anna took a firm hold of Jane's arm and propelled her to a dressing room.

"I said no and I mean it. I refuse—"

"Jane, it's the wedding dress. I could tack up the sleeves and pants on the other items for one of the other models. But Stephanie was the only one tall enough to wear the wedding dress, except for you, of course."

Everything became a blur after that. Jane felt like she was having some kind of a strange dream. Anna bustled her into the dressing area and helped her into the dress. She was rushed over to the hair styling station where Harrison styled her hair and put the white roses and netting on her head just like her wedding day. Then she went to make up. Someone did something to her face.

"What happened?" she asked as she stood with the other models behind the curtain. "I said I wouldn't do this."

"I guess you just lost control of the situation," Victoria said, patting her arm. Victoria had volunteered to model her bridesmaid dress. Hope and Joy were in their dresses as well.

"Do you know what to do, Janie?" Joy asked.

"No, I haven't practiced or anything. I'll probably fall off the runway." Her hands started to shake. The roses in her bouquet were bobbing up and down.

"Of course you won't fall off the runway," Hope said. "You just remember to go to the middle of the stage and turn. Then down the left runway first, across to the right, then turn again in the middle and head to the front."

"That's right," Joy said. "Do you want me to teach you how to turn?"

Jane nodded her head and took last minute lessons from the two bubbling girls. She felt numb and dizzy.

"I hope I don't faint," she said.

"Have you eaten anything?" Victoria asked.

"No."

"Good, you won't throw up, but you should drink a little juice. That'll put sugar in your blood so you won't faint." Victoria disappeared, reappearing in a minute with a small glass of juice.

"Couldn't I throw up the juice?" Jane took the glass.

"No, it's absorbed into the bloodstream too fast. Drink up. It sounds like they're getting ready."

The music started. It was typical runway music, steady rhythm, mostly base, easy to walk to. They could hear Anna's clear melodic voice as she described the attri-

butes of each outfit. One by one the models walked grace-
fully through the opening in the curtain, only to return
from another opening on the side and get back into line.

Hope went through the curtain grinning broadly,
then Joy a little more subdued. Then Victoria went
through. None of them came back.

"How will I know when to go?" she asked Janet,
who'd gone first and was now standing behind her.

"The bridal group will make up the finale. They'll
stay on stage. I'll tell you when to go. When you've finished your walk, stand behind them."

"Thanks," Jane said.

"Then we'll all come back out." Janet tapped her
shoulder. "Go on."

Jane walked through the curtain. All she could
really see were lights. She blinked but started to walk.
She could hear Anna describing her dress. The music
propelled her and she remembered Hope's instructions.
Slowly she started to feel relaxed. She felt invigorated.
Feeling a smile forming on her face, she looked at the
audience. Gordon was there smiling up at her. She felt a
lump in her throat, but it felt good, thrilling. Joe and Jeff
sat beside him. They were smiling at her, too. Everyone
was smiling at her. She smiled back and turned, moving
like in a dream. She felt like she was floating back up the
runway. Victoria, Hope, and Joy were standing according
to height. They were all three beaming at her. She circled
them and came to a stop behind them between Joy and
Hope. The music stopped and the audience applauded.
Jane could feel her heart pounding. She hoped the audience couldn't see it.

Then the music started again and the rest of the
models filed out single file several paces apart. They made
their way down the left runway, then the right, to the front
and back to the stage where they stretched out beside
the bridal group to the right and left. Again the music
stopped and the audience applauded. They clapped for
a long time, then Anna walked to the front of the group,
and holding her microphone she faced the audience.

"Now I'd like to introduce our fearless leader who would like to say a few words to you. Ladies and Gentlemen, the president and founder of *Second Half* magazine, Jane Fox."

Jane took a deep breath, handed her bouquet to Victoria, and moved forward to take the microphone. She held it up to her mouth and said, "That was fun." Again the audience roared with applause.

"I thought you weren't walking down a runway," Gordon said later at the reception. Jane had changed back into her suit and joined them out front. Victoria, Hope, and Joy were out there too. Michael was cooing over his beautiful daughters.

"Well, you gotta do what you gotta do," Jane said.

"You did it beautifully," Jeff said, putting his arm around her waist and leaning in to kiss her. He stopped about an inch from her mouth. "May I kiss your wife, Fox?" He glanced at Gordon.

"What if I said no?" Gordon asked, but he was smiling.

Jeff leaned forward and kissed her. "I'd do it anyway."

"I thought so."

"You really did look like a pro, Jane," Joe said, and kissed her cheek. "I can't believe you didn't even practice. How did you know what to do?"

"Joy and Hope gave me last minute lessons." She put her arms around each girl and squeezed. "I love you guys."

"We love you too, Janie," Joy said.

"The only problem with being in the show was that I didn't get to see the two of you, or you, Tori."

"They were spectacular," Michael said. "I've produced some beautiful girls."

"Yes you have," Jill said, "with a little help from me."

"I've got great footage of it, Jane," Daniel said. "You'll get to see it." He gestured to a small dark haired woman and said, "I'd like you to meet my wife, Ida."

"I'm so happy to meet you, Ida." Jane shook her hand.

"That was a wonderful fashion show. I want one of those silk pant suits," Ida said.

"Hopefully a lot of people will," Jane said.

"Hi, Janie." Jane looked up from her computer as Maggie came bouncing through the door of her office. It was mid-March and the weather had warmed to pleasant. Maggie was dressed in shorts, a T-shirt and soccer shoes.

"Have you been to practice?"

"Yep. Dad took me after school." She climbed into Jane's lap and hugged her.

"How's it going?"

"It's going great. I got a left foot."

Grant came into the room and sat down.

Jane looked down at Maggie's left foot and said, "Don't most people have a left foot?"

Maggie giggled and Grant laughed. "I kick with my left foot," she said. "I write with my left hand, too."

"Oh," Jane said. "I see what you mean."

"It really works in her favor in soccer. Everyone expects her to take another step before she kicks, catches the other kids off guard," Grant said.

"So do you like playing soccer as much as you like watching it?" Jane asked.

"More. I'm good at it too."

"She is," Grant said. "At this age very few of the kids understand what they're doing. Most of them just run up and down the field chasing the ball. But Maggie knows what she's doing. I guess she learned from watching it on TV so much."

Maggie grinned up at Jane.

"Well, I'm glad things are going so well. How does your mom feel about it?"

"She still worries a lot," Maggie said. "But she promised she'd come to my first game. It's March 20th. You'll come, won't you, Janie?"

"I wouldn't miss it, Grampa either."

"Ready to go?" Lauren came into the room. Grant stood and kissed her. Maggie got off Jane's lap and went over to her mother.

"Here." Grant reached into his pocket and took out Maggie's inhaler. He handed it to Lauren. "She didn't need it."

"I hardly ever need it," Maggie said.

"Are you joining us for a pedicure tomorrow, Lauren?" Jane asked.

"I'll be there. It's almost sandal season," she said as she left the room, Maggie in tow.

"Bye, Janie," Maggie called.

"We've got quite a group together for pedicures. It's become a social event." Jane laughed.

"It's good to see Lauren doing things with friends," Grant said. "So, how are we doing on clothing sales since the fashion show?"

"Great. I've got two interviews set up this afternoon for clerical people to process the orders. We've had so many," Jane said. "The cookware is doing well, too. David set up several demonstrations in kitchen supply stores and Christine is teaching a class at one downtown. We're really doing great."

"Just two more weeks until first issue, it's exciting," Grant said.

"It sure is," Jane replied.

Jane followed Gordon out of the bathroom. She had taken the day off and had talked him into spending an extra hour with her in the morning.

"So what are your plans for the day?" Gordon asked.

"Right now, I'm going to take Fred to the park and run," she said as she pulled on her underwear. She reached over and stroked Baby. The cat was lying on her dresser. It had become a favorite place for her. "Then I'm having a pedicure with the girls. After that I think I'll put my winter clothes away and get the spring things out of the closet in the guest room."

"Sounds like fun," Gordon said, watching her stroke the purring cat. "You and Baby have really become friends."

"As long as I don't cross her lines," Jane said.

"Oh, she has clearly defined lines."

"You know, I'd give up all my plans if you'd spend the day with me." Jane looked at him hopefully.

"I'd love to," he said, putting his arms around her. He was fully dressed. She still wore only her underwear. "But I have a number of things going on at the studio that I don't want to miss."

"So I can't compete with the studio."

"If it was a competition, you'd win." He kissed her soundly and released her. "But I believe you'll still love me at the end of the day."

"Right." Jane pulled on her running clothes as Gordon left. She heard the front door close behind him. "Ready to go, Fred?" The little dog scampered around in a circle and they were off.

That afternoon she pondered her closet as she prepared for spring cleaning. She'd had a wonderful run in the park then joined Victoria for lunch at her favorite salad place. Afterward they had joined the girls for a pedicure. The group had taken up the entire shop and Ida had added delightfully to their social circle. Jane was feeling good about life.

She moved several handfuls of hanging clothes off the rack to the other closet, and brought several back. She pulled sweaters off the shelf and brought T-shirts back. She was on her way out of the closet in the bedroom with her hands full when she spotted Fred ready to go in.

"Oh, no," she said. "That's the only place you pee where you shouldn't." She hooked her heel on the base of the door and pushed it shut.

There was an immediate shrieking sound and Jane dropped everything that was in her arms and whirled around to find Baby hung by the tail in the closet door.

"Oh, Baby!" Jane rushed forward. The cat yowled again, hissed, showing long sharp teeth, and started swinging her paws. Jane jumped back. "She doesn't have claws," she reminded herself. Jane leaned forward careful to avoid the teeth that Baby displayed with every hiss, and grabbed the door knob to opened it up.

The cat launched herself at Jane hissing and yowling. Jane turned and ran out the door and down the hall. About half way down the hall she lost the race and Baby sunk her teeth into the back of Jane's leg just above the ankle.

Fred came out of nowhere and jumped on top of the cat. He clamped his mouth over the back of her neck and she let go. Jane ran into the living room and jumped up on one of the bar stools. After a minute, Baby came into the room. Her tail hung down from a point about half way up.

"I broke your tail, Baby, didn't I?" Jane said. The cat seemed to be in a trance. She walked to the couch, jumped up and stared forward. She switched her tail and blood spewed across the room. There was a trail of blood from the hall to the couch. After a minute the cat started to shake and pant.

Jane climbed down from the stool and picked up the phone from the table beside the couch. Baby didn't notice.

"Tori, I need your help."

"What's wrong, Jane?"

"I broke Baby's tail. I need to get her to the vet."

"Take her to the vet then."

"I'm afraid to pick her up. She bit me."

"Jane, clean the bite wound. Cat bites can be very bad."

"I have to take her to the vet first. She's bleeding badly." Jane was crying now.

"Jane, I can be there in twenty minutes," Victoria said. "While you're waiting for me, clean the wound. I'll catch the cat."

"I can't wait twenty minutes. I think she's in shock. She looks strange. Tori, what will everyone think of me? She's Margaret's cat!" Jane was shaking now, too. "Tell me how to pick her up?"

"Promise me you'll clean the wound before you leave."

"I promise."

"All right," Victoria said. "Get the carrier and stand it on end. Open the door."

"Hold on," Jane said. She put down the phone and got the carrier. "All right, I've done that."

"Now, Jane, you have to do this all in one move. Sneak up behind Baby, reach down and grab her by the skin on the back of her neck and lift her into the air. But Jane," Victoria said. "Don't hesitate. All one movement, otherwise she might bite you again."

Jane crept to the back of the couch. She took a deep breath, reached down and scooped the cat up. "She's just hanging there," she cried into the phone.

"That's normal, Jane," Victoria said. "They go into the fetal position when you pick them up by the scruff. Now lower her into the carrier and shut the door.

Jane got the cat into the carrier.

"Jane," Victoria said. "Clean the bite wound before you go. Cat bites can be very bad. I'm serious."

"I will, thanks, Tori." Jane hung up the phone, grabbed the carrier and her keys, and ran out of the apartment.

Two hours later she let herself back in. Gordon stood behind the couch.

"Gordon, I'm so sorry," Jane said.

He whirled around and ran to her. "Jane, thank God!" He wrapped his arms around her.

She dissolved into tears, sobbing. "I'm so sorry."

"What happened, Jane? There's blood everywhere." He held her away from him for a minute. "You're covered with blood. Where are you hurt?"

"I'm not hurt. It's Baby." She covered her face with her hands. "What will everyone think of me? They'll hate me. Baby will hate me." She sobbed as he pulled her close again. "And I love her so much."

"Tell me what happened, Jane." Gordon guided her to a chair. He sat down and pulled her into his lap. Cradling her in his arms, he said, "Tell me, Jane."

"I was cleaning the closet and I pushed the door shut with my foot. I guess Baby was coming through behind me. It caught her tail and broke it." Jane's words were broken with sobs.

"Oh, God, Jane, is that all?"

"Gordon, they have to amputate the tail! They couldn't do the surgery until tomorrow. She was in shock when I got her there. They started an IV and stabilized her. They have to amputate her tail!" Jane buried her face in her hands and curled into a ball.

"Jane," Gordon tried to uncurl her. "That's a shame, but it was an accident. They can take care of it." Finally he pulled her into his arms.

"Your family will hate me. I didn't mean to do it."

"No one will hate you, Jane." Gordon started to massage her back.

"She's Margaret's cat, Gordon. Everyone will hate me."

"Damn it, Jane." Gordon stiffened. "She's not Maggie's cat. She's my cat and now she your cat."

"I'm sorry, Gordon." She felt him take a deep breath. Then he pulled her into his arms again and began to rock back and forth.

"She'll be all right, Jane. You got her the help she needed. No one will think badly of you."

Her sobs calmed after a few minutes. "You don't think so?"

"No." He stroked her back. "Thank you for taking care of her. I'll call the vet tomorrow and tell them to clean her teeth while she's under anesthesia," he said. "She was due for a dental."

"You really don't hate me?" She looked up at him.

"I love you, Jane." He kissed her. "I'm sorry you broke our cat's tail." He got up and settled her in the chair. "I'm going to see what I can do about all this blood.

"I think I'll take a bath." Jane stood. She winced as pain shot through her lower leg. Luckily Gordon didn't notice. "I'm a mess."

"You go ahead and take a bath. I'll work on this." He was looking through the broom closet for cleaning supplies.

Jane went into the bathroom and pulled off her clothes. Her leg was swollen around the bite. She had wiped off the wound at the vet's office and swabbed it with alcohol, but now it was swollen and red. In fact her leg was red all the way up to her knee. She ran her hand over the bite. It was warm. She got into the tub and scrubbed herself.

After she was dry, she went into the bedroom and pulled on a bathrobe. Feeling dizzy, she lay down on the bed to rest.

Gordon was calling her from somewhere far away. She tried to open her eyes, but they were just too heavy.

"Jane wake up, sweetheart," Gordon urged. "What's wrong?" She felt him touch her cheek. "My God, you're burning up!" He shook her. "Can't you hear me, Jane?" He sat down on the bed beside her, bumping her leg. She cried out in pain.

Gordon gasped. "She bit you. Jane! Why didn't you tell me?" Something jostled her. She managed to open one eye just a little. Gordon had her in his arms and was carrying her somewhere.

The next time she became aware, she was in the emergency room. The lights were very bright and she tried to shield her eyes with her arm. But someone was holding her arm.

"Jane, can you hear me?" a woman's voice from far away said. "I'm placing a catheter in your arm. Try to hold still."

People were talking around her, but she couldn't understand them. Then she drifted away again and everything was quiet.

She gradually came awake and opened her eyes. They were less heavy now. She was in a hospital bed. There was a window in the room and it was dark outside. There was something heavy on her hand. She looked down at it. Gordon was sitting in a chair pulled up to the bed. He had his head resting on her hand. He looked up when she tried to move it.

"Jane, you're awake." He picked up her hand and pressed it to his lips. "You've been delirious for hours."

"What's wrong? What happened?" Her voice sounded like gravel. She tried to clear her throat, but she couldn't.

"Don't worry about it now. Just go back to sleep."

She could feel herself drifting off again.

"You need to rest, sweetheart." Gordon's voice faded away.

The next time she woke up a nurse was doing something with her IV.

"What's that?" Jane asked, motioning to the bag she was hanging on the pole beside her bed.

"Antibiotics and more fluids," the nurse said. "You had some serious infection. Cat bites are really bad. It's not at all uncommon to get cellulitis if they aren't cleaned right away."

"But it happened so fast. It was only a matter of hours," Jane said.

"It doesn't usually happen that fast, but it can," the nurse explained.

"Where's my husband?"

"When we told him you were stable, he went home to shower and change. He was here all night. That man really loves you." The nurse was taking her vital signs now. "How are you feeling now? Do you need something for pain?"

Jane moved her leg and winced. "Maybe later," she said.

The door opened and Gordon came in. He was shaved and smelled of soap. "You're awake. Are you in pain?" He came to the side of the bed and took her hand.

"Not too bad."

"She just refused pain medication," the nurse said on her way out of the room. "I'll check back in later."

"Jane," Gordon said.

"I'm sorry, Gordon."

"Stop apologizing to me, Jane," he said. "Why didn't you tell me about the cat bite? We could have gotten you some help before things got so bad."

"I don't know. I was afraid too."

"Damn it, Jane." Gordon ran a hand through his hair. "What have I ever done to make you afraid to talk to me?" He started to pace beside her bed.

"I'm sorry." She felt tears pushing at the back of her eyes.

"I told you to stop apologizing to me. I'm sorry doesn't mean anything unless you try to solve the problem." He stormed out of the room and the door swung shut. Jane pressed the button to raise the bed. She felt along her leg and winced when her hand came near the wound.

The door to her room opened again and Victoria and Jeff came in. Victoria ran to her and put her arms around her.

Jane started crying softly. Jeff stroked her head.

"Tori, I've made such a mess of things."

"You've made a mess of yourself. I told you to clean that wound."

"I know. I'm stupid. I just didn't think it would happen so fast," she sobbed. "Gordon's so mad at me. He'll never forgive me."

The door opened again and Eric rushed in. He hopped onto the chair on the other side of the bed and wrapped his arms around Jane. Katherine came into the room behind him.

"He insisted on coming. I had to sneak him up the back stairs," she said.

"Oh, Eric." Jane's tears rolled down her cheeks. She wrapped her arms around him. "Thank you."

He stroked her hair with his soft little hand. "It's all right now, Janie," he said.

Grant came in next. "We saw Dad storming out the front door of the hospital. Michael's gone after him."

"He's so mad at me. He'll never forgive me," she said. "And I don't blame him."

"Michael will bring him around," Katherine said.

"That's right, Jane. He has a flair with Dad."

"He and Dad formed a special bond when he was a kid," Katherine said. "Dad was always shielding him from Mom."

"Yeah," Grant continued. "She was tough on Michael."

Jane smiled at the two of them. "Gordon's right, though. I definitely don't think very clearly when it comes to anything concerning your mother."

"Is there anything we can do to help?"

"I don't know, but I've got to do something. Her memory is a big part of Gordon's family."

"We're your family, too, Jane."

"We love you, Janie," Eric said, stroking her hair again.

Gordon came into the room with Michael right behind him. "I see we've got both sides of the family here," he said as he walked to the bed and stood beside Eric. "Could I have a minute alone with my wife?" He looked around the room.

"I'm not leaving, Gordon, if you're going to hurt her again," Victoria said. "She's been through enough." She leaned down to kiss Jane's forehead.

"Me neither, Fox." Jeff squared his shoulders. "Before she met you, I never saw her cry. I never saw her faint. And I never saw her in a hospital bed."

Jane reached for Jeff's hand and squeezed it.

Gordon looked down at her, a smile pulling at the corners of his mouth. He leaned forward and kissed her. "I won't make her cry again."

"Is it all right if we leave, Jane?" Victoria asked.

"I'll be all right, Tori, Jeff. Thank you. I love you."

"All right then." Victoria grabbed Jeff's arm and pulled him to the door.

"I'm warning you, Fox!" Jeff said as he went through.

"We need to go, too, Eric." Katherine took his hand. He kissed Jane again on the cheek and let his mother guide him out of the room.

Grant stepped to the side Jeff and Victoria had left. "We'll hold the fort at the magazine. You just concentrate on healing." He squeezed her hand and left.

"Is it safe to leave the two of you together?" Michael put his hand on Gordon's shoulder.

"It's safe." Gordon smiled at him as he left. He lowered the rail on the side of the hospital bed and sat down beside Jane.

"I love you and you scared me to death. I shouldn't react with anger, but I did," he said. "Will you forgive me?"

She nodded her head.

"We have an appointment with the psychiatric resident on call. She'll be here in about an hour."

"Good." Jane sniffed and pulled a tissue from the box beside the bed. "I have a problem I need help with."

Chapter Twenty-Four

Jane limped through her front door with Gordon holding her around the waist. He settled her on an easy chair and carefully propped her leg on a pillow placed on a stool.

"Maybe I should lie on the couch," Jane said.

"The couch is pretty badly stained," he said. "Do you want to reupholster it or should we get a new one?"

"Are you sure the blood won't come out?"

"Pretty sure."

"We'll get a new one. I wasn't all that crazy about that couch anyway," she said, smiling at him, "except for the memories."

"I'm glad they let you come home today. I don't sleep well without you," Gordon said. "Do you want something to eat or drink?"

"No, I'm fine. Have you called about Baby? When will she come home?" she asked. Fred scampered into the room and jumped into her lap. "Oh, Fred!" She hugged him. "You know, Gordon, when Baby attacked me, Fred made her stop. He protected me." She kissed the little dog's head, "...without hurting Baby."

"Good man." Gordon stroked the little dog. "Look, he's got a scratch on his back leg. She must have gotten him with her back claws." They examined the scratch for a minute. It was clean and healing. "I'll pick Baby up this afternoon."

"I hope she forgives me."

"I'm sure she already has." Gordon sat on the arm of the chair. "You know, Jane, I feel a little guilty. The doctor told me today that infections like that are more likely if the cat has dirty teeth. She was overdue for a dental."

"I can't believe you actually get her teeth cleaned. Do I need to clean Fred's teeth?"

"Not yet, he's a little young, but eventually you will," he said, getting up and heading toward the kitchen. "Let me fix you some lunch."

"I can do it. I can walk, you know."

"No, the doctor said keep that foot up until the swelling is gone. That's what you're going to do."

They had a nice lunch of sandwiches and veggie chips. Gordon was about to leave to get Baby when the buzzer sounded. He pressed the button.

"Gordon, it's Lauren, may I come up?"

"Of course." He pressed the release. "I hope everything is all right," he said to Jane as they waited for the door bell. When it sounded, he opened the door and said, "Come in, Lauren. Oh, I see why you're here."

Lauren came into the room carrying an arrangement of flowers. "I thought these might cheer you, Jane."

"They're beautiful, Lauren, thank you," Jane said.

Gordon took them from Lauren and placed them on the table beside Jane. "I was just about to go and pick up the evil cat," he said. "I hate to leave when you've just gotten here."

"That's all right. I really came to see Jane."

"Well, give me a hug before I go," he said. "I guess I'll see you on Saturday at Maggie's soccer game."

"I'll be there." Lauren laughed. "On valium."

Gordon left and Lauren came over to the chair beside Jane. "Is your leg painful?" she asked as she sat.

"Only when I bump it or something." Jane put her feet down and moved the stool. "Gordon was just being over solicitous. I don't have to sit with it up in the air all of the time."

"Well if you need to, don't worry about me."

"I'm fine. So tell me what's on your mind. I sense there's something you want to tell me."

Lauren looked down at the carpet. "It's probably not

fair that I tell you my problems." She looked at Jane. "I don't even know why I'm so compelled to."

"I guess we've just broken down the barriers," Jane said. "Is it a serious problem?"

"Some people might not even think it's a problem." A tear leaked out of Lauren's eye. She sniffed and brushed it away.

"Tell me, Lauren." Jane leaned forward and put a hand on her arm.

"I'm pregnant."

Jane leaned back, startled. "You're pregnant? That's wonderful!"

"I'm scared to death!" Lauren cried and buried her face in her hands.

"Of course you are," Jane got up and went to the chair where Lauren sat. Leaning down, she put her arms around her shoulders. "After all you've been through. But maybe you won't have a problem with this one. How did things go with Gary?"

"It was an easy pregnancy, an easy birth, and he was an easy baby."

"There, you see. That's what will happen with this baby."

"I hope so," she said, looking at Jane. "Shouldn't you be sitting down?"

"No, I'm tired of sitting down. How does Grant feel about it?"

"He doesn't know." Lauren dabbed at her eyes. Jane handed her a tissue from a box on the table.

"You told me before you told him?" Jane asked "I feel a little guilty."

"Me too, but I'm afraid of how he'll feel. We weren't planning it. It just happened." Lauren hiccoughed.

Jane remembered Victoria wondering why her birth control lesson hadn't worked with Ellen and she wondered if Lauren had even had one.

"Why don't you let Gordon and me sit for the kids tonight?" She sat down on the stool facing her. "You and Grant can go out to dinner together and you can tell him.

I think he'll be happy," she said. "He might be a little worried, but he'll be happy."

"You really think so?" Lauren looked into Jane's eyes.

"I do. How do you feel about it? I mean, besides scared."

"I'm excited. I'm thirty-five years old. It might be my last chance."

"How far along are you?"

"Ten weeks."

"If you don't tell him soon, he'll figure it out for himself," Jane said, and then laughed.

Lauren laughed too. "I love you, Jane. You've become a dear friend."

Jane felt her throat tighten. "I love you too, Lauren."

"Even though I called you a bitch?" Lauren stood up and gathered her purse.

"Maybe more because you called me a bitch," Jane said.

"I've got to go. The kids will be home soon. Are you sure you're up to staying with them?"

"Sure."

"When can you and Gordon be there?"

"How about six thirty."

"Sounds good. You know what I wonder, Jane?"

"What?"

"I wonder how many women can say they've called their mother-in-law a bitch." She smiled. "To her face, I mean."

"She called me her mother-in-law," Jane said to Gordon in the car on the way to Lauren and Grant's house.

"Did you feel dizzy?"

"No, but I felt guilty. And I also felt...I don't know... connected to her. It was a nice feeling."

"It is a nice feeling, isn't it? So tell me what's going on that made you volunteer to baby-sit on your first night out of the hospital?"

"I didn't get permission to tell you, but if you promise not to give anything away, I don't think she'd mind."

"She's pregnant."

"How did you know?" Jane punched his arm playfully.

"I've had a lot of experience. I can just tell sometimes."

"So how does it feel to be about to have nine grandchildren?"

"Eleven," Gordon said. "Don't forget the ones on your side of the family. And to answer your question, it feels good, frightening, exhausting, and wonderful."

"Well put!" Jane said as they parked along the curb in front of the house and went to the door.

"I know what's going on, so neither one of you has to pretend," Grant said as he opened the door.

"What's going on?" Gordon asked. "Jane wanted to give you and Lauren a little time away from the kids."

"That's what Lauren said, but she always does something like this when she wants to tell me her brother is coming to stay." Grant shook his head as they followed him into the living room. "Want something to drink?"

"No, I'm fine," Jane said.

"Me too," Gordon repeated.

"You know her brother has a hard time keeping a job. I end up supporting him for months at a time. Oh, and thanks for paying for dinner tonight, Dad. I'm going to need the cash."

"Are you ready to go?" Lauren came into the room looking radiant in a red silk pant suit.

"Is that one of Anna's?" Jane asked.

"Sure is."

"Where are you going?" Gordon asked.

"Four Seasons," Lauren said. "Jane suggested it."

Jane squeezed Gordon's arm and they waved them off.

"I didn't know I was paying for this," Gordon said when they were out the door. "But I suppose I don't mind."

"I didn't tell her you would. I think that was just to throw him off." Jane laughed and sat down.

"Let me prop your leg up." Gordon rushed to put a pillow under her knee. "I think I'll go look for the kids. I wonder if they've eaten."

In a minute the kids came bouncing into the room.

"I wanted to come and see you in the hospital, Janie," Maggie said. "But Mamma wouldn't sneak me in."

"That's all right, Maggie. I wasn't there for very long."

"Janie." Gary held out a picture to her. "I've got a picture I thought you might want for your magazine."

She took the picture and held it in front of her. "Gary, this is really good." It was a picture of an old woman sitting on a bench leaning forward to pet a dog. Everything about it was beautiful.

"She's ninety-six. I got her name and contact info, if you want to feature her in your magazine. Dad said you were planning to do that."

"Thank you, Gary. I would like to contact her. We need to find out who she is," Jane said.

"They haven't eaten, Jane. I was thinking, even though it is a school night, we might go to the pizza place for dinner."

"I think that sounds great. Have you done your homework?" Jane asked.

"Maggie doesn't get homework," Gary said. "And you can believe Mom wouldn't leave here if I didn't have mine done."

"Well, what will we do, then?"

"I've got a soccer game taped from Brazil I haven't seen yet," Maggie said. "You can watch it with me if you want."

"I'm gonna show Grampa around the photo-editing software he got. I have the same program."

"That's great. I'll watch soccer with Maggie," Jane said, but she fell asleep right after the pizza.

"Well, I wasn't much help tonight," she said on the ride home. "And I was the one who volunteered us."

"That's fine. You need your rest. You're still healing."

"Did Grant look a little pale to you when they got home?"

"He looked a lot pale to me," Gordon said. "He'll be all right. It was nice that we didn't tell him we knew. When he gets used to the idea, he'll want to make an announcement."

"Lauren looks wonderful."

"Yes, she does."

On the day of the game, Jane limped out to the field behind Gordon. He carried a folding lawn chair to a spot next to the field where Lauren sat in a similar folding lawn chair.

"Now let me prop your leg up on the cooler," he said.

"No, Gordon, I'm fine," Jane insisted. She looked at Lauren. "He's being very protective."

"You should see Grant. He's starting to get on my nerves."

"I'm enjoying it at this point," Jane said. "But if it goes on too long, it'll get on my nerves, too."

"Are you all right, Lauren?" Grant asked. "You're not too cool, are you? I told you to bring a sweater."

"I'm fine, Grant. Stop worrying about me. Things are going great so far."

He kissed her and looked at Jane. "I'm a nervous wreck."

"About the new baby or about Maggie?" Jane asked.

"Both," he said, pulling Maggie's inhaler out of his pocket. "I'm armed though."

"Janie, Mamma." Maggie ran up to them. "Isn't it exciting? I won't play until the second half. I hope I can wait that long."

"Don't jump up and down too much. You'll use up all the energy you need to play soccer," Jane said.

Maggie subdued herself for a moment then started jumping up and down again. "Coach, Coach." She waved at a stocky young man who had just walked up to the field.

He waved back and headed in their direction.

"Coach," Maggie said. "Come and meet my Mom and my grandmother." The word rolled off her tongue as if she'd been saying it all her life.

Gordon separated himself from the group of men he and Grant were talking to and came to Jane's side. He leaned down behind her and said into her ear, "Are you all right?"

She looked up at him and smiled. "I think so."

The young man stopped in front of Lauren and Jane. "John Fenton," he said. "I'm Maggie's physical therapist."

He shook hands with each of them.

"I'm Maggie's mother, Lauren Fox."

"Jane Fox," Jane said as she shook his hand.

"I was really lucky," John Fenton said. "I always coach soccer in the spring and fall, but when I started working with Maggie last fall, I asked for this age group in the spring. That way I can work with her in soccer, too. She's quite a kid." He smiled down at Maggie and ruffled her red curls.

"Yes she is," Jane said.

John looked at Lauren for a moment with her straight black hair then he looked at Jane. "I guess your hair was red at one time?"

She felt Gordon's hand tighten on her shoulder and put her hand over his reassuringly.

"No, I'm her adopted grandmother."

"Really, I'm surprised. I thought she favored you."

Jane looked at Maggie. "Well, maybe she does a little," she said, smiling at Maggie.

"She won't play until the second half," John Fenton said. "She can't play for long periods of time because of her asthma." He looked reassuringly at Lauren. "She knows the signal to give me if she needs to come out. She's a smart kid. She's not a die hard. She'll signal me if she needs to."

"I hope so," Lauren said.

"I know so. Looks like we're getting started," he said. "I'll see you later."

"I gotta go sit with the team," Maggie said, and scampered off. She sat down on the bench with the coach and watched the other kids go onto the field.

The game started and just like Grant had said, most of the kids just ran up and down the field chasing the ball. Just a few of them seemed to have any control. The ball was knocked into both goals a couple of times, but no one seemed to be keeping score.

"Is there a score?" Jane asked Gordon.

"No, at this age it's just fun and skills building," he explained. "The parents keep score, though."

"I think our team is down by one," Jane said. "Looks like its four to three."

"That's what I counted, too."

When it was halftime, Maggie waved to them as she moved onto the field and another kid came off. Soon the game proceeded. The kids volleyed for a few minutes. Then Maggie got control of the ball, carried it down the field with the pack following and kicked unexpectedly with her left foot to put the ball into the goal.

"I see what you mean about a left foot, Grant," Jane said. "I didn't expect that at all."

After that happened two more times, the coach pulled her out and substituted the other child.

Lauren jumped up. "Grant where is her inhaler? She must have signaled him." Both of them hurried off in Maggie's direction. Gary hurried after them obviously concerned.

Jane stretched to see what was happening. She could feel Gordon's tension as he squeezed her shoulder and looked after Grant and Lauren.

After a minute of talking to Maggie and the coach, they turned and started back. All three of them were smiling.

"He took her out because he thought it was an unfair advantage over the other team," Lauren said as she sat back down.

"Are you all right, Lauren?" Grant asked.

"I'm fine. He said she could play again in five minutes."

When Maggie went back in she continued to control the ball completely. Coach took her out twice more, but by the time the game ended the score was ten to four.

The kids didn't notice it. They stood in a line high-fiving each other. All of them were happy. Maggie and John Fenton walked over to the family.

"Mr. and Mrs. Fox," John said. "I was afraid of this. She's too good to play with this group. I'd like to advance her to at least the next level, maybe two levels."

"But then you wouldn't be working with her," Lauren said.

"I'll talk to the coach. I'll stay involved," he said. "But this isn't fair to her or to the other kids."

Maggie stood next to him looking very serious.

Lauren bent down and looked into her daughter's eyes. "What do you want to do Maggie?"

"I wanna play soccer."

"Do you think they'll let her play with an older team?" Lauren asked.

"I think so when I show them how good she is. You might have to sign a consent form." He looked at the whole group. "But this kid is a natural. It would be a shame not to let her use her talents."

"Get her on a team she can be competitive with," Lauren said. Grant, Gordon, and Jane looked at her, startled. "I'll watch her." She looked around at the gaping group. "I'm her mother."

"Oh, thank you Mamma!" Maggie started to jump up and down.

"I'll be involved, too," Grant said.

"We all will," John Fenton said, and then smiled.

"Well, here it is guys." Jane came in the front door of the nursery. Jeff and Victoria were standing at a display of assorted plants. She pulled a wagon with two stacks of magazines on it. "Where do you want them, Jeff?"

"Over here." Jeff led her to the magazine rack. "I've got a space all cleared for them."

"Are you sure you want to sell them in here? They aren't gardening magazines," Jane said.

"But the gardening section is written by my partner." He smiled and put his arm on Victoria's shoulder. "I want everyone to see it."

"That's right, you're partners now." Jane smiled at the two of them.

"Let me see it, Jane." Victoria took a pair of pruning sheers off her tool belt and cut the straps that held the magazines. She pulled one of them off and looked at the cover. "I'm on the front cover," Victoria said, "with mud on my face. When was this picture taken?"

"That day I came in to tell you my problems and you made me work to get over it. Remember Michael came by with a camera and filmed our little dirt battle. But look at the picture, Tori. You have to admit, it's flattering."

"It is. I look great."

Jeff took the magazine from her and looked. "You do," he said, studying the cover then flipping through the pages. "In fact the whole magazine looks great." He looked at Jane and tilting her chin up lightly kissed her mouth. "You said you were going to do this and you did. I feel proud to be your friend."

"Best friend," Jane said, lightly touching his cheek.

"Hey," Victoria said.

"You're my sister," Jane said, "and my friend."

"Well, I agree with Jeff," Victoria said. "This magazine is beautiful. You've done a great job. I guess you're not burned out on life anymore, are you?"

"How could I be? My life is totally different than it was six months ago."

"That's for sure."

"You'll both be at the celebration tonight, won't you?" Jane asked.

"Joe and I will."

"What about you, Jeff? Please come."

"I'll be there. It's important to David, too. His mother is coming with me."

"Great. I'll see you there." Jane hurried out. She had a few more deliveries to make before she went home to change for the first issue celebration. They had invited everyone involved with the magazine and all of the family. It was going to be a big event.

The following morning, Sunday, Jane sat at breakfast with Gordon. "That celebration party was perfect," she said.

"Yes it was. I think everyone had a good time," Gordon said. "Jane, my sister is coming to town this week to get together with Jerry and me to discuss our parents. I really think they need more help."

"I know that must be hard, Gordon." She reached across the table and put her hand on his.

"It is, but at least I have help," he said. "Anyway, I wanted to rent the room in the Italian restaurant at the mall so the family can go out to dinner together."

"I just want you to leave Saturday night open for me," Jane said.

"Of course I will. It's our six month wedding anniversary."

"I can't believe you remembered that! Most people don't pay attention to that," Jane said.

"I'm sure I wouldn't have earlier in my life. But now, it means a lot to me."

Jane smiled at him. "So when is the family dinner?"

"I'd like to do it Friday night. That way the elders won't fall asleep and the parents of the youngsters don't have to worry about it being a school night. I want them all there."

"Me too, I love the kids. The family wouldn't be complete without them."

"No, it wouldn't.

"You must be Jane Fox," The petite woman standing at the door said.

"That's right, and you must be Rita Bell. It's a pleasure to meet you, Ms. Bell." She shook her hand.

"It's Mrs. Bell. Come in and meet my husband."

"Will I be able to interview you both?"

"If you'd like to."

Jane followed her into the living room of their apartment. A tall thin man stood when she came into the room and held out his hand.

"This is my husband, George Bell."

"It's nice to meet you, Mr. Bell." Jane shook his hand.

"Please call us George and Rita," he said and smiled charmingly at her.

"I hope you'll join us for the interview," Jane said as they gestured to a chair and all three sat down. "It was very nice of you to let my," Jane hesitated for a minute, "grandson get your contact information."

"He was such a polite young man, and quite precocious with that camera. He seemed young to be so serious." Rita smiled.

"He is," Jane said. "A passion for photography runs in the family. Tell me something. How long have you been married?"

"Forty-six years," Rita said patting George on the arm.

Jane looked at them puzzled. "That would mean..."

"I was fifty-years-old when we married. George here is eight years younger than me." Rita winked at Jane. "It's better that way. Men wear out sexually earlier than women."

"Is that so?" Jane said. "I guess I'm lucky then. My husband is younger than me, too. What did you do before you were married, Rita?"

"I was a career girl. I owned and managed a line of children's clothing. It was great fun."

"Really, did you quit when you met George?"

"Yes, I had lost interest by then. I loved what I did, but you can only do something for so long—no matter how much you love it."

"That's true," Jane said, remembering her years in the computer software industry. "What about you, George?"

"I was married before I met Rita. Actually I was married a couple of times," he said. "It never worked out until I met her."

"Did you have any children from those previous marriages?"

"Yes, I have two sons and four grandchildren. Rita makes a wonderful grandmother." He pinched her cheek.

"Stop that," she said. "He knows I hate that." She slapped at him. "We had a child of our own as well."

"You did?" Jane asked. "I assumed..."

"I know. Getting married that late you wouldn't expect it, but we did, a little girl, Jennifer."

"Did she give you any grandchildren?"

"No, she died when she was twenty-eight-years-old. She had Down's syndrome. They have bad hearts, you know."

"Oh, I'm sorry."

"Don't be," George said. "She was the apple of my eye. We don't regret a minute of it."

"She was just as sweet and loving as she could be." Rita smiled as she talked about her. "There was not a mean bone in that child's body."

"Sounds like you were very lucky to have her."

"Yes we were, and lucky to have each other."

"I'm so glad that I decided to do the interview myself," Jane said to Gordon on the drive to Michael and Jill's new house. They were meeting there and driving to the restaurant in a caravan.

"It went well?"

"It was exhilarating. This couple had married when she was fifty-years-old. He's eight years younger than she is. They had a Down's syndrome child and talked about it like it was a wonderful thing. I just hope I can write the article."

"I'm sure you can, Jane. You can do pretty much anything you put your mind to," Gordon said.

"I've never done much writing."

"You've never published a magazine before either."

"That's true."

"Or been a grandmother."

"When I thanked her for letting Gary take her picture, I called him my grandson. I was surprisingly comfortable with it."

"Good."

When they arrived at the restaurant parking lot in the caravan, they all got out. Eric, Teddy, and Alexandra had ridden with Jane and Gordon in Katherine's minivan. The older children were promised to sit with them at the restaurant.

As the group walked in, Jane remembered the first time she had done this with the family. She had felt like a drop of water in the ocean as a wave moved toward the shore. She still felt that way, but she belonged with that wave.

At the table she and Gordon sat with Joy, Hope, Gary, and Maggie.

"Are you coming to my soccer game tomorrow?" Maggie asked Gordon and Jane.

"They have to come to my baseball game sometimes," Gary said. "You're not the only grandchild."

"Yeah, but mine is the first time with an older team. They have to come to mine."

"I thought we were going to the dog park?" Joy looked at Jane.

"Hey, guys," Gordon said. "We'll get it all in. Gary I thought your game was earlier than Maggie's."

"Oh, yeah, that's right."

"And they're both afternoon games," Jane said. "So we can go to the dog park in the morning." She turned to Hope. "What do you want to do? You've been very quiet."

"I'm going to the fish store with Dad. I matted a bunch of his slides for money and he said he'd take me to buy some new fish. I have a saltwater aquarium now. Did I tell you?"

"No, you didn't. Gordon, we'll have to find some time to see that tomorrow too."

"Yes, we will."

"It's a lot of fun, but the fish cost a fortune. So I have to find jobs to do. Do you have anything?" She looked at Jane.

"How do you write? It might be fun to put an aquarium section in my magazine. Gary could take the pictures." She looked across the table at Gary.

"I could. I've always wanted to take underwater pictures. I could get an underwater camera..."

"You can't get into the aquarium, dummy," Maggie said.

"I wasn't planning to, stupid." Gary raised his hand to swing at her.

"That's enough!" Jane said. Everyone turned and looked at her. Gary lowered his hand. "That's much better. Now," Jane picked up her menu. "What's everyone going to eat?"

Gordon squeezed her shoulder and kissed her cheek. She glanced at the rest of the room. They were all looking at her. She raised her glass and said, "To family." They all laughed and raised their glasses.

"What time did you make the reservation for?" Gordon asked Saturday evening. It had been a long day with the grandkids and they were both tired, but relaxed. They had come home about four o'clock and made some new memories on their new couch. Their lovemaking was still as thrilling as first love, but it had become richer with their growing intimate knowledge of each other.

"Seven," Jane said. "I reserved the booth where you asked me to marry you."

"I hoped you would," Gordon said. They were standing at the bar enjoying a cocktail. "I have something for you. He pulled a box out of the refrigerator at the bar and pinned a corsage on her.

"It's Tori's hybrid."

"She had some blooming when I went to the nursery to get it. She made this for you," he said.

"I have something for you, too." Jane went into the kitchen and pulled a box out of the refrigerator. "It's a lapel pin." She pulled it out and pinned it on him.

"It's Victoria's hybrid," Gordon said. "She's always planning, isn't she?"

"She is." Jane put her hands on his cheeks and kissed him.

"Shall we go?" Gordon put his hand on her waist. She gathered her purse and they left.

When they arrived at the booth, there was a bottle of champagne, an arrangement of roses, and a card on the table.

"Did you do this?" Jane asked Gordon.

"No, I assumed you had." He picked up the card. "Let's find out who did." He opened the card. Edging around the booth he squeezed closer to Jane. They read the card together.

"That is so nice. Look Gordon, all of the kids and grandkids have signed it, Teddy, Eric, and Katherine signed Valerie's name with her initials after it. Your parents and brother and sister signed, too."

Gordon smiled at her.

"I went to Margaret's grave last week," Jane said.

"Really?" Gordon frowned. "Why?"

"I know she isn't there." Jane looked into his eyes. "But somehow it helps me to talk to her there. I thanked her for making you so happy that you have those beautiful smile lines beside your eyes." Jane traced the lines with her finger then leaned forward and kissed his temple.

Gordon kissed her warmly. He pulled back just a breath. "Let's just make out like teenagers for a while here in our booth and then go home."

"No way!" Jane said. "I want lobster."

The waiter opened the champagne with a pop. "Will that be two lobster dinners, sir?"

They moved slightly away from each other.

"That's right, Drew," Gordon said. He turned to Jane when the waiter had left. "How does it feel to be President and founder of *Second Half* magazine?"

"It's so exciting, Gordon. I've enjoyed it so much. I just love my team," she said. "Not just because most of them are family, but they're all so enthusiastic and so talented. They've done an excellent job, individually and as a team."

"And you're the team leader."

She laughed. "I have the money."

"Jane, go ahead and take some real credit."

"I did a great job of putting it together," she said, blushing. "And you know what, Gordon?"

"Tell me."

"I have a legacy now. When I'm gone, which won't be for a long time," she said and then smiled as he tensed and put her hand on his, "the magazine will go on with the kids."

Gordon held up his glass. "To the *Second Half.*" They clicked their glasses. "Mrs. Fox, answer another question for me."

"What's the question, Mr. Fox?"

"How does it feel to be the matriarch of such a large family?"

Jane felt her expressions change from surprise, to concern, to happy. "It feels good, terrifying, exhausting, and wonderful."

"Well put."

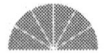

About the Author

Susanna Chelton Sheehy:

Susanna lives in Atlanta, GA with her husband of thirty years. She works as a Veterinary Technician, a job which fulfills her requirement to be happy and useful. Living in the same general area is her family, including aging parents, grown children, and siblings, and her friends, both old and young.

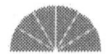

www.ingramcontent.com/pod-product-compliance
Lightning Source LLC
Chambersburg PA
CBHW031426240626

47154CB00001B/221